SHOPPING FOR A CEO'S BABY (SHOPPING SERIES #16)

JULIA KENT

SHOPPING FOR A CEO'S BABY

It's Andrew and Amanda's turn... in duplicate

We're having twins.

Twins.

Which means my shooters are stronger than my brother's. I win.

Yeah, yeah, everyone can say it's not a competition, but it is.

And we all know it.

Two babies at once means double the fun, and double the misery for my poor wife, Amanda. While I'm growing a Fortune 500 company, she's growing two entire human beings out of nothing but orange cheese snacks and ice cream.

Do you have any idea how hard I've worked during this pregnancy, tracking down orange smoothies for her?

Not to mention being forced to Facetime into a childbirth class on perineal massage, rescuing Chuckles the cat from being shaved bald by my two-year-old niece, and fighting with a wife who has named the twins Lefty and Righty.

By the time we hit the ninth month, my entire world revolves around pleasing — and protecting — her.

Even if it means humiliating myself in the name of love.

Wait a minute. Wait a minute, now.

Hold on.

Is she the one who's winning?

Andrew and Amanda are BACK in the newest New York Times best-selling Shopping series book as they "beat" Declan and Shannon in the baby competition, but at what cost? As their future awaits them in the form of twins, Amanda and Andrew face ghosts from the past with wit, humor, and most of all — plenty of love.

Andrew

My wife is orange.

She is caked with orange dust, on her fingers, in her cuticles, and her lips are the color of a traffic cone. She's in the kitchen, standing in front of the blender, drinking something–

You guessed it.

Orange.

"*Mmmmm,*" she moans as she drinks straight from the blender itself. "Isss izz *soooooo* goooo."

"What are you drinking?"

"Eeeto-eenie."

"What?"

A swallow later and she says, "Cheeto-cini." When my sister-in-law, Shannon, was pregnant with my niece, Amanda created a special orange smoothie for her out of Cheetos, marshmallow cream, and orange sherbet.

My wife has modified it to remove the sherbet and replace it with coconut milk, which does nothing to change the fact that it's vile to the core.

It's just slightly less gross now.

"Another one?"

"It's the only thing that stays down."

"And the doctor really says this is okay?" I say, staying far away from the blender, knowing how territorial she is about her food. She's pregnant and still stuck deep in morning sickness.

For the last few weeks, all she's eaten is *this*.

Cheeto smoothie.

And nothing else.

"It's full-fat coconut milk. One big leaf of kale." She makes a gagging sound. "Apple juice. One banana. And Cheetos. I freeze the fruit and it tastes like a milkshake."

"Our babies are made up of *that*." At least she added the kale, banana, and apple juice this time.

"I choke down a prenatal vitamin, too, Andrew." Her eyes tear up and her chin quivers.

Damn.

"It's fine. Good. I'm so glad you can eat something. Really. Not judging you. I know you are doing everything possible for our babies." I rub the spot between her shoulder blades, hoping I can calm her down before a full-blown meltdown kicks in.

"I am! Everything," she says before gobbling down more of that candy corn-colored monstrosity. "I've lost two pounds. The doctor said the placenta looks fine and the babies are growing within range, but this morning sickness is horrible. If I drink water, I puke! If I drink this–" she points at the blender, "–I don't."

"Then by all means, drink *that*." I hold back a shudder. My trainer, Vince, would have an unexpected coronary if he saw Cheetos in a Vitamix.

"I–I know I'm not doing this the way another wife would. A better wife. A wife who is stronger and who..." Her lower lip begins to quiver.

Here we go again.

I come in for the hug before I wince, feeling like a jerk. Being supportive isn't hard. Not at all. Being pregnant with two babies–*my* babies–has to be *impossibly* hard. And poor Amanda has to shoulder that load. I can't do one bit of it for her.

But I could do without the drastic personality change. It's like someone swapped my wife out for the most insecure woman on the planet.

Ever.

The woman who could do anything, fix anything, mediate *anything* has become a sniffling puddle of overly apologetic goo, who makes insecure celebrities look like they invented arrogance.

And who has convinced herself that she's terrible at being pregnant.

"Amanda." I kiss her, gently, tasting salt and cheese and sugar. "You're perfect."

"I'm incompetent."

"All you have to do is let cells divide inside your womb."

"And grow a placenta. I'm terrible at this. I'm failing at basic biology!" Wide eyes, big and beautiful, tear up like someone's pumped her full of salt water.

"It's not a college course," I joke. "It's just nature."

She stiffens.

Uh oh.

"It's not 'just' anything."

Declan warned me about this stage of pregnancy. The super-sensitive stage. The you-can't-say-anything-without-opening-the-portal-to-demonic-possession stage.

That's his phrase. Not mine. Don't pin *that* on me.

"Of course it's not 'just' anything," I soothe. "I'm not trivializing it. I'm saying you're doing a great job."

"If it's 'just' nature, how can I be doing a 'great' job at something I have no control over?"

She's got me there.

"You're the most loving woman I know," I tell her. "Which means you'll be the most loving mother I know. Which makes me the luckiest man alive, because you're going through such a huge sacrifice to give me two children. Not just one. Two. At the same time."

Uncertainty flickers across her face. Aha. *Now* I'm on firmer ground. We're just in the middle of a slippery negotiation. The other party is insecure and needs reassurance.

I've got this.

I've totally got this.

A few more sentences and she'll be eating out of my hand.

Not that Cheeto-smoothie crap, though.

I splay my hand over her belly. It's surprisingly flat, though her nice, curvy hips make it easy to cuddle. "Our babies are right here. You're growing them. Your body nurtures them."

She gives me a shaky smile.

Score! I did it. I talked her down. Declan is such an amateur. He can't compete with my ability to–

Amanda's shaky smile turns into something... green.

My wife has gone from orange to turquoise. She's the Miami Dolphins in pregnant form.

Casually, like I've done this a thousand times before (hint: it's been seven, but I've perfected my move), I reach for a small bucket in the kitchen and hand it to her so she can do the inevitable.

Reject every calorie she's trying to consume.

"I hate this," she moans as I rub her back and try to console her. Secretly, though, I'm relieved.

At least this time, she didn't get my shoes. Can't just hop on a plane to Italy today and get a replacement pair in Milan like I used to.

"I hate it for you," I assure her. I do. I really, really do. You know how some men claim they'd get pregnant for their wives, to spare them the pain of everything they go through to bring a new life into this world?

Yeah. I'm not one of them.

But I'll hire people to help with that pain.

And I'll be there with her, in sickness and in health, 'til Cheeto smoothies do us part.

Because we're definitely parting ways on this. If I'm eating something orange out of a blender, it'll be something my trainer, Vince, made for me, and it won't come out of a foil bag.

Though it might come out of a former Soviet-bloc country's experimental performance enhancement lab.

"Andrew?" Amanda calls for me, the sound of the bathroom faucet stopping. I hear sniffling, then she emerges, red-rimmed eyes and wan smile breaking my heart a little.

Yes, I have one.

"Oh, honey. I'm so sorry." Compassion doesn't come easily for me. It can't, when you run a big corporation. Compassion gets tucked away in a walled-off safe, deep inside a chamber of my heart, the path to reach it one my wife has to traverse everyday. It's like working in a maximum security prison, I imagine.

You're not a prisoner, but you have to go through all the layers of security to enter the facility.

When she's upset, though, all the security measures go into a reverse lockdown, my compassion flying out to find her, protect her, keep her happy.

Sound cheesy? Too bad.

"It's okay. It's temporary. Everyone says it'll be over soon." She frowns. "Except for Carol. She said her morning sickness lasted for thirty weeks."

"You won't be Carol," I say automatically, hoping like hell I'm right.

"But I have *two* inside me. Two! All bets are off."

I rub her belly, moving my hand along an imaginary infinity symbol. "This is the best bet ever."

Her smile spreads. "Yeah. It is. We made babies. I'm growing humans inside me."

"You are."

Every day, we have this conversation. Every single day, at some point, we stare at her navel and pat ourselves on the back for doing what Neanderthals did long before you could order a coffee on a phone or book a seat on a private space shuttle (I was number three in line when they took deposits). From the dawn of man until now, hormones and desire have made it possible to procreate.

And I hear the desire part is optional for some people.

Definitely not us.

"You know what's missing here?" I grab my phone.

"You working?" Her tone goes sour.

A few taps, and the opening chords of the first song on Yes's *The Yes Album* begin on the kitchen speakers. Her shoulders drop, a long, slow inhale making her ribs widen, increasingly bigger breasts rising up, my palms curling in as if imagining how I'm going to cradle them momentarily. Neurology is complex, the complicated weaving of personality, basic functioning, biology, impulse, perception–the whole mix of what makes us fully human–coming to the fore as the melody finds its way through all the interconnected channels to tap into emotion.

That heart of mine, tucked behind the iron door of a safe?

It's tapping its toes now as she lets me put my arms around her, the back of her head pressed into my chest, her weight melting into me as we close our eyes and do exactly what all expectant parents should do.

Be.

Just be.

❧ 2 ❧

Amanda

"I can't believe you gag on saltine crackers but you can eat *that*," Shannon says as she points to the roe resting on top of a carefully molded chunk of rice.

We're having lunch together at a trendy new "we serve a little bit of everything" restaurant in Beacon Hill in Boston, the kind of place where you can order black bean penne tossed with arugula/sunflower seed pesto, or various kinds of sushi, or vegan ice cream with pour-over coffee.

It's like a cafeteria for hipsters.

"It's orange. Apparently, I can eat salty orange things and nothing else."

She snorts. "You told me this when we talked on the phone, but I thought you were kidding!"

"Not kidding."

"I can't believe we're both afflicted by the same orange food problem in early pregnancy."

"You rubbed off on me," I say with a glare.

"Carrots?"

"Only carrot chips, like potato chips."

"Oranges?"

"No. Not salty."

"Salmon?"

"So far, yes, if it's more orange than pink."

"What else is orange and salty?"

"Sweet potato fries."

Shannon waits, as if there's a longer list.

"That's... it?"

I shrug.

"There has to be more. What about Goldfish crackers?"

I smack my palm to my head. "I never thought of those! I'll add them to my list."

"I just expanded your dietary repertoire by twenty-five percent. You're welcome."

"Shut up. You had weird foot behaviors when you were pregnant with Ellie."

"I did. No Cheeto smoothies, though." Her shudder is *so* judgmental.

"You weren't pregnant with twins."

"Here we go again. You're becoming as competitive as Andrew, Amanda."

"It's a statement of fact. Not one-upmanship."

"Okay. Fine." Shannon flags down the server, who stops and gives us a patient smile.

"Yes?"

"You have microcreamery ice creams, yes?"

"Sure."

"Any chance you have something orange and something salty?"

"How about orange sherbet and salted caramel ice cream?"

My stomach sings.

"Yes!" I say. "Can you add a side of anchovies?"

"Excuse me?"

"That was a bad joke," Shannon tells her, laughing and rolling her eyes.

But it wasn't.

"Two servings of orange sherbet and salted caramel ice cream," I say.

"God, no!" Shannon practically screams. "Not two! Only one. I want a double scoop of chocolate peppermint, like *normal* people."

I look at her like she's crazy. "I wasn't talking about *your* order!"

"Okay, then," the server says, backing away slowly. "Two orange sherbet and salted caramel ice creams, one double scoop of chocolate peppermint," she mutters as she walks away.

"'Normal people'?" I throw out at Shannon.

"You know. Women who aren't eating for three."

"You typically eat a pint of ice cream in one sitting, Shannon. Those pints say 'serves four.'"

She pats her stomach. "Then maybe *I'm* having *triplets*."

"The older you get, the more you sound like your mother."

We laugh, but I'm not kidding this time, either.

"How's Ellie?"

"She's marvelous."

"That Mommy and Me class working out?"

"It's going slowly. We're working on getting her used to the play-group at the preschool, and next month, we're going to try leaving her there. We can't have a repeat of the gym daycare fiasco."

I wince. "Did the daycare worker's toupee survive being torn off like that?"

"Yes." She hunches over. "His ego was bruised more than his scalp, thank goodness." Her eyebrows go up. "Dec says the guy got off easy. Ellie kicks Daddy's balls regularly, like her foot is a stick and his boys are a pinata."

"She just loves you. A lot." I bring my water glass to my neck and press the wet side of it under my earlobe, hoping it'll quell the unease in my stomach.

"And I love her a lot, too." She eyes my belly. "Wait until you've spent almost a year holding a human leech against your skin twenty-four/seven."

"Andrew has his moments."

"Hah!" Sympathy takes over her face. "I'm sorry about the morning sickness, though." A single orange globule of fish egg sits on my plate, taunting me, daring me to press my fingertip into it and lick it off the pad.

"Thanks." Who knew one little fish egg could make my entire stomach start to rebel?

The server appears, tray aloft, setting my bowl of ice cream in front of me, delivering Shannon's with a flourish. Two napkins, two spoons—and then one intense whiff of Shannon's chocolate mint ice cream makes eating for three suddenly turn into nausea for three acres.

The server loads our dirty plates onto the tray as everything in the universe warbles. Wobbles. Warbles and wobbles into a sickening vibration that's about to make me spew.

"Excuse me," I say urgently, moving around the server, who

bends her back so she can lift the tray of dirty dishes in the air. Finding an opening, I squeeze around her, walking as fast as I can to the bathroom, where I find–

A line.

"Oh, no," I groan, pressing my palm against my stomach, wondering how I'll make it. My skin tingles, chills overtaking me. Who knew a stomach could change temperature in waves like this?

"Are you okay?" the woman in front of me asks, gray hair framing a kind, worried face.

"I'm pregnant, and, and morning sickness, and smells, and–"

Gray Hair turns into my own personal lead blocker, sweeping aside the women in line like pee wee football players. People move back in waves, backs slamming against the wall as I lurch into a stall and everything comes back up.

Orange.

"PREGNANT!" Gray Hair announces.

"Oh, honey."

"Poor thing."

"I remember those days!"

The chorus of sympathetic voices form a wall behind me as my stomach unclenches, the wave over.

And as I hear them talking among themselves, the shared experience of growing a human being–or two, in my case–with nothing but food and blood, I realize Gray Hair was right.

All she had to do was shout "PREGNANT!" in a group of women and they instantly banded together in solidarity to help.

To help me.

I am a member of a new group now.

One I didn't really understand even existed.

Tap tap tap

"Amanda?"

I peel my face off the cool toilet seat and turn to see Shannon's navy high heels under the door. She really needs a pedicure, because the chips on those nails are big enough to have been chiseled.

"Mmmm?"

"You okay?"

"Pregnant," someone in the background mutters.

Shannon laughs. "Oh, I know. I have a toddler at home."

Murmurs of understanding fill the air.

Shannon's in the club, too. The one I didn't know about. One you only join through trial by fire. And my body decided to enter this new realm with double the impact.

Damn Andrew and his supersperm. Of all the ways to beat Declan at this whole fatherhood thing, he had to do it with *my* body?

"Andrew gets all the glory, and I get all the puking!" I choke out, spitting twice after, disgusted.

"At least there aren't any cameras these days," Shannon commiserates. "The pap are leaving you alone."

"Only because Andrew forced James to stop using us to generate PR."

"And that article about how Andrew stopped being eligible once you were pregnant."

"Pffft. Doesn't stop plenty of women from hitting on him, still."

"Yeah, but it keeps the asshole pap away, and that's something."

She's right. This would be so much worse if my puking were being *documented*.

A hand comes under the door, a box of orange Tic Tacs in Shannon's fingers. "Here."

"What's that?"

"I got them on the way here. Made sure they were orange."

Shaking them, she urges me to accept. Slowly, I move a few inches across the floor, the nausea holding back enough to snatch the little box, pop the top, and shake a single orange pellet into my hand.

Gently, I put it on the center of my tongue, the taste buds on the tip too sensitive to assault quite yet.

I close my eyes. I cross my legs, not caring that I'm doing this on a disgusting women's room floor.

I breathe.

My mouth moistens.

"Shannon!" I call out. "This is working!"

Applause comes from the other side. "Yay! I wasn't sure."

"She gonna be okay?" someone mumbles from the other side of the door.

"In the long run? Yes. She's in her second trimester, pregnant with twins."

"TWINS?" Gray Hair shouts. "WHY DIDN'T YOU SAY SO, HONEY?"

Groans of recognition fill the bathroom, an echo chamber of interconnectedness.

It makes me feel better.

Like this stupid orange Tic Tac.

While the floor is nice and safe, I'll pick up a germ if I stay here, so I slide up the stall wall and stand, testing my balance. So far, so good. My palm goes to my stomach.

"Let Mommy finish lunch with Aunt Shannon, okay, kiddoes?"

"You say something, Amanda?" Shannon calls out.

I open the door, plastering on a smile, but a really sad one. "Just talking to the babies."

"It'll get better, honey," Gray Hair says as she washes her hands. "And if it gets really bad, grab a cigarette. Yeah, yeah, I know... my daughter and granddaughter want to tar and feather me, but one here and there to get rid of that sour stomach won't do you any harm."

The thought of a cigarette sends me straight back to the bowl.

"I'll settle the bill," Shannon says, bending down and calling under the door. "You do what you need to do."

And I do.

Cursing Andrew the entire time.

❧ 3 ❦

Andrew

Vince grabs my hand before I can touch the forties I'm about to do curls with.

"What the hell is that?" He points to my orange cuticles.

"Cheeto stains."

"You're eating *Cheetos?*" He sounds like I just told him I cooked my father's liver and ate it on a buttered croissant. Not sure whether he'd be more outraged at the patricide or the carb count.

"Not me. My wife."

"Yeah, yeah. All my clients blame their partner. You're on a strict program, Andrew. No chemicals, no grains, no–"

"Flavor," Declan mutters under his breath as Gerald smirks. We're working out at this shithole gym Vince likes, only this time is different.

Because I bought the place.

Declan's not the only McCormick who can go out on his own and buy a company. No one, other than Amanda, knows I did this.

And don't ask me why I did it.

Turns out, the guy who created this gym, old Jorg, is one of those under-the-radar types. Quiet, unassuming, scruffy, and curmud-geonly, but street smart.

Sharp.

And ancient.

The guy owns–owned–sixteen gyms across Boston, Lowell, Fitchburg, and Springfield, all of them gritty, intense places where guys like Vince and my old chauffeur/bodyguard, Gerald, like to get wrecked.

This place isn't trendy. It's not fancy. Nothing about it makes me feel seen or displayed, and Instagram can go screw itself if it thinks any of the customers here give a rat's ass about posting anything.

Which is why I bought the entire chain from old Jorg.

Because *this* is the future of gyms.

Not for everyone. But for plenty of guys like me. People want authenticity. They want to belong without being smothered. They want to be ignored but also welcomed.

With a nod. A chin jut.

Not an upsell or an ad push.

Starbucks became huge not from selling coffee, but from selling the emotion you could feel when you got coffee there.

Time to do the same with gyms.

Only instead of market testing to find the optimal emotional experience for the widest customer base that can deliver massive quarterly profits, I just want to build a bunch of places that appeal to *me*.

Why?

Because I can.

"Earth to Andrew," Dec says, grunting through the words as he squats below parallel, staring up. Sweat coats him, from hair follicles to the elastic on the bands of his socks. Drenched and red, he's been busting a nut for the last two hours, clearly working through something more than muscle groups.

"Huh?"

"Vince is nagging you again. Pay attention."

"No."

Vince shrugs. "Fine. Pay me to ignore me. Best gig ever."

Dec lifts up, locks the weight bar in place in the cage, and laughs. "You couldn't be paid to sit on your ass and do nothing, Vince. Within thirty minutes, you'd find a rattlesnake to wrestle, or invent cold fusion. You're one of those guys."

"Those guys?" Vince crosses his arms over his enormous chest.

"You can't not work." He thumbs my way. "Like him."

"I can not work," I argue, Vince folding in half laughing before the sentence is out of my mouth.

"But," I continue, "I choose not to. It's like choosing not to have sex."

"If you're comparing sex to work, you're doing it wrong." Declan gives me his patented older-brother eye roll.

"Both involve being on top." I smirk.

"You're a workaholic."

"And a sexaholic."

"And a hypocrite. I don't work nearly the hours you do. I stopped when Ellie was born. But I don't think you'll stop, baby bro."

"Twins, Declan. I'm having twins."

Vince looks at my belly. "Where? Out your butthole?"

"We. We're having twins," I clarify.

"One out of your butthole, the other out your wife's–"

"Both of you can just shut up and let me lift," I grouse as Vince checks something off a list on a clipboard.

"Stop eating your pregnant wife's Cheeto stash."

"I'm not! If you have to know, my fingernails are stained because I was feeding her."

"With your hands?"

"Yes. Some mornings, she wakes up so sick, it's the only thing that keeps her from puking. Her eyes open and I slowly move a Cheeto into her mouth. She sucks on it for a while, and then she can sit up."

"That is the worst beginning to a porno ever," Dec drawls as he tosses a medicine ball my way, the unexpected hit to my solar plexus making me laugh.

"I'm sure sex is the last thing on Amanda's mind these days," Vince says, suddenly serious. He gives me a pitying look. "Hope you enjoyed your last time sleeping with her, because it'll be a while."

"Says the man who has no kids."

"True, true... but I know hormones. And we know what Declan's described. You shot your wife up with double the trouble, man."

I shoot Dec a big old grin. "That's right."

"Which means she's going to be twice as sick."

My grin freezes.

"And the glorious second trimester is going to be a blink for you. Not that nice, three-month stretch of horny preggo wife Declan got to enjoy."

Are Declan's shoulders shaking with laughter?

A blast of cool air from the main door makes us all turn to see old Jorg walk in. He's the only person in my life other than Amanda who knows I bought the gyms. Even Vince doesn't know, which is about to change when I offer him a huge raise and a director-level role–with plenty of time on the flagship gym's floor–running my new chain.

"Speaking of preggo wives, how's Suzanne?" Declan calls out.

"She's good." Gerald has a face like a concrete block, with a smushed nose and scars to go along with the look. Head shaved bald, he's intimidating as hell, which is perfect for a bodyguard.

But he's a study in contrasts: The guy is also a marshmallow on the inside, teaching sculpting to little kids at a local center for the arts, spoiling his wife's dog, Smoochy, and getting ready for his first kid.

Like me.

Except I've got *two* coming.

"How many weeks now?" I ask.

"Fourteen. You know, I'm amazed," he says in a weirdly reflective tone. Gerald's not one for offering up opinions, insights, or... ugh.

Feelings.

"At what?" Vince asks.

"Suzanne hasn't had even the slighted whiff of morning sickness. She's gained ten pounds. The doctors just told her to stop running five miles a day, so she's fast-walking seven instead. Her caseload at work is the same."

"And the sex?" Vince asks, eyes cutting to me.

One offended eyebrow goes up on Gerald's face, making him look like a villainous Mr. Clean. "'Scuse me?"

"We were just talking about pregnancy sex."

One corner of Gerald's mouth curls up. "Let's just say her caseload has expanded in that area."

I drop the forties in my hand and grunt at Vince. "Next."

"Ropes. Use the wall anchor. Then tires," he orders.

A curt nod is all I have in me. Exhaustion isn't the problem.

Gerald's words are.

No way will I admit this to the guys, but we haven't had sex since morning sickness crept in. Amanda cries–a lot–and apologizes profusely. And she offers other, shall we say... activities as compensation.

But I want her.

All of her.

And I want to give.

Jacking off in the shower (at home, not here, because I'm not depraved) barely takes the edge off.

So if I'm looking at double the morning sickness, double the nausea–double the negatives–in order to have double the children, while the trade-off is worth it, of course, the terms of this deal *suck*.

They're the only thing that's sucking these days, because unfortunately, my dick isn't orange. Amanda would put it in her mouth more often if it were.

Hmmm. Can you buy dye for that?

"Andrew!" Jorg barks, making me look up sharply, the curve of a rope looping up damn near shearing off my nose. The guy looks like he's ninety, but I now know he's seventy-eight. How do I know?

Contracts.

"What?" I call back to the guy, who seems like he's walking with a lighter step. Is this what the curmudgeon looked like when he was happy?

"How you liking the place?"

Vince goes dead still. Damn it. I told Jorg not to blow the secret.

"Smells like an elephant got drunk and took a piss in here," I answer as I wipe down a bench.

"Good. Wouldn't want nothin' to change." Then he cackles. Vince looks at him, then me, eyes narrowing.

Instead of asking what's up, he says, "Your glutes look like something you find in the broken doll bin at a thrift shop."

"What's a thrift shop?" I ask, puzzled.

That must have come out a little too loud, because I can feel everyone's eye roll. Why?

Vince points to the mat. "Hundred burpees. Now."

"What?"

"Do it."

"Why are you punishing me?"

"One, because I'm your trainer. You pay me to punish you. Two, because you're sheltered."

"Sheltered? I'm not–"

"If you don't know what the hell a thrift shop is, you're sheltered."

I look at Dec. "You don't know what one is, do you?"

"Of course I do. Marie and Shannon used to drag me to those places all the time. It's like an antique store for poor people."

"A junk shop?" Now I get it, turning to Vince for vindication.

"You," Vince points at Declan, then the mat next to me. "Hundred burpees with him."

"Why me?"

"You billionaires need to feel more pain. Toughens you up."

"He's not a billionaire anymore," I clarify, earning a glare from my big bro.

"Well, boo hoo," Vince says, the sole of his shoe going flat on my spine the second I drop, reflexes fast enough to move as I stand. "You'll just have to hug your hundreds of millions and listen to the whispers of all those not-quite-billions as they flatter you."

Dec drops to the mat with me, humoring him. "I don't like your tone," he says. "It's funny when it's pointed at Andrew, but not me."

"Are those tears I see? You can wipe them up with hundred-dollar bills. I'm sure Ben Franklin can feel your pain."

Dec opens his mouth to argue. I elbow him.

"Shut up. The more you argue, the more he'll make us suffer."

"Since when did that bother me? Have you met our father?"

Seventeen minutes and half an ACL tear later, I finish.

Before Declan, for the record.

This place is too stripped down for a water cooler. I press my thumb against the ancient water fountain faucet and aim my bottle. The slow gurgle of water arcing in makes me long for touchless water bottle refill machines.

Definitely installing some of those in here soon.

"Hey. You bought the gyms?" Vince says to me in a raw voice, astonishment evident in his tone.

"*Shhh*. Yes. I was going to tell you, but–"

"Hey, man, you don't owe me an explanation."

"I know I don't owe you one. I want to give you one."

"You're moving on. Found a different program. It's cool."

His words don't make sense to me.

"What are you talking about?"

Cold eyes meet mine. "Jorg told me. I'm sure you're moving on the gentrification plan some bean counter at your company came up with."

"Gentrification?"

Vince gestures towards the door. "This neighborhood was a steaming pile of dog crap when I was a kid. No one wanted to live here. Jorg had this place long before he took me in. And now you're razing it and turning it into some co-working place for doggie daycare, or whatever you real estate developers do."

A thousand defensive responses go through my head before I shut the hell up and just cross my arms over my chest, breathing carefully, letting the silence hang between us. Vince is furious. So angry, he won't make eye contact.

"That's why you think I bought the gyms from Jorg?"

"Why else would you?"

"Maybe I like the place."

He snorts, using the towel in his hand to wipe imaginary sweat off his shoulder. "You only come here because of Gerald and me."

"No. I came here the first time because of that. I kept coming back because I like how I feel when I'm here."

"No successful CEO of a Fortune 500 company does business based on how he feels."

"Wrong, Vince. So wrong. That's how you get to be the CEO of a Fortune 500 company. How something feels is one of the best predictors of success. Plus, this place fills a hole in the market. The combination captures my attention."

Now he meets my eyes.

"And I don't want to change anything. Not even the stench of your wrongness."

Vince puffs up. "You seem awfully cocky."

"And you seem pretty negative, for a guy I was about to offer a director-level job to."

"A what?"

"I need someone to run the fitness side of the gyms. Stay true to the concept. I want a chain where people can go and just sweat. Do the hard work. Gritty and authentic, without all the fancy frills. No upselling. No pressure. Just a gym home where you feel like you're part of the community at the same time you're left alone to do your lifting, sweat it out, and head home."

"You're offering me a job?"

"I am. Gina has all the details ready to mail you when I give her the okay."

At the mention of my executive assistant, Vince's eyes widen a little, then settle down. "Why would I want to become a corporate drone? Last thing in the world I want is to sit behind a desk."

"Then we won't put one in your office."

"You're serious."

"I am. At first, we'll stick to the existing sixteen locations. Create procedures, audit staff, make sure we understand what we're marketing and to whom and how best to expand the clientele. And then–"

His hand goes to my forearm. I shut up.

"You want me to direct a chain of gyms? To make sure they stay like old Jorg's created them?"

"Yes."

"This is either crazy or genius."

"Let's go with genius."

"I don't know, man. I have a lot of clients right now. They'll be pissed if I leave them."

"Your call. No rush on a decision. Take a week or two. But I do need to know."

"What about salary? Benefits?"

"Gina has the proposal. You want me to have her send it?"

Over Vince's shoulder, I see Jorg watching us, one eye narrower than the other. A protective, fatherly quality radiates from his look. Whatever happened when Vince was fifteen and the old man let him live in the office here at the gym persists to this day.

"I will never become your bitch, Andrew."

"I'll take that as a yes, Vince." I grab my phone and text Gina, who instantly replies with *Confirmed*.

"I didn't accept the job. Just looking over the proposal."

I grin at him. "I know."

"Don't give me that smug look."

"I'm not!"

"It's embedded in your face. You can't help yourself, can you? Go sweat it out. Hundred burpees."

"What?" My grin falters, sliding off my face like a mountain goat losing his footing.

His glare is tinged with amusement. "You want authentic? We'll start right here, right now. With *you*."

❄ 4 ❄

Amanda

"**M**om?" After all these years of my mother being sick with fibromyalgia, I've reached a point where I know the second I open the front door, even an inch, what kind of condition she's in. The tells are simple: which lights are on or off. Whether I smell home-cooked food or something more industrial from a frozen dinner. The trash can still out by the curb, two days after pickup.

Her teacup Chihuahua, Spritzy, eagerly wagging his tail, and the overly enthusiastic ankle-licking invasion.

"Amanda?" she calls out weakly from the other room. "I'm in here."

In here means she's stationed in her recliner chair, laptop desk in place, a thick rice pad on her kidneys, long cold after being microwaved an hour ago to ease her pain. Her eyelids droop slightly, not from sleepiness, but from the effort it takes for her body to manage so much pain.

There is no extra bandwidth to lift her eyelids more than necessary to see.

"Mom," I say, reaching for her hand, lightly holding the back of it. A hug would hurt her too much. Touching gives her some small comfort, so over the years, we've worked out this gesture.

Her skin is warm. Dry. Her clasp is weak.

"Could you?" Bending forward just an inch or two, she signals for me to take the rice pad from behind her. Instinct tells my hands what to do, my motions suddenly automatic. Two minutes and twenty-nine seconds have passed by the time I realize I'm standing in front of the microwave, the buttons pushed and time just something to get through before bringing Mom some relief.

I look down. Her dog is panting at me.

"Have you walked Spritzy?" I ask, knowing the answer is no, but Mom needs the dignity of being asked.

"Not yet. Could you?"

"Of course!" I find the can of treats to snap one in half, making Spritzy sit for it. The way he chows it down reminds me.

Yup. The dog food dish is empty. Water's full, thankfully, because of a self-watering system that Mom can fill every couple days.

"Don't try to feed him!" Mom says. "You'll make sick all over the kitchen floor like last time."

"I am so sorry."

"It's fine. Wasn't the first time I've ever cleaned up your sick."

Mom calls vomiting "your sick" or "the sick."

"I'm a grown-up, Mom." Ignoring her comment, I shake some dry food in Spritzy's bowl. He eagerly starts chomping away, the back of his little head bobbing as he chews.

"And soon you'll be someone's mom. Two someones." Her eyes jump to my belly. "How's it going?"

My hand goes under my navel and I smile. "I'm fine. I'm into the second trimester now, so things should get easier soon."

"I can't see it with that baggy shirt you're wearing," she says evenly, slowly. "Soon you'll have to wear maternity clothes."

I pull up the hem of my shirt. She giggles. The wide elastic panel on my pants makes it clear I'm pregnant.

"I remember when I was pregnant with you," she says softly, eyes unfocused, clearly going back in the past in her mind's eye. "My friends lent me their maternity clothes. We didn't have so many choices back then. You saved your stuff and passed it around. Why waste money on new when you'd only wear it for such a short time?"

I point to my pants. "These were Shannon's. She lent me her collection of maternity clothes."

"Lent?"

"She wants everything back."

"For when she and Declan have another, I hope?"

I nod. She smiles, but it's weak.

The microwave dings and I walk over to it, the dog at my heels. *One thing at a time, doggo,* I think to myself. Take care of Mom first, then you.

My stomach tightens. Soon I'll add two babies into the mix of people I take care of.

Thank goodness I have Andrew to take care of me.

"Here, Mom," I announce as I return to her, holding the rice pad. Gingerly, she leans forward. I settle it in place, then let her tweak it. As her shoulders relax, eyes closing with relief, I wonder if I'll develop this autoimmune condition, too.

I wouldn't wish it on my worst enemy.

"Marie is going to be thrilled Shannon's planning to have more. She already has three grandchildren, so you'd think that would be enough," Mom says as I click Spritzy's leash onto his collar, which immediately leads to him jumping at my face and licking my nose.

Which makes me gag.

Which makes me–

"Are you about to be sick all over, Mandy?" she calls out as I dry heave, Spritzy stepping back and cocking his head as if to ask, *Was it something I did?*

"Fine, Mom. Need fresh air," I gasp as I lunge out the door, Spritzy's stubby tail jiggling with excitement as I take five steps and he sniffs the hell out of Mom's light post.

Then he pees and I turn away, trying not to watch the long, thin stream.

It's a sunny day, the kind you want to milk for every second it offers. The temperature's in the mid-sixties, a rare nice early-March day in Massachusetts, where the sun seems allergic to paying a visit in winter.

I'll try to convince Mom to go outside and sit in the sun, on a reclining lawn chair, but my chances are about one in four. Mom's an actuary, so I think of her in those terms.

Math.

Too bad you can't math your way out of a flare. If you could, Pam Warrick would have done it long ago.

Spritzy turns to look up at me, an eager expression on his tiny, pinched face, as if I'm supposed to praise him for answering nature's call. Instead, I move forward, enjoying the feel of my legs as I take long steps, walking around the block. He's a tiny little thing, a few pounds at most, and holding my end of the leash feels a bit like walking one of those "invisible dog" gag toys you win at a carnival booth.

But he's very real, and I don't know what Mom would do without his companionship.

Fresh air helps me, the walk getting my blood pumping. My body still feels foreign to me as the pregnancy evolves. I have moments when I'm not sure how to get through time itself, the strangeness of growing two human beings inside me making daily life seem dreamlike, as if I'm forgetting something important.

How can I walk a dog while something so monumental is happening in me? How can I get the mail, sit in a work meeting, pump gas—do all the normal things we do in life—and not constantly stop to marvel at what I am doing through no effort of my own?

Biological processes have an order, a sequence, a systematic ritual. Each step hands the proverbial baton off to the next one.

How do we not spend all our time pondering pregnancy?

Spritzy sneezes, three adorable little snits in a row, then turns around, suddenly ready to head home. He has a homing device in his head, the walks always shorter when Mom's having a flare. I can tell he senses her sickness, and gives her extra attention when she flares.

Like Andrew and my pregnancy.

"We're not so different, are we?" I whisper to the dog as we turn the corner and I see the front of the house, looking at it through a new lens. The bushes need to be trimmed, and the mulch has worn thin along the sidewalk. Mom used to hire a neighbor kid to mow the lawn, but he graduated from high school and went off to college, time passing in a way that upset her routine.

Note to self: Hire a landscaping crew to help her.

"Hey!" I call out gently as the screen door bangs behind me, Spritzy shaking with excitement to be home. I unclick the leash and he goes straight for his food dish, looking at me with eyebrows up as if surprised there's still food there from when I fed him before.

"Thank you. Now I don't have to worry about him."

"Why not do an electric fence in the backyard, Mom? Then he can run free and you don't have to take him on walks."

"It's on my to-do list. But you know."

Yeah. I know. When you're sick like Mom is, you do as much as possible during the good times; when it gets bad, the rest falls by the wayside.

"Let me hire someone for you."

She bristles, unwilling to meet my eye. "I can do it."

"Mom. Let me. Please. Knowing Spritzy's well cared for matters to me because it matters to you."

"Actually, I was thinking about putting in a regular fence."

"Really? Why?"

"For when you and Andrew come and bring the babies."

"Huh?"

"They won't be babies for long. Soon they'll crawl, then walk. And two at the same time! I remember your toddler years, Amanda. You'll need to keep them safe by always having an eye on both. A fence in the backyard here will make a safe place for me to play with my grandchildren, and for Spritzy. It's win-win."

"That sounds extremely practical."

She points to herself. "That's me."

We laugh. It feels good.

"Then I'll hire a company to install a fence," I say, seizing the moment. "You pick the fence."

"I'll have to see if it's in the budget."

"It's in *my* budget," I say firmly.

"Everything's in your budget. You married a billionaire!"

"That's right."

"We've talked about this before," she says tightly. "You can't just—"

"If your reasoning is that the regular fence will help you to watch my children, then I *can* 'just', Mom. My treat."

"Since when is a fence a treat?" But she's smiling, eyes kind and, dare I say it—happy?

"Good. It's settled."

"You always were a fixer, weren't you? Still are."

A wave of nausea hits me, making my skin crawl. Who knew skin could feel sick?

"Amanda? You're green. Here." She sorts through something on her end table, then hands me a wrapped candy. It smells like lemon. I open it and put it on my tongue, the taste instantly helping.

"Get some carbonated water from the fridge. It's in the door. Slim little bottle, no flavor. Sip it slowly. You'll be fine."

I do exactly as she says, my body moving as if someone is pulling the strings, the sick flavor of bile threatening to crawl up my throat. The first sip makes my stomach gurgle, the second makes me gag, but halfway through the small glass, lemon takes over my mouth and I finally feel the crisis fading.

"Sit," Mom says, pointing to the couch across from her. I do, Spritzy jumping into Mom's lap, chin on paws, eyes closing as he sighs.

"Okay."

Wonder where I learned to fix problems for people.

"You'll be fine. Nothing is permanent. How we feel always passes into something different."

"Is that how you handle flares?"

"Sometimes. It's very easy to be calm and composed when you're not the one struggling."

I catch her gaze. She's worried. I see it.

"I'm fine. The babies are great. We have an ultrasound coming up."

"I know. James told me." Andrew's father and my mother have one of the most unlikely friendships I've ever seen. At one point, we assumed there was a romance brewing between the two of them, but Mom rebuffed him. I'm not entirely convinced nothing's going on, and I've often wondered why Mom rejected his advances before.

Sure, he dates other women. When have you ever seen James McCormick without a woman on his arm, four decades younger? So maybe I'm wrong about my mom, but...

When I ask, she changes the subject.

But they still hang out together.

And they obviously gossip about me and Andrew.

"Did he? I've been informed by him that I'd better produce a boy."

"That's all on Andrew," Mom says with a chuckle.

"I understand biology, Mom. Tell it to James."

"Oh, I have. Trust me. I've made it clear he needs to back off and leave you two alone."

"Hah! Fat lot of good that will do."

"I tried." She shrugs. We share smiles that make it clear we both know how difficult James McCormick can be, and how legendary his stubborn streak is.

My husband is definitely his father's son.

Bzzz

I look at my phone. Andrew.

I'll be home for dinner. What do you want?

For the last few weeks, we've ordered takeout every single night, because I never know what my stomach will or won't be able to handle. I close my eyes and ask myself what I want, and reply:

Grilled salmon with paprika. Cantaloupe. Sautéed carrots in honey and cumin.

He texts back: *I see you're sticking with the orange theme.*

I send an emoji of someone sticking out its tongue.

Will do, he replies. *I'll have Consuela make it and bring it home after the gym.*

Then I get a heart.

Consuela owns a private restaurant in the Seaport District, the kind that you can't know about unless you know someone who knows someone. It's our special place, and since morning sickness has ravaged me, Consuela's been gracious enough to meet my weirdo dietary needs.

She also takes it as a challenge. My palate has expanded considerably as a result of her driving mission to find new orange foods.

I reply with: *You mean you'll have Gina contact Consuela to do it all, and have Gerald pick it up and bring it to the house.*

Same thing, he texts back.

"I love how you smile when you think about Andrew," Mom says, making me look up from my phone.

"Huh?"

"You two are so in love."

My smile broadens. "We are."

She looks at my belly. "Those babies are very, very fortunate."

"Billionaire's kids," I mutter.

"No. You could be penniless and they'd be so, so blessed. You and Andrew are going to be wonderful parents."

"How do you know?"

Tenderness floods her face as she reaches for me. I stand and bend before her, her hand on my shoulder, eyes shining with something close to tears.

"Because you have such a good heart. You always did. You're smart and sweet and you care about people and want to help them. And Andrew loves you deeply. I may not understand his ambition, but I do see that he's a loving man."

"Ambition?"

"When you two started dating, I worried he'd be too busy for a real life. I am less worried now."

My turn to bristle. "He's not James."

"Goodness, no. He's certainly not. Andrew will never grow old and have the kinds of regrets James has."

"Regrets?"

A slight wince forms in her features, as if she's said too much. "We all have regrets."

"Tell me. What are yours?"

"Why would you want to hear that?"

"Because I want to try to avoid having them when I'm older. And the only way to do that is to understand what causes them."

A long, heavy sigh pours out of her. "It depends on the kind of regret, I think. Some regrets I have are for things out of my control, like Leo. Your father made choices and you and I paid the price, but I couldn't change him. So that's a different kind of regret."

"I understand that. What about regrets involving things you had control over?"

"Mine are the same as most people's. I wish I'd enjoyed you more when you were little. I'd worry less now about a messy house, or about a problem at daycare or your school, and just relax. Enjoy you for who you were and are. I wish I had understood when I was younger that there is no point where everything's in balance. Something's always askew. Learning to live with that is life."

"What do you mean?"

"I thought that life was what you did when the house was clean, the repairs were done, work's checklist was completed, and the decks were cleared. It was foolish, and part of being so left-brained. It was hard to just play with you when the kitchen was messy, or to carve out open time to just be available to you if a work project loomed. If I could do it over, I'd let all that go."

I open my mouth to tell her something Andrew's tried to get through my head–that I can leave my work at Anterdec and be a stay-at-home mom to the twins. Like Shannon, I'm being offered something very few women get: the freedom to be a stay-at-home mother without worrying about money. At all.

"Do you ever wonder what life would have been like if Dad hadn't been so dysfunctional?" I ask, surprising myself with the question.

"All the time," she answers, upping the surprise.

"How?"

"It would have been easier to raise you. He loved you, but Leo was a tormented man, and he didn't give two whits about being self-reflective, or getting real help. His journey was his, and he didn't really see you or me as people after a while."

"Like a narcissist?"

Mom shakes her head. "No. When Leo was sober, he was a good

guy." Nostalgia softens her tension. "We had so much hope in the beginning. But time wasn't kind to us. And the alcohol made him selfish."

"I think addiction does that to people."

"It sure does. So I can't imagine a life with Leo in it that didn't include his mistress."

"Mistress?"

"The bottle. Hardest relationship to quit."

"Ah."

A sad silence settles in between us until Spritzy's collar begins to jangle. He jumps off Mom's lap and toddles over to the food dish, which is empty now.

"Right! Sorry!" I say to him, moving away from Mom into the kitchen, where I find the bag of dog food and a little more into the bowl. He begins gobbling, making huffing sounds, and Mom laughs.

"I fed him a few hours ago! He has the metabolism of a humming bird. Would you pour a few small bowls and set them on the counter for me? Then I just have to bend down and put them out for him."

"Of course."

"And the mail?" A small stack of envelopes is on the counter. "I forgot to put it next to my chair," she says sheepishly, as if that's some sort of mistake.

"Here." I hand the stack to her and watch as she sorts, then turn away to pour dog food into four small bowls I find. If it makes life a little easier for her, I'm happy to do such simple tasks.

Her flares come and go, and hopefully by the time she's used up these bowls, she'll be on the upswing.

"Junk. Junk. Junk. Another political donation request. Junk. Replacement windows. Junk." She pauses her description of the pile. "Lab."

"Lab?"

She sighs, shaking her head. "James has it in his head that I might not have fibromyalgia."

"WHAT? How dare he? He doesn't have the right to–"

"No, no. He doesn't think I'm faking. Plenty of people think it isn't a real disease, but he's not one of them. He thinks I have Lyme disease."

"Lyme?" I look at her, searching her skin for the red bullseye rash Lyme brings.

"He said there are stories of people with autoimmune conditions who turn out to have Lyme disease. Treat the Lyme, and the condition fades."

"What's the lab work for? Did you get bitten by a tick?"

"Not that I know. And I've had the fibro for so long. I think he's wrong. But there's a special test that can find antibodies if your immune system ever mounted a response, so..."

"He convinced you to do the test?"

She nods and stares at the envelope. Her finger is halfway through the flap, but then she stops.

"You're nervous about the results?"

"No. Just–what if he's right?"

"You know James. He is right, in his mind. Always."

"But what if I've had Lyme this entire time and everyone missed it?"

"You were tested for it, though."

"Not with a test as sensitive as the one James's doctor ordered." She taps the envelope. "I wonder what this says."

"Are you afraid to read it?"

Spritzy jumps up and snuggles in her lap again. Mom looks at me with eyes I don't recognize, the skin around them sagging with age, eyelids half closed, exhaustion turning my no-nonsense mother into someone slower, sadder, smaller.

"Yes?" The fact that she phrases it as a question breaks my heart.

"I'll read it for you, Mom."

"This is silly," she gasps, but doesn't move. "Having Lyme won't change a thing."

"Of course it will! You'd use different treatments. You might be able to get rid of the flares."

"I'll still be sick."

"But you'll be sick in a way that doctors could try to cure. Fibromyalgia doesn't have a cure!"

We both look at the envelope. She thrusts it at me.

"Yes. You read it." Closing her eyes, she uses her right hand to scratch Spritzy's forehead. His eyes tighten and he looks like he's grinning.

"Okay."

I slide the letter out of the envelope, unfold it, and scan the document. My throat tightens, stomach dropping as all the pieces come together in my mind, the implications enormous.

Then I grab her hand and gently, so gently, I squeeze. Years of her pain and suffering, her stoic resolution, of supporting her through it all, have to be expressed in pressure so tender that it conveys love, but not so hard that it adds to her struggle.

That balance is impossible.

"Mom?"

"Yes?"

The tears I'm trying to hold back don't care about what I want, dotting the page as I tell her, "James was right."

Amanda

"Your father!" I say in a voice that even I know sounds accusatory. Andrew just walked in the front door, and he's dripping with sweat, so soaked that I cringe when he wraps his arms around me and tries to kiss my cheek.

"Why won't you hug me? And what about my father? What did he do now?"

I ignore the second part and focus on my husband's sweaty, humid body. "Why didn't you shower at the gym?"

"Vince made me go for a long run."

"How long?"

"All the way home."

"To the condo?" We still have his condo in the Seaport District, though we moved to Weston a while ago, renovating Andrew's childhood home. "There's a bathroom there, with a shower."

"I know there is. We've had some fantastic sex in that shower, but no. He made me run *here*."

"He made you run all the way from the city to Weston?"

Andrew rakes one hand through soaking wet, dark hair. "Yes. Stuck with me the first ten miles, then peeled off to head to his home."

"That's got to be twenty miles!"

"We started at the gym. Fourteen point eight, to be exact."

"I didn't know you could run that far."

"Neither did I, until today."

"Your security team let you do that?"

"Let?" Andrew's glare makes me feel like my skin is being peeled off by lasers. "My team doesn't *let* me do anything." He puffs up. "I do what I want."

"Right." I avert my eyes. "Why is Vince pushing you so hard?"

"Because old Jorg told him."

Uh oh.

The chain of gyms is Andrew's personal project, and I'm so excited for him. Telling Vince about it was presenting a challenge to my husband, and now it sounds like that has just exploded.

Andrew begins to stretch, giving me a chance to admire his body, but nausea is trying to creep back in. This mixed reaction to the world is driving me nuts. How can I be nauseated and sexually aroused at the same time? The two conditions are wholly incompatible, but welcome to pregnancy, where nothing makes sense and all of the inconvenience is on you.

"I'm sorry. How'd it go?"

He lets out a laugh that doesn't sound amused at all. "It went fourteen point eight miles of pain, that's how it went. Vince thought I was firing him."

"But you want to hire him!"

"I know. He misinterpreted everything." Andrew stops at the foot of the stairs and stretches more, a long, slow movement that moves my inner turbulence up a notch.

"So he's angry with you?"

"Fourteen point eight guesses why."

"I don't know. Why?"

"He thought I wanted to remodel the gyms and make them–his word–bougie."

"Bougie! No! You want to keep them authentic and comfortable and… gritty. Like they are."

"Right."

"And have Vince be in charge of keeping them that way."

"I told him that. Gina's sending the proposal to him. Already did, in fact. Not sure he'll bite."

"I hope he does."

Andrew winces. "Vince replaced my arms and legs with rubber bands filled with pain."

"You say that every time you come home from a training session with him. Why torture yourself?"

"Because keeping a body like this takes effort."

I let my eyes comb over his tall, muscular form. "I owe Vince my gratitude, then."

"Oh, really?" The gleam in his eye makes my stomach clench. He wants sex. My joke triggered the always-on-the-surface reaction that makes it clear how ready he is. Gym shorts hide *nothing*.

A war begins in my mind, two very different Amandas squaring off.

"So, about your dad," I blurt out.

Something in his eyes dims. "Yes?"

"He figured out my mother's fibromyalgia."

"I see. The conversation is now about our parents. Got it." Andrew pauses, as though my words are finally sinking in after a time delay. "My father did *what*?"

"Figured out the source of her fibromyalgia."

"My father? James McCormick? Are we talking about the same man?"

"We are. He encouraged Mom to get some complicated Lyme disease test, and it came back positive. It could explain everything with her."

"Lyme?"

"I know, right?"

Andrew guides me upstairs, gently encouraging me to walk up the stairs first.

"Where are we going?"

"I need a shower." He winks at me, eyes going straight to my midsection, his wolfish smile softening. My body is growing two human beings that are part him. It connects us. His loving gaze is endearing, a source of comfort.

The babies are part me, too, of course, but the idea that I have a piece of Andrew in me is so amazing.

Happiness makes me warm. Or maybe that's just hormones.

We walk into the bathroom together, and Andrew turns on the shower jets. The renovated master bath is half shower room, half everything else. Satin nickel frames the creamy white subway tiles of the shower walls, the floors all Carrera marble. We went for a classic look in here, timeless elegance to suit this antique estate. Sconces are mounted on the mirrored wall over the sinks, adding extra sparkle that's both flattering and soft.

It's like staying at the world's most luxurious hotel, but it's also your home.

"You joining me?"

Before I can answer, he stops himself, reaching for my hand, eyes concerned.

"Wait. Sorry. Let me drag my lust-filled brain out of the lake of testosterone it's swimming in and ask: How is Pam?"

"She's stunned. It was hard to leave her alone today," I admit, growing even warmer as he pays attention to me. Andrew has a one-track mind. No, not just sex. It's literally a one-track mind: He focuses on one thing at a time, and one thing only, with one hundred percent attention. Nothing else exists when he's lasered in on whatever captures his focus.

It feels very good to be that object.

"You can go back to her. Honey, I'm sorry," he says, voice dropping. "Is she in danger?"

"Danger?"

"From the Lyme?"

"Oh, no. The tests show she's had it for a long time. Probably years. Maybe even way back when the fibro was first diagnosed. It's not an emergency. Just... it's a lot to process. Mom was furious that none of her other doctors ever figured it out, and then she went into research mode. You know how she is."

He smiles, but it's a muted amusement. "I'm sure she had PubMed pulled up within seconds and created a database of possible treatments before you could brew a cup of coffee."

"Close," I say, smiling right back. My stomach flips, not from the babies, but from knowing he understands my mother so well. This is what families do, right?

They accept one another. They watch each other. They see people and help them feel seen and heard.

"Are there treatments we can help with?"

"Help?"

"Research trials? Specialists Pam can't easily access? I'll pull whatever strings I need to," he says firmly. "Dad will, too. I'm on the hospital board, after all."

"You know Mom hates that."

"Too bad."

That's the other side to family: Sometimes, there's conflict.

"You can't alpha your way through my mother's medical issues."

"Who says I can't? Watch me."

Protectiveness radiates off Andrew like the sweaty musk from his workout. While I'm slightly outraged by his dominance, I have to admit, it's also a relief. And sweet. And hot.

Mmmmm, hot.

I reach for my top button and undo it, his eyes growing wider by the second, attentive to my fingers in that super-focused manner he has.

And then he acts.

Naked in seconds, Andrew reaches behind me and slides his hands under the thick elastic of my maternity pants, the fabric pooling at my feet. Sex has been hit-or-miss these last months as morning sickness has ravaged my whole self. When he kisses me, I taste the salt of sweat and the sweet flavor of something fruity, and then he dissolves into just Andrew.

"You sure?" he whispers as he deftly unclasps my bra, pregnancy-augmented breasts spilling out into the space between us, my nipples rubbing against his chest, the air around us filling with steam.

"Yes. Please, yes."

"You do not have to ask. Trust me. I'm the one saying please."

His kiss stops whatever response was forming in my mind, the day's worries stacked on top of each other in a pile I have to sort, organize, distribute, and dispense with, but as he moves us into the water's spray, the tumbled mess of everything is suddenly over there, off to the side, out of sight. He pulls me back into my body, and the worries fade.

I'm nothing but wet skin and full lips, Andrew's eager hands taking over, making me feel. Far too much time has passed without this, and it feels good to feel good. To feel *great*.

To feel with my body, and not only with my heart and mind.

His palm slides down my wet breasts, cupping the growing hard ball beneath my navel. Then he drops to his knees and kisses me there, twice.

Once for each baby.

But the next kiss he gives, going lower, lower, *lower*, is very much for me.

And only me.

🦋 6 🐚

Andrew

On Sunday, the doctor's office robo-called to remind us about our eight a.m. appointment today. Amanda had to drink a gallon of water and hold her bladder, so she's twitchy, excited, miserable, and fussy.

Which means she's not all that different than she's been since the first trimester.

But now she needs to *go*.

The chairs in the waiting room at the ob-gyn's office are simple, with thin wooden armrests and gray tweed upholstery. They're wider than I'm used to, but then it hits me:

They're wide because pregnant women grow.

"I can't believe that with so many medical advances in modern society, obstetrics still hasn't managed to come up with a way to get images of a fetus that doesn't make me feel like my bladder is the Titanic," Amanda hisses at me, earning an appreciative glance from a woman across from us, who literally looks like she swallowed a whole watermelon and it's trying to escape out of her belly button.

"Your bladder hit an iceberg and cracked in half?" I whisper back to my wife.

"Taking on so much water, it's sinking me. Andrew, I don't think pelvic muscles were designed to clench this hard."

My body and my mind have two distinctly different reactions to that comment.

"Wait until the baby's this big," the woman across the way says, pointing to her belly. "Your bladder will be flatter than roadkill."

Amanda's face turns green.

The woman puts her hand over her mouth in horror. "Oh! I'm sorry! Are you still dealing with morning sickness?" Her eyes drift to Amanda's belly. "You look like you're well into the second trimester."

"Twins," I explain, the woman's male companion looking at me with an expression I can't quite name, but I swear there's pity in it.

And, of course, admiration.

That's right. My shooters scored, big time.

"Twins? Are they your first?" the guy asks, patting his wife on the knee. She removes his hand with a vacant expression.

The gesture makes me shiver.

Amanda nods. "We're first timers. You?"

"Fourth baby," the woman says, eyes cutting to her husband. "And this time, you don't get to listen to the Red Sox game during pushing."

"They were in the Series!" he snaps back, looking to me for validation.

I go full poker face.

I'm not stupid.

"Fourth!" Amanda exclaims. "Good for you. Any tips?"

"Get the epidural in the parking lot," the guy mutters.

"They do that?" I ask.

Amanda elbows me. "Ha ha."

"You going for a natural birth?" the woman asks us.

Amanda tenses up. I'm not sure why she does, but I'm suddenly uncertain what to do.

So I take her hand in mine and smile at her.

"We, well... we're not sure," Amanda says, eyes searching mine.

I kiss the back of her hand. "Whatever gives us two healthy babies and a healthy mom is all that matters."

At the word "mom," Amanda's head pulls back slightly.

Mom.

My wife is about to be a *mom*.

"Get the damn epidural," the woman advises. "Don't be a hero. Besides, you probably won't have a choice."

"What do you mean?" Amanda asks her.

Pointing to Amanda's belly, the woman's eyebrows go up. "Twins are a crapshoot. I've never had them, but my friends with twins had to have c-sections. The worst were the ones who labored all the way through vaginal deliveries and at the last minute, a baby turned and *bam*–they needed a c-section, too. Nothing like recovering from an episiotomy and abdominal surgery at the same time!"

Amanda squirms and hisses, "I need to pee so bad."

"How about peeing on her to shut her up?" I mutter back.

"Karen?" a medical assistant calls out. The pregnant mom stands, her husband shuffling after her like a whipped dog.

"Good luck!" Karen chirps.

"She's like a pregnancy dementor," Amanda grouses, moving to one side, one hip up, the other stretched at a funny angle as she lengthens her left leg as much as possible.

"What are you doing?" I ask.

"Flattening my bladder."

"Flattening it?"

"Lengthening it. Making it stretch. Pick a term. I've got nine gallons of water in a five-gallon container and I'm ready to blow."

Just then, the radio starts a new song. TLC's "Waterfalls."

"COME ON!" Amanda shouts, staring at the speaker. "Are you *kidding* me?"

I start singing along to the first two lines and immediately regret it when she elbows my crotch.

"HEY!" I choke out. "If you want more kids, cut it out!"

"Elbow doesn't do enough damage anyhow," says a pleasant woman's voice from behind us. We turn to find Dr. Rohrlian, a friendly woman we've met once before. Short brown hair, a smile like Mary Lou Retton, and keen eyes taking us in.

I leap up. Amanda moves slowly, but eventually stands.

"Let's get you in for the ultrasound before that bladder bursts. I'm so sorry we haven't found a better way to do this yet, Amanda, but we do our best with the technology we have." She shakes my hand. "Good to see you again, Andrew."

Her clasp is strong, hands dry and smooth. I wonder how many babies she's caught–or cut–out of mothers.

"Good to see you, too, Dr. Rohrlian."

Amanda gives her a wan smile. "In case I pee on your shoes, please accept my apology in advance."

"Wouldn't be the worst thing to land on these workhorses," she answers, flexing a foot, showing off black Crocs. "That's why I wear shoes I can hose down."

We walk down a long hallway. This practice is one of the biggest in Boston. When Amanda learned she was carrying twins, her options immediately narrowed. We agreed we wanted the best, of course, and everyone's health was our priority. Amanda's the one whose body is experiencing everything, so I let her decide.

And fortunately, she decided on this ob-gyn practice with ten doctors, two certified nurse-midwives, and plenty of experience with multiples.

"Normally, one of the medical assistants does this," I say to the doctor, a bit puzzled. "Doesn't Amanda need to weigh herself and do the urine test?"

"Not for this," she answers evenly as she opens the door to a dark room with an exam bed and monitors all over the wall. "Ultrasounds are different. But you're right – normally the tech would come out to see you in, but I happened to be walking by and wanted to say hi again."

I help Amanda up on the exam table as the ultrasound tech walks in. A bright smile greets us, the light from the hallway glinting on braces as she closes the door.

"Amanda? I'm Tanley," she says, giving Amanda her hand. We take care of the pleasantries, the hum of machinery that's about to let me see our children a warm backdrop.

"You won't see me next time," the doctor says as she starts to slip out, "so good luck to you both."

"Why won't I see you next time?" Amanda asks, turning to the doctor with a perplexed look, an edge of panic in her eyes. Aha. This one's her favorite so far.

I knew she'd become attached.

"We try to rotate you through appointments with everyone on the team, and there are twelve of us. That way, whoever is on call when you deliver is someone you've met," Dr. Rohrlian explains.

"We don't get to choose the doctor?" I ask, surprised.

"You can try. And if you do a scheduled c-section, you often can decide. But short of that, no," she patiently explains, looking at both of us, careful to establish eye contact. "We rotate being on duty. If you have a favorite doctor or CNM, just try to time labor for when that person's on duty."

"You can do that?" I ask.

A loud, infectious laugh fills the room. "If pregnant women could decide when to go into labor, our practice would be much easier to run, Andrew," she says, grabbing my arm with affection.

Amanda laughs, then winces.

Instantly, the doctor gets serious, giving Tanley an arched brow. "Let's see those babies. Mama needs to pee."

"Please don't say the word pee."

Laughing at Amanda's please, the doctor slips out and Tanley takes over.

Excitement and dread blend in my blood, coursing through me with a glittering electricity as I look at the monitor. The black, white, and gray imaging is so old-fashioned; later, we know, we can see the baby in 3-D. For now, it looks like the old Commodore 64 machine my older brother, Terry, used to play with.

I'm about to see my babies.

My babies.

Children I'll soon raise, be responsible for, whose entire existence now rests in Amanda's hands. How she cares for her body completely holds them at her mercy.

The crushing weight of that hits me between the shoulder blades as the tech pulls the waistband of Amanda's loose skirt down around her hips, gently moving her shirt up.

A rush of emotion makes the next few minutes pass in a series of images. The tech squirting gel on Amanda's belly. Holding a wand. Pressing it to her skin. Amanda's groan. Talk about Kegels and complaints about ultrasound technology. Eternity yawns before me as I see myself as a piece of something so much greater than just my own life.

I'm passing on new life to other beings.

There will be a time when they are alive and I am not.

A loud groan, this time from Amanda's stomach, fills the room.

"Sorry," she says, sheepish. "I couldn't eat this morning, but I'm starving now."

"How's the morning sickness?" Tanley asks politely.

"Better, but not gone."

"With twins, everything's stronger. You'll probably have it a little longer than someone carrying a singleton, but it should fade."

"Thanks. It already is."

Buh-DUM! Buh-DUM! Buh-DUM! Buh-DUM! Buh-DUM!

The sound of horses galloping fills the air.

"There we go. Found twin number one, here on the left. Let's see if we can find the other."

Twin number one.

"Lefty!" Amanda jokes.

"That's the heartbeat," I say, as if speaking the words makes it more real.

"One of them. Aha! Here we go." Tanley points to the screen. "Twin number two on the right. Both strong."

"Righty!" Amanda calls out, squeezing my hand with emotion, her grip communicating so much.

Tanley watches the display, then looks at us. "You saw the babies earlier, yes?"

We both nod.

"Then you know they're identical."

"One sperm, two humans," I reply.

"Efficient," is her gratifying answer. Amanda, on the other hand, lets out a sound that makes it clear my swimmers don't impress her at all. "One placenta, as well. But it has to work extra hard." She pats Amanda's shoulder in comfort.

"What are they?" I ask.

"Humans," the tech deadpans.

"No–I mean, boys? Girls?"

"It's pretty early to tell, but we do have some new techniques. You're only at twenty weeks, Amanda, but I can estimate..."

For the next minute, we're silent, Tanley taking pictures, analyzing, doing everything with efficiency. I watch the various shades of gray, white, and black on the screen and fixate on those hearts pounding blood as hard as possible.

My children.

"Um, I really don't think I can hold it much longer," Amanda chokes out, her hand going limp in mine. She's sweating now, and a look of pain lingers on her face even when the tech removes the ultrasound wand.

"I'm sorry." Tanley mops up the gel on her belly. "Go ahead to the bathroom."

"But are they boys? Girls?" Amanda asks as I offer her a hand to sit up, which makes her mouth stretch in a miserable grimace.

"I'm not one hundred percent certain, but I'll tell you if you promise not to sue me if I'm wrong."

"You want it in writing? I can get my assistant to draw up a contract right now–"

She cuts me off. "That was a joke, Andrew. Congratulations." She smiles. "You have two boys in there."

Boys.

Sons.

Two sons.

"Oh, my God," Amanda gasps.

"YES!" I shout, arm going up in victory before I can stop it, fist punching the air with satisfaction.

"You clearly have a preference," the tech says to me dryly.

"No. It's just–" I start to explain.

"He's beating his brother at the baby game," Amanda says, sarcasm dripping from her voice. "Now he's knocked me up with *two* babies from a single supersperm, *and* he's delivering the first grandsons to his father, who is a sexist jerk who finds that important."

I look at my wife.

Who then lifts her hand up and high-fives me.

"We beat Shannon and Declan," she crows.

"I thought you didn't care about that?"

"I do when I'm a bloated whale floating on an endless sea of pee and I turn angry."

"Let's find you a bathroom."

"A potted plant will do at this point."

"Right next door," the tech says, pointing. Amanda rushes in and the lock clicks.

"I'd be happy with whatever," I assure Tanley. "Boy, girl, nonbinary, unicorn, or baby android, as long as they're both healthy."

"But..."

"But this is going to really make my brother's teeth grind."

"I thought the only grind he was into was coffee."

My turn for eyebrows to shoot up. "You're a Grind It Fresh! patron?"

"I am. Next time you see your brother, thank him for me. His new roasted cacao latte has made many pregnant patients happy. Not as much caffeine as coffee, and all the good vibes from the theobromine make for happy moms."

"I will let him know." I clear my throat. "Right after I tell him I won."

Did she just roll her eyes like Amanda does?

Speaking of my wife... she's taking a while. Tanley hands me a long strip of photos of the babies, then extends her hand. "Good to see you. Marci at the front desk will make sure your next appointment is a rotation with one of the other doctors or a CNM. Good luck!" She guides me to the hallway then knocks lightly on an exam room door, entering with a greeting. The sound of the door closing leaves me in a daze.

Ultrasound paper is like old-fashioned fax machine paper, with a coated finish, and the fluorescent ceiling light's reflection on the image catches my eye. One big sac, split in the middle by the placenta, babies floating next to each other, stares back at me and whisper, "Daddy."

"Hey, there," I say to them, looking around furtively. No one heard me.

Good.

A chair is against the wall opposite the bathroom where Amanda's taken up residence, so I have a seat. You can admire a grayscale photo of your womb babies for only so long; after a while, I check messages on my phone, answering a few from Gina.

And then:

Help. I can't pee.

Gina can be a little too TMI for my taste sometimes, as her boss, but this one takes the cake.

Hold up.

That text isn't from Gina.

It's Amanda.

What? I reply.

I CAN'T PEE.

"You don't need to shout," I say aloud.

I can hear you through the door, she answers.

I look up sharply, half expecting her eyes to laser holes through the thick wood.

Do you need help?

What do they do to help you pee? This is ridiculous, now I can't. I can't pee.

One of Amanda's best qualities is her ability to fix things, but when she's the one who needs help, she can be slow to ask for assistance. That's where I come in.

I'll get a doctor, I type, standing up.

NO!

NO!

NO!

The three panicked texts make me halt in my tracks.

Come over to the door, she quickly adds. *Put your mouth near the crack.*

"That's what she said," I mutter out of the side of my mouth.

ARE YOU MAKING THAT STUPID JOKE WHEN I AM IN CRISIS? she texts.

"No. Of course not," I whisper into what I assume is the crack she's talking about.

"I need you to help me," she hisses through the door.

"I can't pee for you, honey. No matter how hard we try, it's impossible."

"A good husband would find a way," she snaps.

Oh, boy. This has escalated instantly to Defcon 5.

"A doctor can help."

"I'll be humiliated! And this is the best practice in the city."

"Have you tried running the faucet? The sound of water could help."

"I tried. No luck."

"Relax. Think about sex from last week."

This is how bad things have gotten. I'm referring to sex in terms of *weeks*.

Not days. Or hours.

"Why would thinking about sex help me pee?" she shouts through the door.

Just then, a medical assistant walks by. She doesn't make eye contact, but she bites her lips as if trying not to laugh. I give her my most charming smile and shrug.

She continues down the hall.

"What do you want me to do?"

"I don't know!" she wails.

Then the door clicks and opens half an inch.

"What are you doing?"

"Get in here!" My upper arm is grabbed with surprising strength and in less than a second, I'm in the bathroom with her, back against the door, wondering if I can text Gina to help me figure out how to make my wife pee.

That's a really bad idea, isn't it? She already gets hazard pay for working for me. I don't need to up it.

Amanda is like a caged animal, walking back and forth, her panties in a wad on top of her purse, her skirt swishing around her knees. If she weren't in so much distress, I'd consider this the prelude to an awesome quickie experience in public, but if I suggest that, I believe she will extract her full bladder from her body using only her fingernails and beat me to death with it.

Then empty it, slowly, on my cooling corpse.

"I can't pee, Andrew! I can't! It's like my body clamped down hard to make sure I didn't embarrass myself in the ultrasound room and now it just refuses! My bladder has selective mutism, except instead of being quiet, it's not releasing."

"Do you want me to massage it?"

"Huh?"

"Or... I don't know! I've never been in this situation before. I just want you to feel better."

Her eyes drop to my hand. "What's that?"

"Pictures of the babies."

She bursts into tears. "I can't even enjoy my own babies' first images because I have a bladder that's turned into a prison gate! AAAAUUUUUGGGGHHHH!" she screams.

Immediately, someone's banging on the door.

"Hello? Can I help you?" The doorknob jiggles.

"We're fine!" I call out, regretting the words instantly.

"Uh, who's in there?" A different voice, lower and commanding.

And male.

"It's me, Amanda McCormick," Amanda says, moving closer to the door. "My husband's in here. Don't worry. We're not being weird or having sex or oh, God," she mutters at the end. "I'm just having a problem."

"Can we help?" Back to the female voice.

"I can't–I can't pee!" Amanda gasps. "I came in for an ultrasound and–"

"It's okay," the woman says. "It happens. Did you try running the sink water?"

"Yes!"

"Are you open to essential oils?"

"What?" Amanda says to the door, incredulous. "Are you one of those MLM people, pushing your product on me *now?*"

Laughter, muted but genuine, pours through the door. "No, no. Peppermint oil helps women pee after labor and delivery. It sounds crazy, but it's worth a try. If you open the door a crack, I can give you a small bottle to try."

Amanda looks at me. I hold up my palms in surrender. When I gotta go, I just whip it out, point, and go. I am not an expert on her predicament.

Bzzz

My phone.

At the same time, Amanda opens the door, grabs an amber bottle from an unknown person, and shuts the door quickly.

"Ten drops in the toilet water. Turn on the faucet, too. And tell your husband not to watch."

I make a face at the door and turn my back to Amanda.

"Gina just texted me. I'll go out in the hall and—"

"NO! You need to stay."

"I do? Why?"

She bursts into tears.

That is the universal explanation that requires nothing more. When my wife cries, I do whatever she asks.

"I'll stay. Of course."

"But don't look at me! I'm so mortified."

I turn away again, staring into the corner like one of the teens in *The Blair Witch Project*, waiting for my fate.

And I read my texts.

From Gina: *Don't forget the Myers meeting at 11.*

I check the time. 10:53.

"Is this going to take much longer?" I ask Amanda as the room fills with a thick peppermint scent.

"ARE YOU RUSHING ME?"

Gonna be late, I text Gina.

You can't be much late, she texts back. *Myers is picky about that.*

Amanda's having a medical problem.

The sound of the faucet turning on tells me Amanda's trying. Go, girl, go. You can do it.

None of those baby books I pretended to read (but had Gina summarize for me) mentioned being stuck in an obstetrician's bathroom with your wife using essential oils to try to pee.

Not a damn one.

Is she okay? Are the babies okay?

They're fine. She's fine. It's... personal.

Did she pee her pants? It happens. I can send a new set of clothes, Gina replies.

Why would you think that?

"IT'S NOT WORKING!" Amanda wails.

Because my last boss had a pregnant wife and her body was like Old Faithful. Poor woman.

Do you know a lot about pregnancy, Gina? I ask, wondering if she can get me out of this.

What's Amanda's problem?

The sink turns off. Amanda huffs. "Now I'm nauseated by the peppermint and my bladder feels like it's so big it's massaging my sinuses, and... HELP me!"

Tap tap tap

"Did the peppermint oil help?" asks a woman through the door.

"No," I say on Amanda's behalf. I have to. She's currently sobbing so hard she can't speak.

"Honey," the woman says softly. "We can catheterize you if we need to."

Amanda's face flies up from being buried in her hands, eyes wide. "Catheterize!" she gasps.

What does catheterize mean? I quickly text Gina.

Tube shoved in your bladder to drain it.

Through your abdomen? I ask.

She follows up with a texted image.

"OH GOD NO!" I bellow, nearly dropping my phone.

"Right?" Amanda says, my comment taken as a form of support. "I don't want that!"

"How can we get you to pee?" I ask her.

Bzzzz

Gina says, *She needs to do something pleasurable. Something she likes more than anything in the world.*

I type the words, *Like sex?* But before I can press Send, Gina writes back:

And not sex.

Damn.

You need to send me a Cheeto-cini from Grind It Fresh! I text back, smacking my forehead. What the hell am I doing *talking* about this with my assistant?

She should be fixing it for me.

I can't.

Gina's two-word reply dissolves into a red wall of disbelief.

You what?

I can't, Andrew. I'm occupied.

If you can text me, you can order a Cheeto-cini to be delivered to me.

You'll have to do it. I'm voice texting. Can't use my hands.

"What are you doing?" Amanda gasps, still crying.

"Trying to fix this for you."

That just makes her cry harder. Amanda's the fixer.

Gina, I'm your boss. This is an order, I type, knowing I've lost the frame the second I hit Send.

Gina's reply is a single photo. It appears to be someone between another person's legs, the only thing I can see knees on a table and a masked person's face between them.

I can't, Gina replies again.

What the hell is that?

I'm getting a lunchtime wax, she replies.

A what?

A Brazilian.

"What the hell is a Brazilian?" I shout, which makes Amanda stop crying, face scrunching in confusion.

"Who's getting a Brazilian right now?" she asks.

"Gina."

My wife goes red faced, big eyes popping out, brow rising. "Why would she share that intimate detail with you?"

"She's telling me she can't work right now."

"It would be pretty hard to work when someone's slathering hot wax all over your nether regions so they can – "

Oh. That kind of Brazilian.

Never mind, I type back quickly, deleting the photo.

Good, Gina responds. *Because the next photo was going to make it so we never make eye contact again, Andrew.*

What does that mean? I start to type.

Because I really, *really* don't want to know.

I backspace, trying to think, the moment too much.

And then I remember.

I'm a Fortune 500 CEO. My superpower is focus.

So I close my eyes. I take a deep breath. I go inward. I find the solution.

And I hug my wife.

"I am going to fix this for you. Give me ten minutes."

"What are you going to do?"

"Do you trust me?"

"Of course. But what are you doing, Andrew?"

Before she can finish, I run out of the room and find the stairs. Down, down, down I thump, moving lightly but fast. I've been on the board of directors of this hospital for a long time and I know the layout pretty well.

This practice is in the wing where Amanda and I went to a birthing class, in fact. Back when she still did mystery shops.

I navigate to the cafeteria, finding my first bounty.

Snack-sized Cheetos.

I grab the orange bag and scan the room, spotting the ice cream section, hoping for a smoothie bar.

Score!

A simple orange-vanilla smoothie rests in a cooler as if it's been custom-made for my purposes, victory so close. It even has a spoon taped to the side.

I toss a ten-dollar bill at the cashier and sprint out, clutching my purchases, taking the stairs again. I suddenly appreciate my time with Vince all the more.

When I return, I barrel into the one-person bathroom, Cheetos and smoothie in one hand, the other on the doorknob. I take one step in and the shrieking begins.

"OH MY GOD, GET OUT, GET OUT!" she shouts, the piercing sound turning my eardrums to bleeding shreds.

"Amanda, why are you – "

I do a double-take.

That woman who's shrieking?

That's *not* my wife.

"I am SO sorry," I shout just as a hand–a strong, angry one–grabs the back of my collar and pulls.

Hard.

"Andrew?" the woman squeaks as the door slams shut, yanked by the same beast who has me lifted up off the ground a good inch, which is damn hard, given that I'm well over six feet tall.

How did she know my name?

And who the hell is *this?*

He twists me, tossing me against the wall as a crowd of white coats and green scrubs turns my peripheral vision to a blur.

But I'm clinging to the Cheetos and the smoothie, no matter what. I may have to turn them into a weapon.

A fist is pulled back, cocked by a bulging arm driven by protective instinct, and it takes my eyes a split second longer than it should to see the threat.

And the face attached to it.

"*Gerald?*"

Rage turned him into a red marble statue, but then his mind comprehends who I am and his arm lowers, slowly.

"Andrew? Why the hell are you crashing my wife in the bathroom?"

"*Suzanne?*"

"Hey, Andrew," says a muffled voice from the other side of the door, followed by the sound of a flush.

"What's going on out there?" Amanda calls out, her voice muted, too.

"Excuse me," says Dr. Rohrlian with more authority than I expect, her presence sudden and fierce. "This kind of violence is absolutely unacceptable in our office. You two need to stop immediately."

Gerald releases my shirt.

And rolls his eyes at me, looking at the Cheetos and the smoothie cup, which is now sweating.

But not as much as I am.

"It's a misunderstanding," I explain to her. "I thought that was my wife's bathroom."

"We're good," Gerald says to her. "I didn't know what was happening. We know each other." He glares at me, contempt no man should ever reveal to his former boss pouring off his scarred face like a nuclear reactor melting down. "Not that you're allowed to barge in on my pregnant wife when she's in the bathroom."

"It was an accident!"

Just then, Suzanne walks out, looks at the food in my hand, and says, "Amanda needs an emergency smoothie?"

"Andrew?" Amanda calls out.

"Go help your wife," Gerald grinds out.

"Thanks. I owe you."

"Oh, you'll pay."

This time, I take great care entering, relieved to find Amanda–and no one else–in the bathroom two doors down. Without a word, I take the bag of Cheetos, place them on the top of the toilet tank, and take all my frustration out on them.

"What are you doing?"

Bang bang bang

"Turning this into dust for your smoothie."

"My what?"

Ignoring her, I open the bag. I pour the dust in, untape the spoon from the side of the cup, and stir.

Then I hold my masterpiece before her in triumph.

"A Cheeto smoothie. This will help you relax enough to pee."

She looks down.

And gags.

"What's wrong?" A cold flush turns my skin to iron.

"It's chunky."

"It's *what*?"

"If I take a bite of that, I'll throw up."

"But–but I pulverized it for you!"

"It needs to be blended."

"BLENDED?"

And... she starts to cry again, clutching her belly, making me feel more insanely pissed than I have ever felt in my entire life.

Because I can't give her what she needs.

I grab the cup, open the door, and move quickly to the same medical assistant who checked us in.

"Excuse me, Lisa," I say, looking at her badge. "Is there a blender somewhere here? In the break room, maybe?"

"Blender? Like, a kitchen appliance?"

"Yes."

She looks at me, then the smoothie. "You're unhappy with your... shake?"

"My pregnant wife is duct-taped to the toilet after an ultrasound, her bladder more distended than a beached whale, and I'm trying to find a way to get her to relax enough to pee." I hold the smoothie aloft. "This is my one chance."

"Pregnancy craving?" she asks, standing.

"Something like that."

"Margie has a Vitamix in the cabinet, for some protein-shake diet she's on. Come with me." She takes me down the hall to a beige door marked Employees Only. Inside is a wall of cabinets, also beige.

Lisa starts opening doors, hitting pay dirt on the third try. She pulls the monster out and plugs it in. I dump the smoothie in, clapping the top on, then I–

"Careful. These things don't just blend. They *heat*. You could end up with smoothie soup if you do it for too long."

It's hard to hear above the machine, getting louder as I turn the dial all the way up to Liquify.

"THANKS!" I yell.

The mixture turns a perfect, day-glo orange.

"What is that, anyway?"

"Orange-vanilla smoothie with a bag of Cheetos in it."

She lets out a low whistle just as I turn the machine off. "That's one I've never heard before."

"She's pregnant with twins and her bladder is turning it into triplets. I'll do whatever it takes."

"Good man. Go!" she says, slapping my shoulder like we're in a relay race. "I'll clean this out for you."

"Thank you!"

I race back to Amanda. The sink is running. Poor honey. Must be trying again. I tap, then open the door.

She's standing at the sink, washing her hands.

She looks up and grins. Then her eyes drift to the smoothie in my hand.

"I peed!" she exclaims.

"You did? How?"

"Marie."

"Marie?"

"I texted Shannon, who texted Marie, and Marie did this guided meditation thing she learned for teaching yoga. I imagined my Kegels were dissolving into breast milk that feeds the babies and suddenly, I peed."

"*That's* what made you pee?"

"Mm hmm." Her stomach growls. "Man, I'm hungry." She takes the drink out of my hand, eyes it, then sips.

And winces.

"That is *disgusting*, Andrew." Before I can stop her, she tosses it in a perfect arc into the trash can, scoring three points.

"I–"

"Don't you have a work call?" She kisses my cheek. "I understand if you need to rush off." Her own phone buzzes.

I stare at her.

It is going to be a long twenty weeks.

❦ 7 ❦

Amanda

My two p.m. appointment fills me with a deep sense of amusement.

And dread.

Mostly dread.

Because do you know which two names are written in that time slot?

Agnes DuChamp and Corrine Morris.

That's right. Those two.

The pinchers.

Regulars at my best friend's mother's yoga classes, older-than-dirt Agnes DuChamp and Corrine Morris like to pinch the asses of hot young men they meet. Hot men like my husband and his brother, who now refuse to attend Marie's yoga classes on the grounds that they bruise easily.

But also because they have actual boundaries.

Why, you may wonder, are The Pinchers meeting with me here at Anterdec?

Because I need them, damn it.

And to top it off, Agnes and Corinne are here long before two p.m. Of course they are.

"Pinch and Pincher are here," Carol says in that droll voice of hers. "Who's next? Are you planning to put my mother on the payroll?"

"Marie? Why would we do that?"

"You're hiring her friends, why not Mom?"

"You want me to offer her a job?"

"Hell, no. I was making a joke. You think I want to work full time with my mother? There isn't enough cannabidiol oil on the planet to make that work."

"Why do you and Shannon have such a visceral reaction to her?"

"Have you met Marie?"

"Of course I have. I love Marie!"

Carol just stares at me. Of all the Jacoby daughters, she looks the most like her mother, so it's a bit jarring to be arguing about how tolerable Marie is when I'm staring into the face of a younger version of her.

"You love Marie enough to turn her into a colleague? Think about that for a minute."

"How did we get from Agnes and Corrine to Marie?"

"All crazy women with AARP cards and no boundaries."

"My card is titanium," says a gravelly old voice from the door.

"Shut up, Corrine. Mine is a stone tablet carved by Moses himself."

"Are we really having this conversation, Agnes? Because you're damn straight, you're older than me. We all know it. You have the liver spots to prove it."

"Too bad I can't turn my liver spots into a blanket and cover my face with it so I don't have to look at you, Corrine."

A young woman in her early twenties, with chestnut hair pulled back in a long ponytail, and wide brown eyes, pops her head between the two old ladies.

"Is this the right place, Grandma?" Her voice is lower than I'd expect, and there is something compact and commanding about her.

"It's fine, Cassie. This is it. My new career, where all I have to do is be old and pretend to be stupid."

"Well, that'll be a change from you being stupid and pretending to be old, Agnes."

"That makes no sense, Corrine."

"Neither does that outfit," the old woman sniffs, giving Agnes's red and white caftan some major side eye.

Cassie taps Corrine on the shoulder. "My brother and I bought that for her for Christmas."

Corrine gives her a thousand-watt smile. "That's so sweet, honey." The charm is strong in that one, because Cassie just shakes her head and laughs.

"I'm Amanda McCormick," I say, striding across the reception area, hand outstretched. "And you are?"

"I'm Cassie. I'm just the driver for these two," she replies, looking behind her. "Mind if I wait in the lobby downstairs? Saw a good coffee place there."

"Not as good as Grind It Fresh!" I stress, never missing a chance to plug my friend's chain.

"How far is it?"

"Two blocks to the left, out the main door." Shannon and Declan have opened two more shops in downtown Boston, in addition to the flagship store at their headquarters. It's made drinking good coffee so much easier, plus Anterdec employees get a twenty percent discount.

Shannon insisted.

"Get me a half-caf skinny macchiato with extra whipped cream," Corrine calls out as Cassie starts to leave.

"But skinny means it's made with skim milk."

"I know."

"Skim milk and whipped cream? Don't the two negate each other?"

"Don't apply logic to her, Cassie. Waste of time," Agnes shoots back, earning a glare from Corrine.

"I like what I like and I don't care if it doesn't make sense." Her eyes flit over Agnes. "Like you and that outfit."

And with that, Cassie departs quickly, making me wish I were her, on the way to Grind It Fresh! Anywhere but here with these two old bats.

They shuffle into my office. Agnes leans on her walker and slams her palm on an empty space on the top of my desk. "I want two hundred thousand a year, a parking space by the elevator, and a pool boy of my own, and I won't take anything less."

Corrine flutters her eyelashes, long, fake things that look like a cloud of starlings hovering in front of her corneas. "Agnes, Agnes, Agnes. You suck at business negotiation."

"I'm stating my terms up front. It's like sex: If you aren't clear about your expectations, you end up getting pissed on."

"Sex has nothing to do with getting pissed on!"

Agnes goes quiet in the creepiest way *ever*.

I clear my throat, Andrew's constant offer for me to leave the company and be a stay-at-home mom suddenly sounding *way* more appealing. I'm already close to saying yes. It's not that I don't love my job–I do–but I don't *need* it. Someone else can take my role and the mystery shopping division will function just fine.

It's more that I won't know what to do with myself if I'm not organizing and fixing problems.

And while twins certainly need lots of attention, caring for babies is so different.

Fear spikes through me, sudden and fierce.

"Amanda?" Corrine asks kindly. "Is something wrong?"

My hand goes to my belly and I give her a shaky smile. "I'm fine."

"You're cooking two at a time. That's superhero level. I remember being pregnant with my daughter like it was yesterday."

"You gave birth before ultrasounds, Agnes."

"I gave birth before television was invented, Corrine."

"When was that?" I ask.

"1960."

"We had television in 1950, Agnes," Corrine says.

"We weren't rich like you, I guess," she says with a sniff.

"It's not my fault my dad was the town doctor and had a thing for electronics."

"He sure did pass on that love of electronics to you, didn't he? Too bad you like the perverted kind."

"Agnes!"

"HEY!"

We turn toward the voice. It's Carol, standing in the doorway. I missed her knock, or she didn't bother. Either way, I'm relieved to see her.

"If you two old biddies can knock it off for three seconds, let's get this all figured out." Carol strides across the room and sets two manila folders on the desk in front of me. "Contracts for these two. I have no idea why you're hiring them."

"Because we're old and you need people who are collagen-challenged."

Agnes looks at Corrine like she just sprouted horns. "Who're what?"

"Collagen-challenged. It's a fancy new term for being old."

"We need new terms for it? It sucks being old. Why sugarcoat it?"

"Because it's not our fault time ticks away. *Old* feels like an insult."

"Only if you're offended by the truth."

"Agnes," Corrine says with a playful slap on her friend's arm.

"What? You're old. I'm old. I'm ninety, for goodness sake! If I can't call myself old, who can?"

Corrine looks at her. "What?"

"What?"

"What did you say?"

"I said, if I can't call myself old, who can?"

"What?"

"Aw, hell, Corrine. Quit pretending you can't hear me. I'm onto you." Agnes snatches one of the manila folders from my desk.

Before Carol can leave, I say, "Stay. You're better at explaining what they need to do than I am."

"You just want reinforcements," she hisses.

"Yep."

Agnes chuckles. "I'll go down to a hundred fifty grand a year, but I won't budge on the pool boy." She flips open the folder and begins reading, her mouth so set in a frown, she has grooves in her chin like Thanos.

"I'll take whatever you're offering," Corrine chirps. "I just like being wanted."

"Geeee-*odd*, Corrine. And you say *I* suck at negotiation?"

"What negotiation?"

Agnes spirals her finger around her ear and points at Corrine. I notice a bumper sticker on her walker that reads, *My amygdala is my favorite scapegoat.*

With a pink brain on it.

"Here," Carol says, handing Corrine her folder. I motion for Carol to take a seat.

She shakes her head.

I cock my eyebrow.

Her nonverbal reply says, *Oh, please. You can do better than that.*

She is Marie Jacoby's daughter, after all. She doesn't cower easily.

I change my expression to *pleeeeease*, and add a belly rub for good measure.

Her eyes jump to my hand. Guilting people into doing stuff for me because I'm pregnant with twins has turned out to be far easier than I expected.

"Fine," she hisses, taking a seat and turning to Agnes and

Corrine. Her finger comes out, like she's scolding an errant child. "I'm going to explain the job, and you're going to listen."

Corrine smiles sweetly.

Agnes rolls her eyes.

"We own assisted living homes as well as retail spaces, resorts, and restaurants. It's the assisted living homes that require your help. Quality control is important, but we also need to track other issues. How women are treated versus men. Minorities, immigrants. LGBTQIA seniors. People who don't speak English well. Income level. All of those factors and more. We need to track customer service in every way possible."

"Sounds like a lot of detail. My memory is great, but Corrine's is absolute crap."

"Hey!" Corrine objects.

"Am I wrong?"

"About what?"

Agnes tilts her head and gestures at her friend. "See?"

"Actually," I interject, "that's what we need. Authenticity. Genuine senior citizen behavior."

"Well, you've come to the mother lode," Corrine says, glaring at Agnes. But her expression falters, concern creeping in. "But we don't need jobs. I've got my late husband's pension and social security. And I can't come into Boston every day. Heck, Agnes isn't even allowed to drive anymore–"

"HEY! THAT'S PRIVATE, CORRINE!" Agnes bellows.

"You talk about getting pissed on during sex and suddenly you're offended I told the truth about losing your driving privileges?" Corrine says in a smug voice.

Carol looks at me and whispers, "This will be you and Shannon in sixty years."

"I hate you," I hiss back.

"Corrine. Agnes," Carol says smoothly. "This isn't a regular job. We'd need a commitment of about one to two mystery shops per week, especially when we're dealing with theft issues in stores and have time windows we're focused on. You do need transportation, though. Do you have someone who could drive you there, reliably?"

They both frown.

Until Corrine lights up, her hand going into the air, finger pointing up.

"I know!" She looks at me. "What about Gerald?"

"Gerald?"

"You know. Gerald Wright? Your husband's chauffeur?"

"I know who Gerald is. What about him? You know him?"

"We take sculpting courses from him at the Westside Center for the Arts. And he's a professional driver. Why not have him drive us to these mystery shops?"

"Damn it, Corrine, there you go again."

"What?"

"Just when I've written you off as a typical dumb blonde, you go and get a great idea. Why didn't I think of that?"

"Because you're an angry old bat who only thinks about herself?"

"No. That doesn't explain it."

"Gerald has a job, Corrine," I explain.

"Can't your husband spare him four times a month?"

"No," Carol says firmly, in a voice that surprises everyone. Even Agnes doesn't argue.

"In order to do these jobs, you need three things: transportation, a smartphone, and a younger family member to go with you and evaluate how family members are treated."

"I am not bringing my daughter along! She might like one of these homes and decide to put me in it!" Agnes shouts.

"My children all live far away," Corrine says in such a mournful voice, I'm close to tears.

"And I have no use for those smartphones. My grandson tried to teach me how to use that Facetime thing and I ended up turning it on while I was washing my pits," Agnes adds.

My tears turn to nausea.

"Hey!" Corrine chirps. "What about Cassie?"

"Cassie? The woman who was just here?" I ask.

Corrine nudges Agnes. "Cassie's not in police school now, and she doesn't have a regular job. She could be our driver. She knows how to use a smartphone." Corrine turns to me. "Why does she need one?"

"To answer questions about the mystery shop in the app. Quietly take pictures and upload. Add video when needed."

"Oh, we definitely need Cassie, then. Would Anterdec pay her to help us? She's smart. She was studying to be a cop."

"A cop?"

"She's not anymore," Corrine says quickly. "But she wants to be a private investigator."

"Actually, mystery shopping and PI work overlap," Carol says, giving me a look I quickly understand. She thinks hiring Cassie is worth it.

So do I.

And if she might be willing to do some shops on her own, we could really make it worth her while.

Suddenly, someone's phone goes off, the ring tone the opening bars of "It's Raining Men."

"Gawd," Agnes groans, reaching into her purse, finally pulling out a flip phone that looks like something from 2004. When she opens it, the buttons are huge.

"Can you read that, Corrine?" she asks, squinting at the display screen. It's so big, I can read it from across the desk.

I could probably read it from the Grind It Fresh! Counter two blocks away.

Corrine digs through her own purse, finding readers. Except she already has readers on the top of her head.

Two pairs, in fact.

"It says, *I'm in the lobby, Grandma. Call when you're ready*."

Agnes looks at me. "Are we ready?"

Carol and I lean toward each other. "Why don't you take Agnes and Corrine into your office," I say, formulating a plan on the fly. "Meet with Cassie. See if there's a way to make this work for everyone. We really do need smart, trustworthy shoppers for our properties and so far, we've had nothing but trouble with the elder shoppers."

"It's not their fault they keep dying, Amanda."

"I don't mean that! But transportation is an issue for so many. And this is such an important evaluation. We need to know that our elders are being cared for with compassion and kindness, and the only way to do that is to have people like Agnes and Corrine rise to the occasion. They're special."

"We are?" Corrine gasps, hands clasped over her heart.

"You heard *that* but you don't hear *me* half the time?"

"I hear *nice* things loud and clear, Agnes."

"Hmph." Agnes slowly stands, hands clasping the bar of her walker. "Okay, Carol. Let's call Cassie and bang out a deal. She needs something good in her life after the whole police academy mess, so I'm willing to take whatever offer you have–even without a pool boy– if it helps my granddaughter. Why not hire her full time? She can snoop and drive us around and do the smartphone thing and probably work even harder on other stuff for this crazy corporation."

Agnes' business instincts mirror mine. Not sure whether to be impressed or horrified.

"Why do you call it crazy?" Carol asks, bemused.

"Because you're offering to hire us. Anyone who offers employment to a batshit old woman is crazy."

"I'm so glad you're embracing calling yourself old, Agnes," Corrine gushes as they shuffle toward the door.

"I was talking about *you*, Corrine," Agnes grouses.

Carol turns to me, finger in my face, teeth bared. "I get four hours of comp time for taking this over. And maybe a raise."

My stomach gurgles, a fluttering sensation making me halt.

"What?" she asks, eyes wide, looking like her mom again.

"I think–I think there are a bunch of bubbles in me."

She grins, then moves to the door, clutching the manila folders, as Agnes and Corrine argue about using Agnes's flip phone. "Call Andrew. That's not gas."

"What is it?"

"You just felt your babies move. Congrats!"

And with that, she takes over with the old ladies, and I stare at my bulging belly.

Bubbles never felt so good.

❧ 8 ❦

Andrew

"I am sure you're wondering why I asked you to lunch, Andrew."

"Because you're my father and you love me and want to spend time getting to know me better?"

We both snort.

"Good one," he mutters around a highball glass filled with ice cubes and the remains of his pre-lunch cocktail.

"You want to talk about the Dong-Wei deal, don't you? The sheetrock for the Australian resort was a problem, but the customs officials said–"

He's obviously ignoring me, waving his empty glass in the air like a really bad lacrosse player going for the ball.

"What are you doing?"

"Trying to get more lunch."

"How about we order actual food?"

"If they add three olives to this, that should count."

The server appears, an older gentleman in a white jacket and black tie. "Mr. McCormick?"

Everyone here knows Dad. A very regular customer, he has his table in his corner and his wish is their command.

Also, Anterdec owns the place.

"Another, Paolo."

"Of course." His eyes catch mine. "And will you be ordering lunch, sir?"

I don't even need a menu. "Two tenderloins, both rare, mine with the balsamic fig glaze, his with the bleu cheese reduction. Grilled Brussels sprouts and two watermelon radish salads."

"You're making me eat that crap?" Dad grouses. How many drinks has he already had?

"Very good," Paolo says, taking his leave as I wonder what kind of dressing down I'm about to get.

Silence prevails as Dad looks anywhere but at me until his fresh drink arrives, accompanied by my own vodka and soda. It's one in the afternoon and I have back-to-back calls until six p.m., but if I'm a little loose for my two o'clock, the world won't end.

If I endure this conversation without a little liquid sustenance, though, it might.

"I asked you to lunch because it's time to talk, man to man, about being a father."

Oh, boy. Where's Paolo?

I need a second drink already.

"Okay," I say slowly, then drain my entire cocktail in one smooth gulp.

"You're about to have twin boys."

"Yes."

"Which means you'll be raising *men*." The way he says that last word makes my gut clench.

"Mmm."

"You were so close to the Olympics, Andrew. So close. This time, we have a chance of making it."

We.

"Amanda's tall, but not quite as long-torsoed as your mother. Her genes plus mine gave you the perfect swimmer's physique. And if it weren't for–you know," he says, slugging down the rest of his drink. The "you know" is understood:

My mother's death of anaphylactic shock from a wasp sting.

And my own near-death experience from the same.

I don't make a sound. Don't move a muscle. Don't even breathe.

Because my father can be highly unpredictable in emotional moments. Hell, in *any* moment. And right now, I don't have the bandwidth for James McCormick to get some bull-headed idea in his stubborn brain and expect me to be a minion in its perfect execution.

"You have a chance to get it right with these boys. I built Anterdec from the ground up, so you and your brothers got a head start in life from me. But the third generation is where people like us have the opportunity to really shine. Sometimes they do. Sometimes they fall apart completely."

People like us.

"How so?" I ask, noncommittal, but my jaw won't unclench. I crick my neck, something popping.

Probably my b.s. detector, breaking from overuse.

"You can make certain your boys get it all. Private coaches. Baby swim lessons. If they don't have the physique, we can test them to find their own talent, then nurture it from childhood. You can achieve what I couldn't."

Paolo appears with bread and a charcuterie board. Dad layers prosciutto on rosemary focaccia and takes a bite.

I let his words hang. I'm not buying any of this.

So I make a different choice.

"Did you have this conversation with Declan?"

"What?"

"When Shannon was pregnant with Ellie, did you talk about this?"

"No. Of course not."

"Why not?"

"Because it's different."

"Because she's a girl?"

"That." He takes a sip of the dregs of his drink, not even acknowledging the sickening sexism. "But also because Declan never had the sports success you did. You were my crowning achievement, Andrew. You. And now your boys will be a new opportunity to–"

I stand before I realize I'm doing it, feet flat on the ground, palms sensing every fiber of the tablecloth as I lean on it, hovering over my father, who is seasoned enough not to flinch.

"My children are not opportunities. My children are not chances. My children are not experiments."

He does a slow eye roll, the kind that takes its time. It's infused with contempt but suppressed enough to make sure I know he's not investing enough emotion in me to react more. "Simmer down. You're making a fool of yourself in public."

"I don't care. It's better than being a tone-deaf idiot in private."

That makes him flinch.

It also makes me feel like crap, not that he doesn't deserve it.

"I'm trying to talk to you about legacy."

"So am I."

"My legacy, Andrew. Not yours."

"Your legacy is *this*, Dad: Treating people like they're nothing more than opportunities to make you look better."

Contempt is gone, replaced by a shocked, hollow look in his eyes. "You really think that of me?"

I hate the emotional rollercoaster he puts me on. Dec would have stormed off by now. Terry would have avoided the conversation altogether. I accept Dad's invitations and let him into my life over and over again because I keep trying to elicit that piece of him that's more humane, more authentic, more...

Dad-like.

And then he does this.

"Your actions dictate what I think of you, Dad. And when you start talking about putting my toddlers under pressure to be super-humans who achieve greatness according to your metrics, then–*yes*."

"What the hell is wrong with greatness?" He says it calmly, plucking a piece of fig cake off the wooden board. As he chews, he looks at me speculatively, as if he actually wants to know the answer, as if it's not a challenge.

"Greatness is truly great when it's intrinsic. Not when it's forced by someone else."

"You're just going to waste your boys' childhood? Never encourage or guide or structure their time so they can be molded to do more? Be more?"

"Not your way. No."

"My way? There is no 'my way'! It's *the* way, Andrew." He shakes his head, a slow, sad gesture of disappointment. "One of those boys will run Anterdec someday. It's all you have, and when you're my age, you'll understand why legacy is important. You'll be in this exact position one day."

It's all you have.

The temptation to mention the gyms I now own is strong, but I won't show my hand in a moment of weakness, and make no mistake: I am weak right now. Weak because I brought up emotion.

McCormick men don't feel.

McCormick men *act*. To feel is to admit weakness.

The feeling is distinct and palpable, and it makes me livid.

"What's your point, Dad? I should take pity on you because one day I'll hand the company off to one of my children?"

He bristles at the word *pity*. "I'm trying to warn you. Give you advice. Help you learn from my mistakes."

"Trust me. I already have."

He lets out a long sigh with more emotion in it than I'd expect. "This is not how this conversation was supposed to go."

"Good, because this is pretty bad."

"I also want to talk about inheritance."

"What about it?"

"You have children coming. That means significant changes to wills and trusts."

The hair on the back of my neck begins to stand up. "What do you mean?"

Before he can answer, Paolo appears with a table brush, removing our bread plates, gently brushing the crumbs off the tablecloth. He sets down dinner plates and then a steady stream of servers deliver our food.

"Another drink, sir?" he asks Dad, who gives me a glance before declining. I change my mind on the fly and shake my head. After refilling our sparkling water, Paolo leaves.

I immediately cut into my steak. Can't scream at someone with your mouth full, right?

"A new generation requires additions and changes. After your brother had Ellie, I spoke with our estate attorneys, and with the Montgomery trustees."

"Okay." One-word answers are safe, and the tenderloin is perfect. Maybe that vodka and soda is kicking in, too.

"Of course, I've written Ellie–and will write any additional grandchildren–into my will and your mother's family trust. None of the trusts will actually break, though, for four additional generations beyond your children."

"Sounds good."

"You're not angry?"

"Why would I be angry?"

"There's significant capital tied up in these trusts."

"I know."

"You don't want access to it?"

"I don't *need* access to it. I have my salary, my investments, and my income is plenty."

He snorts. "From the Montgomery trust, surely not." My mother, Elena Montgomery, came from a family with money. Dad has no control over her family trust.

And it kills him.

"Terry lives on it," I remind him, secretly pleased that this is like poking him in the eye with a pine needle.

He gives me a sour look. "Terry lives in a hovel and drives a tin can."

"He owns a duplex in Jamaica Plain and drives a Subaru."

"Exactly." Dad takes a bite of his steak. I use it as an opportunity.

"Why tie up the trusts for so many generations?"

His eyes hold intrigue, as if he's caught me in a snare.

"Not that I care," I add, then take a bite of salad. The watermelon radish complements the bibb lettuce and shaved campo de Montalban, and the pear-lemon dressing is perfect.

"Legacy. I like to think I've founded an empire that people can continue to build on."

"How can we build on it if we don't have access to capital?"

"I did. Built Anterdec from the ground up with absolutely nothing."

"Yes. Of course." We have to acknowledge it, always. And I do genuinely admire what my father managed, but I don't understand his incessant need to have it validated.

Then again, I didn't grow up on the streets of South Boston, stone-cold poor. The divide between the world as he knows it and my own world, a product of his choices, is too great.

Maybe that's the source of so much friction between us. He expects me to be grateful for all his hard work when I never asked him to sacrifice so much in the first place.

"You're upset the trusts don't break with your generation," he says in a goading voice, as if he thinks he's close to riling me up about something I truly don't care about.

"Why is it so important to you to think I think that?"

"You're in denial, son. Every man with some smarts wants the money to prove himself."

"I don't need to prove myself to anyone but me."

Only a double blink shows me I've gotten to him.

"I think it's a strong decision to delay the trust breaking. Prevents future generations from spending your hard-earned money in foolish ways. Keeps the McCormick family on top for a long time," I continue, feeding his ego. Moving him away from specific discussions about my wife and children is the goal here.

Not dominance.

Distraction.

"Good to see you come around," he says after another bite of steak. I ignore the ridiculous barb and focus on my food. Amanda's finally out of morning sickness, so I can eat whatever I want in front of her, but the Brussels sprouts might still be a bit much.

This is good. Not as good as Consuela's meals, but damn close.

We finish our food, lifting the napkins from our laps at the same time, sharing a small smile that feels like a truce. Dad stands, looks at his watch, and makes the most basic of gestures indicating he's choosing to leave me.

I stand, too. He offers his hand to shake and I take it. Grip strength isn't a measure of a man, but it can be a measure of health, and his is weaker over time.

His strength is waning.

He mentioned his age earlier.

And speaking of health...

"By the way, good call on Pam," I say to him, prolonging his exit for reasons I don't understand.

"Pam?"

"Amanda told me you're the one who suspected Lyme disease in her."

"Oh. That." He waves his hand dismissively. "It made more sense than fibromyalgia. All she needed was a special blood test. I just encouraged her."

"You did more than that, Dad."

His hand is still in mine and he pauses, not letting go. "Thank you, son. Pam's a special woman. Any way I can help matters." He finally lets go, straightens the lapels of his suit, and cocks one eyebrow. "You take care of Amanda, and I'll take care of her mother."

"Will do."

"And *we* will take care of my grandsons," he says with an unsmiling wink.

With that, he leaves.

And all I can think about is whether Amanda's torso is long.

9

Amanda

I open my eyes, the words running through my head before I'm fully awake.

Twenty-three weeks, three days.

That's my first thought.

The second is: I need to hump my husband.

Some impulse centers itself between my legs, turning me into a rocking nerve ending, my entire body so horny, it's like some gene in me got flipped and my entire purpose in life is to orgasm in a continuous loop.

"Help," I whisper to Andrew as I slide my bare thigh against his hair-covered one, his body gloriously nude, which only ratchets up my sex-crazed fever.

"What's wrong?"

"I need you to let me have sex with you again."

One eye narrows, the other holding steady as I reach for him, finding him halfway to where I need him.

"Excuse me?"

"Can I please have sex with you again? I know we just did it–" I look at the clock, squinting to read the numbers, "–seven hours ago, but I–"

The kiss answers me.

"You don't have to ask."

"Of course I do! Consent is very important."

His erection twitches in my hand, jumping slightly.

"There's my consent."

This isn't slow sex. It's fast and hard, the kisses hot, my legs parted and my body centered over him in seconds. The grinding need to have him touch the deep ache inside and unclench it is too furious, too intense to ignore.

I'm bent over him, hips rolling up, belly hardening with each curl as I ride, ride, *ride* to climax. My thighs pull him in deeper, knees pressing against his tight ass, my hands on his chest, his head bobbing up to suck one breast at the perfect moment of ecstasy, making me moan into eternity.

And then–*snap*. I'm done.

I climb off and kiss his cheek.

"Thank you!"

"That's it?"

"That's it. Why? Do you want more?"

"Of course, I want more."

"Now?" I look at the time. "Because I have forty-four minutes to make it downtown for a meeting."

"No, not *now*, but..." He frowns. "Is this the magic second trimester the guys always talk about?"

"The guys?"

"Vince. Dec. Gerald."

"You talk about our sex life with them?"

"What? No." He avoids eye contact. "We talk about pregnancy. Suzanne's due around the same time as you. A few weeks behind."

"Yeah, no kidding. We sure do know that. Maybe you could be her doula now that you've seen her half naked in the bathroom."

"Hey! That was an honest mistake," he grumbles.

"You're lucky you don't have an honest shiner from Gerald."

"I'd have deserved it."

Andrew reaches for my hand, pulling me back to the bed, hand on my belly.

"I love this. You're so full and hard."

"That's *my* line, bud."

Resonant, rich laughter, full of a happiness I've never heard from him before, fills the air.

"I love you." He kisses my belly. "And I love them."

"I love you, too." I reach down and wrap my hands under his

chin, cradling his face, the morning beard growth prickly and real. "I am so lucky to spend my life with you."

"I'm the lucky one. I never would have guessed I'd end up with a wife who asked permission to have *more* sex with me."

That stirring starts between my legs. I close my eyes. He chuckles, a deep sound that tells me he's reading my mind.

And then he pulls back the covers, spreading his nude body out on the mussed sheets, and says:

"At your service."

❧ 10 ❦

Andrew

"You guys weren't kidding about the second trimester," I say as I curl sixties, barely making it through eight, going slower on the release. Vince watches my form like he's just eaten a bad pistachio.

"Right?" Declan's eyes go distant. "It's basically the reason I can't wait to have another one."

"Basically..?"

He shrugs. "If the second trimester is the holy grail, the first year after the baby is born is the Sahara desert, bro."

Gerald chokes on the protein gel packet he's sucking down. We look at each other, the shared anticipatory pain a bonding moment.

"You guys make me puke," Vince interrupts. "Whiners."

"Says the guy who isn't married and doesn't have kids."

"Haven't found the right person yet."

I smirk. "You mean you haven't found the guts to ask Gina out yet."

A silence descends, slow and humid, like a tornado rolling in over a prairie.

"What did you just say?"

"You heard me. It's obvious you two like each over. Ask her out."

"My love life is none of your business. You guys might talk about what your dicks do or do not do all the time, but I sure don't."

Old Jorg walks by and says, "That's Vince Code for not gettin' any."

Declan's in the middle of guzzling his water and sprays half of it over the bench he's on. Gerald smothers a grin, wiping his scarred face with a hand towel that looks like it's seen better days. Bleach spots all over it at least attest to being washed.

I hope.

Note to self: Have Gina assess gym cleanliness and up the sanitation protocols for the chain.

"JORG!" Vince bellows, face rippling with a wave of emotion that makes me see the fifteen-year-old punk in him.

"Ask the girl out. Bet she's waiting for you to do it, ya dumbass."

Watching Vince get ribbed is the *best*.

"What're *you* looking at?" Vince growls at me, ignoring old Jorg. "Get your ass over to the sandbags and tires."

I eye that section of the gym. It looks like a reality show set for people too naive to realize their pain is being exploited.

Hey. Wait a minute...

"And you, too," Vince adds, pointing to Dec. "Tug of war."

"There's no rope over there."

"Not with rope. With the tire." He points to one with a five-foot radius.

Even Gerald balks. "You want these two to play tug of war with a monster-truck tire?"

"You make fun of me, you pay."

"I already pay you, Vince," I point out.

"And you and your brother can show us who's stronger."

"We know the answer to that," Declan says smugly.

Instantly, I'm on alert. Did he just say–

"Me," my brother adds.

Yep. He did.

I snort. "You wish. Sleep deprivation has you hallucinating, bro." I flex my arms as I curl a sixty, holding back the internal scream.

"Snooze, you lose," he shoots back, eyeing my biceps with a mocking expression that sends red rage through me.

Competitive red rage.

"Deal." I drop the sixty on the ground and leave it, pumped and ready for this battle. "Get over here," I call over my shoulder, "and prepare to get your ass whupped."

A small crowd begins to form, starting with Jorg, Vince, and Gerald, followed by two teens, a guy who is either their father or a coach of some kind, and two jacked-up dudes with muscles that look like they glued apple fritters to their arms and thighs.

Dec and I get into squat position. Tire tug of war isn't new, but I've never done it myself. Watched Vince and Gerald go at it here and there, but it's not the most efficient way to spend time working out. It's more about using your body to manage the unexpected, which is great for a bodyguard like Gerald, or for firefighters or ninja warrior freaks, but when you're the CEO of a fast-paced multinational conglomerate, you focus on other workouts.

But this? Now it's a grudge match. Vince took his own pissed-off state and turned Dec and me against each other.

And I'm going to win.

"Before we start, let's set some rules," Dec begins.

"The only rule is, you're about to lose," I shoot back.

"Talk is cheap, Andrew."

"So'm I!" Old Jorg shouts. He gets a sprinkling of laughter.

"We hold the inside of the tire. Top or bottom?"

"Which one are you?" one of the muscle-bound dudes shouts.

We ignore him.

"Vince and Gerald stand at the midpoint. First time one of our feet crosses, the other wins."

Vince and Gerald nod.

"That works," I agree.

"This is all about drag," Vince clarifies.

The steroid-poppers look at each other as if they hadn't heard that quite right.

Or as if they interpreted it very differently.

"On the count of three," Vince shouts. "One, two–three!"

I'll give my brother credit: He's stronger than I expected. Those soccer legs of his dig in like tree trunks and don't budge. But where he has me on leg power, I've got him on shoulders and arms. We're equally matched.

Which means this comes down to strategy and sheer perseverance.

So I'll win.

The tire's edge is hard to gain purchase on, my fingers curled in on the thin lip of the ring, the bottom of the tire resting on my forearms, which are on top of my thighs. Declan has chosen a different hold, hands on top, those tree-trunk legs of his giving him more power.

If we were wrestling, I could flip the damn tire and take him by surprise, burying him.

But we're not. This is tug of war, so I need to drag him across that imaginary midline.

Which means I need a better grip.

Veins bulge in Declan's neck as his green eyes, so much like Mom's, taunt me. Sweat blooms on his forehead, pit stains already wide from the earlier workout. He's pulling hard and as I think, I lose my footing, shoe moving an inch forward before I can tighten my core and use it to extend muscle strength to my shoulders, the network of my body communicating to do one job.

Just one.

Don't move.

"Hey, little bro, getting tired?" he taunts. The slip was a show of weakness he is eating up. Thirty-three years of frustration turn my mind to nothing but rage and I do it.

I flip the tire.

Because I'm already in a slight crouch, I have the advantage, Declan's mouth going to an O of surprise that I will cackle at until my last breath on Earth. The heave-ho I give the two-hundred-and-fifty-pound piece of rubber sends him on his ass, his reflexes good enough to move his arms and catch it before it flattens him.

I hold my place.

The crowd goes nuts.

"This is like free WWF!" one of the muscleheads shouts, and the two teens start cheering.

"CHEAT!" Dec calls out.

I cross my arms over my chest. "I'm still here. You're over there. Not my fault your 'nads have tire tracks on them because you didn't see it coming."

Neither of us is strong enough to throw the damn tire, but flipping it isn't out of range. Declan goes into a reverse somersault, hooks the soles of his feet on the thick tire edge, and kicks it off him as hard as possible.

It lands with a thick thump on my side of the floor, the edge brushing down my shin, leaving a black streak. When Dec stands, I see his arms have tire tracks on them. He looks like a tank ran over him.

"TIME OUT!" Vince shouts. "You idiots don't even know how to play tug of war right! What the hell did they teach you at that fancy prep school you went to? Needlepoint?"

Dec crouches, rights the tire on its end, and shoves as hard as possible at me while I'm turned toward Vince. The damn thing barrels at me and if I move the wrong way, I cross the line. As I leap into the narrow space I have left as an option, it grazes my bare shoulder, leaving behind a mark and the scent of rubber burning through me.

I grab the thing and send it right back. Dec's prepared, though, so it just hits the ropes and rebounds, halting next to him like a good, loyal pet.

"Douchebags," old Jorg mutters. "You're ruining the floor!" Our eyes meet and his widen. I know exactly what he's thinking.

I'm the one who owns the place. This is on my dime.

"Do it right!" Gerald shouts, his voice holding enough command in it to make Declan and I give him twin looks. Dec sends the tire into the center again, the beast circling over and over like a kid's slowly spinning top until it flumps down.

And we begin again.

This time, I grab from the top, but Dec grabs from the bottom and the bastard outmaneuvers me, flipping the thing like I did, using my own trick against me.

And he ups the ante, flipping it so the thing ends up on its side, rolling right at me, my legs split, thighs engaged in a squat.

I get a face full of rubber and a sac massage all at once.

Have you ever wanted to kill someone? Really kill them? Watch the light drain out of their eyes, their flesh going limp, all the parts of their humanity draining out of them like water in a bathtub?

Me, neither.

But I'm so damn close right now.

"You are so dead!" I scream, standing and using a roundhouse kick to send the tire back to him, then running after it. I rip my lats and triceps to shreds as he dodges, but I change the course of the massive tire.

Running him over from behind.

"Anyone recording this? Because YouTube'll make this go viral," one of the teens asks, looking around as Declan's head gets run over by the now-slow tire bounding off the ropes. He sputters and rolls, looking up at me.

"Man, you can really tell you guys are brothers. Look at that hate," says Vince, who is laughing.

The phone in the office rings, the sound hard to discern from the ringing in my head, but it's clear. Old Jorg answers it, then holds up the receiver.

"Declan!" he shouts.

"WHAT?" Dec screams back.

"Yer wife. Says yer ignoring yer phone. Something about dinner plans and how you and Andrew need to get yer asses to yer house or she's gonna cut off sex."

"WHAT?" Declan's voice goes up an octave. "She SAID that?"

"Nah." Old Jorg lets out a phlegmy laugh. "Just the part about dinner plans. You two need to go."

"Damn," I mutter. "We're babysitting for you guys. Remember? Shannon and the *Hamilton* tickets."

Dec says a curse under his breath. "I forgot. What time is it?"

We look at the wall clock.

"You idiots. Finish this by running all the way to Declan's apartment. Then think about how weak you both are until our next workout," Vince says as Dec and I run into the locker room, grab our gym bags, and start the run to his place. I slip my arms through the two handles and wear the bag like a backpack, running easily. Dec's right next to me, huffing harder.

Years of swimming give me the lung advantage. Dec's a better soccer player, but short-distance running doesn't help after that kind of workout.

You need stamina.

By the time I reach the main door to the building where he and Shannon live, I have to wait a good minute for him to catch up and let me in. The doorman, Barry, gives me a wave but doesn't offer.

Smart guy.

Dec uses his card key to take us to the elevator, both of us simmering. It isn't until we're at his floor that I take a look at his body.

And mine.

And realize we're up shit creek with our wives.

"Dec?"

"Huh?"

"Look at us."

His eyes take me in first, going over my arms, then my legs, bouncing to his own body. He stretches out the arm not carrying his gym bag, chest huffing from exertion.

"Oh, hell," he says. "We need to go downstairs to the building gym and shower before Shannon–"

Opens the door. Which she does.

Right then, on cue.

"Declan!" she hisses, their toddler daughter, Ellie, on her hip. Dec's wife is furious, and why wouldn't she be? We're nearly an hour late.

Dec's eyes drop as he passes her. "I'll be in and out of the shower in three minutes and we'll be fine, Shannon," he says.

"It's our first date in months!" She's in the *I Can't Believe You Did This to Me* zone. My brother is making a huge mistake.

"Let me fix this for you, Dec."

Dec's back is to me, hunched in anger.

"What?"

"First, tell your wife you're sorry."

Shannon beams at me.

Ellie's pudgy little fingers reach for me, eyes wide with delight as she catches my eye and shouts:

"Uncadoo!"

Declan falls over, laughing so hard, he starts wheezing. Talk about a mood change.

"There's your nickname for the rest of your life," Shannon tells me. "Uncadoo." Whatever pissed off self-righteous anger she was holding dissolves on the spot, too.

"I... can't wait... to tell Vince and... Gerald," Declan gasps, holding his sides.

"You do that, I'll tell them your nickname from the lacrosse team at Milton."

Declan freezes. Shannon gives me an extraordinary look, the kind I only thought I gave people when they threatened to spill the secret on an opponent.

"What was it?" she gasps as Declan lunges for me, hand over my mouth before I can react.

He may have the element of surprise, but I have superior muscle strength.

Thanks, Vince.

"Don't. You. Dare," Dec says, grabbing my arm, which makes Shannon look at us.

Really look.

"Declan, you're a mess!" Shannon says reproachfully, reaching for Dec's hands, mouth turning down as she eyes the black all over them. "What on Earth? You look like you bathed in grease!" She sniffs. "And you smell like tar."

"Close," I mutter, wondering if I can grab a quick shower before my wife arrives and I get the same lecture.

Ding! The doorbell snatches my defeat from the jaws of victory.

Damn.

Amanda appears in the doorway, the seconds before she hugs Shannon a moment for me to take her in. The maternity clothes have finally taken over her wardrobe, belly swelling with a grace that mirrors my heart as I watch her. That belly grows my children. That body sacrifices so our sons can be born.

That body gives so much for me.

But it's not her body I have to watch out for.

It's her mouth.

"Andrew!" She looks me over, eyes going to my face, my hands, my arms, then centering on my knee. She points. "What *is* that? A TIRE TRACK? Did you get run over by something?"

"More like some*one*," Declan crows as he ducks into the master suite. His laughter booms until a door closes, then a shower begins. Good thing they have three bathrooms, because I'm taking over the guest one.

"What is Declan talking about?" Amanda asks, coming to me, walking a little slower than usual. Is she... waddling?

No. Can't be. She's only at twenty-six weeks.

"Dec and I got into a fight with a monster-truck tire. Dec lost."

"I HEARD THAT!" a muffled voice comes from down the hall. "*YOU* LOST!"

"We tied," I explain to her and Shannon.

"DID NOT!"

"Declan!" Shannon calls out. "Take your shower. We're going to be late for dinner reservations if you don't hurry up."

The bathroom door opens and steam pours out. Dec's soaking wet head appears, and he yells, "Uncadoo is lying!"

"TAKE THE DAMN SHOWER!" Shannon shouts in a voice that makes me see how similar she really is to her mother, Marie.

Ellie looks at her mother, fascinated and a little nervous at the change in her demeanor. Shannon's definitely not a yeller, so even I'm a little nervous, too.

"Mama loud," Ellie says, pointing.

"Yes, sweetie." Shannon scoops her up and balances her on one hip. "Sorry."

"Too loud!" she admonishes in a voice you'd expect from a librarian, not a small toddler.

"Yes," Shannon says in a calming voice.

Ellie's little fingers cover Shannon's lips. "*Shhhhhh.*"

Something in my chest melts. We're about to have *this*.

In duplicate.

"Uncadoo *shhhh*," Ellie says, reaching for my mouth. Shannon's eyes flash with horror, making me wonder what I actually look like.

"Let Uncadoo take a shower first. And brush your teeth. You have black streaks on the two top ones," she says, making me reach up.

Huh. Slightly swollen lip, too.

"Did you two get into a brawl at a tire factory?" Amanda asks, giving Shannon so many covert looks they might as well give up on trying to be subtle.

"Something like that." I hold up my gym bag. "I'll just shower in the guest bathroom."

"Uncadoo owie," Ellie says as I walk away. In the bathroom, I stare at my reflection.

Yeeesh.

Dec got me good.

But I got him better.

The bottom of the bathtub has a small pile of black residue around the drain by the time I'm done showering, body still pumped from the competition that–to be entirely, utterly objective–was a tie, whether Dec will admit it or not.

My shoulder screams as I reach into the armholes of my clean polo shirt, and I know my thighs will join the pain chorus later, too, but once I'm done, I'm presentable enough. The swollen lip isn't that bad, and my jeans and shirt cover the red marks left from rubber being dragged across my skin.

But at least I wasn't dragged across the tug of war line.

I call that victory.

Dec and I emerge from our separate bathrooms at the same time. I'm dressed in my casual clothes, he's in a nice suit and a tie I personally would donate to a homeless shelter, but if he likes it, whatever.

"You two are incorrigible," Shannon pronounces, her mouth tight with annoyance, her gaze taller.

Taller?

I finally shake myself out of my gym state and look at her. My sister-in-law is a hot, full-figured honey blonde who any man would be lucky to pin down, but she chose Declan.

Which means she has weird taste in men.

She's dressed in deep, dark blue–a dress that hugs her curves. It's cut low in front but with long sleeves and skirt, and tied at the waist. Diamonds sparkle in her ears, sapphires on her wrist. And she smells great.

Dec's fastening his cufflinks.

One wrist shows a black streak he couldn't get off in the shower.

SCORE!

"You two are positively medieval," Amanda says to me as she examines my face like a mother, one hand clenching my chin, turning me from side to side. She sure does have the maternal seething expression nailed down already, huh?

"That's right," I agree. "Because I'm the king."

"More like the court jester," Declan says calmly, pulling at one cuff. Shannon whaps him.

He kisses her cheek.

He grins.

And then his eyes widen as he really takes in his wife.

"You look hot." He pulls her in for a deeper kiss, one that makes me wrap my arm around Amanda's waist.

Her *growing* waist.

"I tried," Shannon says breathlessly as they break the kiss. "I waxed and everything."

"You waxed... everything?"

Another whap.

Laughter pours out of both of them as Ellie toddles over and wraps her little arms around Declan's leg, clinging to the fine cloth of his pants. She sits on the top of his foot, legs wrapping around his ankle.

"Horsey!" she says.

Dec obliges, looking down and laughing as he moves her, inch by inch, across the floor. A sudden flash of our childhood, Dad in a tux and Mom in an evening gown, hits me. Dad never goofed around like this. He was always too busy, impatient, showering attention on Mom but treating us like soldiers in the McCormick Men army he controlled.

Dec's got it right.

We don't have to be like our dad.

Emotion chokes me, and my grip on Amanda tightens. She frowns.

"What's wrong?"

How does she know?

"I'm just..." I shrug, the words thick in my throat. Her eyes track mine and she softens.

"He's a good father, isn't he?" Giggles float up like bubbles from little Ellie, her face turned up in a full smile at her daddy.

Who is my brother.

Who is nailing this father thing.

"He is. I hope to be as good at being a dad as Declan is," I say.

He freezes. Damn. He heard that.

Then he turns to me with an expression I have never seen on his face before, and trust me, I know my brother pretty damn well. I've seen it all.

"Thank you," he says in a voice as strangled as mine. "That means, well..." He clears his throat. "That means a lot to me."

Amanda nudges me. "This is the part where you hug him."

"What? No."

"You're having a moment."

"I paid him a compliment."

"You did it without being competitive, Andrew. In your family, that's the very definition of a moment."

"DADDEEEEEEE!" Ellie screams as Shannon bends down and peels her off Declan's shoe.

She catches my eye and says, "We're late. Help? This is the part where she becomes an octopus."

"Huh?"

"Separation anxiety is in full force. She'll scream for twenty minutes after we leave, but then she'll be fine."

"Twenty minutes?"

"It'll pass in no time," Shannon says cheerily.

"Plenty of beer in the fridge if you need it," Dec says. "Limit yourself to two, though. That's my daughter you're watching."

"EEEEEEEEEE!" Ellie's reaching for Shannon as she tries to hand her off to Amanda, who is doing her best, but no match for frantic octopi.

"Let me hold her." I step in when Ellie starts kicking and firmly grab her torso. Dec reaches over and pries her limbs off Shannon like a professional poison ivy puller following a root to the end. Finally disengaged from her mother, Ellie's in my arms.

It's like holding a twenty-pound bag of cats.

With tentacles.

"Have fun!" Dec shouts over the fray as Shannon blows kisses and runs out the door.

Click.

"EEEEEE DADDEEEEE MAMAMAMAMAMAMAMAMA-MAMAMAMA!!!!"

And here we go.

Our first night babysitting.

"WHAT DO WE DO?" I shout to Amanda as I pat Ellie's back. I think it's her back. I'm patting whatever part of her is under my hand as she squirms.

"Put her down."

I start to crouch. Ellie clings harder, still wailing.

"No, no, hold her."

"But you said to put her down."

"She needs to be held."

"But–"

"AAAAEEEEEEEEEE!!! MAMA!!"

I'm starting to understand Declan's smirk when I told him it couldn't be that hard to babysit, when he asked.

Amanda's eyes catch mine and she's tearing up.

"What's wrong?" I ask in a louder voice than I want to use because of Ellie's screams.

"Look at her! She's terrified!" Amanda's hand goes to her belly. "It's just–I guess it's primal? I feel, I feel…"

And then my wife starts sobbing, too.

Great. Two women bawling their eyes out and I can't make either of them feel better.

Where was that beer again?

Suddenly, Ellie stops crying, watching Amanda with fascination. She tucks her index and middle finger in her mouth and starts sucking.

With her other hand, she points to Amanda's face and says, "Owie?"

"Are you hurt?" I ask her, looking over her hands, arms, legs.

"Manna owie."

"Manna?"

Amanda smiles through her tears. "She started calling me Manna a few weeks ago, Uncadoo."

I give her a sour look as Ellie giggles and points to me. "UNCADOO!" she screams, shredding my right eardrum.

Amanda starts laughing and crying at the same time, hand rubbing her belly.

"Ellie, say uncle," I instruct. This shouldn't be hard.

"Unca."

"Say an."

"An."

"Say Drew."

"Doo."

"Now, say Uncle Andrew."

"UNCADOO!"

If nothing else, the exercise in futility amuses my wife, which makes my humiliation worth it. Sort of. With a long sigh, I look at my niece and say, "Fine. Uncadoo it is."

"Dow."

I carefully set her down. She toddles to the front door and points. "Mama?"

"Mama will be back tonight."

"Daddy?"

"Daddy will be back tonight, too. We're here to play with you," I explain, crouching down to her height.

"I'll get a snack," Amanda whispers, wiping her eyes. "Shannon said she'll do anything for a yogurt treat."

"Yogurt treat?"

"I'll show you."

Ellie walks up to me, eyes shining, the tears drying on her cheeks. Long, thick eyelashes frame eyes just like my brother's. She has Declan's coloring and eye shape, but the contours of her face are like Shannon's. It's so weird to see Dec's features superimposed on a toddler.

What'll it be like to see me in my own boys?

"OHGURT!" Ellie screams, right in my ear, like a laser blaster to the trigeminal nerve. The kid can be harnessed and weaponized if this whole toddlerhood thing doesn't work out. Damn.

Ellie walks over to the high chair and lifts her arms to Amanda. "Uppie, Manna!"

Amanda bends to pick her up. I rush over. "I've got her."

Amanda frowns. "I can pick her up."

"You shouldn't. Not in your condition."

"I'm not *that* out of shape!"

"I don't mean your muscles. I mean the babies."

"I can pick up a twenty-pound toddler, Andrew. Our bodies are designed for pregnancy and for managing toddlers at the same time, you know. It's basic evolution."

"You sound like Pam."

She pauses. "I think I did hear that from Mom."

"OHGURT!" Ellie repeats as we click her into place. I grab the foil pouch from the counter.

"Yogurt dots?"

"Freeze-dried yogurt." She takes the package from me, opens it, and sprinkles some on the tray. Ellie acts like wild geese at a pond after someone throws stale bread their way.

"Here. Try one," Amanda offers, handing me the package.

"Sounds gross."

"Try it."

I pop a piece of blueberry yogurt in my mouth.

And instantly realize how wrong I am.

"Gimme more," I mutter around the chewing. "These are fantastic! We have to get some." I look at the label.

YoYo Baby Belly Snax.

I look at the ingredients. Pure yogurt, natural sugars, no colorings, no preservatives.

"Even Vince would approve of these," I say to Amanda, who gives me a smug grin.

"MO!" Ellie shouts. I half expect her to toss a beer stein to the ground and call for her hammer next. If they remake "Thor" in twenty-five years, they can cast my niece.

"We'll get some next time we're at the store," I tell Amanda before popping another one on my tongue.

"You're going to the gym carrying a pouch of baby snacks? I'll pay good money to watch that unfold."

I grab another handful from the pouch and toss the whole thing in my mouth. "Mmmm."

Ellie watches me, mouth open, a yogurt drop attached to her lower lip.

"Careful," Amanda says, beginning to search the cabinets. "Let's hope that's not the last pouch. These are the only thing that calms her down."

I sprinkle ten more on Ellie's tray.

She turns into a shark with fresh lamb thrown in the water.

"I feel you, kid," I mutter as I eye the pouch, then look at Amanda on her search, hoping for more.

"Pay dirt!" Amanda calls back. "Four more pouches."

Awesome. One for Ellie and three for me to devour after she's asleep. Shannon and Declan can pay us in yogurt dots.

Amanda eyes me eating more. "I can't believe you're eating baby food."

"What? It's good."

"I know. It's just..." Her laughter warms me. Full and strong, happy and hopeful.

I shrug, then tip the end of the foil pouch to my mouth, tapping the dust in.

"Wata," Ellie says, turning to look at the water filter on the fridge.

Amanda finds a sippy cup, fills it with water, and plunks it on the tray. Ellie begins gulping, eyes on me the entire time.

I look at the clock. It's 5:49 p.m.

Dec and Shannon are home at midnight.

We've totally got this.

Bzzzz

Amanda's phone. She picks it up and reads. "Our food's coming."

"Food?"

"I ordered takeout."

My stomach growls. "Excellent. So, what do we do with her?"

"Do?"

"We have nearly six hours."

"She goes to bed at seven, Andrew. We eat dinner, then she gets a bath, then we read to her and sing a lullaby and put her to bed."

"That's it? That's the whole night?"

Amanda picks up a piece of paper with Shannon's handwriting on it. "Yes? That's what this says. Shannon fed Ellie at five."

"Well, that's boring."

"Boring? Of course it is. We're watching a toddler. It's not like we're taking her to a Bruins game or going on a harbor cruise."

"We could, though."

"That's not the plan."

Ding!

The apartment buzzer sounds. Amanda waddles to the door, talks to someone on the intercom, and pushes a button.

"Food's here."

"What did you order?"

"Cheeto smoothies." She smirks, eyes big and sparkling with mirth.

"I hope you made sure they're blended extra fine."

"You're never going to let me off the hook for that, are you?"

"Do you have any idea how much work it took to make that smoothie?"

"Do you have any idea how much pain my bladder was in, Andrew?"

Ellie's watching us. "MOOVIE!" she squeals.

Amanda opens a cupboard, finds a glass, and pours herself some water. "I got Thai. Pad Thai and spring rolls."

"Are they orange enough?"

"Ha ha."

"Ha ha." Ellie's a perfect mimic for Amanda's sarcastic tone.

We all burst out laughing, Ellie clapping for added amusement.

"Let's eat at the dining table," I say, pulling Ellie's high chair up to the place she clearly sits at, as there's no chair in that spot. Just then, the door buzzes and Amanda handles the food delivery, the scent of peanuts and fish sauce soon filling the air.

Plates come out, containers get spread on the table, and within a few minutes, we're feasting.

Bzzz

Amanda groans as my phone goes off. "I thought you were on Do Not Disturb."

"I run a corporation, Amanda. I can't do it forever."

"But this isn't forever. It's just until midnight."

"Midnight? I thought Ellie went to bed at seven."

"BED!" Ellie screams, taking part in the conversation, then puts a Cheerio in her mouth. Amanda has poured some on her tray.

"She does. But sometimes she gets up. And I thought we could watch movies together."

"You did?"

Instant regret floods me, because even I cringe at my tone. Damn. I had no idea Amanda had this all planned out.

"I did," she says tightly. "If you didn't come here to be a true babysitter, Andrew, why don't you just go home and work and I'll take care of Ellie."

"That's not what I want."

Bzzz

"I know you want to answer it."

I pick up the phone, stand up, walk over to the refrigerator, and put the phone in the butter compartment on the door.

"What are you doing?" she asks.

"Putting it where we won't hear it."

"Do Not Disturb mode isn't good enough?"

"I want it out of sight."

Her shoulders drop, corners of her mouth turning up. "Thank you."

"I should have done it sooner."

Now her body melts, tension gone.

Sure, I'm desperate to do what I need to do. Decisions come from the top down at Anterdec, and even an hour out of touch can make a huge difference. I just spent all that time at the gym ignoring my phone, and my behavior is catching up with me. The unknown of texts and emails and decisions I should be weeding through grows as time passes and I don't check in.

But a slow dawning is happening as I take a bite of my noodles and watch Ellie carefully picking up her Cheerios, one at a time.

This is life.

It's boring because it's life. Dinner with your wife and kids *should* be boring. Watching a toddler for a few hours *should* be mundane. Chilling on the sofa while the kids are asleep *should* be a waste of time.

Productivity isn't the measure of a good life.

I might not know what is, but answering texts and emails sure as hell isn't it.

Amanda carefully picks out all the orange foods and eats them first, slowly moving on to the chicken and the noodles in her pad Thai. The bizarre orange-and-white-food thing has diminished, but this pregnancy is going to leave all kinds of marks on her body and her eating habits.

"BAF!" Ellie shrieks, looking toward the hallway. "WAN BAF!"

"She's really good at talking," I marvel.

"You're right. She's way ahead of where Tyler was at this age."

"Tyler?"

"Carol's son. You know."

"Right. Weird little kid, but he's happy. What about him?"

"Remember his language disorder?"

I frown. "I guess so. I don't know much about it."

"He spoke a little until he was almost two. Then he lost a lot of language. Came back when he was older. But he was never as expressive as Ellie at this age." She tilts her head as she looks at our niece. "Tyler's the last baby I spent major time with until her."

"You're going to get all the baby time you could possibly want in a few months," I say, reaching for her hand and giving it an affectionate squeeze, then moving to her belly.

"BAF! UNCADOO BAF!"

Our queen has issued her command.

"Does she have a special bath?" I ask, unsure what to do next.

"You mean, like, holy water? I know Declan worships her, but I doubt they've gone that far."

I ignore that. "How does a little kid take a bath?"

"She doesn't take a bath. You give her one. You have to turn on the water, plug the tub, pull out all the toys, and watch her like a hawk."

"Le Hawk," I joke, which makes Amanda smile. It's been years since she saved a Chihuahua from a random hawk attack at a park. It was good work but it wasn't pretty. And it took a lot of effort for the reputation management company I hired to get that video off the internet.

"AWK!" Ellie shouts, looking at us both to see if we respond.

"You really don't know how to give a child a bath?" Amanda asks, something in her voice making me pause.

"No. Why would I?"

Her brow knits as she thinks, then she shrugs. "Good point. I only know about taking care of little kids because of Carol and her two boys. You don't have any small children in your life."

Ellie bangs her fist on the high chair tray as if to protest.

I smile at her. "I do now."

Amanda's hands go to her belly. "And you'll have more soon," she adds.

"Let me learn this," I say, standing and walking into the bathroom off the hall.

Amanda's voice is muted as she calls out, "I think they bathe her in the master bath."

Which makes sense. I follow her lead and go into Shannon and Declan's bedroom, a sprawling affair with a huge window looking over the city. Unlike my condo in the Seaport District, they're not right on the water. This is the same place he's had forever, though I know he and Shannon are looking for a home in the suburbs. Amanda's pushing Shannon hard to move to Weston, near us.

When I reach the bathroom, I see Amanda is right.

It looks like an aquatic toy store exploded all over my brother's bathtub.

There's a plastic elephant over the bathtub spout. It looks like the elephant has the worst runny nose ever as water pours out of it, the color of the plastic changing over time. Amanda appears, carrying a very sticky Ellie, who looks at the bath and shrieks, "WAN BUBBAS!"

"That tone is subatomic," I say, rubbing my ear.

"Get used to it. It's all we're going to know for a few years," Amanda says, hand to her belly again. This time, I join her, her other hand reaching for a shampoo bottle that turns out to be bubble bath solution. As she pours, the room fills with the scent of fresh apple.

And bubbles explode over the surface of the water.

Ellie lifts one leg and starts to climb in, monkey toes curled under.

"Wait! We have to take your clothes off," Amanda says patiently as Ellie looks at her, then holds her little arms up.

My wife takes the hem of her shirt and pulls north, Ellie's face disappearing for a moment until she's shirtless. Within seconds, Ellie is bath-ready, in the water, and squealing with delight.

"Here." Amanda hands me the dirty clothes and a rolled-up wet diaper. "Can you take care of those?"

"Take care of?"

"You know."

I stare at the pile in my hands. "No. I don't."

She snorts. "You sound just like James when you say it that way."

"What do I do with this?"

"What do you think, Andrew? It's laundry and a dirty diaper."

Uncertain and hating that feeling, I walk to the laundry area and throw it all in the hamper, then return to find Amanda using a washcloth and soap to wash Ellie. She's a natural at it, knowing exactly what to do, and then out comes a visor.

"Is she going to play tennis in there?"

"Hah. No. It's for washing her hair. I've seen Shannon use it." Narrowing eyes meet mine. "You threw the dirty clothes in the hamper?"

"Of course."

"And the dirty diaper in the diaper can?"

I stare at her. She stares back. Seconds tick by.

"Why would you ask me that?" I challenge, instantly defensive because —

"Because knowing you, you threw it all in the hamper, and if I don't ask, Shannon and Declan are in for a disgusting laundry surprise."

I sigh.

I go back to the hamper. I find the dirty diaper. What the hell is a "diaper can"?

"The diaper can is in Ellie's room! It has a clear plastic cover on it, next to her changing table!" Amanda calls out, as if she's reading my mind.

Or she assumes I'm exceptionally incompetent at this.

But we're not going to entertain that possibility, right?

Ring!

In the distance, a phone goes off. Can't be mine, because mine's keeping cool with the beer and the butter. I set the dirty diaper on top of a contraption that meets Amanda's description and go back into the bathroom.

"Ignore it," Amanda murmurs, smiling at Ellie. "Can't be more important than this."

Ring!

She frowns, then her eyes flare wide. "What if it's Mom? She's been sick."

"I'll get it," I tell her, half jogging into the living room. I find her purse, the phone tucked away in a pocket. I punch in her six-digit code and find my own assistant calling...

My wife?

"Hey, Gina." I start walking back to the bathroom.

"Andrew? What happened? Are you all right? Has there been an accident?"

"What are you talking about, Gina?"

"You never, ever go this long without answering a text? And you didn't answer your phone, or email either? I thought you DIED, Andrew?"

Every sentence out of my executive assistant's mouth sounds like a question.

"I'm alive."

"I can tell? But why?"

"Why am I alive?"

"Why did you ignore all my messages?"

"Because I'm taking a break."

"A break?"

"It's Saturday night. Amanda and I are babysitting for my niece, Ellie, and I wanted a break from the phone."

"ARE YOU REALLY ANDREW MCCORMICK?" she screeches into the phone, making me wonder if she and Ellie are distantly related. "Andrew McCormick never takes breaks from his phone? What is this 'Saturday night' business? You never cared before?"

"I do now."

"You could have told me? Given me some warning? I got so desperate I called Vince?"

"Vince?"

"I didn't know if you were on some crazy workout with that jerkface?"

"What did he say when you called him?"

"He asked me out?"

"Really?" Go, Vince.

"YES?"

"You sound upset about that."

"I thought you were dead, and I'd have to initiate the Dead CEO PR Protocol? So I wasn't thinking about going out with someone?"

"Hold on. What's the Dead CEO PR Protocol?"

"The one Mr. McCormick created?"

"I'm Mr... oh. You mean my dad."

"Yes?"

Amanda's glancing at me here and there as she finishes pouring the water over Ellie's head, the visor keeping it out of her eyes. I don't know how much of my conversation with Gina she can hear, but it's getting harder and harder to avoid the temptation to put this on speakerphone.

Dead CEO PR Protocol? Amanda mouths.

I shrug. "What is this protocol?"

"Your father had your obituary written up the week you became CEO? And I inherited all the information from Grace?"

"I have an obituary?" My question makes Amanda freeze.

"Yes?"

Amanda's hand goes to my forearm. Gina and *Vince?* she mouths.

Great. My wife cares more about Gina and Vince's love life than the fact that my father initiated an obituary for me.

"Did you say yes?" Amanda calls out.

"Hi, Amanda," Gina says, loud.

I give up and go to speakerphone, which makes Ellie reach for my phone and shout, "Wan phone!"

"Is that Ellie with you?" Gina asks in a cooing, sweet voice clearly designed for small children, though I know she also uses it on my dad when he comes to the office and tries to be important.

"We're giving her a bath before bed," Amanda tells her as Ellie stares at my phone like it's a wallet hanging out of the pocket of a tourist in a Marrakesh market. She's just waiting for her chance.

"You want to know about Vince?" Gina offers up, which makes me groan.

"Great. Fraternizing between employees who are my direct reports," I mutter.

"I'm your employee and you fraternize with *me*," Amanda points out.

"I'm the CEO. I'm allowed."

"I can date who I want to, Andrew?" Gina's question-like statement is emphatic, scrambling the signals to the speech and comprehension centers of my brain.

"Yes, you can?" Damn. Now I'm doing it, too. "What's the emergency, Gina? Let's clear it up so I can get back to important matters, like giving my niece bubble beards."

Silence.

Dead silence.

It ticks on for an eternity before finally, in a small, nervous voice, Gina whispers, "You're serious?"

"Huh?"

"You're really not working?"

"I am not."

"I think I might faint?"

"Ha ha. Very funny. Now tell me what I need to do to get off the phone as fast as possible."

"AH DONE!" Ellie shouts, standing suddenly, pulling the visor off her head and flinging it at me, marking my polo shirt with soapy foam.

Amanda finds a hooded towel that has spikes up the back like a dinosaur. It's pink and yellow and adorable.

"Tell me later, Gina?" Amanda says, then clamps her hand over her mouth.

It's truly contagious?

See. It is.

Within five minutes, I've given Gina a series of decisions and she's off to execute them, leaving me standing in the living room,

Amanda wrestling Ellie's right arm into a pair of Dalmatian-inspired pajamas, her dark, wispy hair in need of combing.

"Here." Amanda thrusts the wide-toothed comb at me. "You do this part."

How hard can combing a toddler's hair be?

I pick her up and set her on the floor in front of the sofa, then put the comb on top of her head, barely pressing.

She becomes a fire-engine siren in petite human form, then runs across the room, scrambling over the cocktail table like she's in Special Ops training and a bear is trying to eat her.

Amanda snickers.

"Ellie," I say in a goofy voice. "Time to comb your hair."

"No."

"It's messy."

Her hand goes to the dark brown tangle. "No."

"You have to."

"AAAAAIIIIIEEEEEEEEEEE!"

Amanda sidles up next to me, her finger in her ear as she says loudly, "Are you sure this is the hill you want your eardrums to die on?"

"You told me to do it!"

"Comb your own hair and smile while you do it."

I look at the princess comb. "What?"

"Show her how combing your hair doesn't hurt. Then she'll be more likely to try it."

"There is no way that will work."

"AAAAAAIIIIIIEEEEEEEEE!"

"And your current approach will?"

I lift my hand with the comb in it, spines down, and make sure to catch Ellie's eye.

She says, "Uncadoo comb."

I nod. "I'm combing my hair. See?" I move the princess comb down my hair from scalp to end, making a mental note to have Gina schedule a haircut for me sooner than usual. Did Amanda's pregnancy make my hair grow faster?

"Comb Uncadoo."

"I am."

"WAN COMB!!! AIIIIIIEEEEEEEE!"

Yet another woman completely and utterly confusing me.

"I think," Amanda shouts over the fracas, "she wants to comb your hair."

For the first time all evening, Chuckles appears. He's Shannon's old cat, Lucifer himself shoved into fifteen pounds of furry beast, and he looks at me with half-lidded eyes that clearly say, *Sucker.*

I lift the comb from my scalp and bend down, offering it to Ellie. "You want to comb Uncle Andrew's hair?"

She snatches the comb, then lasers in on Chuckles. "Comb kitty!"

By my estimate, Shannon's cat is pushing fifteen or sixteen, which isn't ancient by cat standards, but he's no spring chicken. But his legs sprint like Vince is on his ass, threatening to make him drink a melted beef-heart-fat energy drink with a grape-seed extract anti-mold chaser.

"You can't comb the kitty, Ellie," I patiently explain, taking my role as morality shaper for my niece seriously.

"AAAAIIIIIIIEEEEEEEEEE!"

"She really doesn't like being told no," Amanda says under her breath as I wipe imaginary blood off my earlobe from the eardrum rupture I'm certain just happened.

Chuckles runs into her bedroom. I see a giant stuffed animal in a corner wobble a bit. That cat is smart. I eye Amanda, who is looking more and more elephantine these days.

At the rate Ellie's going, I might need to take cover behind my wife.

"Want to comb my hair?" Amanda asks. Ellie's scream turns into a single sniffle, then a huge grin as she toddles over to Amanda and shoves the comb in her hair so hard that Amanda gasps.

"Practice," she mutters.

"Practice?"

"For our boys."

I snort. "We never combed our mom's hair. Put a frog in it? Sure. Comb? Never."

"I think," she grunts as Ellie yanks the comb down Amanda's waves, "I'll take a frog over this." She reaches for Ellie's wrist and gently grasps it. "Ellie? Can you comb softer?"

"Soff," Ellie repeats.

"Yes. Gentle."

Ellie's downward stroke yields about 20 strands of hair in the comb as Amanda grimaces.

I look at the clock. Forty-four minutes to bedtime.

Little kids can't read clocks, so how would she know the *actual* bedtime? We can aim for 6:45, right?

"What's next?" I ask Amanda.

"We still have to comb her hair. Then read some books. Then brush teeth."

"We only have forty-four minutes to do all that."

"You're watching the clock?"

"AAAAIIIIIIIIIEEEEEE!" Ellie screams as the comb hits a knot in Amanda's hair.

"Damn right," I say as I scoop my niece up, careful to disengage her hand from the comb first, and we go into her bedroom. I plunk her on the chair and give her a raspberry on the tummy.

The screams turn to giggles. Still ear shattering, but qualitatively different.

A long time ago, Declan told me the secret to dealing with his two nephews, Jeffrey and Tyler, was to talk about poop and turn everything into a game. The poop part won't work with Ellie, but the second part fits: turn everything we do into a game.

Just then, Chuckles makes a lazy appearance.

And Ellie pounces.

You need to understand that while Chuckles loves my brother, he hates me. *Loathes* me. It's as if Declan intentionally turned his cat against me as sublimation for his jealousy of my success.

Yeah, I know it sounds far fetched.

But my brother is *that* disturbed when it comes to competing with me.

Ellie grabs Chuckles' tail, and while I know the cat's not going to hurt her, I go into protective mode.

"SPPPHHHT!" Chuckles emotes, glaring at me as if I'm the one shoving the comb into his back.

"No!" I say firmly, carefully lifting Ellie's comb-clutching hand off the poor cat, while Amanda works on her tail hand.

"UNCADOO!" Ellie wails, as if I've wounded her.

Chuckles shoots me another killer look. If he had fingers, two would be pointed at me, then at his eyes. Jimmy Hoffa may have been offed by this cat's ancestors.

"AAAAAIIIIIIEEEEE!" Ellie screams, the comb held against her chest. "Wan Chuck!"

"How much beer can I reasonably drink and still be responsible for a child?" I ask my wife.

"This question reminds me of New Year's Eve in 2018."

"Hey! We weren't babysitting, and I could still walk after all those shots with Vince."

"You *were* the child that night, Andrew, and the answer is three. Three beers."

Ellie abruptly stops crying, holds the comb out to me, and says, "Comb."

Giving Amanda a wary look, I start combing her damp hair as Amanda gives her a doll to play with. One minute later, we're done.

Storm over.

"I know you want to check on work," Amanda whispers. "I'll handle reading time."

"What? No! That's the best part."

"Shannon says they read *Goodnight Moon* every night, then two other books. I'll do the two, and you come in for *Goodnight Moon*."

"What's that?"

She reads the first line of the book. Some piece of my heart starts to wake up.

I recite the second line with her and she gives me an appreciative look.

"You do know children's books!"

"No. Not really. Just a memory of my mom and dad."

"And *dad*?"

"Yeah. When he was home around bedtime–which was rare–if Mom read us that book, he'd say "hush" for the role of the quiet old lady. Dad's head would pop into the room suddenly, the word "hush" would come out in his baritone, and we'd giggle."

"We?"

"Me. Declan. Maybe Terry? I think he was too old by then."

"How old are you in the memory?"

I shake my head. "No idea. But young."

"Book!" Ellie gasps, toddling across her bedroom to the book-shelf. She begins flinging books off the shelf as if she's looking for something.

Was Amanda's offer a test? If I take her up on the offer to go work, do I fail somehow? It's certainly more appealing to sit with them and read picture books, the experience a glimpse into our future as parents, but reality needs to be acknowledged, too.

I'm the CEO of a major company.

I have responsibilities.

For the next twenty minutes, I triage my texts and emails, answering the hair-on-fire situations, amazed at how quickly I can work when I know time is limited.

Maybe parenting is the ultimate form of essentialism. Time spent away from your kids comes at a cost.

Better be worth it.

"Andrew?" I look up to find Amanda standing there, holding Ellie on her hip, our niece yawning.

"Oh. Right. Tooth brushing and–"

"It's all done. Just need *Goodnight Moon*."

"Moooonnnnn!" Ellie yawns.

Her room has a crib, an upholstered chair, more toys than a toy shop, and a shelf of books. *Goodnight Moon* is an orange and green square on the chair's seat. We settle in, Ellie against my chest.

She turns the first thick board-book page and before I can say a word, she recites:

"Gay gee oom, teyfone. Yed boon..."

I guess I'm just the holder. She's the reader.

Amanda's got her phone out, snapping pictures surreptitiously. As Ellie "reads," I find the chair too comfortable not to relax, the intonation of her words hypnotic. Here, I'm in a world I don't control, where the hardest decision is whether to comb a toddler's hair, and where just being present is all that's required of me.

I could get used to this.

"Nite ey whey," she says dramatically, closing the book and giving me a closed-mouth smile that reminds me of Shannon. "Ah done."

"All done," I repeat, kissing the top of her head.

Tucking her into her crib is easy. She settles down fast, and I tiptoe out, feeling accomplished. The distance from her room to the living room is short, and Amanda's been gone for less than five minutes, but when I arrive, I find my wife fast asleep on the sofa, her head on a huge throw pillow, body curled on her side, feet propped on an ottoman.

How often do you get to just watch your gorgeous partner in stillness?

My laptop pings with a notification, and next thing I know, I'm deep in work. Hours pass, punctuated only by Amanda turning slightly, or my body's need for bio breaks. I go into a work flow state, hyperfocused.

The click of the front door opening makes me look up from my laptop, a smiling Shannon and Declan walking in, her eyes immediately landing on my sleeping wife.

"Ellie tire her out?"

"Everything tires her out." I close my laptop. "How was your evening?"

"Great." Declan looks down the hall. "Ellie okay?"

"Sleeping like a baby."

He gives me a sour look. "You're about to learn how vile that saying really is."

"We fed her. Bathed her. I combed her hair," I say pointedly, earning a squint from Shannon, "read to her, put her to bed, and–"

"MAMA!" Ellie screams, suddenly in the hall, running for Shannon like she's an Olympic sprinter.

"Uh huh. Put her to bed. Right."

"How'd she get out of her crib?" I ask, incredulous.

"Monkey toes," Shannon says with a look that makes it clear this isn't Ellie's first breakout.

"She's been asleep for four hours!"

"Sure, bro." He gives me a hug and a yawn at the same time as Amanda sits up, rubbing her eyes.

"I fell asleep?" she asks, picking up Declan's contagious yawn.

All I can do is nod, now in the throes of my own jaw stretching. Exhaustion washes over me.

"Here," Shannon says, returning from the kitchen with Ellie on her hip, holding a glass of water. "Drink this."

Amanda takes the glass without comment and does as told, rubbing the small of her back with her free hand.

Shannon yawns. Ellie pats her chest and says, "Milk," then gives her the saddest little pouty smile, big eyes used to her advantage.

With a laugh, Shannon heads toward the bedroom. She waves. "Thank you so much, guys, but the queen demands me at court."

"So does mine," I say as I put my arm around Amanda's waist and guide her to the door. She leans into me, my instincts correct.

"Thanks," Dec says, eyes tired, but face filled with more emotion than usual.

"Thank *you*. She's adorable, and I learned something tonight," I tell him.

"What's that?" he asks as Amanda yawns again, moving into the hall.

"When they write my real obituary, sixty years from now, it needs to include Uncadoo."

Amanda

"You want a piece of white cheese," Tyler says to me as Carol and I sit at her dining table, a plate piled with cheese cubes and carrots in front of us. The roasted cauliflower hummus is half gone, most of it in my stomach, feeding the babies.

"Go ahead, Tyler, but that's the last one," Carol says to him. He snatches two and runs off.

"I thought you said one piece?" I point out to her, chuckling as Tyler glares at me from the door for even mentioning his thievery.

She laughs. "He refuses to take anything in an odd number. Has to be even. If you give him nine Skittles, he'll ask for a tenth. If you don't have any more, he'll make you take one and eat it, so he has eight."

"That's quirky."

"That's Tyler."

Now nine, he's a tiny little thing for his age, and he reminds me more of a five- or six-year-old than the third grader he is. Carol kept him back a year, his summer birthday making it easy. But he turns ten soon, and yet he's so little-kid-like.

"I really like him," I confess, feeling self-conscious for reasons I don't understand.

Carol beams, but asks, "Why do adults always say that, but poor Tyler can't make a friend his own age to save his life?"

"Really? He's so–"

"Amanda! Four ropes on the rescue game!" Tyler pipes up.

"Yeah?"

"Four! Four more!"

He runs back into the living room, the distinct sound of a video game playing. Then he appears again, iPad in hand, and sits on the chair next to mine, leaning on my arm, chewing what I assume are the two pieces of cheese he took earlier.

"He's so sweet. And happy."

"Try teaching him to shower," Carol says with a shudder.

"NO SHOWER!" Tyler yells, but his eyes are fixed on the screen. "See?"

"Why don't you like showers?" I ask Tyler, who reluctantly gives me a split second of eye contact before going back to the game, but he snuggles in at my side.

"Don't like water in your eyes."

"I don't, either," I tell him.

That makes him look up. "It feels yucky."

"Yes, it does."

"Yucky is bad."

"Hmmm. Sometimes," I say, earning myself a skeptical look.

"Yucky is always bad. *Always*," he emphasizes. And then he spends a full minute repeating something from a video game he watches, the words and numbers not making sense.

"Twenty minutes of screen time left, Tyler," Carol says to him. "See the timer?"

He looks up. "Okay." Then back to his game.

Carol sighs, motioning for me to follow her outside to her patio. She and the boys live in a simple little Cape, smaller than her parents' home and definitely more run down, but it's a decent place. Until a few years ago, she didn't have a steady, full-time job with benefits like the one she has with Anterdec. I know Shannon and Declan try to get her to accept their help, but other than help with Tyler's expensive therapy or access to certain specialists, she turns them down.

Pride is very real in the Jacoby family.

"He's talking to me more," I say as we settle down, my back groaning from the Adirondack chair. Carol's eyebrow goes up.

"He is. Most of it's nonsense."

"I thought it was his way of trying to participate in a conversation."

"It is. It's part of the reason why the specialists say he's not on the autism spectrum. But it's still nonsense half the time."

"It used to be most of the time, though, so that's progress, right?" Some piece of me needs to be hopeful right now. I'm not sure why, but it's important to think of Tyler as getting better. Progressing.

Improving.

A wan smile is all I get. "You sound like my dad."

"There are worse things in life than being compared to Jason. I'll take that as a compliment."

Carol's eyes drift to my growing belly as she takes a sip of wine that I instantly envy. "You're asking me because you're worried."

I blink. Is it bad manners to admit that? With so much of this pregnancy stuff, and the prospect of actually parenting two little human beings, I feel like I have been dumped into the craziest work project ever without a map or any tools. And there's a looming deadline in twelve weeks that has no room for leeway.

Or mistakes.

"It's normal to be worried," she adds, as if reading my mind. "Although I wasn't." She frowns. "When I was pregnant with either of them. I was more worried about Todd than I was about either of my fetuses."

"He was an actual problem. The kids were just potential ones." I clap my hand over my mouth before I say more.

See? I was about to call her kids problems.

"I get it. I know what you mean. And Jeffrey was so easy. Smart and talkative and adventurous, and I assumed that's what Tyler would be like. But then we got a totally different kid. He was smart, but wouldn't talk. Didn't seem to listen. Kind of floppy, too. Low energy."

"I remember when Shannon told me you'd enrolled in early intervention. How scared you were, and how you had to fight Todd about it."

She groans and rolls her eyes. "He was such a jerk about it. All he kept saying was 'He's fine! I don't produce defective kids.'"

"Ugh."

"The only thing defective about my children is their father," she whispers. "He's still in prison and–"

Her turn to clap her hand over her mouth.

Just like that, the tables turn.

"It's okay, Carol. I know. My own father is in prison."

"I know you know. It's just, you know... your dad–I forget. You never talk about him. I shouldn't have made that crack. And your dad is in for reasons that are really different than Todd's. Todd was a master at fraud."

"Leo killed people. Drunk driving," I say, hearing a robotic tone in my voice. Talking about him hurts. A lot. Having a father in prison is hard, but being rejected when I tried to see him or have contact has been even harder.

"I'm sorry."

I touch her hand and squeeze. "It's fine. And if Jeffrey ever needs someone to talk to, he can come to me."

"Why would he–oh." A long, painful sigh comes out of her as she closes her eyes and winces. "Thank you. My dad is *so* not the same type–the kind of guy who–" Carol cuts herself off by taking a very long drink from her wine. "I'll shut up now."

"Jason is the exact opposite of Leo and Todd," I summarize. "He's been more of a father to me than my own."

She nods. "Same for Jeffrey and Tyler. My dad is the überdad."

"You ever wonder if it's too much for him?"

Her expression tells me that idea has never occurred to her.

"Too much?"

"Being a father figure to so many people who aren't his children. It's a big responsibility. Plus he does those workshops at the Maker Center for the after-school program, and he teaches Sunday school. Jeffrey said something about Boy Scouts, too?"

Carol laughs. "He can't seem to help himself. Now he's chaperoning the Boy Scout camp weekends for Jeffrey's troop."

"Is Tyler in Boy Scouts?"

"Cub Scouts. Yes." A shadow passes across her face. "But it's not going well."

"Why not?"

Leaning in, she taps the bottom of her wine glass on the scarred wooden table top. "Because Tyler is weird."

"Little boys are weird."

"But Tyler's weirder than the other little boys, and his peers don't know what to do with him. So they either bully him or ignore him. Dad's stepping in to take Tyler, but I think it's hard."

"Hard?"

"Dad's a softy. He loves Tyler deeply. And he just wants him to fit in. You can't make a kid fit in, you know?"

"Aren't there other kids with special needs in the troop?"

She shakes her head. "Not that I know of."

"Maybe move to a troop where there are some? Or one with leaders who–"

Her turn to squeeze my hand. "You're trying to fix this. It's not your job."

"I know. It's just–"

Her palm goes to my belly, our friendship the only permission she needs to touch my babies.

"Your sons have a loving father. A wonderful grandmother. Aunties and uncles who have resources and families and an extended network of people who will help you and Andrew, to make sure they thrive. No matter what."

Tears fill my eyes.

"My sons have my parents. They have Shannon and Amy. And they have you."

I'm openly crying now.

"We're all part of a big village that works to help each other. But that doesn't mean it's easy, or that we don't get stupid ideas in our heads that make life harder than it has to be."

She hugs me, bending her body in that awkward move friends now do to avoid my baby bump.

"I'm scared," I whisper in her ear.

"About having a child with special needs?"

"No. It's actually, well–if it happens, it happens. But I'm not scared about it. I'm scared I won't be good enough. There's no test you can take ahead of time that tells you if you'll be a good parent."

"Hah. No kidding."

"So how do you do it?"

"One hour at a time."

"That is one of the worst things you can say to a planner."

"I know. But it's the truth."

I sigh. "There's a lot of truth to this whole having children thing."

Tyler comes running into the backyard, completely naked.

"I need my bathing suit!" he shouts, turning around.

Carol lights up. "Would you look at that!"

I can't help but laugh. "He's a streaker, huh?"

A blank stare is her first reaction, then a grin. "Oh. That." She waves me off. "I've gotten so used to him having zero self-consciousness. I wasn't talking about that. I meant what he said!"

"What did he say?"

"Correct pronoun use! He said *I* instead of *you!*" She fist bumps me.

We take our victories where we can find them.

And as Tyler comes back out into the backyard in his swimsuit and turns on the sprinkler, tossing LEGO blocks into the spray, I realize parenting is nothing but small victories, stacked up on top of each other, one at a time, leading you along a line on a map you didn't draw and only see part of at any given time. Which is so freaking unfair for a strategic thinker.

But I didn't make this world.

I'm just helping populate it.

❦ 12 ❧

Andrew

"Will you be on your phone the entire time we're eating?" Declan asks as he stabs his salad with his fork like he's a caveman killing a wild boar.

"Only if you're going to use that tone." I finish my text and set the phone down to my right. "Happy?"

"No."

We spend the next five minutes eating, my baked haddock perfectly seasoned with green shallots and tarragon, the mushroom risotto pure perfection, but the side of Cranky Declan is leaving a bitter taste in my mouth.

"Why," I finally ask after finishing my meal, turning to my pint glass to clear out the taste, "are you being such a dick?"

"*I'm* the dick? *I* am?"

"I was answering texts from Gina. You do the same with Dave."

"Not during social time with family."

The snort comes out involuntarily. "Social time? Since when is a meal with me social time? It's always about business."

"It *was* always about business. I don't do that anymore."

If my throat could scoff in seven different languages, it would, but I'm left with just one sound to make.

It appears to work.

His shoulders drop, the tension releasing as he reaches for his full pint glass, the deep lager leaving a line of foam on his lip before he licks it off. Declan would look terrible with a moustache.

Most guys do.

"You'll see. Once you have kids, it all changes."

"Of course it does. But you still run the company. That doesn't go away just because you have a child."

"No. But it's different."

"Dad said you'd say that."

"James McCormick is the last role model you should take for how to be a father. Especially on the topic of being a workaholic."

Defending our father wasn't what I expected to be doing at this dinner with Declan, but it's what rises up immediately.

I tamp it down.

"He definitely wasn't around as much as he should have been."

"That's like saying the pope is a little bit Catholic."

Can't help but chuckle a little. He's right.

Plus the beer's kicking in after a good meal.

"You're a great dad to Ellie. I'll do my best for these boys who are coming. I think, in his own weird way, Dad did his best." I hold up a palm to stop Declan before the protest even begins. "I'm not saying it was good enough. I'm saying the man has limits, just like all of us, and he did his best."

"Did he?"

"Within his limits, yes. And I know that's hard to accept."

"You sound like a therapist."

I hold up my empty beer glass. "Here's my PhD."

The server takes the gesture as a sign to come over, pluck it out of my hand, and go directly to the bar for a refill. Instantly, my mind calculates, using a formula involving time, distance, vehicle, conversation topic, and safety.

I don't stop her.

"I can crash at your place if I have to, right?"

"Sure. Why?"

The server delivers another dark lager and I point. "That."

"As long as you don't pass out on my sofa and ogle my naked wife when she shows up in heels and a trenchcoat, yes."

"That happened once, Declan. Only once! And first of all, I didn't ogle her. Second, she wasn't your wife yet."

His eyebrows shoot up. "As if that's germane to the topic?"

"Fine. I'll have a driver take me home."

"Or you can walk to your condo. It's not far."

"Amanda wants me home every night in Weston, unless we're together in the city. It's one of those marriage things."

He grins and leans forward. "I know all about those."

"And now we have baby things. Babies," I correct.

"Like what?"

"The books."

Rare sympathy floods his face. "Right. The books. Did you have Gina summarize them for you?"

"Amanda's too smart." My glare tells him the truth: Shannon tipped her off, which means my brother ruined my plan. "We sit at home on the sofa and listen to the audiobook form together. You ever hear a verbal description of a c-section? I've learned everything about fascial tearing and uterine blood flow that I've spent my entire life trying *not* to know."

He sighs. "I'm going to have to go through this all over again."

"Again?"

"We're trying for another."

I laugh. Can't help it. "I'm having two at once and you're trying to catch up?"

A sour look is all I get back.

"It really isn't a competition. If we only ever had Ellie, I'd be the happiest man in the world."

"If the only child I could ever have was Ellie, so would I."

Hard blinking, a sign he's surprised, makes me realize how important my words are. This is Declan's version of emoting. When he's not stone faced, he's irritatingly condescending or jocularly sarcastic, so getting a better range of emotions is a nice change.

Then again, maybe I'm not giving the guy enough credit. Shannon has definitely softened him.

And Ellie has turned him into melted butter.

"Thanks. Those babies are lucky, too."

"Are they?"

We both gulp a lot of beer, then sit in silence, holding back the inevitable carbonated sounds that want to replace words from our mouths. This restaurant isn't top of the line, but it's pleasant, and right now, pleasant counts for a lot.

"Did Dad talk to you about the trust? About inheritance?"

Ah. That's what this meal is about.

"Yes."

"Is he being a jerk about Ellie?"

"Ellie?"

"She's the wrong gender, in his eyes."

"Oh, Dec. God. No. Don't worry about it. If he does the wrong thing, I'll make it right."

"It's not about the money, Andrew. We have more than enough. And he can't change Mom's trust, so there's that."

"He tried, with Terry."

Declan lets out a nasty sound. "Sure did." Concerned green eyes meet mine. "What kind of pressure is he putting on you to turn your children into little James McCormick Perfection Bots?"

I let out a curse.

"He did," Declan says, banging the table with one fist. "I knew it."

"You, too?"

"His big thing was that Ellie wasn't a boy, but yes. He tried."

"What'd you say to him?"

"I told him to go to hell and stormed off." Anger has a way of settling in comfortably on Declan's face, as if his features were made for it. "You?"

"Something like that."

"He's a piece of work."

"Will we be?"

"What?" Declan covers the top of his beer as the server comes by. My own glass is enough, and I'll have to call José or one of my other drivers soon.

"A piece of work to our kids. Mom was our shield against Dad. Are Amanda and Shannon going to have to act as shields for us because we put too much pressure on our kids to be clones of us?"

"Why would I want my kids to be clones of me?"

"Dad has a point."

"Oh, geez, Andrew. Come on."

"Bear with me. He has a point. I didn't say he's right."

"That's some heavy-duty parsing you're engaging in, bro."

"He worked his ass off to build Anterdec. We're all where we are because of him. Even Terry benefits from Mom's family trust. We've never had to build anything from scratch."

Dec starts to argue, but I stop him. "You bought Grind It Fresh! with money from Mom and Dad. I bought the gyms that way, too."

Damn.

"Gyms?"

I stare at the beer and blame it. "Never mind."

"Gyms?" he presses.

"Fine. I'll tell you. But you have to keep it a secret."

He pretends to zip his lips. The gesture looks so stupid on him.

"I need more than that."

"Like what? Pinkie swear? Blood rites?" He perks up. "The Turd-mobile! You can have the–"

"A basic promise is enough."

"No, no, no. Taking the Turdmobile off my hands is the ultimate in helping me keep a secret."

"I thought your assistant, Dave, took it?"

"He gave it back. Said the miles-per-gallon wasn't good enough, and he couldn't convert the engine to run on old french-fry grease, so we're stuck with it again."

"I don't want it."

"Fine. Tell me about the gyms."

"How did we get from Dad wanting to use us and our kids to secure his legacy to the Turdmobile?"

"The gyms, Andrew. What kind did you buy?"

Once the words are out, I can't put them back in.

Finally, he gets it. Dec isn't stupid, but he's a wee bit slow on the uptake tonight.

"Old Jorg sold to *you*?"

The way he says *you* makes me bristle, even through the beer.

"He did. Sixteen gyms. *Mine*," I growl, like some beast dude in a werewolf film.

"Sixteen." He says it like he's comparing.

"Size doesn't matter," I blurt out, instantly regretting my words.

Slinging back a skeptical sound like I threw at him earlier, he eyes me, suddenly serious. "You bought old Jorg's gym chain?"

"I did."

"Does Dad know?"

"Hell, no."

"Good. Don't want him mucking it up."

"What do you mean?"

"He'll try to take control. The old guy loves to rest on his laurels with Anterdec, but if he knows you have something new, he'll jump in."

"Why would he?"

"Duh. Control. Trust me. I know from experience."

"He tried to control Grind It Fresh!?"

"He's a coffee expert, Andrew. Didn't you know?"

"Ugh."

We sit in silence, finishing off the beers.

"Why does he make everything more difficult?"

"Because he is who he is and makes the world bend around him."

"I'm that way, too," I mutter.

Dec shakes his head. "Not even close. You're good, I'll admit. Strong, and smart at reading people. But he's an asshole to the core, and we're not."

"*I'm* not," I correct him.

That earns me a laugh.

"We inherited more than enough asshole from Dad's genetic code, but it's muted by Mom's kindness. Terry got a little more of that than we did."

"Imagine what Dad would be like if Mom were alive."

He rears back slightly.

"You've thought about it. Right?" I press.

"Sure. They'd be celebrating..." he pauses to calculate, "...wow, forty years together. He'd be the same guy, only more..." Dec fumbles for words.

"Human?"

"Right."

"What ifs," I say with a sigh.

"Too many what ifs."

"I wonder what kind of men we'd be today if Mom had lived," I confess, the beer making me more emotional than usual. Letting my guard down around my brother is hard.

Especially about feelings.

"We'd have a filter," he says simply, my signal not to pry or press further.

Line touched.

But not crossed.

"She was our filter. And when she died, we didn't just lose our mom. We lost our filter. Dad lost his buffer."

"Grace tried."

"Oh, sure. And she was great. But she wasn't Mom. No one else in the world was Mom."

"No. No one else was. She was one of a kind. I wish Ellie could meet her namesake. Mom would adore her."

"And my boys. They'll never know the great Elena Montgomery McCormick."

"She never got to be a grandmother. Marie and Pam get that, but not Mom."

Oh, no.

No, no, no.

The back of my throat is tightening because I'm tired, right?

Not because of–

Are Declan's eyes shining?

"You're not... *crying*, are you?" I ask, needing to toss the accusation out first, before he throws it at me.

"What? No! Bug off, Andrew." Dec clears his throat. "If anyone's crying, it's you."

"Nice deflection."

"You didn't deny it." He pauses. "You know what? Mom would hate this conversation. She'd tell us we sounded just like our father at his worst, and that we were better gentlemen."

Dec's words cut me to the core.

Because he's right.

"If Mom were here, we wouldn't be crying," I point out.

"I'm not crying. You're crying."

"You're proving Mom right."

His laugh is a little hoarse. His fingers twitch to wipe the obvious water from his eyes, but he's too stubborn to do it. Can't blame him.

So am I.

"Can we agree that it's a damned shame our mother didn't get to meet her grandkids?"

"Yes," I say immediately as Dec flags down the server.

Holding his credit card between two fingers, he waves it slightly. She comes over, looks at me, and tells him, "It's taken care of."

Dec insists on paying every other time, but I beat him to it today. He rolls his neck and slides the card back in his wallet.

"Again?" he grinds out.

"Always."

"You're such a dick."

"Well," I say, standing and patting him on the back, "I *am* James McCormick's son, after all."

❦ 13 ❧

Amanda

E verything is in pairs at this baby shower.
Everything.
When you're having two children at the same time, of course, this is how it works.

The only thing we don't have two of is the cake, which–hey! There are multiples of every kind of alcohol.

Where's the second cake? Especially a Cheeto-vanilla cake?

I demand parity.

Or, at least, my stomach does.

"Hey. You look upset. What's wrong?' Andrew asks, rubbing my back right in the spot that's been aching recently.

"Thinking about how unfair it is that there's only going to be one cake. Mom said Marie is bringing it."

"It's yours."

"What?"

"Pam has trays of cookies. If you want the entire cake, go for it."

Mom's hosting the baby shower. We're at her house, which is spotless. I look at the cookies on the table and perk up.

"Marshmallow treats!"

The doorbell rings and I hear the jingle of Spritzy's collar as Mom answers it. Thankfully, she's having a good day. The Lyme disease protocol she's been on for a few months now seems to be slowly leading to some improvement, though I have my doubts sometimes.

"Pamela," my father-in-law says with deep affection from the front door, their conversation turning to backdrop as I make my way to the Cheeto marshmallow treats, grab one, and take a bite of the crunchy, gooey stuff. The roof of my mouth argues back a bit, and I know tomorrow it'll be sore from the rough texture, but I don't care.

One of the babies does a flip, making me laugh. Andrew immediately puts his palm over my belly, feeling it.

"This just doesn't get old," he says, kissing my cheek.

The baby kicks in affirmation.

"Get a room!" says a bubbly voice as I'm side hugged by Shannon's mom, Marie. Her hands join Andrew's on my belly, the fingernails perfectly manicured, any idea that there might be a boundary about touching my bump inconceivable to her.

"Hi, Marie." She takes a deep breath, closes her eyes, and presses gently on both sides of my personal, attached blimp.

"Hi, babies," she whispers, her lips inches from my belly button. "What are their names?"

"Sun and Moon," Andrew deadpans.

"Sun and Moon?" Marie repeats, incredulous. Is her eye twitching?

"Sunshine and Moonbeam, shortened to Sun and Moon."

"Ha! You would never do that to your children. Those are horrible names!"

"How about James the Second and James the Third?" Declan says from behind us, voice filled with sarcasm.

Not that this is any different from his normal voice.

"That won't work," Marie says, turning to give Declan a hug.

"Why not?" he asks, winking at me.

"Because James had his chance for a namesake and he blew it. He gave you his name as a middle name," she says to Andrew, who nods. "You get to pick whatever names you want for your sons." She plucks a piece of lint off Andrew's shirt, scrunching her face. "Except Sunshine and Moonshine."

"Moonbeam."

She waves her hand. "Whatever. Don't give your kids weirdo names. We stuck to Carol, Shannon, and Amy, and look how well they turned out!"

At that exact moment, Carol walks in carrying a cake that looks like... a baby being born out of a woman's vagina?

"MARIE!" Mom shouts. "What *is* that?" For my mother to raise her voice means whatever's been done is a big, fat negative.

"The cake," Marie answers, clearly pleased with the result.

"I asked for a Cheeto-vanilla sheet cake."

"It is. On the inside. But you wanted a boring, white rectangle with orange roses and that was just so... *boring,* Pam!"

"What's the brown fudge under the baby's head as it's being born?" Andrew asks, peering at the cake with increasing alarm.

Like all of us.

"It's, um...." Marie struggles to explain, which is very unlike her.

"Oh, ewwwww," Mom whispers, eyes wide, hand going to her stomach as if in pain.

Horror at Marie or Lyme disease antibiotics? You decide.

"We'll just cut this up fast and hope no one realizes what they're eating," Carol says, reading the room. The oldest of the Jacoby girls, she's the one who fixes her mother's social messes most often. "Put a scoop of ice cream on top and no one will notice they're eating the sugared-up version of an umbilical cord."

"Did you say Cheeto-vanilla cake? Let me come with you and help," I venture.

"You just want to sneak a piece."

"Yup!"

"Here." She picks up a spoon and scoops some chocolate frosting.

"This looks just like the top of the Turdmobile," I say as I pop it into my mouth.

Andrew's turn to clutch his stomach.

"Mmmm. Chocolate coffee cream," I gasp.

"Really?" Carol takes a taste. "Yum!"

"You two are disgusting."

"No," she says, patting Andrew's cheek. "We're mothers."

He's definitely not convinced.

"How is childbirth class going?" Carol asks, eyes twinkling. "*Real* childbirth class, this time."

Just then, my friend Josh walks over to us.

His eyes cut to the abomination on the table before us. It looks like Carol is dissecting an alien baby with orange insides.

"Uh, hi?" he says to me, hugging me with thin bands of steel that pretend to be arms. Josh worked with Shannon and me at Consolidated Evalu-Shop, a mystery shopping company that Anterdec acquired a few years ago. Josh is a techie, and still works with me at Anterdec, though he was moved out of mystery shopping and consumer evaluation and into accounting.

Plus he swears the pool of eligible bachelors is better there.

"Josh! I am so glad you're here!"

He thrusts a present at me. It's two boxes stacked, wrapped in white and navy-blue stripes. An adorable card with two little baby feet dangles off the red gift bow. "Happy babies." Nervous eyes drift to my belly.

"Can you believe there are two in there?" Marie says, grabbing what I think is a Swedish fish posing as the clitoris from the cake and chewing on it. Her hand drifts to my belly again.

Josh peers at my midsection and says, "Absolutely."

"Hey! I'm not *that* big."

Everyone in the room goes quiet.

Oh, crap. I *am* that big.

"Speaking of childbirth class," Carol says, clearing her throat and looking at Josh, "I was just asking Andrew and Amanda how it's going."

Andrew squeezes my hand. "It's fine. Really simple. No instructors wanted by the narcotics squad this time."

Josh looks at me, mouth a little shaky as he whispers, "Vulvatron."

"Hey!" I give him an elbow jab, but the memory of mystery shopping a childbirth class at the local hospital–the very same place where I'll be delivering–hits me.

Josh just laughs.

I grab his arm, horror ripping through me as his mention of the past kicks in. "Josh?"

"Yes?"

"*I'm* Vulvatron." I look down at my crotch. Can't see it, of course. All I can see is my innie belly button that's turned outie, the nub outlined by the stretchy jersey of my dress. "Me. *I'm Vulvatron*," I repeat.

"That was a joke. We were pretending to be an expectant couple for that stupid childbirth class mystery shop," Josh hisses. "Don't hold it against me now!"

"Were you joking back then when you told me I wasn't fit to raise a sea monkey?" I shoot back.

"Of course I was! The entire mystery shop was a joke." He runs his hands up and down his body, pointing. "I was pretending to be hetero. We were acting. You're *more* than capable of raising a sea monkey."

"Thanks for the vote of confidence."

"Hey," he says, brow furrowed in concentration. "Remember how we learned that some women eat the placenta? Are you planning to do that?"

"Yes. I'll eat half right after the birth and freeze the other half. Then I'll wait a few months, until I'm back at work."

"Why wait until you're back at work?"

"So I can cook it up, slip it into my lunch bag, and put it in the staff kitchen at Anterdec. Then when you steal my food, you'll eat it."

"You wouldn't!"

"What good is making an entire organ with my body if I can't use it to torment you? And aha! You didn't deny being the leftover thief!"

"Of course I'm not." But his shifty eyes give him away.

Of all the moments for my father-in-law to appear.

He looks at the carved-up alien baby on the table.

"I see Marie made the cake herself," he says dryly, reaching for an unopened bottle of whisky of such high quality and expense I'm one hundred percent sure he brought it as a contribution to the celebration, but with the intent of consuming most of it himself.

"No! I found someone on Facebook Marketplace who does baby cakes," Marie chirps.

"That's supposed to be a baby? It looks like someone hit a clown with a Humvee and you scraped it off the turnpike."

We all do a double take, because that's *exactly* what it looks like.

"It's nothing some good ice cream can't fix," Carol says patiently.

James shakes the whisky bottle midair. "This will suffice as my dessert."

I grab the slice with the baby's nose and chomp down. Mmmm. Caramel.

Jason joins us. The bottle in *his* hand is amber, and must be some kind of locally brewed beer.

"Andrew." They shake hands, Jason turning to James to do the same. Then his eyes settle on–take a guess.

My attached boulder.

"Two in there, huh? We never had two babies at the same time. That's going to be so much fun."

"You have a warped idea of fun, Jason," James comments.

"I love babies. You two ever need a babysitter, let me and Marie know."

"Hey!" Declan says to his mother-in-law. "You're *our* babysitter."

"Ellie's growing up. We need a *new* baby to hold," Marie says pointedly. She actually sniffs.

"Is that a subtle hint?" Shannon asks, coming in next to Declan to slide her arm around his waist.

"Since when do I hint?" Marie replies. "I've been saying Ellie needs a sibling since..."

"Since we conceived her," Dec mutters.

"If you two want to get started on another, go for it. I'm sure there's a closet somewhere here at Pam's where you can have privacy," Marie says to Declan.

Who points at Andrew and me. "They're the ones with a thing for closets."

"Maybe that's how we stop fighting about cribs," I say to Andrew with an elbow nudge. "Just give them a walk-in closet to sleep in."

"Who does that? Sounds cruel. Besides, we can afford new cribs."

"You can afford to build new walk-in closets," Jason says drolly as he offers up a piece of poop.

Which I accept gratefully.

"Why are we eating cake first? Don't we normally do this later?" Declan asks, spearing a chunk of red cake that must be from the placenta and chewing thoughtfully. He scoops a piece of poop off his plate and eats it.

Andrew turns green.

"What kind of party games did Shannon come up with?" Marie asks, eyes bright with excitement. "Remember Porn, Labor, or Constipation?"

"How could we forget, Mom?" Amy says, frowning as she enters carrying a red and white polka-dotted gift. She looks at me, teeth gritted, eyes shining maniacally as she adds, "I'm never having kids after playing that game."

"Come on! The pain isn't that bad."

"I meant the constipation pictures."

"Oh. Yes. The first postpartum poop is–"

Amy shoves a piece of chocolate poop in her mom's mouth. She moans.

"I love these chocolate shavings around this pink cake!" James says, appearing with a slice. "How inventive. The shades of pink and purple are so vivid."

"It's a hairy vulva," Marie explains.

Instantly, Andrew turns on one heel and leaves.

"A what?" James inquires politely.

"Hairy vulva."

"Is that a Latin term?"

"Like cunnilingus?" Marie replies, clearly perplexed. James begins to choke.

Good to know my father-in-law knows the meaning of *that* word.

"Don't you dare mention Cardi B. and Megan Thee Stallion's song," Shannon whispers in my ear. I laugh, which nearly makes me pee, which confuses my central nervous system, and suddenly, I'm hiccuping and have an eyelid twitch.

"If we're going to talk about vaginas at a baby shower, it should be mine. Not the one on the lovely cake Marie brought," I say, trying to divert attention.

It works.

"And have you seen the album?" Mom says loudly as she picks up on my cue and changes the subject. "Amanda's baby photos." Mom looks at James. "We have one of Andrew, too, thanks to his father."

"You do?" Andrew says, surprised.

"Of course. Remember the copies I made years ago and gave to you for Christmas?"

Declan looks at Grace, who is now across the room, chatting animatedly with Gina. "You mean the copies Grace made and put into the albums we all received."

James waves his hand dismissively. "You have them. I assume the boys will look like Andrew," he says in a tone that is so annoying it's as if it's all affect, but it's not. James came out of the womb clutching a mergers and acquisitions contract and an ego the size of Missouri.

"You can't assume that."

"Why not? My sons resemble me."

"They have some of Elena in them, James," Grace points out, joining our group. I notice Gina now at the table, picking up a Cheeto marshmallow treat, sniffing suspiciously.

"Fine. And the boys would certainly be well served by big, smart eyes like Amanda's," my father-in-law says, offering an unctuous–and rare–compliment.

I blame the scotch.

"Thank you," I say politely, earning a dazzling smile from him.

The guy may be in his sixties, but I see how he manages to get women in their twenties to date him. Charm doesn't fade from men like James McCormick.

Or from his sons.

Andrew's arm wraps around my expanding waist and squeezes my hip, his nose in my hair. "I hope our boys take after you. But when we have a girl, she'll–"

"Hold up there, bucko. Let me get through *this* pregnancy first."

Mom watches us, eyes rolling from Andrew to me. "You want *more?*"

I rub my belly. "Eventually."

He kisses my cheek. "Four."

"FOUR?" James and Mom gasp in unison.

Andrew gives his dad a flat look. "Sure. Have to do one better than you."

"Hmph. I'm not too old to produce another child, you know. Don't poke my competitive streak," James replies.

Poor Jason has just wandered over to us.

"Are you crazy? You'd be dead before the child turned eighteen!" A booming, unexpectedly caustic laugh makes everyone stare at him in surprise. For a mild-mannered guy, this is out of character.

"Clint Eastwood had a baby in his seventies," James huffs. "I could, if I wanted to."

"And I could have a surgeon cut off my arms and attach them to my forehead like horns if I wanted to, but I'd be crazy and there would be no point," Jason shoots back, but his entire demeanor softens, as if he's realizing the fight isn't worth it.

"It doesn't matter," Andrew interrupts. "You're not having more kids," he says to James, "and even if you did, we'd just beat you by having another."

"We would?" I squeak.

"What about us?" Declan demands, pointing between himself and Shannon, who startles like she's been hit with a cattle prod. "We could have five, if we wanted to."

"FIVE?" Shannon screams in horror.

"FIVE?" Marie squeals with sheer delight.

Shannon turns on her mother, finger in her face like she's ready to give her a nasal swab test with her fingernail. "We are NOT having five kids!"

"But Declan just said–"

Shannon turns to her husband, same finger in his face. "We are *not* having five kids to fulfill some sick competitive streak of yours."

"We'll talk later," he says smoothly. He turns to Pam. "How are you doing? Shannon told me you learned the fibromyalgia might be caused by Lyme?"

Pam and Declan begin talking as Shannon stands there, gape-mouthed. Her husband has just smoothly finessed his way out of a fight.

"How does he *do* that?" she hisses. "I can't complain publicly because he's expressing compassion for Pam. But he left that grenade hanging without a pin!"

"He'll have to put the pin back in the slot someday," I say with a wink.

Her eyebrow cocks. "Ooooo. Leverage."

"*Awwwwwwww,*" comes a collective outburst from the living room. Shannon and I share a perplexed look and follow the crowd.

A slideshow is being projected on the wall.

Terry is holding baby Andrew in a photo, Declan behind them, playing with a toy truck, the 1990s on display.

In the present, James has a funny look on his face, arms folded over his chest. Andrew stands next to him, looking like his dad.

A hand goes to my shoulder and I turn to find yet another McCormick man in my Mom's house.

"Terry!" I say, instantly in a hug with my brother-in-law. Of the three McCormick boys, he's the most distanced from the family. The eldest, with the deepest voice, he's the rebel. He was groomed by James for greatness, but he quit Anterdec after their mother died and James handled it all so poorly, turning Declan into the scapegoat.

Terry lives in a duplex in Jamaica Plain. His income is from his mother's family trust, an annual sum that would support most families comfortably but that Andrew and Declan consider pocket change.

"Amanda." His voice always gives me shivers, because Terry sounds like Barry White. Like everyone else, his eyes drift to my belly. "Can't believe I'll have two nephews soon. How are you feeling?"

"Heavily occupied. Literally."

He laughs and looks around. "Nice place your mom has."

"You've never been here before?"

He shakes his head. "No. I like Newton, though."

"It's not quite JP."

Before he can reply, Andrew walks over, thumbing the slideshow. "Can you believe Dad gave Pam those photos?"

"He has a soft spot for her. And it's great to see them again." Terry frowns. "But notice how none of them have Mom in the picture?"

"I'm sure those just haven't been rotated through yet. Plus, she was probably taking the photos." Andrew's involuntarily first response is to defend James.

"Right. Sure." Terry doesn't back down so much as he backs off, easily. "I'll bet that's it."

Andrew's eyes narrow. "How's it going, bro?"

"Fine. I'm working on a cool hydroponics project."

"Growing pot? Great growth market. We have some advisors helping us to look at capital investments in marijuana that might–"

"No. Tomatoes."

"What?"

"Tomatoes. Hydroponic tomatoes."

"Does that scale up?"

"I'll donate the extras to a food bank."

It's like they're speaking two completely different languages with just enough overlap to make them think they aren't.

"You're learning hydroponics to... garden?"

"Yeah."

"Oh." Andrew blinks. "Want a beer?"

Terry glances at their dad. "Hell, yeah."

When Shannon and Mom asked me about throwing a baby shower, I had some terms:

1. NO GAMES. MARIE'S ROUSING RENDITION OF PORN, Labor, or Constipation at Shannon's baby shower scarred me for life.

2. We'll do a video present opening. That's right–nothing live. I have a bladder the size of Ellie's attention span, and also, the thought of smiling nonstop while we open two of everything gives me hives. Carol told me that videotaping the presents was a new thing. I'll add the video to a private YouTube channel and send the link later. This also means giving every single gift its due attention, something I just can't do at a big bash like this.

3. Cheeto cake.

· · ·

So far, so good.

A small gasp to my right makes me turn. It's Mom, hand to her mouth, staring at the screen. Following her eyes, I see a picture of my dad cradling baby me in his right arm, holding a wrench in the other hand. Shirtless and very muscular, he has a huge streak of grease across his cheek and is grinning with abandon.

"Who's that hot dude?" Marie asks, spellbound.

Jason clears his throat and whispers in her ear.

"Oops," she hisses, stuffing a piece of cauliflower in her mouth and chewing with an *I'm sorry* look at my mom.

"That's Leo?" James asks with a *harumph* of disapproval.

"Yes," Mom says. "I–I put that in here because I felt the show should be balanced. I wanted to be fair."

James suddenly looks a bit sick.

Terry nudges Andrew and gives him a *Told you so, bro* look that makes me realize he is, without question, a McCormick man.

And then James reaches in his jacket pocket, pulling out an old-fashioned photo envelope from the days when you had film developed. His fingers don't shake as he finds three little square cardboard pieces with film in the center. Mom connected an old slide projector to her more modern one.

James goes to the older device and slips the slides in.

Suddenly, Elena Montgomery McCormick is on my mother's wall, almost life size. She's sitting on a beach, wearing a late-1980s bikini with a high hip cut. There's a baby at her breast, two young kids who must be Declan and Terry building a sand castle, and a dark-haired man next to her. Both of them are laughing, the wind whipping through their hair, the picture clearly impromptu.

"Elena," James says quietly.

"Oh, my God," Terry says under his breath, emotional restraint barely there. "Mom."

"I've never seen that picture before," Shannon says, awe in her voice. "Ellie looks like her."

"You chose your daughter's name well," James says gruffly, sucking on the last drops of whisky in his glass. His eyes jump to the sideboard, where spirits rest in bottles.

And, in this house, on walls, too.

Click

The machine pushes the slide to the next one, Elena face-to-face with a cherubic, older baby, one who can't quite walk.

"Is that you?" I ask Andrew, who nods without taking his eyes off the wall.

"You were such a fat baby!" Marie declares, nearly making Andrew choke.

"All of our boys were," James says, voice going soft. "Elena joked that her milk was Vermont cream."

For James to comment publicly about breastfeeding is a surprise.

"She was a wonderful mother." Terry's deep voice cuts through. "And she would have been a tremendous grandmother," he adds, looking at Pam. "Thankfully, Andrew and Amanda's boys will have you."

Mom blushes. I can tell she's trying not to cry, and she'll succeed. Never overly emotional in public, Mom has the ability to experience something without reacting to it in real time.

She'll fall apart later.

Click

Toddler Andrew in a pool, swimming with Elena next to him.

The indoor swimming lanes attached to our house, put in place when Andrew was a competitive swimmer, have been under renovation, a crack in the pool disrupting everything. Of all the times not to be able to float and defy gravity.

I rub my belly. The work will be done soon. Seeing a picture of my husband with his mom, his tiny head floating above water, face screwed in intense concentration, makes me melt.

"How old is that baby?" Josh asks, moving closer to the screen. "He can't even be two!"

"Andrew was twenty months when he learned how to swim. Early start and proper training. You were so close to the Olympics," James says in a rueful voice.

Andrew's face hardens.

James looks at my belly. "Those boys have good genes and every advantage in the world. We'll make champions out of them. Take their raw talent and maximize. Optimize. They'll go beyond anything my own sons have done."

Anger washes over Terry swiftly, changing him, McCormick anger filling out his face, making my breath halt in my throat. He opens his mouth to speak, but Andrew puts a hand on his shoulder, ready to intercede.

It's my mother who cuts through it all.

"You love them," she says simply to James. "You loved Elena. You love your sons. You love my daughter. And you love these grandbabies. That's what's so wonderful about love, James: We love people for who they are. Not for who they could be."

Stunned, he says nothing, the click of the projector moving on to a picture of me at four, wearing a Wednesday Addams costume for Halloween.

The room bursts into laughter.

And I reach for another slice of Cheeto cake.

❧ 14 ❧

Amanda

He's late.

It's the third meeting of our childbirth class. There are only four couples in the class, and they have all managed to be on time. Eighty-seven point five percent success. Andrew is the remaining twelve point five percent of the students.

I'm going to cut that point five percent off if he doesn't walk through the door in the next thirty seconds.

Where are you??? I text furiously, as if being angry will make him more likely to respond.

Nothing.

Not a word.

Hope, our childbirth instructor, gives me that raised-eyebrow look, the one that hints at wondering where my husband is, but doesn't outright ask in case the answer is something uncomfortable. I smile back, shrug, and furiously type another text.

Nothing. No answer.

The tears are so close now, sudden and fierce. I'm an emotional wrecking ball, swinging wildly on a long chain. Here I am, looking like I'm nine months pregnant in a class for seven-monthers, sitting all alone. I've been abandoned by my husband, who is too busy to bother spending time with me learning how to bring his own progeny into the world.

How pathetic.

Big, fat tears well up in my eyes, which makes sense because I'm nothing but big and fat, too. I can't cry, because if I start, I won't stop.

My hip starts that nerve pain that's been triggering lately, so my ass cheek aches, on top of everything else. Shifting slightly, I blink and twin drops fall from my eyes onto my light-gray top.

Great. Now I look like it's raining on my breasts.

"Amanda?" Hope says softly, her hand on my shoulder. She smells like orange eucalyptus. "Are you okay?"

"I'm fine," I say with a laugh, trying to pass my emotions off as nothing. "Being silly. Andrew's running late."

She leans in and whispers, "He's the CEO of a major company. And on the board of this hospital. I get it. No problem."

Her compassion makes me feel even worse.

I sniff. "Thanks. We can just start and I'll do both parts."

Hope laughs softly. "I'll fill in for him. Today it's all about massage and supporting your partner through the discomfort."

Oh, no.

A sob escapes me, full and ripe, which only makes Hope feel worse for me, which elicits more tears. The other couples are doing their best to ignore me. One woman gives me a pity smile, the kind I hate more than anything in the world.

"Do you have a friend who could come over?"

I nod and grab my phone. "Let me try my friend Shannon."

She straightens up and moves to chat with another couple. I know she's buying me time.

You had better be trapped by an evil villain and your only excuse for not being here is you have to save the world from certain doom, I text Andrew.

On second thought, I add: *Or you've discovered a source of Cheeto ice cream and are getting me some as a surprise.*

As I switch over to text Shannon, a tap on the door makes me look up, a familiar face giving me a wide-eyed, sheepish look.

"Gina?" I gasp. "What are you doing here?"

Hope waves to her. "Hi! Oh, good." She smiles at me. "You got a friend to fill in for Andrew!"

You have got to be kidding me.

That's *exactly* why Gina's here.

"So, Andrew can't make it?" she says, walking to me, peering at the other couples as if she's a cyborg studying how to mimic being human. She crouches behind me, spreads her knees, and starts kneading my shoulders.

I startle. "What are you doing?"

"I'm filling in for Andrew?"

"You're what?"

"He sent me? His flight back from New York was delayed by mechanical failure there?"

"Why didn't he text me back?"

"His phone died?"

"He could text you, but not me?"

"I haven't heard from him in two hours? He said if he didn't call back, to come here and be with you just in case?"

"So he texted you to fill in as the father in this childbirth class? This takes the cake, Gina. Andrew leans on you to do everything for him, but come on! I can't believe he–ah, God, right there," I moan as her fingers do magic on the spot in my shoulder that's been aching forever.

"Like that?"

"Mmmm. Where did you learn to do that?"

"I was a licensed massage therapist before I got computer training to be an admin?"

Hope waves a book in the air, smiling at Gina and me. "I'm so glad everyone has an assistant today! We're going to work on massage, and how to use massage to increase blood flow, decrease pain, and make our moms comfortable."

"Ooooooh, perfect! I know this inside out?" Gina purrs.

"And," Hope says, leaning in, "we'll also focus on perineal massage." She reaches for a bottle of olive oil.

Gina's fingers come to a dead halt on my shoulders.

"There is no bonus Andrew could give me to justify this, Amanda." Her voice goes down at the end of the sentence, making my blood run cold. She pauses. "Unless a private jet is on the table, and even then I'd need a large dose of scopolamine. And a–"

"You're not touching my perineum, Gina!"

"I chose massage school over esthetician after the first term because there was no way I was learning how to wax a labia. I can unknot a piriformis in no time flat, but hand me a labia and I'm dangerous."

"What does that mean?"

"Let's just say I'm really glad that in the student clinic, I only did one shift and they had liability insurance. There's a woman in Melrose who I still light a candle for at Mass."

"What did you *do* to her?"

Before she can reply, my phone rings. Hope gives me a look that reminds me of being hushed by my preschool teacher.

Pressing one ear shut, I put the phone up to the other one and whisper, "Andrew! What are you doing?"

"I finally got my phone working. I'm sorry. It's been malfunction after malfunction."

As I peer into the phone, I realize he's wearing headphones. And shouting.

"Where are you?"

"On my way!"

Hope starts waving her arms for me to simultaneously pay attention to her and be quiet.

"*Shhh!* Hope's teaching us today's lesson." As I speak with him, the instructor hands something to Gina.

Whose mouth drops into an O of shock.

I peer over my belly. "Is that a..?"

Gina moves it so I get a better look.

"I'm Facetiming you," Andrew says into the phone. "Let me see. I can't be there, but I can be there," he emphasizes.

"I'm not sure you want to see this."

"Of course I do. If I can't be there, I can watch."

That sounds porny, but I don't say that because another look from Hope like the one she shot me a moment ago and I'll burst into tears.

Gina's eyebrows go up and she moves the item in her hand within view of the screen as she waves half-heartedly at Andrew.

His brow drops in confusion, then shoots up. "Is that a–"

"Sex toy?" Gina asks.

"Labia," Hope says loudly. "We're looking at a silicone replica of the labia, vulva, vagina, and perineum."

"Where's the clitoris?" one of the women across the room jokes.

"That's what *he* said," someone else calls out, making everyone fall into middle-school giggles.

"Andrew," I hiss into my phone, staring at his übercalm face. I know that face. It's the expression he gets when he knows he's done something wrong but he's going to Mr. Cool his way out of it. He has a presence, a kind of command that takes over in moments like this.

It pisses me off to no end.

Because it implies I'm being unreasonable, and I am anything but.

"Yes?"

"If you don't get here in the next twenty minutes, I'll have to let Gina massage my fake perineum, and there are some lines your executive assistant should never cross."

"I'm, like, getting the platinum health insurance plan for bronze prices?" Gina says, grabbing the phone from me. "And if I'm touching that silicone replica thing, I get a better parking place than the one on the third floor?"

"Have facilities see what they can do about the parking," Andrew says.

"You said that last time? And I got a spot by the elevator but it's next to the dumpster?"

Hope clears her throat pointedly. "We're about to begin the massage." She looks at my phone. I turn it around so she can see Andrew's face.

"Hey, Hope," he says from the screen. "I'm on my way, but stuck in some bad weather here in New York." A deep, sexy chuckle emerges. "Can you do me a favor and let me Facetime in for this session? I want to support Amanda in every possible way, and your classes have been top notch."

Her hands fly to her heart, mouth pressing into the universal expression of a woman whose heart has been touched by a flattering schmuck who is trying to get his way.

"You are so sweet, Andrew. Of course, we can let you Facetime!" Hope looks around at all the couples. "Anyone mind? Amanda's husband is Andrew McCormick, a member of the board of directors for this hospital, and he's caught in New York in bad weather. Amanda's got twins in there, and at thirty weeks, no less. He needs the up-close experience with her perineum!"

"It's been so long, I'll need a map," Andrew mutters.

"HEY!"

"YAY! I'm so glad you said YAY!" Hope says to me as everyone else in class nods to give Andrew permission to be here virtually.

"Platinum for bronze," Gina hisses at Andrew, who gives her a wink.

"You are such a piece of work," I say to him quietly. "I can't believe you flirted with our childbirth instructor like that!"

Genuine astonishment fills his face. "That wasn't flirting. You know what flirting looks like from me."

"I do. It's a bulldozer filled with testosterone."

"Exactly."

"Ewwwww?" Gina huffs. "I want platinum health with free massages and no deductibles?"

"The perineum," Hope announces, "is here. Colloquially referred to as the taint, because it ain't this and it ain't that (she pauses for obligatory laughter), the perineum is a thick muscle that does a huge amount of work in the final stages of labor. The baby's head stretches it, thinning it out. Most women consider it to be the most painful muscle of all when it stretches–sorry, moms–but it's one that partners can help with."

Hope holds up her replica and uses two fingers to press and slide along the lower rim of the vulva.

"Gina," Andrew whispers. I hand her the phone.

"Yes?"

"Take notes."

"Excuse me?"

"Take notes for me. Add them to my daily audio summary."

"You expect me to take notes while standing in for you at your wife's childbirth class, and make sure they're put into your audio software so you can listen to this tomorrow on your morning commute?"

"Of course."

"THE TAINT?" she says loudly, making Andrew go back to Mr. Cool Face.

"Just do it."

"You need a reminder about THE TAINT? Shall I write up an executive one-pager for you?"

He smiles, as if now she understands. "Exactly."

"Up here, on the table, we have a bowl of olive oil. Partners, dip your index and middle fingers–"

"Andrew?" Gina asks sweetly.

"Yes?"

"Does she mean this finger?" She flips him the bird.

Mr. Cool Face becomes Mr. Sour Puss.

"Fine. Platinum plan, no deductibles, better parking spot, and no audio summary."

I turn to her. "You can go home."

"I can? I–I didn't mean to be unsupportive to you, Amanda?"

"Oh, *pffft*. I know that. It's just–you negotiated well. Got what you wanted. Now let's watch Andrew stew as he doesn't win. Letting you go home means he doesn't win."

"HEY!" he bellows from the phone.

"If I don't learn how to do perineal massage, how will Andrew learn?"

I arch one eyebrow at her.

She reddens.

"Gotcha? Okay? Bye?" I've never seen someone back out of a room like that. How does she know where the open door frame is? Somehow, her body manages it, and soon I'm alone.

Alone with my Facetime husband.

"You do understand there is no Facetime at the birth. You'd better be there in full."

"In the flesh," he says–and he's right.

Because his voice gives me shivers as he says those words directly behind me.

"Andrew!" My in-person words are echoed on the screen, as he pulls me in for a hug, careful around my belly. All my irritation fades as the familiar scent of him makes me grin. "I thought you were in New York?"

"I realized I could get back faster by helicopter. Wasn't fully certain I'd be there in time, so I hedged my bets."

"I'm so glad you're here."

"I wouldn't miss touching your perineum for anything."

"I think that's the most romantic thing you've ever said to me, Andrew."

Hope gives us a look that says, *Are you done now? I have a curriculum to get through*. Andrew sits behind me and I lean back, hips aching but happy, his arms around me the best cocoon I could possibly have. As Hope picks up where we left off, I look at the silicone model, imagine my own tissues, and see Andrew doing the same.

We're learning.

Learning how to help my body experience even the tiniest bit less pain, given what it's about to go through.

That's what childbirth class boils down to, isn't it? We're not here to master a process. Optimizing it isn't quite right, because the optimal outcome is a live, healthy baby–or two, in my case.

But there's definitely a way to mitigate the negatives and accentuate the positives, and that's what we're doing, as Andrew takes two fingers, oils them up, and begins stroking the fake perineum like he's applying lip gloss.

"We're not painting the flesh, Andrew. We're massaging it. Dig in. You want to help direct blood to the area," Hope explains.

"Blood?"

"Inside the muscle. That'll help it stretch."

His hand halts. "Hope?"

"Yes?"

"Statistically speaking, what are the odds of a primiparous twin birth being vaginal?"

"I–I don't know." She gives him a flirtatious look that makes me want to rip her hair out. "But I'm very impressed that you know how to use 'primiparous twin birth' correctly in a sentence."

I snort.

"Amanda."

"Yes?"

"Text Gina that question."

"What?"

"Text her. She'll know."

"Why would Gina know that?"

"She doesn't *know* it, but she knows how to get me the answer."

"You realize you can just Google it."

"Why? It's easier to ask Gina."

"You're adding a step, Andrew. Pull up the browser on your phone, type the question, and–"

"That's an added step."

"*Gina* is the added step!"

One of the fathers across the room holds up his phone. "While you two were arguing, I looked it up. About twenty-five percent of twins are delivered vaginally. And then there's the dreaded vaginal c-section."

Hope clears her throat. "Please don't use negative words."

A sheepish look covers his face. "Sorry."

"Twenty-five percent?" Andrew looks like he's weighing his options, fingers now deep in the muscle. "And vaginal c-section is when one twin is delivered vaginally, but the other gets stuck and needs a surgical birth?"

Hope nods. "It's rare, but it happens."

I shudder.

"Are you calculating the value of your time spent learning this by weighing the statistical likelihood that I'll need perineal massage at some point?" I accuse him.

"Yes," he confesses. Except it doesn't sound like he has any guilt whatsoever about being so cold and calculating.

"You should do it because you love and support me!"

"Of course I will. Just being pragmatic."

"Pragmatic!"

"Your mother is an actuary. She does this for a living."

"My mother is not supporting her partner in giving birth to twins. But at the rate you're going, she might replace you."

"Hey!" He holds up his hands, one covered in oil. "I'm doing my best here."

"I'm your wife, Andrew. I know what you look like when you're doing your best, and this isn't it."

He leans in and whispers, "Normally when I do this, the only lube is from my mouth and I'm using my tongue, not my fingers."

I freeze him out and watch one of the other fathers use a technique that makes me think he's a middle school band director, using his fingers like a conductor's wand. I get seasick within seconds.

"Okay, then, everyone!" Hope announces. "I know this puts us well into the discomfort zone, but it's so important to make sure blood goes to the right places."

"It's definitely doing that right now on me," Andrew mutters as he wipes his fingers on a paper towel.

"Seriously? You're getting *aroused* by this?"

"It's a pretend vagina and vulva, Amanda. I'm biologically primed to be aroused by it."

"Are you going to sport an erection when you're watching my vagina during the birth?"

"You're probably going to be strangling me, so I assume the blood won't be able to travel south."

I smirk in spite of myself.

He waits.

I say nothing more.

His eyes cut over to me, face slack, but I can read him as his eyes drift to my belly. Andrew is a tough, direct, self-contained CEO who schmoozes everyone but is close to few. I'm in his inner circle, at the core, and I know he'll do literally anything to make life better for me.

Including feeling up a plastic pus–

"EEEEEEEeeeee!" Hope squeals, staring at her smartphone screen, the sound one of joy rather than fear.

"Hope?" I ask. She's standing just a few feet away. When she looks at me, her eyes glisten, mouth broad and grinning.

"One of my students just texted me." She turns the phone so I can see it.

It's a picture of three little burrito babies, all in the row, wrapped in the classic hospital receiving blankets with pink and blue stripes.

"Triplets?" Andrew gasps, mouth setting in a piqued line.

Yeah, yeah, someone outdid him.

"Vaginal triplets," Hope says, triumphant. She looks at me–the only person in class not having a singleton–then she looks at Andrew's hand. "See? You never know when you'll need to feel your way around a vulva."

Andrew's nose twitches, but he looks at me to avoid making an obvious joke.

"Right, Hope. You never know."

§.

HIS HAND SLIDES BETWEEN MY THIGHS AS I DRIFT OFF TO sleep.

My eyes fly open.

A kiss on my bare shoulder, then the long, hot, hard length of him up against my back makes me take a deep breath. I don't mean to, but I hold it.

"Amanda?" he murmurs, that hand between my thighs intent on doing more than finding a resting place.

"Mmmm?"

"Are you...?"

Am I what?

INTERESTED?
　Willing?
　Horny?
　Scared?
　Turned on?
　Desperate?
　Aroused?

HOW ABOUT ALL OF THOSE?

"I'm... I don't know."

His hand stops moving.

"*I don't know* is a no." He snuggles in. "Affection's fine."

The baseball bat between his legs, poking my tailbone, tells me it's not fine.

"In this case, I don't know is... too many feelings to just say yes."

"Which is a no."

"It's not a no. It's a..."

"A what, sweetie?" He strokes my hair.

The "sweetie" makes me burst into tears.

"Oh, Amanda," he whispers, holding me in his arms, palm running from my shoulder to my wrist, a soothing gesture that shows how much he cares. "What's wrong? Did I do something to upset you?"

"No. It's not you. It's me."

"You were fine until I reached for you, so it's me."

"It's not. It's... it's a little bit of everything. I'm so big, we can't do my favorite position. I'm so swollen that one touch between my legs and I come–and no, that's not some superpower, because it doesn't feel as good as it did before the pregnancy. Then I worry that I'll never orgasm like I did before the pregnancy, and that I should have appreciated it more when I could come like that. Plus, I'm a house. Literally a house. I'm housing two womb mates. And I know you find me attractive and sexy, and I feel attractive and sexy, but I'm pretty close to either having my vagina split open or my abs cut by a scalpel, so sex is complicated and tough and, Andrew," I sob, the hitched breaths feeling completely untethered. "I don't know. I don't know who I am anymore. I don't know what I want. I don't know what this body is. So... I don't know."

"There's a lot of emotion behind those three words."

"It's not the only three-word sentence packed with emotion," I reply. "There's *I love you*."

"And *Yes, I swallow*."

Through tears, I hit him in jest, but his comment does what it needs to do. The melancholy that swept over me earlier breaks free, as if I've been bound by tiny ropes of despair that are frayed by his abiding attention and diligent presence. Rolling over is hard now, but I manage, then kiss him, my tongue moving fast to find his, to connect and savor, to thank and rejoice.

Being understood is a luxury.

Being seen is a holy act.

When every part of your body expands to accommodate new life, being touched by the outside world takes on a new feel. Andrew's familiar touch reconfigures to elicit different reactions from me, his hand cupping my full breast something old and new at the same time.

When I move to be closer to him, his hand on my hip and the glide of my calf between his feels heated and arousing, lust rising with fervent emotion. Intimacy is hard. We have to work constantly to keep the threads of connection woven tightly.

My naked skin craves his touch.

"I love this. I love you," he murmurs, hand going to my belly, then traveling lower. I'm wet and eager, ready for his mouth, his fingers, his thickness in me, but wanting to draw this out, too.

"I love that you love this. Mmmmm," I murmur, his touch making warmth and energy spread through my ever-expanding body. The aches and tensions of pregnancy fade when I'm under his spell, the constant connection of bare skin sending messages to receptors that say *stand down. Relax. Rest.*

Release.

His body is never the same twice as I touch him, eyes closing to accept his offer of pleasure, my own senses heightened as I find the smooth curl of muscle in his shoulders, the fine layering of hair along his chest, the deep grooves of ribs and strong abs when my hands take their normal journey into Andrewland.

Every day that I get to touch him like this is another day of joy, and the combination of his touch, his deep stare, and our wild kisses makes me love the world we create in bed.

Lefty kicks me and Andrew moves back, looking down between us with wonder.

"Does that mean I should stop?"

"No! No," I whisper, moving my hips against his hand, needing to finish what he's started. "You know you can't hurt them."

Amusement and lust make his eyes dance. "I know. It's still a little strange."

"Let's stop thinking, then." I reach down and stroke up once. His eyes close, mouth dropping open, the tip of his tongue emerging.

I want that tongue elsewhere.

"I stopped thinking a long time ago, Amanda. When we're like this, all I do is feel. And there's no one else in the world who can make me just feel. Only you. Only us."

His hands slide under my nightgown and I reach down, his movement halting.

But I pull my nightgown up over my belly, breasts pendulous and full, the cool chill of the air hitting my nude, ripe body making me shiver until Andrew cocoons me in the covers.

And warms me up.

"I won't last long," I whisper before he kisses me, a long, lush kiss full of tongue and smiles and heat.

"That's my line," he says as his knee shifts, thigh mingling with mine, and I feel what he means. "What do you want?" he asks.

"You."

"Always here."

My hand strokes him. "I hope I can say the same."

A sound from the back of his throat makes my heart squeeze. "What does that mean?"

When you're with someone long enough, and love intensely enough, a near-psychic connection makes you damn close to being a mind reader. Or maybe a heart reader? I instantly regret my words.

"Oh, no! I don't mean that. I just mean I'll change. After the babies. Shannon said it took a while for her sex drive to come back."

He pauses.

"This is my version of dirty talk, Pregnancy Edition," I joke as his palm broadens, moving up my body, curling over my navel. He smiles.

"Every word out of your mouth is a joy."

"Even when I call you a jerk?"

"Especially when you call me a jerk."

"Why especially?"

"Because it means I'm right."

Before I can answer, he shuts me up with a kiss, the kind that sets nerves running off to hide and blood racing through me, chasing my worries away, bringing in the love and lust that connects me to my husband in ways profound and profane.

Suddenly, every anxious thought is gone, and all I am is this lush body, biologically primed to be no more, no less than what I am in this moment. The taste of Andrew lingers on my lips as he leaves a trail of kisses down my swollen breasts, tongue going to an exquisite spot between my legs for the flitter of a moment, just long enough to make me keenly need him.

I roll to my side and we spoon, his hard, muscled body behind me, my hand between my legs, guiding him in.

His groan of pleasure makes me nearly come, but as my lower belly tightens to hard muscle like his torso and pecs, I find the orgasm holding itself patiently at bay, wanting more.

In the wonderland of our marital bed, I can be the new version of myself that came into being when we found each other, releasing all of the frayed pieces of the old me that don't hold together well. I'm real without him, but every stroke of my back makes me find that part of who I am. Each thrust into me makes the whole of our time together, shared breaths and memories, more complete.

For now, I am my body only, his hands and mouth on me, his breath on my neck, his power giving me pleasure as our pace quickens. My pleasure expands as his does, and soon I'm moving against him, needing him deeper, drawing him in. Who we are when he kisses my neck, biting my earlobe as I climax, is nothing but instinct.

The space between us is gone, our joining complete.

His hand moves between my legs and a few simple strokes make me gasp, unable to speak, the orgasm a wave I ride and ride and ride as he quickens, finally coming hard against me, his hand on my hip, fingers digging into me with possession and fierceness.

Intense vulnerability is one of the greatest forms of love.

So is wild abandon.

We drift off wordlessly, my body loose and loved. I turn to spoon Andrew and Lefty follows his father's heat, the partial flip making me swallow hard.

"I love you," Andrew whispers into the cool air, the words unnecessary.

So unnecessary, I just hug him harder.

And fall asleep.

❦ 15 ❦

Amanda

"Right there," I tell him, on my side, one leg propped up on his shoulder, the scruff of a day's unshaven growth tickling my inner thigh. He's doing something that makes my belly tighten, the waves taking my breath away. It feels good, hands crawling up my body, but the band around my hips and back is piercing the pleasure.

"More," I whisper, urging him on, but his tongue isn't there. All I feel is the press of that band, tight like a belt, then loosening, over and over, until the next time, it hurts.

Hurts.

"Andrew, stop," I murmur, but he's gone, a cold wave of ache replacing the loving touch.

And then it hurts more.

And more.

"ANDREW!" I GASP, SITTING UP, SAYING THE WORDS IN the dream and in reality. My mind straddles the two, body firmly in this realm as I place my palm on the space above my hip and feel it grow taut.

"Wha–?" A sleepy head appears on the other side of my enormous body pillow. "Wh'd I do?"

"Help," is all I can choke out as the belt-like feeling across my hips cuts off my words.

Andrew rubs his eyes, sniffing once, moving his fingers across his chin slowly, cricking his neck. The sound of snapping filters through the pain I'm feeling, but all I can do is ride it.

Ride it out.

Except nothing fades away like it should.

"Did you just say *help?*" he asks in a low voice. It's finally kicking in that something's wrong.

All I can do is nod, his eyes going to my belly as I suddenly let out a sound I associate with marine wildlife documentaries.

"Are you–are you in *labor?*"

"I–I–" A long, impossibly stretched out inhale twists my lungs into toy balloons as I try to answer him, but can't. My butthole tightens like it's a piece of pain taffy. Those inner thighs, deliciously tickled in my dream mere seconds ago, become painful wooden boards wedged under my skin.

"Amanda! What's wrong?" His hands are on my shoulders, his sleepiness replaced by deep concern.

"Contraction," I finally hiss.

"Contraction? You're only at thirty weeks. It's not time yet."

The pain washes out like the tide. Fear spikes through me. "I know. But I'm pretty sure that's a contraction."

"We need to call the doctor."

"Wait! Maybe I'm just dehydrated." All of my muscles that were tight feel noodly, loose and stringy, and a deep exhaustion seeps in.

Andrew leaps off the bed, runs to the bathroom, and I hear the faucet running. He returns with a half-filled glass and hands it to me, a bit of water sloshing over the edge.

I drink. He fumbles for his phone.

"Don't!" I shout, but a bit of water goes down my windpipe, and suddenly I'm coughing, which turns the hard pull above my pubic bone into a wall of tight rubber.

He freezes, eyes wide, hair a complete mess. He's shirtless, underwear askew, chest rising and falling faster and faster.

Is this what Andrew looks like when he's panicking?

"Why not? We need to call the doctor."

"Let me think." Thrusting the glass back at him buys me time. "Fill this again. I need more."

"I'm calling 911." His voice fills me with terror, because when he sounds like that, he's in action mode and there's no stopping him.

I need time.

"NO!"

"Amanda."

"Please. Water first, hospital next." The words are out of my mouth. I said it. This is inevitable.

But my fear needs a few seconds to get used to the idea.

His finger is an inch away from his phone's screen, but he stops, gets me more water, brings it back, and starts getting dressed. Then he picks up the phone again.

"I said I need more time."

"I'm telling Gina to clear my schedule."

My terror turns up a notch. This must be bad if he's doing that.

"An entire day?" I squeak.

"Are you bleeding?" he asks calmly, and that's what breaks me. His calm. His concern.

And clearing his schedule.

My hand moves reluctantly between my legs, praying for dryness. Peeling back the covers is an act of will. What's there?

What isn't?

As I twist to look, one of the babies moves in a long, rolling line, and a bump of a tiny joint pokes out my skin. It's an inch of heaven.

"He moved! One of the babies moved."

And then the tightening happens again.

A rush, all the air in my body moving out of me, paralyzes my lungs as someone stretches me impossibly. A dull ache turns up in intensity as Andrew holds my shoulders. Strangely, I notice that his shirt is buttoned up wrong, one buttonhole off.

"I'm calling," he says, but I reach forward and clutch his shirt, pulling him closer. He whispers, "Breathe. Use what we learned in class. Just breathe through it. Imagine oxygen pouring into your cells, opening everything."

I take a breath, pushing past the wall that makes air stay on the other side.

"Breathe," he says, making breathy sounds like he's trying to do it for me. His hand is still gripping the phone, but he's not calling.

I do. It slows down, then fades suddenly, like someone stopped wringing a washcloth. The water suddenly tastes like ambrosia and I gulp greedily.

"Call the OB practice," I whisper, grateful for the break. My legs begin to shake. "Let's start there."

"But–"

"Call the OB," I respond in a low, commanding voice neither of us recognizes. I sound like him when he's being brutally firm.

It works. He calls. Someone answers on the second ring.

"This is Andrew McCormick. I'm calling for my wife, Amanda. She's thirty weeks, twins. She's experiencing contractions. Yes." He hands the phone to me.

I take it.

"Hi, Amanda. This is Morgan. I'm calling Dr. Parnathi right now, but as I ping her, can you give me more specifics? Are you bleeding?"

"No."

"How far apart are the contractions?"

"I've had two." I put the phone on speaker.

"How far apart were they?"

Helpless, I look to Andrew, who frowns at the bedside clock as if it's derelict in doing its job.

"I'm not sure. Maybe five minutes?"

"Okay. I'll ask you a few more questions, and let's see if we can stay on the line for five minutes. If there's another one, that'll tell us a lot."

"Okay."

"Has this happened before?"

"No."

"What were you doing when it happened?"

"Sleeping." Andrew takes my empty water glass and walks to the bathroom, refilling it.

"The contraction woke you up?"

"Yes."

"Did you do anything different yesterday? Something extra strenuous?"

"Nothing more than normal."

"Did you have intercourse before bed?"

Andrew freezes on his way back to me, hand clutching the now-full glass. He looks at his crotch.

"Er, um... yes."

"Any suspicious discharge?"

"No."

"Any nausea? Fever? Headache? Heart racing?" She goes through a longer list and I say no between sips of water.

"Then it's the contractions only?"

"Mmm hmmm."

"Okay. Amanda?"

The phone suddenly shows Dr. Parnathi calling on another line.

"Oh! The doctor's on the other line."

"I'm going to hang up now and the doctor will take over from here. I hope everything goes well."

I accept the doctor's call.

"Amanda," her soothing voice says, "I understand you're having contractions. Can you tell me more about it?"

As I give her all the same information I gave Morgan, I drink to the point of needing to pee, but hold it. I climb off the bed and stand, the pressure on my bladder shifting.

"Do you feel the babies?" she asks.

As if in cue, Lefty moves, then Righty.

"Yes. Pretty sure they both just moved."

"Good. That's very good. Have you had another contraction yet?"

"No." I look at the clock. It's been at least five minutes.

And it's 5:59 a.m.

Another series of questions. I ask Andrew to get me a glass of orange juice, per the doctor's suggestion. I drink it.

"At thirty weeks, Amanda, I'm still concerned about the babies' lung development. I hate to send you to an emergency room when our office opens in just ninety minutes, so here is what I suggest: hydrate. Elevate your legs. Pack a bag–"

"A bag! You think I'll be hospitalized?"

"In case. You and your husband should get ready and be at the office at 7:30. We'll make you a standby appointment. We're adjacent to the hospital, so if we need to admit you, we will. But given we're now at eight minutes since the last contraction, I'm suspecting dehydration and sexual activity might be the culprit."

Andrew's eyes change at that last part.

"But–"

"Do you need to go straight to the ER, Amanda? I can make sure–"

I walk a bit, doing an inventory of my body. Babies moving? Yes. Back aching more than usual? No. Need to pee?

Badly.

Contractions? No.

"I think I'm okay. It's been nine minutes and nothing new. I'll keep drinking water. We'll be there at 7:30."

"Good. In the meantime, if anything changes..." She rattles off a list of issues to watch out for, and then I hang up the phone.

My eyes meet Andrew's.

"We're going now."

"No. Please, Andrew."

"And we're never having sex again."

That makes me laugh. Which makes my abdominal muscles (what's left of them) tighten.

Which makes the air whoosh out of me.

Which terrifies my husband.

"We're going," he demands. "I'll have José drive us."

"Hold on." I hold up a finger to denote the need to pause.

He storms across the room and then I hear the shower running. He comes back naked, holding my again-full water glass.

"Drink. Check on the babies' movement. I'm taking a one-minute shower and you're next, then we get ready for the doctor's office."

The tight feeling fades much faster than before. "Yes."

Relief makes his whole body relax. "Thank God."

While he's in the shower, I waddle into the bathroom and pee. The water turns off before I even flush.

He wasn't kidding. That really was a one-minute shower.

My wet, anxious husband opens the shower door, steam billowing around his tall, muscled frame. A wave of arousal pours over me, so wholly inappropriate that it fills me with the weirdest mix of lust and shame.

Who feels this?

Apparently, me. I do.

"Another contraction?"

"No."

"Good," he says tersely. "Need me to pack a bag for you?"

"I'm not packing a bag."

"Then I will."

"I'm not staying at a hospital! This is just an office visit!" I'm breathing hard, and trust me, it's hard to breathe with two babies treating your lungs like kickballs.

"Amanda." Naked, wet, with underwear half on, sticking to his ass, Andrew's hold on my shoulders is tight. He bends down, eyes boring into mine. "You are the most important person in the world to me. The babies rely on you to survive. *I* rely on you to survive. I can't have anything go wrong with you or the babies. Do you understand?"

"I'm sure I'll–"

Raw, vulnerable fear pervades his every cell. I swear I can smell it on him as his fingers dig into my shoulders and he repeats starkly, "Do you understand?"

Suddenly, I really can't breathe. The emotion is too much. My body's sensations are too much.

Gravity itself is too, too much.

And my womb is filled with two babies who need to be okay.

"I do." His kiss is short, a perfunctory brush of lips that says there's no time for more, because we have to act now.

"I need to get dressed," I say, body in a new state of vigilance. Every twinge could be the next contraction, and I'm going mad reading my nerves as they send messages to my brain about where my skin and bones are in space and time.

Everything pinpoints. For this second, all that I am is my hand, clasping the cloth of my nightgown. And in the next second, I am my arms, going up, pulling the cloth over my head. And for the following second, I am my nose, snagging on the cloth, pulled over my chin.

And so on, and so on, each second a world I inhabit.

Enough seconds piled on top of each other become a breath. And each breath a heartbeat.

Three, in fact.

I'm moving for three.

"You want me to pack the bag for you?" Andrew asks, my answer on the tip of my tongue, a reflexive *no* that isn't good enough for this moment.

My *no* is a relic of a time when I had the luxury to think I didn't need help.

"Yes," I say, giving in, his terse nod more of a relief than I wish it were. Slipping my feet into simple flat shoes, I waddle to the nightstand, find my half-empty water glass, and drink. Then I stretch slowly, arms back, shoulders popping slightly as blood flows under my skin, legs aching with weight but gratified to have movement.

I sigh.

"Another one?" he asks, floating to my side so fast, it's like he's levitating.

"No. Just..." My tears take over.

"You're fine," he says, kissing the tear off my cheek. "The babies are fine. Everyone will be fine, Amanda."

"How do you know? We have no control over anything."

"We sure as hell do," he counters. "I'm getting you to the doctor now. You're hydrating. We're following the expert's advice, and that's control."

"That's not control."

"It's as close as I can get, so I'll take it."

Bang bang bang

The door downstairs opens, Gerald's voice floating up. "Andrew? Amanda? I'm ready when you are. You need help carrying Amanda down?"

Gerald's presence takes the reality of this crisis up a notch.

"What are *you* doing here?" I gasp.

"Andrew texted José. I'm filling in for Mort while he's on workman's comp. I was worried." Gerald and Andrew exchange a powerful look that instantly makes me feel safer and terrified.

"I can walk," I whisper. If any two guys in the world can carry a pregnant me down a flight of stairs, it's Gerald and Andrew, but this is already going sideways.

I don't need the memory of *that* added to *this*.

"We're good. Give us a minute," Andrew shouts. "You're sure you can walk?" he whispers to me.

I nod.

I take one, two, three steps toward the door, gaining confidence as no contractions hit. The clock says 6:33. We're only twenty minutes or so from the doctor's office, but Andrew's insistence on going now makes sense.

Better to wait in the parking lot there than to worry here.

I'm slow. Really slow. And our stairs are big.

Really big.

The estate Andrew's dad and mom bought when the boys were little is a sprawling home designed to impress. The staircase wraps around the wide entry hall, and there are twenty stairs from the second floor to the first. My hips rotate as I take each step down, ligaments recalibrating, babies moving with each step.

Thank God.

"I've got your purse and bag. Do you need my arm?"

"The bannister's fine. I'm just slow."

"Take all the time you need. Any more contractions?"

"No–"

Damn it.

As I start to reply, one grips me, hard, lower this time, then suddenly lighter, spreading up over my belly like fingers playing tight piano strings. It's easier to breathe through and fades faster.

"We need to go directly to the ER," Andrew says.

"Would you just STOP?" My voice starts soft and low, but by the last word, I explode. Bending down a little, I take a deep breath, eyes fixed on my hand. I listen to him breathe behind me.

The last breath comes out like an exasperated sigh.

"I know you're worried," I grind out, literally gritting my teeth. "But I don't need the pressure, either. We have a plan. What time is it?"

"Six forty-seven."

"That means it's been over fifteen minutes since the last contraction. They're slowing down. If you want to help, stop barking orders at me about the ER and get me some damn water." That came out harsher than it should, and two different Amandas suddenly take up residence inside me.

One feels guilty.

One feels terrified.

One feels angry.

Guess there are a few more Amandas in there.

"Here." A bottled water is in my hand before I can blink. Andrew's heat radiates behind me, his body close. In my peripheral vision, I see he's got my small bag open. He must have put the bottled water in there.

"Thank you." I unscrew the cap and drink half the bottle, hoping the hydration really does stop the contractions.

"I'm sorry."

I halt with the water still upright, tongue blocking the flow before I choke on the spot. Andrew isn't exactly free with his apologies, so this catches me off guard.

I slowly lower the bottle. "You are?"

"I'm not trying to add to your stress. Or your pain. The opposite. I just–you're right."

An apology *and* a "you're right"? Did I die and somehow not notice?

"I am?"

"I–I–I just..." Something in his voice makes me turn as his shadow changes, lowering. When I look behind me, I expect to see his face, but instead he's sitting two steps above me, one hand over his face.

And he's crying.

Crying.

He's not sobbing; silent tears are running down. The bag is

resting on the stair tread beside him, and I see he has a backpack on his shoulders. He reaches for my hand, threading our fingers, lacing him into me.

"Take all the time you need," he says slowly, earnestly. If I could bend forward, I would kiss him, wipe his face, hug him until he squeezed the fear out of me.

But he has fear, too.

And he's mature enough to show it to me.

We make it to the car, emotion radiating off him, but we're silent. Gerald is, too, moving the car smoothly on the roads, the silence a strange comfort in the enclosed space. By the time we pull up to the medical building, the contractions are there, but they're bearable.

Still present, but not as dire.

It's when I climb out of the back of the car that I realize I've been lulled into a false sense of security.

Because one rips through me as I have one foot still in the car.

One breath is long enough and too short by far, the pain in my belly taking on color. The rip is so intense, I can't even close my eyes. I feel like webbing covers me, all of it pulled tight under my skin.

"Oh, no," I hear Andrew grunt from a million miles away, his hands going to my shoulder, my hips, steadying me.

"I'm. Oh. Kay," I gasp.

"Breathe," he murmurs, slow and low, meant to calm and soothe. "I called ahead. They know you're coming. Dr. Armaji is on duty."

I remember her. A flash of memory hits me, no words attached, just a wide smile, slightly crooked front teeth, deep brown eyes with impossibly long lashes. Her older son plays lacrosse and Andrew gave her some tips to pass on.

And just like that, the grip lessens.

Shuffling, I notice each muscle of my inner thighs, how they stretch and tighten, my mind telling them what to do even as other muscles in me take over and do their work, heedless of my command.

"The doctor's office texted. Said to go in through the ER entrance but she's ready for you."

We make it to an admitting desk, where we're waved onto an elevator to go to the labor and delivery wing. When we came here for childbirth classes, we entered a different way. I'm lost.

Andrew isn't.

"Do you need a wheelchair?" Andrew asks. For some reason, the question angers me.

Apparently, my glare is enough of an answer.

"Here," he says, hands never leaving me even when he has to push the elevator button for the third floor. He's got the backpack over one shoulder now and my bag in his hand.

My hair must be a mess. We're not presentable. We're not–

"*Shhhhh*," he murmurs, wiping away tears I don't even realize are there. "Here." He hands me another water from the bag.

I sip slowly, then drink faster. If hydration takes the pain away, hook me up to a five-gallon jug and a hose.

Ding!

The elevator doors open and we're suddenly in soft light, a nurse's desk in front of us.

"McCormick?" a woman in scrubs calls out.

"Yes," Andrew answers.

She points down the hall. "Room 14. Dr. Armaji's already there."

"It must be really bad if we're getting this kind of treatment," I gasp as we make our way to the room.

"Or she happened to be here at the hospital and we're lucky," he counters, making me smile.

"Amanda!" Dr. Armaji is in scrubs, hands on her hips, the friendly, crooked smile making me relax instantly. "Fancy seeing you here."

"I know, right?"

"Tell me what's going on."

For the next five minutes, she checks the heartbeats, the soothing sound of twin galloping hearts making Andrew's jaw unclench, her long list of questions automatic for her. How do obstetricians handle the responsibility? Life itself is in their hands, literally.

Every decision they make in giving advice and counsel to pregnant women has a possible bad outcome. The weight of that must be enormous.

And speaking of enormous...

Dr. Armaji sits on a stool at the base of the exam table. I'm still fully clothed, leaning back, palms flat against the paper strip covering the cool vinyl.

"I'm not going to examine you, especially because the tissues are likely delicate from the sexual intercourse you engaged in last night. But my guess is that the cervix is starting to thin, though not much.

You've been with me for eleven minutes and haven't had a contraction."

"I swear I was!"

One hand goes to my knee, reassuring. "I believe you. And it must be very frightening. But the babies are fine."

As if on cue, my lower belly pulls in. She senses it, but looks to the monitor.

"Here we go," she whispers, watching. We all do. It's amazing. What my body does is being tracked on that thin strip of paper, documented in a way that medical professionals will interpret, then act on.

All to save lives.

I breathe through it. It's painful, but in a shallow way. If nothing else, I feel grateful: My body is showing the doctor what's going on.

"Just breathe. You've crested the peak. The rest is downhill."

I let out a long, slow sigh.

"Now drink."

Andrew hands me the water.

"Here's what I see, Amanda. You're experiencing early contractions. Twin pregnancies have their own rhythm, so you can't go by singleton timelines. You're at thirty weeks. We want these little boys to cook for a while longer. We can do a cervical exam, but I'd prefer to wait and have you come into the office tomorrow and we'll do a full workup then."

"I'm not–I'm not having the babies now?"

"No. Definitely not." She looks at the water in my hand. "Keep drinking that."

I obey doctor's orders.

"They need more time, don't they?" Andrew asks. "What if–"

"Let's not play the what-if game, Andrew," she says kindly. "That will drive you crazy."

"*This* is driving me crazy, too."

"Amanda, you're fine. The babies are fine. We'll see you tomorrow in the office–it'll be a chance to meet another doctor in the practice," she says with a chuckle.

"I do have two left I haven't met."

She nods. "And I want you on bed rest."

"What?"

"Bed rest is best, until you reach thirty-six weeks."

"That's six more *weeks!* I can't just sit around for *six weeks!*"

Andrew interrupts. "You can, and you will."

"I have a department to run!"

"We'll argue about this later," Andrew says tersely as Dr. Armaji gives us side eye, using a stylus on a tablet to document something.

"Don't you mean *discuss?*"

His failure to answer fills me with dread.

Right. Argue it is.

The doctor hands me a short list of instructions that define exactly what *bed rest* means, but then her phone beeps. She looks at it and frowns.

"Excuse me. I have to take this. Laboring multipara." She slips into the hall for a moment.

"How are you?" he asks, wincing the second the words are out because duh—how does he think I am?

But I also get it. I know what he means.

"I'm terrified."

"So am I," he confesses, surprising me.

"You are? Damn." The tears fill my throat. "You're never afraid. That means I should be even more scared."

"No! No, honey. That's not what I want. I was just being open."

"I think I liked you better when you were an emotionless automaton fixated on work."

"You've changed me enough that I can't go back to being like that anymore."

"Is that a compliment?"

The doctor slips back in at that moment, so we shut up. I read the paperwork.

My eyes skim the part about sex.

No intercourse.

"None?" I gasp, Dr. Armaji clearly understanding exactly what I'm reading.

"There are plenty of safe sexual practices you and your husband can engage in, but at this point, intercourse isn't one of them," she begins.

Is Andrew blushing?

His brow tightens—jaw, too—as he keeps his eyes on a spot at the hollow of my throat.

"We'll figure it out. That's the least of our worries," he says firmly, making the doctor smile slightly.

"Good to hear. Not all partners are as understanding."

"I'm not all partners, Doctor."

He definitely is not.

In so many more ways than this one.

"Amanda, it's been twelve minutes since the last one."

"It has?"

She nods. "How do you feel?"

"Deflated. Scared. Embarrassed."

Andrew recoils. "Embarrassed?"

She pats my shoulder. "Never feel embarrassed. You're at thirty weeks with twin boys, who have underdeveloped lungs. You woke up to contractions coming close together. You did the right thing to come in."

"But–"

"And you need to come back tomorrow. Just because I'm sending you home with strict bed rest orders doesn't mean this isn't serious."

"Strict bed rest?"

"You need to be in bed or in a chair with the exception of bathroom breaks."

"That's it?"

"That's it. Car rides to doctor's appointments are fine. But no dining out, no travel, nothing."

"That sounds horrible!" I grumble. "But I'll do it."

"Of course you will." Andrew kisses my cheek.

"And no sex?" I ask again, struggling to process it all.

"We'll do it." He frowns. "Or won't do it." His hand rubs my shoulder. "We'll figure it out."

I lean toward him and whisper in his ear. "I can still blow–"

Dr. Armaji clears her throat. "I'm sure you're capable of figuring out details. Just make sure nothing foreign enters your vagina, Amanda. And no orgasms."

Andrew starts choking.

"None?" I squeak.

"I'm sorry. They increase blood flow to the uterus and cause contractions. We're trying to prevent contractions, so none." She glances at Andrew. "The orgasm restriction only applies to Amanda, obviously."

Did he just drop his shoulders in relief?

I nod. "I'll be fine. I understand. The babies are worth it."

"Of course they are," Andrew jumps in.

My breathing slows, the band above my pubic bone going taut again, but this time, it's light. A discomfort, but not pain-filled. Dr. Armaji watches me, observant but non-judgmental, as I take three deep, slow breaths.

The tightness fades.

"If the contractions intensify, or come closer together, come right in."

We nod. She leaves.

I go numb.

Climbing off the exam table is an engineering feat, but Andrew helps me. Each step I take feels like I'm a Marvel movie monster made of stones aligned together to approximate a human form. We make it to the main entrance, and Gerald appears as if conjured by Andrew's telepathy.

He emerges from the black SUV, concern etched into his hardened, scarred face. "Everything okay?"

"For now," Andrew says tersely.

I stare at the SUV. Lifting my leg high enough to climb in feels like being asked to summit Mount Everest.

"We need a sedan from now on," I tell him.

"Noted," Gerald says, frowning. "Should have thought of it. Suzanne's struggling with our SUV, too."

Andrew says nothing, one strong arm going to my hip as I lift my foot up and leverage my way into the seat. He climbs in after. Twisting to grab the seat belt is an act of faith, but I do it, clicking in, then resting the back of my head against the seat.

Tears fall, fast, silent, and uncontrolled.

Andrew's arm is around me as Gerald pulls away from the neon glow of the hospital sign. My belly is loose.

But my heart is tight with fear.

"This is all my fault," Andrew whispers, his tone making my eyes fly open.

"What?"

Gerald turns up the radio in the front seat, clearly signaling he's trying to give us privacy.

"I... I made a pass at you. Initiated sex. And that clearly triggered the labor." His jaw is tight, hand in a fist as he punches his right thigh. "I won't be so selfish again."

"Andrew."

"It's different now. I can't just assume that if I want something, I can find a way to get it."

"*Andrew.*"

"If I hadn't reached out for you, if we hadn't done that position, if I–"

My fingers fly to cover his mouth. His chin is scratchy from not shaving.

"Stop. You did nothing wrong. We didn't know." My whisper is low, too, lips against the curve of his ear.

"I'm a fool."

"Maybe. But not because of this." I smile.

"And now I'm making this all about me when it should be all about you." His hand goes to my belly. "And them."

"We're fine." I swallow hard. "Or, at least, we will be."

Andrew looks down at his crotch. "*You* are dead last in terms of priorities now," he chides.

"What? No! *You* can still orgasm."

"That's not a priority."

"Since when?"

"Since three hours ago when you woke me up in bed and told me something was wrong and you and the babies were in danger," he says softly.

I can't breathe.

"*Are* in danger," he adds, squeezing my hand. "I'm not putting anything–not Anterdec, not my body, not my libido–nothing–at a higher priority than you and our babies."

I want to argue, counter his words with something that takes the urgency away, that soothes the burden of terror I share with him. I hate being the center of attention like this, and knowing he's so deeply affected makes this all feel even bigger.

Andrew tends to underreact because he has a big-picture perspective of life that comes from a place of deep certainty.

In every way but the safety of people he deeply loves. Losing his mother to a random, freak event he had no control over is something he's had to overcome,

He *has*.

But I can feel how shaken that foundation is right now.

And I hate it.

"Drink," he urges, handing me yet another water bottle. The cool, sweet water tastes good, and my bladder twinges. By the time we get home, I won't make it upstairs to our bathroom. I'll have to use the downstairs powder room.

Stairs.

My heart sinks. "The discharge directions say no stairs."

"Then we can sleep in the guest room on the first floor." He sighs. "Or you can sleep there alone, if you prefer."

"Why would I prefer that?"

"Because..." His Adam's apple jumps with emotion, but he says nothing more.

"You'll sleep with me," I say firmly. "And we'll use the guest bedroom. We're doing this together, Andrew. *Together*. I won't let you pull away from me now. I need you more than ever."

"You don't need my morning wood poking your ass."

"I sure do! It's how I know you didn't die in your sleep."

Surprised laughter fills my ear. "What?"

"Every morning, as I slowly emerge from the haze of sleep, one of two things tells me you're awake. If you're spooning with me, it's the wood tapping at my ass. If not, it's the tent in the sheet."

"My steady breath doesn't provide adequate proof of life?"

"It's not as amusing. Or as predictable."

"Why are we talking about my penis so much, Amanda? I'm trying not to make it the center of attention, but you're making it hard."

At his phrasing, my lips twitch.

He groans.

I squeeze his hand. "I need this. Being silly. Playful. Goofy. The serious part of it all is a given, Andrew. Of course, I'll go on full bed rest. Of course, you'll do whatever you can to make life safe for me and the babies. Of course, we'll both do the responsible thing. I married you because you're the full package–smart, sexy, and most of all–a grown-up. Mature and always ready to do what needs to be done so that everyone you love is taken care of."

"You think that of me?"

"I *know* that of you."

He nods slowly, methodically. "We're in this together. Forever."

"Right. Together. So if I'm on bed rest, we're binge watching all those series we've been ignoring. Together."

"Oh, hell."

I give him an evil grin. "That's right! I get to pick everything we watch."

"Not the baking show. It's like Ambien."

"Then get ready to fall asleep to British accents and have cream filling dreams."

He kisses my temple. "As you wish."

❧ 16 ❧

Amanda

The door shuts and I find myself alone.

Completely alone for the first time in two days.

For the last twenty-nine hours, Andrew hasn't left my side. We've binge watched all the baking shows I wanted to see, a round-the-world motorcycle show from the early 2000s, and a documentary series about a cult.

Andrew's begging for fiction, so *Outlander*'s next.

But right now, he's at the office, tormenting Gina, and it's my turn to get work settled. "Clear the decks" is a horrible phrase for someone who prides herself on fixing problems, because it means *I'm* the problem. The stuff on my plate can't be there any more.

I have to transfer it to someone else.

So my notepad has a long list of tasks, starting with number one: Call Carol.

Except... she beats me to it.

Carol's name pops up on the screen as my cell rings. I answer.

"Amanda! Shannon called and told me. Are you okay? What's happening?"

"Early labor. I'm fine. On bed rest, though." I cross her name off my list. "And it means I need to make some big changes."

"Right. Legs elevated, drink lots of water, no sex–" She gasps. "Poor Andrew."

"Poor me," I mutter.

Giggly, girlish laughter pours through my phone. "Okay. Let's change the topic. Back to work. What do you need from me?"

"For you to accept a new job."

Silence. As the seconds tick on, I grow more nervous. Why isn't Carol saying anything?

"A new job?"

"Right."

"Like, I'm fired?"

"WHAT? No! Of course not!"

"Whew." A shaky series of sounds, like she's almost crying, come through. "You scared the hell out of me."

"I want to promote you, Carol. I need you more than ever."

"PROMOTE? Like, a raise? More power?"

"Not sure about power, but yes. A raise. A promotion. Interim director of market research."

"Director! But *you're* director!"

"I won't be for a while."

"Are you doing this because of the babies?"

"Of course. That, and now you have to manage Agnes and Corrine." I smile.

A low, feral sound pours through the speakers. "Ah, God, I forgot you hired them. Hmmm. I don't know..."

She knows, and I know, that she needs the money.

I quote her new salary.

"You're serious? What about Josh?"

"First of all, he has different skills, and his IT work doesn't cover what we do. Second of all, it's cruel to foist Agnes and Corinne on him."

"And it isn't cruel to shove them on me?"

I ignore that.

"Plus, I need someone who can manage people and details, and you're good at that."

"Plus, you're desperate."

"That, too."

"How are you feeling, though? Really? Early labor is scary."

"Did you go through it?"

"No. But I can only imagine."

"Well," I say, going into logic mode, because processing how I feel right now is too hard, "the babies are thirty weeks, so they're viable. If I had delivered yesterday, they would have gone to the NICU but chances of a problem are small. The big issue is lung development."

"Right. Which means they need to wait a little longer."

"Yes."

"What can I do for you, Amanda?"

"Take the job."

She sighs. "Not as an employee. I know what you want me to do at Anterdec. What can I do for you as your friend?"

Now the tears rise up.

"I don't... I don't..." Words dissolve into salt water as emotions render me mute. I'm the fixer. I fix other people's problems. I'm not used to having other people offer to fix *mine*.

"Look. I'm at work, but there are papers for you to sign. How about I hit your favorite micro-creamery and get the Cheeto Special, the one they make just for you? I'll charge it to our department, come to your house, and we'll drown our sorrows in ice cream while figuring out a transition plan."

"Transition means something really different to me now. And you're just trying to get free ice cream and halfway closer to your house so you can blow off the afternoon at work and miss the traffic."

"Yes."

"You're not even denying it!"

"Nope."

"Because you know the words Cheeto Special made this a done deal."

"Yep."

"Then get over here! Now!"

She hangs up before I can say another word.

If there's one thing about Carol you have to know, it's this:

She's a doer.

I'm a fixer.

And right now, she's my savior.

🐚

Ding dong!

The doorbell jolts me out of the doze I'm in on the sofa, enough to make me startle.

"ICE CREAM DELIVERY!" Carol shouts from the other side of the door.

"I know their code, Carol. You don't have to yell," Shannon snaps at her.

"You know the code? What is it?"

"I'm not telling you! That's private."

Bickering sounds follow, then the click of the front door opening.

Shannon appears ahead of Carol, the two clearly related, though different. Shannon is a blend of her mom and dad, with Marie's hair color and bright brown eyes like Jason's.

Carol, on the other hand, is smaller and looks exactly like a younger version of Marie.

"Shannon?" I gasp as they walk in carrying plastic bags filled with bakery boxes, another bag weighted down by what looks like two–no, three–pints of ice cream.

Ahhhhhhhhh.

They brought one serving each.

"Maple fritters?" Shannon pulls giant bear-claw pastries out of the box, the telltale beige maple coating making me drool.

Except–is that orange on them?

"I got Paula at the bakery to roll their maple fritters in crushed Cheetos. I think she gagged a little doing it, but I threw a $10 bill in the tip jar after and she told me to call ahead for custom orders any time."

Carol shudders. "How can you eat that?"

"Like this." I take a bite, baring my teeth. "Mmmmm."

"Your babies will be born orange."

"That's better than being born too early."

Shannon sighs, giving me a shaky smile, eyes worried. "How are they?"

"Lefty is learning the tap dance routine to *Long Way Round*, while Righty has decided to nap for long stretches and scare the hell out of me. He only moves when I eat a lot of sugar." I lift my maple fritter in the air like a wine glass. "Cheers! This'll get him moving."

Carol stares at my belly. "Two. Wow. One is hard enough."

"It's not like I know any different."

"Right. It'll make future kids easier."

I stop chewing.

"Mmmmpfh?"

"You know. When you guys have your third kid, a singleton will be a breeze."

The mouthful of fritter turns to glue. It's impossible to swallow. As if she knows, Shannon hands me my water bottle. I clear out my mouth and say, "Third?"

Carol and Shannon burst into laughter.

"We all think we want four kids, don't we? Then we go through pregnancy and childbirth. The sleepless newborn phase."

"Teething," Shannon chimes in, patting her breasts. "Ellie gave me a free nipple piercing."

Here we go. The battle-weary parenting stories. I'm stuck, aren't I? Can't escape.

Carol nudges her sister and then peels the top off her hand-packed pint of ice cream. I smell peppermint. "You're the ones trying for another."

Shannon pokes my belly with her unused spoon. "Dec wants to know how to conceive triplets so we can beat Andrew and get our four out of the way in two pregnancies."

"Declan is insane."

"I know, right? Why would I want to give up all that sex?"

"All that sex?"

"If we get three kids with one pregnancy, we miss the conception sex. The second trimester sex. The–"

I grab a chocolate-coated horn from the bakery box and shove it in her mouth. "We are not talking about sex. I am not allowed to orgasm."

Carol snatches the pint of ice cream out of my hands.

"Then you definitely can't eat this," she declares.

"Come on! It's not–" I halt my words, knowing I'm wrong.

One arched eyebrow is all I get in response.

"Fine. It *is* that good. But I'm still eating it!"

"Bed rest means no orgasms?" Shannon asks, already done with the chocolate horn and now peeling the top off her ice cream.

"For me. Andrew can have as many as he wants."

They snort in unison.

"Of course he can. We're the ones who are biologically forced to take on all the work. We singlehandedly grow new generations!"

"And they want a say in naming the kids."

"Do you have any picked out other than Lefty and Righty?" I don't need the eye roll Carol tosses in with that question.

"What's wrong with those?"

"Hah."

"Andrew has suggested Anderson and Bruford."

"BRUFORD?"

"And then our third and fourth kids will be Wakeman and Howe."

They stare at me. The joke goes over their heads.

"You know. Yes?"

"Yes?"

"The band?"

"What about them?"

"They split up and later formed–oh, never mind. Let's just say Andrew wants to name our kids after rock stars."

"Wouldn't be the first. Tyler has a kid named Kanye in his class. And I know someone who named her son Prince after Prince died." Carol taps her front teeth with her spoon. "Now I'm wondering about Jimmy Page in Jeffrey's Boy Scout troop and Gaga McFarland. Hmmm."

"Six years from now, how many girls are going to show up in kindergarten named Cardi B. and Meghan Thee?" I muse.

"What are the names?" Shannon demands.

"Not telling."

"COME ON! I'm your best friend!"

"We don't know," I confess.

"Liar."

"No. Really. It's hard to name one baby, I'm sure, but two..."

Shannon gives me the stink eye. "Anything but James and James Too."

I nearly spit out my mouthful of Cheeto ice cream. "Don't give him any ideas!"

"Declan is incensed that James is favoring your twins over Ellie already."

"He's such a sexist pig."

Carol watches us like a gossip-chasing paparazzo. "You two are hilarious."

"What?" we say in unison.

"You're married to *billionaires*. Your father-in-law is a billionaire. Your children will be raised with the ultimate luxury. They'll never worry for a thing. And you're making fun of the guy who forged the path for your husbands and your babies."

We pause. Shannon and I look at each other, frowning.

With a quick lick of her spoon, Shannon turns to Carol and says, "And your point is?"

"Have you ever spent more than ten minutes with James McCormick? His ego fills the room like a bad fart," I add.

"And there might even be a scent of sulfur after he leaves." Shannon points the spoon at me and we high five.

Carol's head shake makes me waver. "You make it sound like he's all bad."

"He's not," I jump in.

"But he's.... he's...." Shannon struggles, like me, to explain it to an outsider.

And then it hits me.

Outsider.

All my life, I looked at the Jacoby family and wanted desperately to be a part of it. Marie and Jason loved me–and still love me–as if I'm one of their girls, but of course, I'm not. I never will be.

And Carol's watching Shannon and me from the outside right now, looking in.

She'll never be married to a McCormick. Never understand what it's like to have James as a father-in-law. Shannon and I are in a club she can't join, and I wonder if she's jealous.

But I don't think that's what's going on here.

"You know the old saying that the only people who understand what a marriage is like are the two people in the marriage?" I ask her.

"Mmmph," she says affirmatively, mouth stuffed with ice cream.

"It's like that, having James as your father-in-law. The guy tried to exploit our weddings on social media. Used us as leverage to get the company's stock price up. He views his kids and his extended family members as pawns for his own gain."

Carol swallows and gives us a curious look. "But he's not like that with Pam. Look how he helped her."

She's right.

With a sigh, Shannon stops eating and glares at her sister. "Do you have to be so empathic? Now I feel like a total jerk."

A smug look only an eldest sister can master comes over Carol's features. "Empathy's all I've got, sis."

"Quit calling me *sis*. You never did that before you heard Declan call his brothers *bro*."

"Okay, sis."

"Oh, my *God*, you're so annoying."

"I know, sis."

"Carol! You're thirty-five! Quit acting like you're twelve."

"Fine." She shoves her spoon in Shannon's ice cream and takes an enormous chunk of peanut butter cup.

"HEY!"

"Morry, fis."

"I'm suddenly grateful I never had siblings," I mutter.

Shannon smiles and pats my belly. "Your boys will never know what that's like. They'll always be tormented by their asshole sib."

"HEY!" Carol's turn to be outraged.

"What, *sis?*" Shannon shoots back. "Just telling it like it is."

I stuff my mouth full of ice cream and sit back to watch as they bicker, then hug and laugh it off like it's nothing.

Consider it research on what's in store for me.

"You know what I need next?" I say as they peel themselves off each other.

"A crane to help you get out of chairs?" Carol snarks.

"Hah. No. Well, yes, but that's not what I was going to say. I need a soak."

"Oooo, the pool!" Shannon's eyes light up. "You must love having that!"

"It's been under repair until just a few days ago."

"Can we swim?" Carol wipes something off the corner of her mouth with her thumb. "We have my old suit here, right?"

"We left everything in the closet the way it was months ago, so I guess?"

Carol and Shannon make quick work of putting the ice cream away as I guzzle water.

"Did the doctor say it was ok to be in the water?"

"As long as it's not a hot tub, yes. And we're low-chemical with the saltwater filter, so the OB said it's fine. The temperature's on the low side but not cold."

"Sounds perfect to me. At least it's not winter," Carol says as I stand, moving slowly. Walking down the hall to the pool wing is a slow process, but once we open the doors the blast of moist air makes me smile.

Sunlight pours into the solarium, shining off the water, giving the room a cheerful, almost Victorian feel, a steampunk-like blend of modern and antiquated. Time and sunlight has baked the large wood beams that support the glass windows, and we've preserved the look and feel even while upgrading the pool systems.

"You have this whenever you want," Carol says breathlessly. "So nice."

"Now that it's fixed, bring Jeffrey and Tyler over whenever you like!" I urge her.

"Oh, trust me, I will."

"I mean it. I'm stuck on bed rest. I need the company."

"Speaking of which," Shannon says sternly, "get in the pool and quit standing."

The two of them find their suits in the closet, then go into the small rooms off the pool deck, one a bathroom with a shower, the other a small room for changing. When James created this indoor pool, it wasn't for fun.

It was for achievement.

A single lane, fifty meters long.

A pool Andrew's mother never saw.

After his mother died, and Andrew's deathly wasp allergy was evident, he stopped all outdoor sports, but James was adamant he have a sport, so Andrew switched to swimming. Turned out to be outstanding at it.

And if nothing else, James McCormick loves achievement in his children, even if he doesn't love them in normal ways.

Hence the long, narrow pool attached to our house.

"Oooo," Shannon says as she finds the ladder and slowly steps in. We added a ladder when we first bought the house. Andrew wanted to put in a regular pool, but I stopped him.

There's something very unique about this one.

Other than the ladder and the conversion to saltwater, we haven't made big changes.

I wait until Carol comes out of the bathroom and change slowly into my suit, taking the time to pee and stretch before climbing into the water. Shannon hands me a floatie, my arms going to the sides of it, my body weightless.

The babies feel so weird like this.

"I wonder if this is what it feels like for them in me," I mutter.

Lefty moves, pushing down, making Righty shove up against my lung.

Until I was in the water, I didn't realize how much pain my hips and lower pelvis had been in. The relief is palpable, and I sigh with contentment.

Shannon swims slowly all the way down the lane, keeping her head above water, her lazy breaststroke drawing my attention. When Andrew uses the pool, he's a model of ruthless efficiency, long torso like Michael Phelps, strong and swift strokes moving him though the water like he's oiled up and shot from a rocket.

Shannon's form is like watching a raccoon take a swim from the shore to a rock.

"How are you?" Carol asks, treading water. She's letting her hair get wet, the ends turning dark. Like Marie, she's a natural blonde. Unlike Marie, she's still her natural color. For whatever reason, Marie's gone lighter over the years.

At this rate, she'll be bright gold by the time she's seventy.

"I'm... I don't know. I feel useless."

"You're baking babies. What could be more useful."

"I know."

There's more to say, but I can't find the words. Being asked how I am is a mine field. It's much easier with a full stomach.

And good friends.

Shanon swims halfway back, then calls out, "Carol! Aren't you swimming?"

"I am!"

"Swim swimming!"

"Nah. I like treading water."

"You need to bring Ellie over," I tell Shannon.

"It's summer. Plenty of outside time at the pool," she says. "Mia takes her to the club almost every day." Shannon and Declan found the best nanny through an agency Andrew's insisting we use.

Two nannies, he says, plus a night nurse.

Unlike Shannon, I am all about taking *all* the help.

"Sure. But I'm bored and you don't have to put sunscreen on here here. Come here," I insist, earning a laugh from Carol.

"Done."

"Do you hear that?" Carol asks, arms moving at shoulder level, her ability to tread water for long stretches quite admirable. I feel pathetic clinging to a floatie, but I also don't care.

My job is to just be.

And let these babies cook.

"Hear what?" Shannon calls out.

"Nothing! I hear nothing! We left our cell phones in the main house and no one can bother us!"

The laughter that echoes up and pings against the solarium glass is the sound of tired women who feel like they're getting away with something.

I get the strong sense I'm going to laugh like this a lot for the next eighteen years.

For the next half hour, we swim and float, the water easing tension I didn't know I had in my joints, our conversation drifting to the mundane.

Until Shannon turns, Carol right after her, and they look at the door from the house to the pool.

"There you are!" Andrew shouts, voice flooded with relief. Immediately, he speaks into his phone. "Found her." Then he taps the screen, shoves the phone in his jacket pocket, and walks swiftly to the pool's edge by me, crouching down. "You scared the hell out of me."

"Scared?"

"You didn't answer your phone. So I tried Shannon. No answer. Carol. No answer. Gina called Dave, who told her Declan said Shannon was coming here." He gives her a harsh look. "None of you bothered to bring a phone in here?"

"Why would we?" Carol answers. "It's bliss without it."

"I'm sorry," I tell him, trying to reach out to touch his hand but wobbling in the water, my shoulder dipping in.

Worry and concern is etched into his features, so much so that first Carol, then Shannon, reach the ladder and climb out. Both know where the towels are, still stacked neatly in a closet the maid service handles.

"It's - it's fine." He smiles. "I'm relieved. I'm also surprised to see you in here."

"I'm surprised to see you here. I thought you were in New York. And you could have sent security to check on me."

"I hadn't left Boston yet. We were on 95, headed to the helipad, when I realized you weren't answering phones or texts." He reaches out enough to touch me.

He's *shaking*.

The shower in the bathroom starts as Carol sits down, closes her eyes, and cranes her neck up, relaxing on a small chaise longue chair.

"Andrew," I whisper. "I didn't realize you were so upset."

"Am I overreacting?" The question itself is unnerving. Always so self-assured, Andrew's not the type to ask if his reaction is out of line.

Rapidfire thoughts rip through me as I try to see the situation from his perspective. Pregnant wife on bed rest, home alone, not answering the phone.

"No. I understand."

He squeezes my shoulder harder.

"Swim with me," I plead.

Shannon emerges from the bathroom, towelling her wet hair. Carol whispers in her ear, their eyes cutting over to us. Carol goes into the bathroom and the shower starts as Andrew lets go of me and begins texting quickly.

"Too much work?" I ask, knowing the answer.

"Yes, but I'm clearing an hour."

"A WHOLE HOUR?" Shannon calls out sarcastically.

Blinking rapidly, it's clear her comment hit a nerve.

He bends down to kiss me and I laugh.

"I'll take the sixty minutes. It's better than nothing."

"You are worth much more than 'better than nothing.'"

"Don't fall in."

Midway to kissing me, he halts, an extraordinary display of emotion crossing his face.

To my surprise, he pulls back. Have I offended him? Pushed the teasing too far?

Stripping out of his jacket, he loosens his tie, throws it on a chair, and kicks off his shoes.

"What are you doing?" I shout as Shannon begins whistling a pathetic version of a strip tease song.

Andrew is not known for being inhibited about his body, though he has nothing on Declan, who models for nude sculpture classes at a local arts center.

Within moments he's down to his underwear, Shannon shouting, "OH MY GOD, STOP THERE! I DON'T NEED TO KNOW THAT MUCH ABOUT YOUR BODY!"

The shower ends.

"WHOSE BODY?" Carol calls out.

"ANDREW'S GETTING NAKED."

"HOLD ON! I'LL BE OUT IN A MINUTE! I NEED TO SEE THIS!"

There is no question these two were raised by Marie.

At the edge of the pool, my husband, wearing boxer briefs and a grin, bends down in competitive swimmer's launch pose and flings himself expertly into the water, down the lane faster than you can imagine. In his wake, the waves splash water out of the pool, making

Shannon laugh as Carol bursts out of the shower, frantic eyes searching for Andrew.

"Did I miss the show? I missed it, didn't I. Damn it!"

"Why are you so eager to see my husband naked?" I shout over the sound of Andrew showing off his butterfly stroke as he returns.

"I'm eager to see *any* man naked, Amanda. Haven't seen one in real life in three years!"

Andrew surfaces, looking like a hot, wet seal, grinning and breathing hard as he treads water. Somehow, he does that one handed, the free hand going to my belly.

Righty kicks him, hard.

And then Lefty kicks my cervix even harder.

"Ooof," I gasp, legs scissoring hard in the water as I try to get the pain to dissipate.

Strong hands grasp my hips, pushing slightly up. "What's wrong?" Andrew asks, his body moving rhythmically with his own kicks to keep us both afloat.

"Nothing. Lefty decided to play soccer with my cervix."

"Again?"

"Mmm hm." I smile at him, admiring his wet, athletic body as he moves his hands slowly away. "You don't do this."

"Do what? Touch you?"

"Jump in the pool midday to just hang out."

"I should do it more often."

"We'll see ourselves out!" Shannon hollers, Carol and Shannon blowing kisses our way. Their departure is perfunctory and so speedy I'm almost suspicious.

Then again, if Declan jumped into a pool in his underwear while I was visiting their home, I'd get out of Dodge fast, too.

"Finally," he whispers, coming in for a kiss. "Just us."

Bzzzzz.

"And your phone. Funny, when I imagined having a threesome, I never thought your phone would be the third."

"You've imagined a threesome?" he asks in a tight voice, waving his hand toward the phone. "And I'm ignoring that."

Bzzzzzz.

"It's not ignoring you," I point out.

"My phone doesn't get to tell me what to do."

"Since when?"

"Since I — "

RING!

Hoisting himself out of the pool and giving me a fine eyeful of his ass, Andrew walks carefully to his suit jacket, slides the phone out of his pocket, and starts with, "I told you, Gina, I — "

And then shuts up and listens.

Every second that passes tells me what I already know: this was too good to be true. Andrew doesn't just strip down and take a few hours off with me spontaneously like this.

His life is scheduled to the quarter hour.

A series of sighs tells me what I already know: he's leaving. Back to work. But how to untangle himself from the wife?

I'm thirsty now, and my bladder's about to burst, so I carefully ascend the steps and go straight to a chaise longue chair, my water bottle next to it. Stretching out, heedless of the dripping mess I'm making in the chair, I drink half the water bottle, then close my eyes.

The tears come unexpectedly, the rush of emotion undefined. As they slip out of the corners of my eyes, the cloth cushion absorbs them.

I open my eyes to find Andrew gone, the shower on, the sounds of water splattering hastily coming through. He says nothing, but within a minute he's back to his pile of clothes, sliding one leg in his pants after the other, clearly going commando.

"Amanda? I'm sorry. I have to — "

"I know how it works."

"But this was going to be different."

"Mmm hmmm."

"No, really."

"I know."

"I'll make it up to you."

"You always do."

"Please don't be like this."

"Like what?"

"So — " But he can't find the words as he buttons his shirt and tucks it into his pants. We just breathe together and try to find a way not to let the growing distance between what I want and what he wants become impossible to bridge.

Bzzzz.

If Andrew had a mistress, I could scream and wail, feel justly betrayed, sue for divorce and hate her guts. I could hang out with my friends and wallow in sugar sorrows, and I would get support.

When your husband's "mistress" is his job, though, you're "lucky."

Lucky to be married to a CEO. A billionaire. A "hot man." A success.

As he kisses my cheek and promises to spend more time with me tomorrow, Righty moves in a muted way, like a scoff.

Yeah, kid.

That's right.

I don't buy it either.

And as I hobble to the shower for a quick rinse before heading back to bed rest in the house, I remind myself how lucky I am.

At least Shannon and Carol left me a fresh pint of ice cream.

❧ 17 ❧

Andrew

Gina storms into my office with a red face, phone clutched in her hand, and I can tell this is going to be an expensive conversation.

"He is such an ass?"

"You're going to have to be more specific than that, Gina. Are you talking about Declan? My dad? The Paulson project? Rathi Industries in India? I know the guy was condescending to you, but–"

"Vince?"

"Vince who?"

"Your Vince?"

"I don't have a–wait. Vince? My trainer, Vince?"

"Yes?"

"Oh. Sure. He's definitely an ass. We're in agreement there. What else about him?"

"You told me to schedule a dinner at Consuela's for the two of you? He wants a list of all of the ingredients in every food she'll be serving?"

"Okay."

"And I did that?"

"Good."

"Now he wants a list of all the farms where Consuela buys her food?"

"Okay?"

"And you know how she grows some herself?"

"Sure."

"He wants to know where she sources her soil and fertilizers and worms?"

"Worms?"

"THAT'S WHAT I SAID!"

Whoa. A statement from Gina. This is serious.

"Call him back and–"

"No need to call." Vince appears in my doorway, filling the frame with his huge body. Dark eyes take in Gina with a flicker of appreciation that reminds me I know very little about Vince beyond the gym.

"Vince," I say, standing and crossing the room to grip his hand. He gives me a quick shake, then turns his full attention to Gina.

"What's wrong with caring about what I put in my body? Don't you care about who–er, what–you put in yours?" he says to her, the stumble uncharacteristic.

Her face flames even more.

"I'm not your admin?"

"Then give me Consuela's number so I can ask her myself."

"I'm not allowed? That's personal info?"

"You told me that already. That's why we're at an impasse. I'm in the process of shredding and it matters."

"Shredding?"

"For a photo shoot."

"Like, paper shredding?"

"Muscle shredding."

"What does that mean?"

Vince reaches for the hem of his shirt and pulls it off, revealing a roadmap of anatomy and veins. "*This* is shredding."

"This is Magic Mike!" Gina screams.

"Hell, no. Channing Tatum's a Ken doll compared to this," Vince grunts, pivoting to show off muscular hypertrophy of the finest kind. "So I need to source my food very carefully. Big endorsement shoot in two days."

"This is a lot of bother for a business meal?" Gina says to me. I shrug. Her eyes aren't on me, though.

They're attached to Vince's pecs. If Gina keeps staring at his chest like that, in a few thousand years straight women will evolutionarily evolve to have velcro on their corneas.

"You want to touch it, don't you," he says. It's a statement, not a question.

"What? No? Of course not?" Is that a thin line of drool coming out of her?

"Look," I announce, grabbing my suit jacket and shrugging into it. Rarely does another man's naked chest make me feel inadequate, but Vince has managed it.

"Take that off. And your shirt," Vince orders me.

"What?"

"Let's show Gina the difference between a cut chest and... yours."

"HEY! My chest is fine!"

"Prove it."

"I'm not taking off my shirt to prove a point."

"Then your pecs aren't doing their job."

"What job do my pecs have?"

"To hold you upright."

"My abs do that."

"The pecs make the man. Your confidence is up here," he says, tapping his temple, "but the body knows. And your pecs, lats, abs, and all the smaller muscles matter." He glances at my suit with disdain. "Besides, go change into workout clothes. Screw eating out. Let me pick where we eat."

Gina's shoulders drop with relief. "That would be great? Because I don't know how to find the flies that age the composted cow manure that the farmer put on the carrots Consuela uses in her gazpacho?"

"You should," Vince says, deadpan.

Her eyes don't go to his face.

Ignoring them, I head into the small dressing room off my office and quickly change into workout clothes. I emerge in shorts, a tight Under Armour shirt, and wearing my heart rate variability tracker.

"Shirt off," Vince says, grabbing my hem, pulling it up as Gina protests.

I can't see in front of me, the vision field covered with black, until I hear my brother say loudly, "Vince is your personal valet, now? Need help dressing?."

"Hey," Vince says as I pull the shirt off and glare at Dec. "Whose chest is better?"

Tilting his head slightly, Dec pretends to care. "Yours, of course," he says to Vince. "Why the chest-off?"

"Because Vince is insane," I inform him, wondering why my brother's at Anterdec, and how to get him out of here so I can hire Vince for my set of gyms. That's the point of this business dinner, and now the whole situation is FUBAR'd.

I'm shirtless. Gina is drooling at my shredded trainer. My brother is making fun of me.

Just another day at the office.

"How's Amanda?" Declan asks me with concern. "Shannon's over at your house now, hanging with her."

"Did she bring ice cream?"

"With Cheetos," Dec confirms. "And a case of those YoYo Baby Belly Snax you love so much." Declan gives Vince a smarmy look that makes it clear he thinks he's scoring points by revealing my new love of baby snacks.

"Those are the bomb," Vince says, surprising us both as he asks me, "which are your favorite? Mango or peach?"

"Did I mention the Cheeto ice cream?" Declan reiterates.

That gets the expected response.

Vince starts to gag, then eyes my brother's chest. "What do *your* pecs look like?"

"I am not taking anything off," Declan flatly declares.

"Um, Andrew? If you're done with me?" Gina glares at Vince. "You can find your own meal?"

"I'll feast off your obvious admiration for my shred," Vince says to her with a wink.

"No clean diet can compensate for a man who is, well... compensating?" Her eyes drift lower on his body.

And on that note, she exits.

Dec lets out a low whistle as a stunned Vince scrambles back into his shirt, shooting looks of outrage at the empty doorway.

"Why did you keep asking Gina for all that info? You never drill down like that when we eat at the gym," I ask Vince, who starts stretching.

Damn. He meant it. We really are working out.

"I was just yanking her chain."

"What else were you yanking while bothering her like that?" I ask.

Before he can order it, I drop to the ground and start doing burpees.

From above, Declan says, "While this impromptu workout looks great and all, I came here for a different reason. Dave told me you're thinking about partnering with us for a real food bar in your gyms."

I go flat on my belly and look at Vince, who is now doing crunches. "What?"

"Right. That," he says, sitting up and looking at me. "I was going to tell you."

"Tell me what?"

"I've been working with Dave."

Dec shoves his hands in his suit pants pockets and lowers his brow. Any other guy would be intimidated, but Vince just smiles.

"On what?" Dec asks.

"A whole new way to make people get real food."

"We serve real food," Declan begins.

"Not real enough. Let me show you."

"Show me?" Dec and I say together.

"C'mon. Let's go to Grind It Fresh! Dave's already there waiting for us."

I look at my workout clothes. "We're not doing a workout?"

"Of course not. We're having a business meeting."

"Then why did you make me change?"

"I wanted to see if I could convince you to strip down. I succeeded. You're surprisingly easy to manipulate, Andrew."

Declan bursts out laughing as I storm back into my dressing room and put on my suit of armor, shouting, "Does this mean you accept the job with my new company?"

Silence.

"New company?" Declan calls out.

Oh, damn.

Vince clears his throat and says, "You never told your brother?"

Silence is a fine weapon when wielded appropriately.

Like now.

Finishing up, I re-knot my tie and make them wait. When I come out, Declan has an expectant look on his face, brows raised, eyes unblinking.

"Spill. You're hiring Vince to run your chain of gyms?"

Vince gives Dec an appreciative look. "So you *do* know."

"I didn't realize this was so serious," my brother says, grabbing my arm. "Is it?"

"Not talking about this until Vince answers my question."

"What question?"

"Does this mean you accept the offer?"

"Duh."

"You could have told me sooner."

"That wouldn't have been as much fun as this." He points to Dec. "Now I get to watch you squirm."

"You're seriously planning to run this chain?" Disdain fills his eyes. "Old Jorg's gym?"

"No. Not the gyms. A different chain," Vince helpfully answers.

"Of what?"

"Coffee shops," I say as we walk to the elevator bank and I push a button. Also Dec's buttons.

A bark of laughter escapes him. "You didn't."

"No. I didn't. I have too much respect for you."

Vince laughs through his nose.

"Thank you," Dec says pointedly.

"I would never want to humiliate you by becoming a competitor and wiping you out."

Ding!

He stands there, eyes murderous, as Vince suddenly turns to the stairs and announces, "Let's just take the stairs and get some cardio in."

We're in suits. Vince is in shorts and a muscle shirt.

But obedient clients do as told.

Five flights before the end, Declan huffs and says, "Why the hell are we doing this?"

"Because Vince said to."

"*We* pay *him!* He's not our boss."

I just grunt.

"And you never answered my question." The metallic echo of our voices makes even a hushed whisper feel like a scream. He stops. "Day-to-day operations?"

I just shrug.

"For Anterdec? An acquisition?"

I could lie. It would be easy. It *is* easy.

Instead, I stop. I take a deep breath. I let time pass, enough time for Declan to cross his arms over his unbuttoned jacket and watch me, his judgment fading by the second, replaced by a curiosity I don't see in him very often.

"No."

"An investment? Something you'll dismantle and sell off for pieces?"

"No."

"Andrew." His voice is firm, but frustrated. "Get to the point."

"I bought a chain of gyms. I'm planning to run them. Hiring Vince is the first step. I told you about the gyms when we had dinner."

"You mentioned it casually. I didn't understand the implications of it. Dad is going to lose his mind over this."

"Why?" I round on him, in his face, pissed that of all the things his mind gravitated to, Dad's reaction is on top.

"Because you're the CEO of Anterdec, Andrew! Dad picked you!"

"Is that what this is about? You're still jealous?"

"No. It's that Dad picked you and you're about to have two babies and you are the CEO of a Fortune 500 company and now you're talking about adding a chain of gyms as a hobby? You're not superman."

"You're worried about my time management skills?" I laugh in his face, but an image of disappointed Amanda in our lap pool makes the chuckle cut in half in my throat.

"If that's what you think I'm saying, then you really don't get it."

"Oh, I get it all right, bro. You're playing the role of Dad. Thanks but no thanks. I don't need a lecture on priorities."

The way he grabs my arm makes me cock my other one, elbow ready to punch him. Rage blooms in both of us, fierce and sudden, violent in the way that only authentic emotion can produce.

We're both very, very dangerous right now.

His chest rises and falls, eyes dark, mouth tight and grim. Before he can speak, Vince bursts through the stairwell door. He looks pissed, too.

"Where the hell are you?" He takes us in, then rolls his eyes. "Fighting? You two act like you're eight and arguing over a toy robot."

"I'm trying to reason with Andrew," Declan says through gritted teeth.

"Reason? Hah. You're trying to bring me down a peg."

"No." The word echoes up like a piece of ash from a funeral pyre. "I'm not." He sounds just like Dad. "I'm warning you."

"You're threatening me?"

"I'm warning you. Adding all this to your plate is too much. Your wife is at home on bed rest. The twins could be born prematurely, and you're talking about balancing being a CEO and running your own company, too? You're on track to be like Dad. Don't let those boys go through what we went through, Andrew. You're already Dad's protégé. He groomed you for CEO. Don't treat your kids like he treated his."

Peering intently at us, Vince reaches for my tight arm, fist still ready, and just rests his fingers on my forearm. He doesn't say a word.

"You're crazy," I spit out at my brother, hating his words, knowing the reason I hate them is because there's a shred of truth in them, and if there is, what does that make me?

Even more controlled by Dad then I ever realized.

And I refuse to admit that to my brother.

"I'm the father of a toddler, Andrew. I left Anterdec to grow my own company, and there's a lot of pain that goes into being away from my family. I'm not in your role–"

"And it kills you."

A light huff, the kind of laugh you make through your nose, emerges from Dec, but it's not mocking. No derision. The lightness of it, followed by his wry smile, spears my heart.

Somehow he gets around the armor I think I'm wearing.

"No. It really doesn't. That's the thing, Andrew–it did. At first. When Dad picked you. And then over time, I realized I was relieved."

"Sure. Right," I shoot back, mind and heart spinning out of control as Vince's fingers on my coiled arm keep me from floating away.

Or beating my brother to a pulp.

"What the hell are you doing? I didn't come here to break up a fight. I came here to show you how you can be industry leaders with a new idea that is going to change how people eat, drink, and work out, you dumbasses."

Dec and I slowly turn to look at Vince, who is shaking his head at us.

"But," he continues, "maybe this is a mistake. I don't want to work for two billionaires who can't get over their daddy issues."

"I don't have daddy issues!" Dec and I burst out at the same time.

"And what do you mean, industry leaders?" I follow up.

"Get your asses outside and let me show you." A disgusted glare follows. "Not that you deserve my time, but might as well finish this."

I follow him, ignoring Declan, moving on pace with Vince. Dec catches up and flanks his other side.

Just then, a wasp floats into my field of vision on my left, where Vince is walking. It's almost black with white markings on the face, a bald-faced hornet.

My Epipen is in my jacket pocket.

Dec moves a step ahead of us, eyes on the damn thing, inserting his body between me and the insect. It moves to the left, away from us, as Vince realizes what's happening.

No one says a word until the flagship Grind It Fresh! store comes into view.

"This is my store," Dec announces, as if we didn't know that.

"No kidding," Vince mutters, yanking the front door open and barging in, turning right to head to the Test Kitchen Counter, a special section Shannon developed for this location only. When Grind It Fresh! tests new products, customers get a fifty-percent-off price break, and they conduct focus groups in the evenings and on weekends.

Declan's executive assistant, Dave, is behind the bar, dark brown hair like Declan's, though the guy is shorter, slimmer, and manages to have even less expression than my brother. It's like cardboard with eyes, nose, and mouth.

"Hey," Vince says to him.

"Hey."

"What are you doing here?" Declan asks Dave, who gives him a no-blink stare that would impress any psychopath.

"Saving your company."

"My company doesn't need to be saved!"

"It will if you don't partner with Vince and Andrew."

"Partner?!" I burst out. "What does a chain of gyms have to do with coffee?"

"See? Told you," Vince says sadly to Dave, whose eyebrow twitches as he gives me a condescending look worthy of my brother. "Limited imagination, these two."

"Get to the point," Declan grinds out.

"Ultraclean eating," Vince says. "All natural, all organic, carefully sourced."

"Everyone's doing that," Dec scoffs.

"No. Everyone *claims* they're doing that. Most 'organic' food has crap in it. Rosemary extract? That's MSG. Xanthan gum? Converts to glutamate in the body. Natural flavors? Could be MSG, could be beaver anal glands."

That last part sounds familiar, but I can't quite remember why.

"People feel better when they eat real food. Healthy food. Salad dressings made from high quality olive or MCT oil, a pure vinegar, simple seasonings, and a shake of sweetness like maple syrup or coconut sugar. People feel better when their chicken breast is grilled in unrefined coconut oil or olive oil, Himalayan sea salt, and cracked green peppercorns. Smoothies don't need sweeteners, they need properly ripened organic fruits, vegetables, coconut milk, or A2-sourced dairy. See where I'm going?"

"Yes," Dec says. "And it's been done."

"Not like this," Dave says flatly. "Because it's done in farm-to-table settings on a small scale. Not in large chains."

"Food loss," Declan says simply. "Without preservatives, you have too much loss."

"That's where you have to be willing to think outside the box. Upcharge in a gym where people already spend the monthly membership fee. In coffee shops where four bucks for a coffee is no big deal. And partner with food insecurity charities, composting services, and small environmental non-profits to manage waste." Dave's eyes light up. The guy has an emotional range wider than a lamppost. Who knew?

"What does this have to do with our separate companies?" I ask Vince. Dec walks behind the counter and begins using the coffee machines with a smooth grace I admire. As much as I hate my brother sometimes, he surprises me with random tidbits of personality like this.

He's an enigma. Emotionally tight, brutally competitive, and completely wrong about anything related to me.

But he can master a ristretto pull like it's nothing, and Amanda swears his breve lattes are as good as the master barista's. I make a mental note to have Gina set me up for training on how to make espresso.

Because I'm sure I can be better.

"Your separate companies are yin and yang," Vince answers, looking at me funny. "Add a food bar in the gyms. Use Grind It Fresh!'s food distribution and purchasing power to upgrade to even higher quality food. *They* have a test kitchen, and *we* have members who want to eat clean. Who are motivated," he explains before Dave cuts him off.

"Imagine," Dave continues, "all the small, local producers who could benefit from this. Food allergies are on the rise. We have a spike in people coming in with celiac disease and egg allergies, asking about products they can safely eat. Individualized food is the new trend. Give people exactly what they need, and they'll become loyal customers. Mass and fast foods are out."

"Not convinced," Dec says, and I nod in agreement.

"We know that eating clean leads to health benefits," Vince adds, looking a little too confident. "So we reached out to one of the newer apps being marketed to health insurance companies and primary care physicians. We can calculate the macro- and micronutrient breakdowns and get our foods into their apps. Then co-market to drive their subscribers into our stores and gyms, and vice versa."

My spine starts to tingle.

"Now you're talking." Dec and I exchange a glance.

Damn it. This might work.

Which means.... partnering with my brother's company.

"Wait," I interject, needing to cut through the fog of possibility that threatens to overwhelm me. I've just had a furious argument with my brother about taking on too much. "Why not partner with Anterdec? Why shouldn't I just do this as CEO there?"

Dave and Vince shake their heads. "No."

"No? What do you mean, no?"

"Anterdec is too corporate."

Declan is in the middle of sipping a latte and nearly chokes.

"What does *too corporate* mean?" I challenge.

"Big conglomerates don't have the level of trust needed for this market segment," Dave says smoothly. "And it's a growing segment. People are looking for health factors they can control, and pure food is one of them. Anterdec's too tainted."

"*Tainted?*"

"Would you trust a fast-food chain to produce high quality organic food? Or a huge international hotel chain to provide personalized boutique bed and breakfasts? No. The branding is too strong for what they've done well. Anterdec does what it does very well. This isn't part of your brand," Dave elaborates.

Dec and I stop, blinking hard.

Because Dave is right.

"This won't work," Dec says.

"Why not?" I ask, turning to him.

"Because you have too much on your plate."

"I'll hire people." I point at Vince. "He's on board."

"I am," Vince agrees. "But only if you two work together. I refuse to work in a tense, high-stress environment with two wusses who can't stop arguing like littermates fighting over a bone."

Dave gives Vince a look of love. Pure love.

"I need time," I snap, just as Dave slides a small bowl of salad toward me.

"Try this."

"What is it?" I see chopped dried fruit, avocado, carrots, and–

"Dried organic bing cherries, shaved celeriac, and roasted golden beets on arugula and micro-green pea shoots in a dressing of MCT oil, roasted blended pumpkin seed, maple syrup, cumin, turmeric, and ginger. Slivers of smoked salmon on top."

I take a bite.

"This is good," I mutter around my mouthful. "Really good."

"I just listed every actual ingredient in that." Vince slides a small smoothie toward Dec. "You try this."

He takes a sip. "What's in it?"

"Cashew milk made here on the premises with filtered water and cashews. Mango. Dark cherries. Fresh cranberries from Truro. High-polyphenol olive oil. Hemp seeds. Overripe bananas. Lacinato kale. Organic English seedless cucumber, peeled."

"I would never, ever drink this if I knew what was in it." But Dec keeps drinking. "And it's really good."

"Your body is sucking up the nutrients," Vince says. "Guarantee you'll feel better all day. Imagine eating that well, and tracking your dietary needs in an app. Cross-check it against productivity at work. Against sex drive and sex life–"

"Now you're talking," mutters an employee from behind Dave.

I finish my salad, chewing and thinking. I finish, and announce, "Let me think this through."

Both Vince and Dave nod, then turn to Dec, who sets the empty smoothie glass on the counter.

"No," he declares.

"No?" All three of us are surprised.

"If we're going to do something this complex, I need a partner who is all there. You're too distracted, Andrew." He looks at Vince. "But I'm happy to lure you away from Andrew's gyms, if you're interested."

"I'll help you negotiate," Dave says to Vince out of the corner of his mouth.

"What do you mean, no? I said I'm thinking about it. And you don't get to decide whether my life has too much in it, Declan. That's not your job."

"Maybe not. But when my company is asked to invest and work with another one, it becomes my business." He gives Dave and Vince a nod, then turns to me, pivoting on one heel before he heads toward the elevator to the corporate offices.

"While you're thinking about it, bro, think about your priorities. Because when you want to do it all, it means nothing is more important than anything else. And kids and wives don't work that way."

With that, my brother has the last word.

And I can't stop him.

Because I have no response to *that*.

$$ \text{❦} \quad 18 \quad \text{❦} $$

Amanda

"**D**o it again," he insists.

"I just did it twice!"

"But it feels so good."

"Fine."

"Mmmm. Like that!" he says, grinning down at me.

"This isn't as easy as it looks, buddy."

"You're good with balancing, and man, when you clench like that..." He descends into non-verbal groans and sighs.

"You're really that jazzed when I do it?"

"I've never found your body more exciting."

"Your balls certainly seem to enjoy resting there."

"Until they–oh!" he grunts, then laughs. "That one slid off the side. Look at it go. Ping, ping, ping."

We're staying at our place in the Seaport District, with a small renovation project going on at the house in Weston. Neither of us wants to be exposed to fumes and dust, so we're here for the week.

Nostalgia is everywhere. My first night sleeping over. Our first morning coffee. Our first argument...

He picks up another ping-pong ball and puts it in my navel, which has become an outie, but has a small ring around it that can hold a ball – but barely. The white, lightweight orb nestles in place, and then–boing!

It jumps up an inch and rolls down my right side.

"I love playing ping-pong with my unborn kids."

"I'm surprised."

"You are?"

"So far, they're beating you."

"No one's keeping score," he mutters, but I can tell that's a lie. He bends forward, trying to balance two balls in my belly button, when suddenly, Lefty's elbow pokes up and the ball hits Andrew in the eye.

We descend into laughter, my side hurting from giggling so hard that Righty kicks my ribs. It's like he's curling little monkey toes around them.

Warm, big palms cover the sides of my belly, like a football player sizing up a watermelon.

"Lefty got you."

"Or maybe Righty?" I question, poking the right side and receiving no response.

"You mean Joshua did."

"I am *not* naming our kid Josh. Can you imagine? The real Josh would die and go to heaven. I'm not giving him the satisfaction."

"Well, we're not naming either one James. We have to find some good options."

"We have time," I assure him, but he's right. I hate to admit it.

"Not much. We at least need a shortlist."

I stop him right there. "And we are not naming them Tom and Brady."

"What's wrong with those names?"

Hard stares don't actually melt people, I've learned.

Too bad.

"How about Lexington and Concord? We could call them Lex and Cord for short." This is an old joke. He pokes my belly and laughs.

"Cord McCormick? Sounds like the lead in every cheap Western movie from the 1960s," Andrew mutters.

"Lex is too close to Lex Luthor," I add.

His stomach growls. I look at the clock. 11:46 a.m. on a Sunday.

He brings up food before I do, which is rare these days. "I made brunch reservations for us."

"You did? Where?"

"Consuela's." He holds out his palm. "And before you protest, the doctor said you needed to gradually come off bed rest. You've been so good. You can handle the walk."

"I've been so bored! Carol hardly needs me. She took over at work and is running the division like she was born to do it."

"And you come off bed rest tomorrow," he says softly. "You're supposed to walk a little."

"Still no sex," I say sadly.

He's uncharacteristically silent for a while, and then:

"Dr. Jeffs said you could walk to Consuela's. Use the elevator."

"When did he say that?"

"When I called two days ago to make the reservation at Connie's."

"You mean when *Gina* called."

"No. *I* called."

"You? *You* actually called a place? Dialed a phone and spoke to someone? Wow, Andrew. I had no idea you were evolving like that. Next thing I know, you'll learn to pump gas."

"Let's not be too hasty."

My phone buzzes. I grab it from the nightstand. It's Mom.

Can you send me the link to all the baby products you've ordered for the twins? The Consumer Product Safety Commission just declared some products hazardous to babies and I want to double check your list.

I read Andrew the text and he shakes his head. "Good old Pam."

"Yeah." I type a response and include the link. It's easier to go along with her than to fight. "She's so cautious and analytical."

"Nothing wrong with that. She also seems to have more energy since the new treatments took hold."

I nod, finish the text, and snuggle into his arms, my belly rising up like I'm Mauna Kea, emerging from the oceans as tectonic plates shift.

Which is a good metaphor for what is happening in my body and heart.

"Who knew it was Lyme disease this entire time?"

"In a way, Dad did."

"James is so weird," I blurt out. "He treats you three so differently than he treats me, or Shannon, or Pam. And then there are the women he dates..."

"You mean the gold digger Barbies?"

"Andrew!"

"What? Dad calls them that."

"He does? I had no idea he was so self-aware."

Andrew's cheek is pressed against my belly. When he laughs, the vibration radiates through to the babies, who both suddenly move at the same time.

"I think he considers it a badge of honor."

"Why does he like my mom so much?" I ask as Andrew pokes Righty.

"I don't know."

"She's nothing like Elena, right? Our mothers aren't similar."

"Not one bit. My mom would have gotten along with Pam really well, but they're different. Mom was more social. More into networking and parties and gatherings. She would have found Pam's analytical side charming, though."

"Your father certainly does."

He sits up, questions in those brown eyes. Will our boys' eyes be his shade of brown or mine? Whose nose will they get?

"Nothing's going on there," Andrew says slowly. "We know that. No worries about becoming accidental stepsiblings."

"Not for want of trying on James's part."

Andrew goes still. "What?"

"Come on. You know he likes my mom."

"My dad isn't attracted to anyone who was born before Clinton was president."

"So," I say, holding up my empty glass of water. "My feet have fallen asleep, I have to pee, I'm dehydrated, and I really want to pig out on brunch. How much time do we have to make it to Consuela's?"

Andrew looks at the clock. He has to stretch over my belly, which gets a not-so-gratuitous kiss along the way. "Five minutes ago. We had to leave five minutes ago."

"Good thing Consuela loves you."

"Not as much as you do."

I toss a ping-pong ball at him. "Okay. Let's walk there. Haven't had a contraction in two weeks."

He looks outside at the sunny day, blue sky inviting us to come join it. Hesitation isn't in his nature, but his shoulders square and I realize why he's not saying anything.

"I know. There are wasps out. We don't have to walk. It's just, you suggested it, and–"

"No. It's fine." His eyes drift to his sport coat, casually draped over the back of a chair. "I have my Epipens."

"And I have extras in my purse," I assure him. As he nods, his eyes drift to my belly. Anaphylactic insect allergies aren't new to me. I don't have one, but my best friend did growing up. Andrew's is well documented.

His mother's death–and sacrifice for him–haunts him.

The specter of either of our children having the same allergy is one we barely talk about. In a sense, we don't have to. He's careful. I'm careful. His mother's death means that he has at least two Epipens on him at all times now, so no one ever has to make the choice Elena forced on Declan in the moment both she and Andrew were stung.

I understand that choice better now.

Understanding it doesn't make it less painful.

"Hey, beautiful," Andrew says to me as he buttons his dress shirt, seeing my tear-filled eyes. "It's fine. We'll walk in the sun. I'm not a vampire anymore," he teases.

"You worry about the boys."

He stills, eyes on mine. "Of course I do." A sad smile comes over his face. "But time will tell. And Epipens come in pairs for us." Kissing me softly, then more deeply, our embrace grows more intimate by the second, his body mine to lean on, my body growing his children.

When we untangle, it's with a sniffle from me and a sweet touch of my jawline from him, followed by dueling stomach growls.

Ah, hunger.

Ten minutes later, we're dressed and in the elevator, the sudden drop of the car making my lower belly feel like it's a wave pool. Andrew senses the change in me and gives the boys a good rub, the kind of affectionate touch he never gave before the pregnancy. As we walk out to the Boston streets, heading toward Congress and Consuela's secret rooftop restaurant, I breathe in the salty city air.

My hand seeks his and finds it instantly, our fingers threading comfortably. He slides his sunglasses on and I take him in, deeply grateful for a life with a man so strong, handsome, caring, and most important–all mine.

If you had told me five years ago I'd have this someday, I'd have assumed you got into Chuckles' catnip stash and were pulling my leg.

As we walk, I adjust my stride, Andrew's long legs covering more territory per step than mine. The bigger I get, the more I waddle, but keeping up with him feels good, though he slows down to make it easier on me. My body needs to stretch and move, the blood flow important. I've never been one to work out much, but I do fine.

Pregnancy makes me feel more in my body than ever before.

Sunny days like this make me appreciate having a place on the water. The city is busier than you'd expect on a Sunday morning, easing into the afternoon. It's July, which means the tourists are pouring in, the Tea Party re-enactment boat packed with people and a long line at the ticket window. The scent of garlic and sweet sausage wafts past us as we get closer to Consuela's, then ginger and peanuts. Plenty of trendy places have moved into the area, but Connie's food can't be smelled from the street.

She's high above it all.

You can't call Consuela's to book a table. There is no website. It's the kind of place a billionaire like Andrew knows about because he's Andrew McCormick, CEO of Anterdec, and that's that. Celebrity chefs like Consuela don't hire mystery shoppers, they don't advertise, and they certainly don't have two-for-one specials on Monday nights.

"You okay? The walk isn't too much?" he asks me as we wait at a crosswalk, his hand warm and strong in mine.

"Fine as can be."

A lazy little honeybee bounces from blossom to blossom in a planter outside a café. Shannon is allergic to them, but that little puffball covered in pollen could sting Andrew and he'd be fine. The randomness of anaphylaxis is something I'm not educated enough to fully understand, but on an emotional level, I am an expert on anticipatory danger from creatures that weigh less than .00025 pounds.

Until you carry around forty-five extra pounds of baby (okay, fine, babies and Cheetos...), you don't realize how hard stairs can be. My mother would note that my pregnancy weight is equal to 180,000 bees.

How do I know this?

Because she actually calculated it for me. When your mom's an actuary, you learn these details.

"What are you doing?" Andrew asks as I head toward the stairwell. He's pointing at the elevator.

"Elevator" is a stretch. It's a flat door, the old-fashioned kind, with the accordion grate and everything.

I look pointedly at my belly. "We can't fit in that thing, unless you have a shoehorn."

"Then you go without me. I'll take the stairs."

Claustrophobia is not an issue I've ever experienced, but I get a whiff of it now.

"Nah. Let's do the stairs."

Skeptical eyes meet mine. "Are you sure?"

"I need the exercise."

"No." He jabs the elevator button.

"What do you mean, no?"

"You're not climbing the stairs."

"I said I'm fine!"

"And I said you're not overexerting yourself as you come off bed rest."

"There isn't room for both of us in there!"

"Then I'll walk, you ride."

But the elevator doesn't come.

As we wait, a guy in a white kitchen uniform walks in, carrying a bag of produce. He pauses, then says, "it's broken."

"Broken?" we answer in unison. His eyes drift to my belly and he practically chokes.

"Yeah. Sorry."

"See?" I turn on Andrew as he leaves. "I'll take the stairs."

"We can go to a different restaurant."

I ignore him and start up.

The rooftop part of Consuela's bistro becomes annoyingly apparent as we trudge upward. Behind me, halfway there, Andrew pauses and sighs. I turn around to look at him and he makes a face of chagrin.

"I wish you'd taken the elevator."

"Why? Because my fat ass is hard to look at?"

A hand goes straight to said body part. "That entire sentence is an abomination."

"So is my ass. I thought baby weight was supposed to be for the babies."

"You've never been more gorgeous."

"You always say that."

He steps up to my level, both hands groping me now, making me laugh. My belly's so big, we can't squish together enough to kiss, but by God, the man can do a proper reach-around.

"Andrew?"

"Hmm?"

"Are you just going to stand here holding my butt?"

"Maybe. It's not bad as hobbies go."

My stomach roars indignantly, hunger turning into a verb.

His growls back.

Unclenching his paws, he presses his palm to my sacrum, urging me up. "If you can't walk the rest of the way, I'll carry you."

"Hah! As if."

The air around us changes as I realize my grave error.

I have challenged the most competitive man in the world.

Feet out from under me in an instant, I'm in his arms, my cheek against his shirt buttons, hair caught in the crook of his arm, and let me tell you, Lefty and Righty are not happy with what their father is doing.

"Andrew!" I squeal. "The babies are rolling around like they're protesting, signs and banners and all! Put me down."

The jerk starts running up the steps.

"Vince said I need to do more weight-bearing exercises."

"I am not a sandbag!"

"No. You're not. Sandbags don't complain," he says in an amused tone. I can't wiggle out of his arms or we'll fall.

"Put me down at the next landing," I insist. He ignores me and keeps going.

And going.

Until finally, we burst into the open air of the rooftop to find Consuela's deeply amused face staring at us.

"Renewing your wedding vows? Carrying the bride across the threshold?"

"We did... get married... here." Andrew very carefully sets me upright again, the skirt of my maternity dress now wedged up my butt. He's perspiring heavily, and he can barely catch his breath, but he's trying his best to speak normally.

"Show-off," I call out, just loud enough to turn a few heads of fellow patrons, but not enough to get scowled at. Straightening my dress, I square my shoulders. Consuela's gaze drifts to my belly.

"Oh, so sweet," she says in her lightly accented English. "Your babies. Señor and Señora McCormick are going to be Mami and Papi soon."

"Times two," Andrew says proudly. My mouth starts watering when a server passes by with a plate covered in what appears to be thinly sliced smoked salmon, eggs, and artisanal toast.

"You have eyes only for Amanda, but she has eyes for sustenance," Consuela says with a laugh, giving me a big hug and a kiss on both cheeks. "Let us get this woman some Pan con Tomate!"

"How's business, Connie?" Andrew asks as he helps me sit, gently gliding the seat under me, gentlemanly manners on full display.

"Could not be better. People are acquiring a taste for fresh, real food," she says, earning a... frown?

Her eyes cut to me. "Why does that bother him?"

I shrug.

Shaking his head quickly, as if shooing away a gnat, Andrew smiles. "It doesn't. It's just a hot topic lately."

"Good food is controversial? Since when?"

"Do you think there's really been a turn in the market for high quality, pure food?"

"I do. And it's about time. Americans tolerate so much, what is the word?" She struggles to find it, finally exclaiming with a finger snap, "Crap! Yes, that is the word. Crap."

"That's true," I agree.

Andrew leans toward me and whispers, "Cheetos and marshmallows qualify as crap."

"Then hand over the crap and save the real food for yourself. It's a sacrifice I'm willing to make."

Pan con Tomate, crusty bread rubbed with garlic and oil and topped with tomatoes, appears as if an angel delivered it. Sparkling water in a wine glass, with lemon and lime floating in it, is the perfect accompaniment. Lefty and Righty start chanting "Eat! Eat! Eat!" and the vibrations of their little voices travel up from my womb into my mouth. My tongue and teeth operate before I've even grabbed a napkin for my lap.

Connie is deeply gratified.

"Good food, Andrew. Real food. Quality food cooked with love. That's the secret ingredient, the caring. We feel seen when we are fed well." She pats my shoulder. "Is this not true?"

"Mmmph?"

They both laugh as I take a sip of water and swallow.

"Connie," I say, "See me. See me as clearly as possible. I especially want to be seen through your dessert eyes."

A half hug from above follows, her spicy perfume subtle but distinct. "I knew Andrew chose well with you. Knew from the moment he brought you here, that first time. Shall I choose your menu, taking great care with the sweets?" She looks to Andrew.

"You are the expert. I defer to you."

Her eyes widen. "When does that ever happen? A McCormick renouncing control over something? My goodness!"

I have to swallow quickly before I choke on my own laughter.

Andrew cocks one eyebrow but says nothing.

A call from the kitchen, barely audible, makes her turn and wave to us as a tray of breads and oils appears, and I find myself facing a speechless husband.

"We're not that bad," he mutters as he reaches for a piece of bread.

I laugh. "Andrew, you carried me up here because I made a joke. You insist you're 'winning' the baby-making contest with your brother because I'm carrying twins. You and Declan tried to outdo each other showering Shannon and me with gifts in Las Vegas, including a seven-foot animatronic–"

He pops a piece of tomato bread in my mouth to shut me up.

"Let's talk about something else. Oh, I know!" he says in a bright voice that instantly sets me on edge. "How about baby names?"

"Mmmmp pfttt iss eyem."

"Perfect! Your mouth is full and you can't talk. I'll suggest something other than Lefty and Righty. How about Paul and Dominick?"

I shake my head.

"Richard and Oliver?"

I shake harder.

"Erik and Roger?"

I make a face.

"Well, Leo and James are out."

I finally swallow and reply, "Your father and my mother would kill us if we name one of them Leo. But you're right."

Smug looks always find their way to his face. "Of course I am." He frowns. "About what?"

"We need names. Why not Andrew Junior?"

His turn to make a face.

"How about Al and Barkin?" I suggest. Al Barkin was my prom date in high school. He's a town cop now, and we had a run-in with him years ago, right after Shannon and Declan's wedding.

If Andrew's fingernails could make sawdust out of the table top, they would. "That's not funny."

"Why are you jealous of a guy I haven't dated in forever?"

"I'm not."

"You are!"

"How about Coffin and Raleigh?" A diversion technique: Those are the last names of the two people Shannon is most likely to call me in the middle of the night to help her dispose of their bodies.

"Hah!"

"Everyone's asking, Amanda," he says as a seafood stew appears, along with an assortment of grilled vegetables, pastries I can't pronounce, and refills of our water. I stare at the loaded table and have just one question:

What is *Andrew* going to eat?

Rubbing my belly as the babies move and kick in response to the rush of calories hitting their bloodstreams, I sigh in contentment. This is going to be a fun food marathon.

Andrew had better clear the rest of his day.

For real this time, too.

"We said we wanted classic names. No children named after movies or television."

"Baskin and Exotic are off the list."

"And no family names," I confirm before taking an enormous spoonful of soup, careful not to turn the top of my belly into a bathmat.

"That doesn't leave much."

"It leaves plenty!"

"I want to bring up something more delicate," I say, reaching for his hand. "It's about work."

"What about it?"

"I think I want to quit."

"Quit?"

"Quit. Give Carol a promotion to take over the division."

"And do what?"

Pointing to my belly is the only answer that question deserves.

"Of course! The babies! Of course," he emphasizes, face filling with joy as he leans in. "Are you sure? I never wanted to pressure you, but if you want to stay home with them, I'd be overjoyed. We'll still have nannies for support, but it would be a great honor to know our boys are being loved and guided by so much of you."

"I'm increasingly sure. I need a few more days to make certain, but between Carol doing well, the trust fund money I get anyhow, and the reality check of two babies almost being born pre-term, I've been re-assessing my priorities."

Something dark passes across his eyes. It reminds me of Declan.

"Right. I feel the same way."

"You want to quit your job? Leave Anterdec?"

"What? No. The reassessing priorities part."

"What's wrong? You suddenly seem different."

"Nothing."

"Andrew."

A long sigh, then he leans back in his chair and scratches his chin. "It's Declan. And Vince. Dec laid into me for buying the gyms."

"Why?"

"He says I can't run Anterdec *and* the gyms *and* be a good father and husband."

All the air of this outdoor paradise seems trapped in my lungs.

Beseeching eyes meet mine. "Do you think he's right?"

Andrew doesn't falter very often. Asking me a question like this feels like minor key change that comes across as discordant. Dangerous.

A warning.

"I think," I say carefully, feeling like every word is a step in an active landmine field, "you have a lot on your plate and will need to scale up support to make it all work."

"That's a diplomatic dodge."

"It's not untrue."

"You're my wife, Amanda. Not a COO being asked to give a report or a forecast." He looks down, then back up at me. "That day at home, in the pool. I know you were upset that I left. You can be honest here. I want the truth."

My phone buzzes. It's Carol.

Quick question about the North Shore nursing home account. Are we focusing more on narrative reports, and can we use AI transcription for those, directly from a dictation app? Might make it easier for seniors to explain vs. type.

"Hang on. Work question," I tell him, giving her a quick yes.

"Role reversal," he murmurs as he plucks an almond and an olive from a tray and eats them.

I look up from my phone and smile. "I won't need to do this for much longer."

Suddenly, I can breathe.

Because those words feel true. Right. Open and ripe with the space I want to raise my kids. Privilege is a double-edged sword, and being married to a billionaire means I acquired a heaping dose of it when I took him as my husband.

Why not use it?

Shannon struggles with guilt about the money, but I don't. I view it as a joyful abundance I can share with others. What if I give Carol the opportunity to grow at work, to make more money to raise her kids, while I take the time to be a stay-at-home mother?

What if?

There isn't a what if.

I know what I want to do.

"Really?" he asks as the server removes our finished plate, my stomach full but still ready for more. As I shift in my chair, Lefty does a slow roll. Someday–soon–they won't be in me.

I need to treasure how this feels.

Putting my napkin over the top of my belly, I smile at Andrew. "Really. And I'm so happy you're fine with this."

"Fine? Better than fine. But it seems so easy for you."

"Easy?"

"How do you just walk away?"

"Because I know what I want. And fixing other people's problems isn't my role anymore." I rub Righty. "Fixing *their* lives is."

"Fix. You're a fixer. You told me that from the start, when I met you. I didn't understand it then, but I do more and more as time passes. We're different," he says with a contemplative smile, hand on his chin again, watching me. "I don't fix problems. I find solutions that promote growth."

"You're more ambitious."

Something troubled comes into his expression. "Is that bad?"

"Of course not. It's who you are. Something drives you. It doesn't drive me."

"I don't want to be like my father. I can't let work consume me."

"Work already consumes you."

He nods, his eyes moving slowly to the right. It's a tell that he's thinking, hard, but trying not to be defensive. The long, slow inhale through his nose is another tell.

"It does. Are you worried?"

"No. You're a good man with a huge heart. I know you'll always put us first."

"Us. Us means more than just *us*," he murmurs, pointing me between him and me.

"We're doubling our *us* in one fell swoop."

"I wish I could double my time so easily."

I laugh and move back slightly as a dessert plate appears, covered in an assortment of panellets and two small ramekins of Crema Catalana. "Don't we all."

Fierce eyes meet mine, the tight grasp of his hand over the back of mine jolting. "Don't let me do the wrong thing."

"Andrew," I gasp, surprised by the sudden tone change. "What's wrong?"

"Fathers. Fathering. My dad, your dad, Declan as a dad. Me. Vince was a street kid and old Jorg stepped in like a father for him. Vince accused Declan and me of having daddy issues, and he's not wrong."

"Hey. At least James was around. My dad..." I let my voice drift off, unsure what to say.

"It's hard being a grown-up, isn't it?"

I eye the one and only chocolate pastry on the tray and point. "Am I being childish if I say I want that all for myself?"

Big, booming laughter pours out of Andrew as he lets go of my hand and slides the entire dessert plate in front of me.

"Not childish at all. You're eating for three."

"Then let's flag down Connie, because I need two more."

"You deserve it, Amanda. You deserve everything."

The bite of creamy chocolate is in my mouth as he says this. I answer with my mouth rudely full:

"You've given me everything I need or want, Mr. Ambitious."

"Is there anything I've missed?" He's eyeing the treats on the table.

I look him over, carefully weighing my words as I swallow and reach for his hand.

"There is one thing."

"Name it. I'll make it happen."

"You."

"Me?"

"I want more of you."

CHAPTER 19

Andrew

"We need to talk."

My words make her look at me with so much fear, I instantly regret them, kicking myself for not being better at this. But how can you do better when trying to tell your wife that her deadbeat father is about to be released from his prison term for vehicular manslaughter–and wants to see her?

If someone's an expert at this, Gina would have found them for me and I'd have paid whatever price they quoted.

Balancing Amanda's health and stress levels, the babies' safety, the very real possibility that Leo could go around me, and Amanda's need to know is damn near impossible.

So I'm going to do the adult thing.

Tell her.

Questions float in her eyes as she walks over to a chair, hands on the wooden back, and begins to sway. Her hips hurt less when she does this.

Which makes me think of her pain.

Which makes me think of early labor again.

Which makes me not want to say what I need to say.

Damn Leo for putting me in this position.

Damn him.

"What's wrong?"

"Nothing's technically wrong, but I have something sensitive to tell you, and I'm trying to figure out how to do this without upsetting you. You have the whole early labor thing, and I don't want–"

"Andrew."

I sigh. "Right. Here goes: Your dad wants to see you."

"My *what?*"

"Your dad."

"I'm not going all the way to Iowa to see him. Not now."

"He's not in Iowa. He's in New Hampshire. Got out a year or so ago. He lives an hour and a half away."

"He's that close?"

I nod.

"How long?"

"You mean, how long has he been there?"

"How long have you known?"

Damn. Caught.

"Long enough."

"Andrew."

"A few months. Security checks on him regularly."

"And Leo–my dad–he reached out to you? Why not me?"

"He didn't want to upset you."

"Andrew."

"Fine." One hand rakes through my hair nervously as I eye her belly. "A long time ago, I wrote him a letter."

Oh boy. The look she gives me.

"Told him if he wanted to contact you, to go through me first."

"You threatened him?"

"What? No! Of course not. I simply asked him to contact me if he wanted to talk to you."

"Or else you'd...?"

"You make me sound like a gangster."

"At best, what you did was paternalistic and infantilizing of me."

"Excuse me? I was protecting you."

"I didn't ask you to insert yourself into my relationship with my father."

"Yes, you did."

"When?"

"The day you married me."

"See? Paternalistic!"

"I didn't want to see you get hurt."

"But you did hurt me, Andrew. You took away my choice. I can handle being contacted by Leo just fine."

"I wanted to keep you safe."

"No, you wanted to control the outcome."

"Same thing."

"NOT the same thing! And I've wondered why my father stopped contacting me. Now I know!"

I am so confused. "What?"

"Leo used to write me. Here and there. It wasn't more than every six or eight months, but it was something. And then the letters stopped." She thinks for a moment, suspicion growing in her expression. "Right around when we got married."

My shoulders drop. "Damn."

"You kept his letters from me?"

"I don't understand what you're asking."

"You've been blocking me from seeing Leo's letters," she says slowly, anger building.

Oh, no. She's got this all wrong. "No." I shake my head. "I haven't received anything from him until today."

"Why should I believe you?"

"Because I don't lie to you."

Silence ticks by like hope dying. How did we get to this point? I take in her gorgeous form, so big and round, her body a sacrifice to my own blood. Nothing in the world allows me to give to her what she is offering me in the form of our children, but I have to try.

And being her shield is all I can offer.

"Honey." I walk over and take her hand, which hangs in mine. The pit of my stomach drops as she looks away from me. This is a new level of anger, uncharted emotional waters. I'm treading water. I've capsized my own boat and have no idea where to find land.

Better figure out how to stay above water before I lose my strength.

Her silence makes the waters choppier.

"I haven't received any other letters from him, Amanda," I say softly, my heart pleading with hers for connection. "Just this one. And I'm coming to you about it."

"You have a father," she says, her voice hollowing out my gut. "Our children get James as a grandfather. You see your dad every week. He's a blowhard and has some seriously controlling tendencies, but he's here. He's around. He's engaged. Our kids will *know him*." Those last two words come out hard, raw, and her voice shakes at the end. "I don't even know my own father."

Her hand squeezes mine.

"I'm sorry." A part of me wants to mention that our children only have one grandmother–her mother–but now isn't the time for that. Amanda needs to say her piece.

I need to just listen.

This isn't something I can protect her from, is it? I was wrong.

And I should have realized it sooner.

"I don't even know how to process this, Andrew. It's bad enough my father crawls out of the woodwork after years of not hearing from him, but," she gestures at her midsection, "now we have two babies coming soon, and my own husband isn't who I thought he was."

A discordant note clangs through my brain.

"No." I pull her to me, wrapping my arms around her. She doesn't fight the contact, but she doesn't look up at me, either. Her hands hang by her side. "Amanda, no. That's not where this needs to go."

"It's not? Then where does it go, Andrew?" She finally looks up, and I hate what I see in her eyes.

Disappointment.

All of it for me.

"I–"

"Do you remember, when we were first dating, how you handed me that manila envelope with the research you did on my father? How horrified I was to know you went snooping into my past?"

"And you already knew where he was. And that he had three years to go."

"Sure. I knew he was out but didn't know where he was. And here we are. Nothing changes, does it? You were intrusive and paternalistic then, and now you're still the same. Except I'm even more vulnerable." Her hand pushes me away and she rubs her belly.

"That's not true."

"Of course it is! My entire body is being stretched from the inside out–I'm growing two babies! Your babies! And you treat me like I'm some kind of child who can't handle the realities of her own life!"

"I do not."

"You do! Why would you screen my contact with my own father?"

"Because I knew it would be painful."

"This is *more* painful, Andrew."

"I'll never do it again. Ever. You have my word."

"Your word?" She lets out a scoffing sound that damn near breaks me.

"I promise that I will never, ever try to protect you without talking to you about it. Without making sure you are an equal partner in whatever worries I have about keeping you and your heart safe."

"That's a start. But you did the same thing when we first met and here you are, doing it again."

"I didn't make a promise to you then. I am now."

She takes a moment to think about it, then concedes. "Fair point. You didn't promise then." The hard look in her eyes loosens, but barely. "I've been so sad my father didn't answer my letters."

"I'm sorry, honey. If it's my fault, I'll fix it."

"How?"

"By talking to Leo."

"No."

"Fine. I won't."

"No–I mean..." She sighs, then puts both hands on her belly, rubbing. All her attention is on the babies as seconds tick by, the beat of time making me feel pregnant, too.

"I'll do whatever you want."

Suddenly, she looks up, tears making her eyes shine.

"He wants to see me?"

"Yes."

"Does he know about them?"

"No."

Squaring her shoulders, she stands as tall as she can while holding forty-five pounds of baby in her torso. "Well, then, he's about to find out."

"Huh?'

"Do you have his number?"

"Yes."

"Text him."

"Now?"

"Yes."

"You want to see him now?"

"I am thirty-eight weeks pregnant with twins, Andrew. It's now or never."

"But–"

The glare I get tells me I'm in the doghouse, so don't argue.

So I don't.

Amanda says she'd like to see you, I type to Leo's number. I slip the phone in my breast pocket and look at her.

Ding!

We both jolt.

"Probably Gina," I mutter, but when I look, it's Leo.

You free now? I'm in Nashua.

He types an address. I map it.

"He says he's free now," I murmur, surprised.

"Then let's go."

"Are you sure?"

"Andrew."

"You're sure." I text José, who replies immediately that the car will be ready in five.

She's bereft but determined, soft but firm. "He's my father. He wants to see me. How could I not?"

And then she slips her arms around my waist, leaning in, muttering into my chest. "And wanting to protect me is sweet, but if you go all alpha like that again and cut me out of my own decisions, I'll just end up hating you."

"I would die if you hated me."

And then she weeps into my shirt until José appears, the front door open, his face changing as he sees us.

He slips out quietly, ready when we are.

❧

WHEN YOU HEAR THE WORDS *HALFWAY HOUSE*, WHAT DO YOU envision?

We pull up to a large, white home with black shutters, two doors off a porch indicating it's a duplex of some kind. I realize I expected something seedier.

This looks like a pleasant nursing home on a quiet side street.

Except there are five men in folding chairs, all smoking, all looking ragged and worn out.

"Andrew," Amanda says, clutching my arm. We're in the Tesla Model X. On second thought, I didn't have José drive. This is too personal, too raw. We need to be alone.

I text Leo.

The oldest of the men on the porch, a guy in a Red Sox ball cap, checks his phone. Then he looks up and stares at our car.

"That's him," she gasps.

I see the resemblance, but barely. Amanda's got big eyes, brown and warm, with a face that's confident but sweet. She used to change her hair color frequently, but with the pregnancy she's gone back to her natural color, a soft brown that suits her.

Leo's a gaunt man with gray hair, bags under rheumy eyes, and a hangdog, closed-off expression that makes it clear he's lived a hard life.

But man, does his face transform when he sees us.

When he sees *Amanda*.

"Mandy!" he calls out, taking off his baseball cap and waving it in the air, his smile warm, eyes eager but damn scared. Over the years, I've acquired a finely honed ability to sense fear in other men, and to use that fear in negotiations. His fear has nothing to do with competition or domination.

It has to do with rejection.

How does a father get to this point? Reeling from the thought, I have to hog-tie my emotions and get them in check fast, because this isn't about me. I'm about to be a parent, and my brain fast forwards to a time when our twins will be Amanda's age–what would it take for me to be like Leo?

I can't even imagine it, because the gap between who I am and what I'd have to do is so vast.

Maybe Leo thought that, too, when Amanda was born. Thought he'd never be a father who wasn't there.

"Dad?" The question in her voice makes my heart crack in half, because I've never had that tentative, timid tone when it comes to my father. James McCormick is a deeply flawed man in so many respects, but he was always there.

I don't just smell the fear of rejection on Leo.

I smell it on my wife.

And that enrages me.

Leo walks up to us and halts, uncertain, his body language respectful and eager at the same time, the hand waving the cap moving it to his head, the other patting his thigh, fingers twitching. He wants to hug her, but Amanda is a statue. A big-bellied stone statue who is frozen beside me, her hand in mine, crushing my bones like I'm her only way to prevent being sucked into a black hole.

One centered over her heart.

Politeness dictates that I offer my hand to the guy, shake in connection. When you meet your father-in-law for the first time after being married to his only child for three years, isn't that how it should be?

I don't move.

I just stand here, holding Amanda's heart in my palm.

"You, wow–you're so grown up!" he says, eyes jumping all over, once in a while catching mine for a split second, the corners of his wrinkled mouth going up. He smells like drugstore aftershave and dryer sheets.

Tobacco, too.

Amanda shrugs, eyes wider than normal, her throat working double time to contain emotion. The pressure on my hand lessens and irrationally, I worry she'll float off into the ether, as if decades of not seeing Leo have turned into helium that will carry her off like a balloon.

"May I hug you?" he asks, so softly that I feel it in her before the words click, her foot taking a step toward the guy, her hand releasing mine.

Maybe something in me needs to be tethered, too.

When they embrace, Leo leans forward, pulling his lower half back, her giant, twin-filled midsection impossible to avoid. He closes his eyes as I watch him, his chin on her shoulder, her arms under his, head nodding slightly.

"It's good to see you again, Dad."

At the word *Dad*, he winces.

"Whoa!" he calls out suddenly, backing up, the spell broken as she giggles. "What was that?"

"One of the babies kicking," she says, turning to look at me as if to assure me she's fine.

Because that's what she does. Amanda checks in, makes sure her people are okay, and she fixes problems. Leo's a thorn in her side for the same reasons all estranged parents are, but it works overtime for her, because he's also a problem she can't solve.

This time, I'm checking in on her.

As if he finally realizes I'm there, Leo turns to me, shoulders higher, jaw firmer. He reaches out a hand for a shake. "Leo Warrick. You've gotta be Andrew."

I take the man's hand. It's sandpaper pretending to be a palm.

"Yes." I hold back the *sir* that rises in my mouth. "Good to finally meet you, Leo."

The *finally* makes Amanda blink rapidly.

"You, too." He lets go, then goggles at Amanda. "How many you got in there? A baseball team?"

The word *baseball* starts a sequence inside me, a flash of images based entirely on Amanda's story about the last time she saw her father, when she was five. He took her to a Red Sox game at Fenway Park and lost her.

Lost her.

Then got into a wretched car accident, leaving poor Pam to think her daughter had been thrown from the car, dead in the weeds where the rescue workers couldn't find her.

My wife was a precocious five, though, a kid who wandered the streets of Boston until she found a police station and asked for help finding her dad.

Joking about baseball doesn't just leave a bitter taste in my mouth.

It leaves me out for blood.

"No," Amanda answers simply. "Just two."

"Two? I didn't–I knew you were married," he says, cutting me a nervous look that says we all know how he knows. "But children?"

Amanda just smiles.

"Your mom must be pleased as punch. Pam always wanted more kids."

A pale, shaky look washes over Amanda's face, and I move closer to her side.

"She's happy to have grandchildren," Amanda says softly. I can feel the thousands of questions she has for him, but also the restraint, the terror of being told no, of being dismissed, of being pandered to.

Of being confirmed.

Confirmed to be unimportant.

"I'm so sorry, Mandy," he blurts out. A cloud of cigarette smoke hits us full on from a group of men and women sitting at a hexagonal, weathered picnic table to the right of the house. Leo frowns and looks at Amanda. "How about we move? You like ice cream like you did when you were little?"

"What?" Amanda's in a trance.

"Ice cream?"

I speak for her. "That sounds like a good idea, Leo. Is there a place we can go?" I hit the locks on my keyfob and my car unclicks.

His eyes narrow as he takes in the Model X Tesla SUV. "Nice car. Looks safe."

"Mmm hmm."

"We can walk. There's a great diner just a block from here. Has peppermint ice cream and good coffee."

I lock the car.

"You said the magic words," Amanda jokes. "Ice cream."

Leo grins and looks at Amanda's belly. "Can you walk a block?"

"Sure." She gives a wan smile, but then laughs. "As long as they have a bathroom and ice cream, I can go anywhere."

Awkward seconds pass as we figure out how to align ourselves on the walk. Leo takes Amanda's left side and I move to the right. As time moves us forward, we say nothing, Leo slightly in the lead, guiding us to wherever he has in mind.

The seconds turn into a full minute that feels like an hour. I watch her father, his gait stiff and hunched. He's at least ten years younger than my dad, but seems like he's ten years older. Thin and wiry, he has the look of a guy who has been taught the hard way that reality doesn't bend to you.

The diner he's talking about is a total dive, an old Quonset hut that's seen better days.

Like, in the 1940s.

But there are outdoor tables with wide umbrellas providing shade, and a walk-up window that Leo leads us to. We get in line behind three other people. He points to the menu board.

"My treat," he says.

I nearly swallow my tongue.

Amanda cocks her head and stares at him like he's suddenly sprouted antennae and gills.

Leo reaches into the back pocket of his jeans. He unfolds a very used wallet that looks as soft as the inside of a dog's ear and mutters, "I started getting Social Security disability three months ago. My life's on track now. Living at the house for now," he adds, thumbing back toward the place where we met him. "But me and some guys are looking at a three-bedroom house to rent. Gary and George are vets, like me."

"Vets?" I ask politely, deciding on a coffee and a butterscotch dipped soft-serve cone. Haven't had one of those since...

Since my mother was alive.

"Served in 'Nam. Pulled a bad number. Got drafted in the very last wave. Turned eighteen, and two days later, I was on a goddamned ship."

"Navy?"

He nods. "Got me VA healthcare and some bad PTSD." He says it slowly, like he's still getting used to the idea, then looks to Amanda, who is studying the menu like it's childbirth class and she needs to be an A student.

I know she'll order a peppermint sundae with hot fudge and crushed Oreos, so the reason she's taking so long isn't a mystery.

She's stalling.

Listening.

Absorbing.

"Sounds harsh," I say to him.

Leo snorts and says in a broad coastal Massachusetts accent, like a lobster boat captain, "Harsh?" The word comes out with a long *ahhhhh*, like the R went into hiding. "Prison's harsh. PTSD got to me there. But I'm doing better now. Never going back to who I was." He takes the chance, touching Amanda's shoulder. "I promise, Mandy."

The people in front of us leave, fists full of ice cream cones and cups. My hand goes to Amanda's sacrum and her shoulders drop at my touch. She doesn't say anything to him at first, but as her lips part to speak, I jump in.

"Peppermint sundae with hot fudge and crushed Oreos," I say to the clerk on her behalf, which makes her laugh.

"How did you know?"

I kiss her temple. "Because I love you."

Leo's turn to study the menu board more carefully than he needs to.

We place our orders and I let Leo pay. Pride must be important to a guy like this. As we thank him, he beams but waves us off.

"It's the least I can do," he says as we move laterally to a large water cooler, pouring big cups of the free stuff, waiting for our ice cream and coffee.

No shit, I want to say, but don't, suddenly filled with a jumble of emotions that must be a tiny percentage of what my extremely pregnant wife is feeling.

This isn't about me.

First comes my cone, an enormous tower of soft serve covered with gold hardshell in a waffle cone, then a paper cup of coffee.

Amanda ordered the three-scoop sundae, but this place must be run by pregnant women because every scoop is the size of three.

There has to be a quart of ice cream in there.

Amanda is delighted.

Leo has a frappe the size of a grain silo and an orange soda.

Overloaded with drinks and ice cream, we make our way to an empty table near a large beech tree, shade at a premium. We sit. We use our mouths to eat.

It's a convenient excuse not to talk.

And for me to think.

The guy knows how wealthy I am. Saw my Tesla. He'd have to live under a rock not to know. He got out of prison a year ago; Anterdec security has been keeping tabs on him for me for a long time.

Why wait until now to make contact? Did he see Amanda somewhere, realize she's pregnant, and he's tugging her heart-strings?

A long time ago, Dad warned me that money brings the cockroaches out, ready to feast on whatever they can find. "The only way to get rid of a cockroach is to kill it, Andrew," he said. "Squash it. Make sure it doesn't dig in and breed."

If this guy is like that, though, he's playing it smooth.

The ice cream is surprisingly good, the butterscotch coating instantly transporting me back to childhood. A light breeze lifts Amanda's hair, and her tongue pokes out to lick a dab of hot fudge at the corner of her mouth. Leo says something to her and she laughs, her smile making my heart sink.

This guy has no idea what he's doing to her emotions.

And I'm the one who has to make sure the damage never happens.

With less enthusiasm, I eat more of the ice cream, using time as an advantage. After the cone, the coffee tastes more bitter than usual, but the order makes sense.

I need all traces of sweetness washed away for what I have to do next.

"Leo," I say, balling up my napkin and shoving it into the empty coffee cup, "why did you want to see Amanda?"

A guarded look kidnaps Amanda's face, like my words hold her hostage.

Damn.

"Uh, ah–I know it's been a long time. I said I was sorry, Mandy."

No one's corrected him on her name. Mandy was her childhood nickname. I'll let it slide if she's not saying anything.

"I heard you. I can tell you are."

A coldness washes over me, brain clicking into robot mode. Emotion has no place in me. This is a transaction. If he crosses the threshold for ending conversation, we're gone.

Otherwise, we're here, but conditionally.

"I don't..." His voice is thick, choked with emotion. "I don't know how to use words to make up for years, Mandy. All those years. I was a bad father. An absent father. You turned out so well. Your mother did real good by you." He wipes his eyes with the back of his hand, avoiding conflict.

If this is a performance, I give him points for faking earnestness.

Suddenly, he's looking at me, red-rimmed eyes unembarrassed. "And you. Your secretary sent me the letter. I know what you're doing."

Amanda stiffens.

"Any good man would do it, protect Mandy from someone like me. I got no right to ask for your time like this, but you're here and so am I. I'm making amends. You know what that is?" Narrowed eyes meet mine.

"You're in AA?"

"Recovery. Yeah. Working the program." He reaches into his front pocket and pulls out a shiny round object, thrusting it at Amanda. "That's my two-year chip."

"Two years?" she says with marvel.

"Been more like ten now, in fits and starts, but two years is the longest I've gone in one stretch. Took me this long, and getting settled after getting out, to finally dig up the courage to ask to see you." Leo's eyes cut to me. "Hey. What's wrong?"

"I have to ask, Leo – how do you get alcohol in prison?"

He's taken off-guard by the question, but a sheepish laugh comes next. "Man, until you're inside, you'd never know. Toilet wine. Pruno."

"Toilet wine?" Amanda asks, making a face.

Waving off the question, he scratches his nose and lets out a long sigh. "You just need sugar and something that ferments, like a moldy piece of bread. Some fruit. A bag to put it in and store it. People use toilet tanks sometimes to store it all in a plastic bag."

"Or people smuggle it in for you," I add, thinking it through. Leo gives me a fingershoot that says I'm right.

"Oh." Amanda's little gasp kills me.

Then she does it again, face filled with astonishment, hand going to her lower ribs on the right. "Oh, goodness, Righty!"

"Righty?"

She laughs. "We don't have names for the babies yet, so we call them Lefty and Righty."

Leo shakes his head. "I knew a Lefty in prison. That's no name for a kid. He could dislocate his own shoulder, elbow, and wrist to get out of handcuffs, but only on the left."

"They'll have names soon," I declare. Leo's staring at Amanda's belly like it's a nature show on the National Geographic channel.

"They're your grandchildren," Amanda says softly. He looks at her, frozen. "Do you have others?" she asks.

"Others? Where would I have others?"

One shoulder goes up as she clearly tries to find a way to ask something. "I–Mom never told me much about you. Were you ever married to anyone else? Did you have other kids?"

"God, no, Mandy. You're it. My only kid."

"Oh." Relief fills that single syllable.

"Grandkids. Two at once. Who ever imagined old Leo would have grandkids?" He seems overwhelmed by the idea.

So much that's unsaid fills the air, choking me.

"Why are you in Nashua, Dad?"

Her use of the word *Dad* almost makes me jolt, but I hold it in. I'm very accustomed to restraining emotional reactions. My guard goes down when I'm with Amanda, but Leo isn't her.

And *Dad* isn't a word I've heard her say directly to any man.

Ever, until today.

A shaky smile dissolves and he nods slowly. "I had some choices. Guys like me don't get many, so when we do, it's scary. I came to this place." He nods in the direction of the halfway house. "It's close to home."

I assume by home, he means Boston.

But I'm pretty sure he also means my wife.

"And me," she says, courage coming forth.

"Yes, Mandy. And you."

"Do you..." Her voice breaks. My heart goes along with it. "Do you think we'll just suddenly have a relationship, Dad? I tried. I tried to come to the prison to see you and you refused."

An *oh, shit* look takes over his entire being. I sit up taller, leaning toward Amanda.

Not that she needs my strength. She has plenty of her own.

Leo's eyes close, his throat spasms with a thick swallow, and his nostrils flare as he inhales. The non-stop nodding is a tic, maybe learned in prison, a stalling technique for time.

The guy isn't rushing to give an answer.

And we have all the time in the world.

When he finally opens his eyes, decades of pain shine in them.

"I couldn't face you, Mandy. I was so ashamed. Didn't know how to be a dad in prison. It was easier to pretend you didn't exist than to face up to what I'd done and be human. I'm so sorry. I should have done more. I understand if you want to pretend not to have a dad."

"I don't... I..." Amanda stammers.

Leo stands, hands flat on the table, head down, shoulders curled in. It's a stance of pain, of a wounded warrior struggling to re-center.

"I'll leave you. Grateful you came at all, Mandy. And those babies are so lucky to have a mom like you."

"Dad, wait." Amanda touches the back of his hand. "This isn't all or nothing."

He flinches, then lets out an enormous sigh. He was holding his breath.

"You sound like the therapists in group. Is that what you do for a living?" he asks with a tender smile.

"I run the market research department at Andrew's company."

"Yeah?" Grateful for a less fraught topic, he looks at me. "What's your company do?"

I just blink.

"I'm the head of Anterdec."

Zero recognition.

"What do you guys do?"

I play it safe. "Real estate."

"Gotcha." Uncertainty makes his eyes shifty, until finally he looks at Amanda and says, "I don't know what to do next."

Her hand flies to her throat, nervous and flittery. "Oh, Dad. I think you're doing it."

"But I'm not doing anything."

"You're here. That's more than you've done in decades."

"Jesus, Mandy. I owe Pam one hell of a life debt. She raised you right."

And then Leo's shoulders begin to shake, all pretense of holding it together draining away. His butt plunks down on his seat, the umbrella tilting slightly from the force. Head down, the bill of his hat covering his eyes, he rests weathered elbows on his knees and cradles his face. I'm sure he's crying.

Guys like this don't sob in public. I'm embarrassed for him.

Admire him a little, too.

The guy I thought I had to protect my wife from turns out to be more complex than I ever expected.

Maybe I'm the one who needs some lessons in all-or-nothing thinking.

Amanda's crying now, and gives me a look that says, *What do I do now?*

I shrug. I squeeze her hand. I look at Leo.

How the hell do I know?

Abruptly, he wipes his eyes with the backs of his hands and stands, red-rimmed irises the color of Amanda's own staring at her.

"Look, Mandy, I–I gotta go. Not to be rude or anything. I'm–I'm breaking patterns, you see? And right now, this is me making amends. Sorta. But I have to confess, I want a drink right now, real bad. Awful bad. And when I get like this, I have to go call my sponsor and talk it out. Do the work. So I need to leave. Not because I don't–I don't..." His voice cracks. "Not because I don't care, but because I do. I need to change, Mandy."

"You have changed, Dad." She stands and waddles over to him, taking his hand. He jerks, eyes going down to where their skin meets. "And I understand. This isn't the last time we'll see each other."

"It's not?"

"Of course not." She holds her arms out. "Can I have a hug?"

Leo pulls her in, hard. He whispers something I can't hear.

"Yes. Of course," she says.

And then he lets her go and offers me his hand. I shake it.

And Leo Warrick turns abruptly on one heel, walking like a man with ghosts chasing him.

We walk slowly back to the car and climb in. Amanda lets out a huge sigh of relief, but her hands are on her knees, forearms pressing against her belly, head down, eyes wide.

"He didn't ask for money," I comment as I turn on the car and the air conditioning kicks in. Amanda's turned toward the halfway house, staring at it.

"What?"

"I thought he would."

She tilts her head. "I can see why. But he didn't. All he asked for was a chance to see the babies after they're born."

"All," I murmur.

Her voice is shaking now. I reach for her hand, the fragile shell of my wife needing me.

"He spent all those years not seeing me. And now all he wants is..."

All that my wife can do now is cry. And all that I can do is hold her.

Because all I can do is this:

I can give her my all.

CHAPTER 20

Amanda

I'm drinking my one and only daily breve when my back starts aching like crazy.

And for someone carrying fifty-eight pounds of extra weight around, back pain has to be *bad* to be worse than baseline.

"Ohhh," I say, the little pity sigh leaking out, then turning into a longer, lower, deeper groan. Andrew's head pops up from the report he's reading on the couch, lounging in sweat pants and no shirt. I've told him his new reading glasses give him a hot-geek look, and he thinks that's silly, but I find it incredibly arousing.

But not now.

"What's wrong?"

"I'm fine," I start to say, but as I lean forward to start the arduous process of getting up out of a soft chair, all I can say is, "Fi–"

Followed by another "Ohhh."

The frown he gives me makes his glasses slide slightly down his nose. He takes them off, stands, and offers me his hands to help me up. As I stretch, I roll my pelvis forward and realize I can't.

I can't move.

"My back," I gasp.

"The doctor said this might happen. Back labor can be the start."

"But I'm not supposed to labor at all! The c-section is scheduled for Thursday!"

"Maybe the boys decided Sunday is a better day to be born."

"They need to listen to their mother!"

"They are. Just not the right mother. Mother Nature has entered the game and she has a different mission."

I walk slowly to the kitchen, Andrew right behind me. I'm reaching for a water bottle when my hips turn into wrenches. Bones grind against each other as the contraction pulls on my swollen midsection with a fierceness that is nothing like the contractions that hit me nine weeks ago. I grip the edge of the counter.

All the air in the world is sucked away, my body unable to so much as blink.

And then I'm wet.

Andrew looks down at the ground, eyes widening. "That's–you're–your water broke!"

"I have to call Shannon," I gasp as the grip on my womb lessens. I'm wearing light socks, now soaking wet around my ankles.

Giddy laughter chokes my throat.

"It's time," I tell him, the look we share too poignant to describe. Then he starts texting as I pick up my phone and hit Shannon's number.

This is really happening.

"Hey," she says, sounding bored. "Did you know that there is an actual, quantifiable number of times you can tolerate picking dropped cups off the floor from a toddler who's discovering object permanence? It's 238, for the record."

"My water just broke."

"*What?*"

"My water just broke. I'm in labor."

"You can't be! You're having a scheduled c-section."

"Well, tell that to the twins, because they have other ideas."

"Oh my GOD! DECLAN!" she screams. "Don't leave yet! You have to stay home with Ellie till I can get a sitter here!"

"WHY?" he bellows back.

"AMANDA'S IN LABOR!"

She sounds like her mom.

"LABOR?" I hear him boom.

"I'll meet you at the hospital!" she gushes. "Maybe you'll have a vaginal birth after all!"

"Maybe?" I've become so resigned to the idea of the c-section that her comment makes adrenaline spike through me.

Or maybe I'm just dehydrated. The floor looks like Walden Pond right now.

Andrew's phone rings.

"What?" he snaps.

Declan's voice comes through, though I can't hear the words. A great whoosh of fluid pours out of me, and I freeze.

Cord prolapse. Cords and amniotic fluid. Random portions of childbirth class start flooding into my brain.

"We really need to go now," I urge.

"José's pulling the car around. He already covered the backseat with plastic."

"He did?"

"Last week. Just in case."

"Wow. That's... thorough."

"Suzanne's right behind you, so Gerald told José and it was on his mind."

José's knock on the door makes us both look. The bag has been sitting by the door, ready just in case, but I never thought we'd reach *in case*.

Once we scheduled the c-section for Thursday, I thought that was it.

Thought we had four more days.

Shakes take over my body as I stand there. Andrew hands me a stack of kitchen towels and I hold them, staring dumbly.

"For between your legs," he says.

"I'm going to gush the entire time and have to be in public like this?"

"Is it any worse than having your breasts exposed at a wedding and falling into a pool to rescue a dog?" he quips.

"I guess we're about to find out."

José takes in the scene as he comes into the kitchen, eyebrows shooting up as he watches me waddle/drip.

Waddle/drip.

Waddle–

"Stop!" he says firmly, running upstairs, emerging within seconds as Andrew thumbs toward the front door, my bag in hand. As my husband disappears, José rushes down the stairs, a bedsheet and stack of towels in hand.

He thrusts one big bath towel into my hands. "Here. Put it

between your legs." Then he takes the sheet and twists it, as if he's going to tie it to a joist and escape out a window. He places it on the floor between my legs.

Andrew returns and halts dead in his tracks. "José? What are you doing?"

"Andrew. Take that end." He points behind me. "Amanda, hold the towel up between your thighs. All the way up." One end of the sheet in his hand, he juts his chin at Andrew. "We're making a toga."

"A toga?" Andrew asks incredulously. "What are you talking about?"

"It's genius!" I gasp. José's fixing my problem.

"How did you know what to do?" I ask.

Kind, dark eyes meet mine. "My sister had a baby six months ago. And Gerald warned me."

Within ten seconds, I have the ends of the sheet tied over one shoulder, the thick towel absorbing my amniotic fluid, and we slowly make our way to the car. Halfway down the porch stairs, my back starts to crack my hips in half.

Andrew pulls out his phone, presses on the glass, and suddenly, "Love Will Find a Way" by Yes starts playing. I close my eyes, breathe slowly, and let my mind take me to a quieter place, turning inward until the pressure eases.

We climb in the back of the car, my ass jutting up because of the weird toga-diaper thing I've got going on, but at least I'm not in pain.

"My sister says that hypnosis stuff doesn't work," I hear José mutter to Andrew.

I don't say a word, my hands on my belly, doing an inventory of the boys. Lefty eases to the right just enough to confirm he's fine, but Righty is being awfully quiet. I can't find his head, the location different now.

Maybe he's not transverse anymore.

Maybe I don't need the surgical birth.

Instantly, panic fills me. I didn't think I had a choice. But the idea of possibly being able to deliver vaginally fills me with diffuse terror.

"What's wrong?" Andrew whispers, hand on my knee. I can tell he doesn't know what to do with himself as José navigates the car quickly on the back roads, hitting the entrance to the Pike with a professional precision that infuses me with gratitude.

"I'm not sure I want a vaginal delivery."

"Why would you have one?"

"Righty's head isn't where it was last night. Maybe we can do both twins vaginally after all. I spent a lot of emotional energy accepting a c-section, and now..." I make a helpless sound, hearing it echo in my ears, down my throat, nestling under my heart like a cold, scared mouse.

"Here." He hands me a stainless steel water bottle and I take a sip. It's honey ginger water, with a touch of lemon. Ice cold, too.

"You made this for me?"

"I've had a few in the fridge, ready for this. You said you didn't want to puke orange Gatorade all over the place and never be able to touch it again, so I followed Hope's electrolyte solution."

The concoction is perfect, like drinking in Andrew's love.

And not the kind with a high protein count.

I sit up slowly, back muscles pulling in toward my spine, my hips cranking in as if someone's turning a gear. The tightness makes it hard to breathe, the band of pressure pulling my pubic bone up, down, in, out, everywhere at once. The deep, searing stretch and contraction is something I have to ride through.

We hit a pothole and I feel like my nerves turn into fireworks.

"Andrew," I gasp, losing control. "I can't. I can't I can't I can't–"

Strong hands go immediately to my hips. He twists his torso to accommodate me, eyes within inches of mine, laser focused and intent.

"Breathe," he says, counting a long inhale. "Expand your belly as you inhale."

"I can't!"

"You are."

The confidence in his deep baritone unlatches some of the stubborn muscle fibers encasing the babies and I feel a lurch, a softening, a smidgen of relief as I exhale, then push through the tightness for another long, slow inhale.

"You are. You are. You are," he says, low and slow, the words turning into a vibration that takes my fear to a place where it can flitter and fret but doesn't get in the way of the rescue I need.

And then the pain recedes, slowly replaced with a brisk tingling that saps all my energy.

"Seven minutes away," José announces as Andrew lets go of my hips, unclicks his seat belt, and positions himself better in front of me.

"That's not safe if we get in an accident."

"José's good and I need to be able to get to your hips better."

"I'm fine, Andrew. The contractions aren't that close."

"That was four minutes, and it lasted almost a minute."

Pregnancy math happens fast in my head. "Uh...."

"Drink," he orders. As I tip the bottle up and take my first swallow, the twinge at my back grows again.

"Oh," I gasp.

He takes the heels of his hands, finds the spots on my hips where Hope taught the partners to push in case of back labor, and works with precision to do whatever it takes to make the contraction easier for me. This one fades faster.

This one feels like a giant red alert.

"That was four minutes," he says calmly. "Hydrate. Breathe. We're doing fine."

Bzzzzzz

My phone.

I'm here at the hospital, Shannon texts. *What entrance are you coming in? I'll meet you there.*

Bzzzzzz

Hi Amanda. This is Alex Derjian. I'm the doctor on call this weekend. I'll meet you at the hospital.

"Oh, no!" I groan.

"What's wrong?"

"I can't believe this!"

"You're giving birth?"

"No. Not that. The doctor is the one doctor in the practice who I haven't met. Alex Derjian."

"Why is that name so familiar?"

"Isn't he the guy who coached Declan on how to catch the baby when Shannon went into labor in the elevator?"

"Dec is going to rib me for copying him."

"It wasn't like we planned this! Dr. Rohrlian was supposed to do the c-section on Thursday!"

José pulls the car up to the ER entrance. I see Shannon there, hair in a ponytail, a backpack slung over one shoulder.

She lights up when she sees us.

My heart hugs her from a distance.

Having a bestie is the best in a crisis.

Especially a BFF who's already been through childbirth, even if it was in a broken elevator and involved turning her vajayjay into a possible Pulitzer Prize opportunity for the right photographer.

Rushing the SUV, she opens my door and offers a hand. I'm mid-step when my lower belly tightens and it feels like someone's stabbing my cervix from the inside out.

I freeze.

I can't move.

Behind me, I feel Andrew's arms lock in place, his body rigid to support mine. Shannon puts her hand on my hip. I groan.

"Contraction?" she asks.

"Uh," is all that comes out of me.

Suspended in midair, I can't even move the few inches to set my foot on the ground, the sensation of being a thousand pieces of glass held together by a spiderweb too much. One millimeter and I'm in bone-grinding pain.

So I wait between two realities, car and ground, until enough time passes and I can let gravity continue to do its job.

"Wow," Shannon finally says, fishing around in her backpack. "Let's get you inside. That was a full minute long. How far apart are they?"

"Two to four minutes."

Time changes, as if someone snaps their fingers and I experience everything in extended time. The pain itself doesn't intensify, but it elongates, stretched out and settling in.

The check in. The nurse pointing. Andrew's hand on my back. Shannon's worried face. It's all there, but as backdrop for my own heart beat. The brush of the ball of my foot against linoleum. My refusal to ride in a wheelchair. The pressure of my cervix expanding.

The march of inevitability.

We're in an exam room when a long, low contraction hits, hard and grinding. Shannon sees it before Andrew does and moves my hands to the wall, palms flat, pressure suddenly on my sacrum. Andrew's hands go to my hips, but the sweet relief from his strength isn't enough to combat nature.

These babies are coming.

But everything I see and hear, aside from pain, is so slow. So full. Gravity works on my body but my mind floats. Mouths move, words come out of people with eyes on mine, machines are deployed, measurements are charted.

None of it makes sense.

Andrew speaks for me, with me, translating.

"Transverse," I hear.

Still transverse.

"C-section," he says, bending down, looking up at me with love and a kind of deep, aching empathy that makes my lungs fill with as much of his air as I can.

"Okay," I reply.

Because it is.

And it will be.

A water bottle with a straw is thrust before me and I sip, grateful. Nurses come and go, then a man bigger than Andrew comes in.

No small feat, that.

He's in scrubs, with the matching green cap on his head, and carries himself with an affable competence that makes me want to be held by him. Tall and broad, he has the body of an athlete, the groundedness of a guy you want to spend time with. Friendly eyes take me in as he thrusts his hand to me, then jerks when he sees Shannon.

"*Shannon?*"

"Dr. Derjian?"

I'm shaking his strong hand as he turns to her, but he corrects himself, eyes on mine. "Amanda. I'm Alex Derjian. And very shortly, you get to meet your sons."

"I–"

The contraction steals my breath.

The doctor leaves, Andrew in slo-mo as he moves the water bottle and turns his arms into a vise again, Shannon's body heat to my right. The only awareness I have of anything is concentrated entirely between my hipbones.

It's the center of the universe. Right there.

In me.

"You'll be fine," Shannon whispers in my ear, rubbing the lacrosse ball as hard as she can, digging it deep into the small of my back as the contraction fades. "The anesthesiologist is on his way before they prep you for surgery."

"I can't believe this is happening."

"I know."

"Amanda? Andrew?" Dr. Derjian walks back in, calm and cool, tall and big and warm and–I hope–a skilled surgeon. "We're ready." He gives Shannon a direct look, but somehow it's caring, too. "Only one support person can be in the OR."

"Andrew, of course," she says, sparing me from having to say it.

He walks over to her, kisses her on the cheek, and says, "Thank you."

Tears well up in my best friend's eyes. "No. Thank you." She squeezes his shoulders. "Take care of her." Looking at the doctor, her eyes narrow, mouth set firm. "And you most of all. I hope you're as good in surgery as you were coaching my husband to catch my baby in an elevator."

"I'm even better with a scalpel and a plan," he says with assurance, eyes cutting to Andrew, then me. "It's time."

"Can you call my Mom?" I call out to Shannon, who waves near the electric doors.

"Pam's on her way. Already texted her. I texted my mom, too."

"You invited Marie to come?" I gasp, horrified.

"Invited? God, no. I texted her a warning not to come." Shannon gives me a careful hug. "Next time I see you, you'll have my twin nephews in your arms. You get to meet your children!"

We both burst into tears, a quick hug necessary.

And I'm wheeled away, going through double doors that feel like a birth canal.

CHAPTER 21

Andrew

For most men, watching your children being born involves staring between your partner's legs.

For me? It means trying very hard *not* to stare at a screen displaying her organs, spread out before her like an advanced biology lab project.

It's not that I'm squeamish. I actually love science, but that's my wife's large intestine on the other side of that screen. If I'm going to be intimately acquainted with a body part of hers, that's not at the top of my list.

"We're dealing with adhesions," I hear Dr. Derjian say to someone else in scrubs, then complex language about organs. It's tempting to sit just a little taller on this metal stool and peek over the drape they use as a curtain.

Too tempting.

Declan never had to go through this equivalent of the marshmallow test. He may have delivered his child in a broken elevator, but my two children are being cut out of their mother while I keep her company and try not to look at the string of slimy balloon animals that are her intestines.

Hah. Beat *that*, bro.

"Adhesions?" I ask.

"Nothing's wrong," he says smoothly. "Sometimes women have tissue, a little scar tissue, that makes this a little more complicated." He flashes Amanda and me a confident smile. "I've seen it before. Just means we'll be here for a little longer."

Amanda made me watch enough videos of c-sections that I understand the basics of what he's doing. Now the placenta needs to be removed. Each baby has a team, and beyond the surgical table I see the babies being lifted up, rubbed with towels, weighed and talked to, thin little cries whinnying out of them.

In duplicate.

"I need to see them again," she whispers to me, as if wanting that isn't okay.

"Give us five seconds," Dr. Derjian says, pausing with his hands to give Amanda a compassionate look. "I promise."

"Remember that article I told you about, the maternal assisted c-section?" Amanda says to me.

"The one where the midwife asked the OB to let the mom pull the baby out herself?" Dr. Derjian asks calmly. He moves with coordinated grace, but I can't bring myself to look over the drape.

"Yes!" Amanda replies.

He pauses. "Are you asking to do that? Because the babies are already on the–"

"HELL, NO!"

He chuckles. "Try not to use your abdominal muscles like that. Message received."

"At least she got to hold her baby," Amanda grouses. Her head is obviously connected to the rest of her, but she feels disembodied, detached. Her lower half is cut open and she's chatting away up here as if blood and organs weren't being rearranged like a game of Three-card Monte a few feet away.

"Dad! Want to cut the cords?" someone calls out. I stroke Amanda's hair and smile.

She looks at me, eyes slowly shining as they fill with tears. "Don't you want to?"

"Want to what?"

"Cut the umbilical cords?"

"What? That wasn't me they were asking."

"Of course it was," Dr. Derjian says, happy eyes meeting mine over our surgical masks. "They said Dad. That's you."

Amanda nods me on. "Go help them."

"William," one of the nurses says, and I realize that's my child.

My child. I have two, both squeaking and crying, sounding like billy goats with muzzles. On legs made of helium and concrete, I move to the staging area where William is screaming, eyes shut tight, arms out, naked and new to the world, the umbilical cord bulging and clamped with two clamps, a two-inch spot centered.

I'm handed a pair of scissors.

And I perform the ritual. I'm surprised by the feel of cutting it, how much effort it takes.

The nurse takes him and rubs him with a blanket, then wraps him like a burrito, another nurse moving me to Charlie, who could not be more different from his brother.

Brother. Amanda and I made brothers.

Charlie is calm, almost preternaturally so, staring up at me with dark eyes that take in everything.

As I reach for the scissors, eyes on him, his hand brushes mine, clinging to my glove-covered pinky.

"*Shhhh*, Charlie. *Shhhhh*."

"Daddy's here," one of the nurses says.

I've spent the entire labor and birth carefully restraining my inner turmoil, emotions there but pushed off to the side, in a sector with firm boundaries. Saying my son's name, giving him comfort, having him reach out to me like this–it's permission.

Permission to feel.

Tears don't come naturally to McCormick men. We're taught from a young age not to show emotion. The tacit message is: Don't express.

Even better?

Don't feel at all.

I'm breaking that cycle right now, letting the tears come, feeling them roll down my cheeks, tears of joy and gratitude, of connection and transition. I'm no longer the keeper of my genes, roaming the Earth as a self-contained entity, my heart lent to Amanda but not passed on to another generation.

But now? We've created one.

A new generation who won't just carry on the McCormick name, the McCormick genes, the McCormick business.

They'll break patterns that need to be shattered, and forge new ones.

Starting now.

I clip Charlie's cord, his eyes on mine for a few seconds before they slowly close, then open again, a nurse holding the clamps steady so I can do it one-handed. Then he's rubbed with the towel and burrito-wrapped.

Both of my sons are placed in my arms, Will still crying, Charlie quietly observing.

And I bring them to Amanda.

Hearts, as organs, have finite capacity.

As instruments of love, they're capable of holding infinite space.

All four of us fit inside my heart, tucked away in a small, quaint space where we're protected from the rest of the world, living in joy and happiness, our little family all I need.

Amanda can't move her hands, so I brush the boys' cheeks against her, tears streaming down her face as we look at each other. My eyes are connected to my heart, too.

"Thank you," I choke out. "You did it."

"Did what?"

"You won."

CHAPTER 22

Amanda

I t's a good thing women have two breasts and I didn't have triplets.

And it's even better that the hospital has plenty of breast-feeding pillows to prop up the babies, because avoiding the c-section wound is a full-time job.

Andrew is sitting next to me in a chair, holding Will, who just fed and is sound asleep, swollen eyes showing tiny spikes of lashes. Charlie's still attached like a vacuum cleaner, and I peel my tongue off the roof of my mouth.

Everything is a haze.

"What do you need?" Andrew asks in a voice just above silence, his tone so reverential.

"Water."

Moving his knees carefully, Andrew lifts up, the ripple of thigh muscle under his workout pants something I admire.

Not sexually. Because that layer of hormones is just not present. If I'm sticking something between my thighs right now, it will involve multiple absorbent layers.

Visually, though, he's fun to watch.

Especially when he's holding Will.

"Here," he says, handing me a stainless steel bottle. "It's the electrolyte solution. Hasn't been opened before."

I drink greedily, to the point where it overflows the corner of my mouth, a drop landing on Charlie's head.

"Wow. What else do you need?" he asks.

"Food."

Gingerly, he moves across the room, Will in his arms, and I can't stop watching. My husband is holding my baby. Our baby. A baby who was inside my body until a few hours ago.

A baby who is finally here.

We're parents.

I'm a mom.

"I made sure to bring these," he says, setting a ziplock bag full of Cheeto marshmallow treats on the tray in front of me, using one hand to awkwardly open the bag.

My laughter wakes Charlie up. It hurts, too, my ab muscles completely sliced open.

"Ow. Don't make me laugh," I groan.

Tap tap tap

My mom's face comes into view, her eyes filled with tears, right arm cradling a huge fresh fruit and chocolate basket with two little teddy bears in it.

"Oh!" is all she says as she walks into the room, puts the basket on the small, circular table by a chair, and comes to me, her hug tentative, her tears wetting my shoulder. She's curled away from me so the baby doesn't get hurt, and as she pulls back, she looks down, hand going to Charlie's head but halting just before touching, hovering.

"He's–you're–oh, my little Mandy is a mommy."

And now I'm crying all over my poor baby.

"Say hello to your grandsons, Pam. This is Will," Andrew says, pivoting closer so she can touch his head, too. "William Warrick McCormick."

"And I'm feeding Charlie. Charles Warrick McCormick."

"Such big–names–" she's sobbing, "–for such little boys!" Mom puts her hand on Andrew's shoulder and stares at Will. "May I?"

"Of course."

Careful and methodical, my mom walks into the bathroom, the sound of the faucet making it clear she's washing her hands before touching the babies.

It occurs to me that this is part of the delicate work of protecting brand new humans. Mom does it instinctively.

I need to remember this ritual. This request.

This demand when someone wants to hold the new life I created.

The transfer from my husband to my mother is a visual transition, a moving through time that can't be done any other way, one generation handing the new one off to the old. Her smile is incredible, decades peeling off as I see–right here, right now–what my mom must have looked like the day she first held me.

The day she became a mother.

"Grandma?" I say aloud, the question only hitting me now. "Do we call you Grandma? Grammy? Something else? We always called your mom Grandma."

"That sounds good to me. I'm not fussy. Call me Grandma, Will. I'm so, so happy to finally meet you."

Charlie pops off at that exact moment. He hasn't gotten much from me, because colostrum is all I have, but I'm following the lactation consultant's instructions. I make eye contact with Andrew and he comes over, lifts Charlie from me, and gives him to Mom.

She's full up in the grandchild department.

"Good thing we have two arms," Mom jokes, the comment not particularly funny, but so joyful. I grab my phone and start taking photos, texting them to Mom's number so she'll have them to show off.

Show off.

My babies aren't just mine anymore. Not just ours. They're out in the world now.

"William and Charles. Like the royal family?"

Mom's question makes Andrew and me freeze.

"Huh?" I ask, perplexed.

"You know. Prince Charles. Prince William. Did you pick those names on purpose?"

"God, no," Andrew says, alarmed. "We wanted to give them old-fashioned, traditional names and..."

"Oh, no," I groan. "We didn't connect the two! We're never going to hear the end of this!"

"I'm sure no one will notice," Mom says nervously. "I'm a pattern-matcher. Most people aren't." Mom's phone buzzes in her purse. A weird, guilty look washes over her.

"What's wrong?"

"That might be Marie."

"Marie?"

"She's here."

"*Here?*"

"With Shannon. And Carol."

"They're *here?*"

"Mmm hmm. Down the hall." Mom's shifty eyes make it clear she's been holding them at bay.

Andrew puffs up, hands on his hips. A protective streak that was already strong is gaining power like a Cat 1 storm over warm waters off the Gulf Coast. "We're not dealing with a crowd right now."

"Tell that to Marie." Mom's eyes don't move from the babies.

"I'm fine with it," I say, "but only when Mom's done hogging the babies." I adjust my bra and top, and reach for the giant water bottle Andrew got me. It has a built-in ice section and a huge, easy-to-bend straw.

"Marie will have to wait a year, then," Mom murmurs. "Oh my goodness, Will looks just like Andrew, but he has your nose, Amanda."

She's back to my full name. Emotions are under control.

"They're identical, Pam," Andrew says softly.

"How do you know the difference?" she asks, eyes immediately going to his feet, which are wrapped in the blanket. "I assume they tag the babies with ankle bracelets?"

"They do. And Will's hat has a green stripe on it. Charlie is blue."

"Ah," Mom says, her low-grade OCD satisfied. Her shoulders relax. "Then I won't confuse them."

I sip, swallow, then add, "So far, the only way I can tell the difference is Charlie is a lazy sucker."

That makes Andrew chuckle. "Don't say the word 'lazy' around Dad," he cracks. "Nothing about his grandsons can be lazy."

Mom looks at Andrew and asks, "Has James seen them yet?"

"No. Dad said he'd wait until we're home."

"Then I'm your first grandparent to meet you," she says to Will.

A shadow crosses Andrew's face.

Mine, too, I'm sure, but for a different reason. He's mourning the loss of his mom in a whole new way.

I'm thinking about my dad, which is a different kind of loss.

Bzzzz

Andrew looks over at his jacket, which is buzzing. "Hang on," he says, looking at his phone's screen. "It's Gina."

"Gina? I thought you weren't working!"

"I'm not. She says Marie has texted her eighteen times and wants help getting in here to see the babies." He taps quickly on the screen. "Marie's offering free Unicoga classes for life and to tell her all of Marie's secret Yankee Swap shopping locations."

Mom and I share a shocked look.

"Hmmm. Might be worth letting her in if she'll spill the tea on her Yankee Swap magic," I mutter to myself as Mom grins.

"Hmmph," Andrew grumps as he thumbs his way through a text.

"What're you telling her?"

"I'd rather not repeat it in front of my children."

His phone buzzes again. He looks, and smiles.

"This time it's Shannon. She says she's got Marie under control. Threatened to tell my brother all about Marie's secret thrift shop for that thing you just said. A yankee swap?" Bewildered, he looks to me, then Mom, for help in understanding what Shannon means.

"Oooooooo," Mom and I intone in unison.

"Shannon went there," I mutter.

"I still don't understand," Andrew asks with a smile, "but I'm assuming that means we have privacy?"

Bzzzzz

"Mom is offering to go on a coffee run for everyone while we wait," Andrew reads from his phone. *"What do you guys want? From Grind It Fresh! of course."* He looks at his phone with admiration. "Shannon has figured out her mother, hasn't she?"

"Only took her thirty years," I say with a laugh.

"Who wouldn't be impatient to meet these two?" Mom's voice is gooey sweet as she stares at the babies. The problem with holding twins at the same time is that you don't have a free hand.

Will begins to fuss.

"Here," I say, waving toward Andrew, my other hand going to my gown. "I'll nurse him. Mom can have Charlie to herself." Their handoff is awkward but the goal is finally achieved.

Will's in my arms, little lips rooting. He attaches, but it takes a few tries.

Bzzzz

Andrew's head rears back as he reads his phone. "It's Jason."

"Jason? Jason *Jacoby*?"

"Yes."

"Since when does Shannon's dad text you?"

"Hardly ever."

"What's he saying?"

"I'm holding her back, but even I have limits."

A giggle emerges from Mom. "Marie is a force of nature."

"Marie is a pain in the ass," Andrew corrects her.

"Marie is about twenty minutes away," says a warm male voice from the door. We all turn to find Jason standing there in a polo shirt with a boys' baseball team logo on it, holding a box of chocolates and wearing a grin. "I came to warn you."

"She'll have coffee, though!" pipes up Shannon, who moves past her dad to my bed as if I'm iron and she's a magnet. "Sorry we're crashing!"

"No, you aren't," Andrew murmurs, but he smiles, like me.

"Once Mom arrives, I'll never get to hold the baby."

"Babies," Andrew corrects her. "Everyone gets a turn because we have *two*," he adds loudly as Declan walks in.

An immediate scowl covers his brother's face.

"You are never going to stop bragging about that, are you?"

"No. Only way to beat me is triplets."

Jason crosses the room, gives me a kiss on the cheek, and opens the chocolates with a flourish. "Marie had these handmade for you by a chocolate shop in Agnes' town. Said you'd appreciate them."

Large clusters of chocolate-covered Cheetos, a dozen of them, rest in a plastic tray inside the gold box.

"Oh, my!" Mom exclaims, looking skeptical. "I know you love your salty-sweet Cheeto treats, but this is going a bit far. What are those?"

"Maple Cheeto creams," Shannon explains, pushing the box toward me. "Try one!"

"That's disgusting," Declan opines.

"It's testing really well with the fourteen-to-twenty crowd."

"Testing?" he chokes out. "You're running market tests on that as a product for our stores?"

"No! Even better. As a coffee flavor."

Jason, Mom, and Andrew start gagging.

I high-five Shannon over Will's little head.

"Can we talk about your babies?" Shannon asks.

"Please. Anything but Cheeto maple abominations," Andrew says as he gives her a hug. "Hug me while I have two free arms."

"That'll be a rare moment for the next year. I'll take you up on it," Shannon whispers in his ear as they embrace. "Congratulations."

Declan crashes their hug, the three of them in a big, happy tangle of limbs.

"Congrats, bro. Now introduce me to my nephews."

Will unlatches and fusses, sudden low-grade warmth in his diaper an obvious hint at his distress.

"Perfect timing," I say to Declan as he reaches for Will, averting his eyes as my gown slips. Once the baby's in his arms I pull the blanket up and smile.

"Why?" Declan waits two seconds, then laughs. "Got it. Someone needs a change."

If you had told me five years ago that the suave billionaire dating my klutzy best friend would one day hold my son in his arms and matter-of-factly change his diaper when needed, I'd have said you were as crazy as Meghan the mystery shopper. She's the one who called in sick six years ago, leaving Shannon to cover all her bagel-shop visits.

On that fateful day, she met Declan in the men's room of one of the Anterdec-owned fast-food restaurants. Yes, the men's room.

And now he's my brother-in-law, my sons are his nephews, and my children are my best friend's daughter's cousins.

Life doesn't get any more perfect than this.

For the next fifteen minutes, we play pass the babies, and I sample the special chocolates, loving Marie from afar for finding such a personal treat for me. My sons are attention magnets, as we revel in the joy of new life.

I yawn.

As if my yawn summoned a caffeine genie, Marie appears, holding two full trays of coffees, her eyes eager and her hands clearly itching to get a baby in them.

The trays go on the table that rolls over my bed and she glares at Jason and Shannon.

"You could have come and helped me!"

"We were busy," Jason says to Will, who is in his arms.

"Busy hogging the babies! Give him to me. What's his name? Oh, hi, Amanda."

"Get used to that one," Shannon grouses. "We spend nine months building them, go through pain to produce them, and then they're born and we're just wallpaper to the grandparents."

"Did you say something, dear?" Marie replies as Jason hands off Will to a rapt Marie.

"See?" Shannon throws her hands in the air, then examines the coffees. She pulls one with her name on the lid out of the tray, then finds mine and hands it to me.

I sip the breve carefully to check the temp before giving my bloodstream a healthy infusion of caffeine.

Andrew's cocked eyebrow says he's not sure about my coffee.

"One is fine," I insist.

"It gets in the breast milk."

"Now you're the caffeine police?"

He kisses my cheek. Jason gives him a look of approval, then comes to me, arms open.

A Dad hug is exactly what I need right now, especially as Jason whispers, "Can I consider them my adopted grandkids? Because I know they have James as a grandfather, but what kid couldn't use more?"

Maybe I was wrong.

Maybe Marie and Jason do consider me one of their own.

And maybe that means we find the family we need, blood related or not.

Because blood doesn't make a family.

Love does.

CHAPTER 23

Andrew

"I can't help," Amanda says in a mournful tone as we pull up to the front door of the house. Rather than having someone drive us home from the hospital, I've done it, wanting this to be a special moment.

Just the four of us.

"Of course not. I'll get the babies inside. You can wait and I'll come back out for you."

"YOU CAN'T DO THAT!" she hiss-screams.

"Why... not?"

"The babies will be alone in the house! What if something happens to them?"

"Like what? A random bear in the woods finds its way into the living room out of nowhere?"

"YES! Or a piece of the ceiling could crack off and fall on Will's head. Maybe you lock yourself out of the house after putting them in there and coming back for me. Or a fire alarm could be set off by a faulty wire, and then there's an electrical fire, and the babies are trapped in the – "

I gently press my fingertips over her frantic lips and lean in.

Amanda blinks slowly. "Wow. Mom was right," she mutters under my touch.

"Right?"

"She said there would be a rush of hormones as my body adjusts to being not pregnant, and to cut myself some slack."

"Pam is *definitely* right."

"But you can't just leave them in there alone."

"Sure," I say slowly. "Then I'll help you out first."

"You can't. I'm between them back here."

"You insisted."

"And I was right. Will needed me to stroke his eyebrow just right so he wouldn't cry."

I smother a smile. She's so maternal. So territorial.

"It'll be okay. I'll use the stroller."

"The stroller?"

"I'll unload Charlie. Click him in. Unload Will. Click him in. Then I'll unload you and click you in."

"Ha ha. But the stroller? How will you wheel it to the door?"

"I'll go around back. It's only one step there. And in the meanwhile, I'll text Gina to hire someone to install a ramp at the main door. We'll have this fixed in no time. It'll come up again and I don't want you to worry."

The air around her changes.

"I have a feeling my life is going to involve nothing but worry going forward. It feels like I suddenly have to fix everything, and at the same time, have no power to do any of it."

"You're not alone. You have me. And I have plenty of power because of you."

She snorts. "You had more than enough power before we met and I'm certain I didn't give you any."

I point to Will, who jolts as I reach into the backseat and unlatch him. "You gave me plenty. Fourteen point one pounds' worth."

Our eyes lock.

I've never loved her more.

"WAAAA!" Charlie's shrill cry pierces the moment. I go to the trunk, pull out the double stroller, and unlock the long contraption with a snap worthy of Jason Momoa opening a lawn chair. Three minutes later, I've got their car seats clicked in, and they're wailing in unison.

But first things first.

"Get them inside!" Amanda urges me, sitting in place, clutching a pillow to her midsection.

"They can cry for a moment. I have to help you down."

Turns out, it's easier to get two screaming newborns out of the back of an SUV than a mother who just had abdominal surgery, but we manage.

As I push the stroller toward the back of the house, Amanda glares at the car's back door. "We need a four-door sedan."

"We'll get whatever you want," I call out, speeding the boys around to the back porch, up the single step, and coming to a halt next to the kitchen island. Charlie's screaming, but startles as I place his seat on the counter. Will's next, and then I unclick my older son, his sniffling face on my shoulder in seconds.

"Andrew?" Amanda calls out.

"In here."

Shuffling sounds precede her, then she's in the doorway, frowning. "Is he okay?"

"*Shhhhhhhh*," I murmur in his ear.

Magic happens: He calms down.

"Will?" she asks, wincing as she walks, clutching the pillow like she's holding her guts in.

Which, actually, she is.

As if on cue, Will stops crying, eyes going wide at the sound of his mother's voice.

Mother.

My wife is a mother, I'm a father, and we're home. Our life as parents begins *now*.

"You sit," I order her, worried she's going to pop a stitch. Strength is a given in Amanda, and she'll work herself into the ground to do whatever needs to be done in any given situation, but right now, having her rest on the sofa so she can recover is more important than any notion she has of contributing.

"I will. But..." Helpless wonder covers her face as she looks at the twin chorus on the counter.

"I've got this. They'll calm down in your arms. Go sit down. Now."

One corner of her mouth goes up in a wry smile. But she listens.

That is a miracle in and of itself.

Working double shouldered is a new skill I need to acquire quickly. The learning curve can't be slow. Fortunately, I work with one of the finest personal trainers in the world, and Vince's lessons haven't just been about building muscles.

Coordination and balance have been key.

Holding Will and lifting Charlie at the same time is easy, as long as I pretend it's fine to have kebab skewers poke out my eardrums. These boys have *lungs*.

By the time I get to the living room, Amanda's on the sofa, pillows arranged, top down, breasts lovely and full.

Funny. A few days ago, that sight would have my junk twitching in my pants.

Now? It's just beautiful.

And besides, those breasts aren't mine anymore. Not for a long while.

She's as efficient as she is gentle, the babies' cries upsetting her, but we power through together. Her finger goes under Will's lip to unlatch him twice before she's satisfied with how he's feeding, Charlie fussing against her ribs before finally moving less, suckling more.

A long, slow sigh comes out of her when they're all in place.

It's my chance to look around.

Our house is different.

Fundamentally changed.

Because I'm the father now.

When we left the house, amniotic fluid pouring out of my wife, the boys ready to make their entrance into this strange new world with cool air and bright lights (but hey–boobs with milk, too, so there's a consolation prize), my father was the only man who had lived here with the title of Dad.

Not anymore.

A smattering of gifts covers the front hall table, but the Red Sox-themed box with a huge card on it that says FROM GRANDPA LEO makes me stop short.

Damn.

I pick up the box and stare at it. Amanda can't see this now. She's too fragile. I'll put it in the closet for later.

"Andrew?"

I freeze and look up. I'm directly in her line of sight.

"What's that?"

"One of the gifts."

"Do I see my dad's name on it?"

Damn her good eyes.

"Yes."

A wide moon gaze meets mine. "Can you open it?"

She's so vulnerable, breasts out, babies nursing, her face haggard and glowing at the same time. Doing this to her now feels harsh. Hard.

Unfair.

"Why don't you open it later?"

Her hands reach out. "Give it to me." There's no quarter in that voice. I have to comply with the order.

So I do.

With careful fingers, she opens the present, saving the card for last. Inside the box are two little baseball hats with Red Sox logos, and onesies made to look like jerseys.

Her hands shake.

But she opens the card.

"Dear Kids," she reads aloud. "You haven't met your old Grandpa Leo, but I hope to take you to a game with your mom and dad one day, and get it right this time. Love, Grandpa."

Get it right this time.

Air whooshes out of her like a tire going flat. I bend down, eyes at her level, and put my hand on the cocktail table, careful not to upset the delicate balance she has going on with the babies and nursing.

"Leo's trying. He really wants to meet the babies," I say, watching her closely.

"I know."

"We can cut him back out of your life again if it's too painful," I whisper, as if the truth is too hard to say in a full voice. If I had complete control over the mess with Leo, this would be easier.

But I'm not Amanda. This is her call.

"It's painful having him come back, but I'm not sure it would be any less painful to pretend he's not trying."

There are layers to being an adult. Seeing the world as a nuanced, complex place where people aren't all bad or all good is part of operating at a mature level. Watching Amanda work her way through the choppy waters of that journey is an honor.

It's also heartbreaking as hell.

"Andrew? Can you get me more water?" Amanda asks sheepishly, moving carefully to stretch her shoulders.

"Of course. What else? Are you hungry? Need more pillows? Need a–" Before I can finish, a long yawn escapes from me. I try to hold it back as if it's a sign of weakness.

I fail.

"Just water." My yawn is contagious, Amanda's arms going up to stretch, pain taking over her expression as the stretch proves to be a bad instinct.

She clutches her midsection and breathes, hunched over the babies, who are quietly snacking.

"Need your pain meds?"

A nod is the only answer.

A minute later, I'm handing her the water and an ibuprofen pill the size of a water softener salt pellet, when there's a light knock at the front door. My phone buzzes.

So does Amanda's.

"That must be Mom," she says, yawning again. Panic takes over in her eyes. "Hide the gift from Leo! I haven't told her he's back in my life."

I grab the box, card, and torn wrapping paper and shove it in a big basket in the closet.

The sound of a code being punched into the front door means it's–

"Dad?" I say loudly, trying to warn Amanda, whose breasts are laid out like they're on a charcuterie board. She's no prude, but given this is the first time my father's been near her since the babies were born, she grabs a small blanket and quickly covers her chest.

Pam comes in right on Dad's heels, carrying a brown paper bag with the logo of Amanda's favorite Greek restaurant in Newton.

"Hello, hello," Dad says, the second word turning to a whisper as Amanda holds her finger up to her lips in a polite *shhhhh* gesture.

To my surprise, Dad complies, tiptoeing backward with an impishness that makes me do a double take.

Dad doesn't *do* silly.

Is he drunk?

Pam bursts into a huge grin as she sets the bag of food down on the table, the scent of spiced lamb and beef mixing with garlic and freshly baked pita. My mouth waters. My stomach growls.

Dad is staring at Charlie's head, his gaze filled with so much emotion I have to turn away.

"When they're done, you can hold them," Amanda whispers, then yawns, trying to hold it back.

"Let me make you a gyro you can eat one-handed," Pam offers to Amanda, who smiles gratefully. I was prepared to help my wife, but Pam's doing just fine mothering her.

Mothering the new mother.

"Congratulations, son," Dad says, coming in for a handshake that turns into a hug.

"I didn't do anything, Dad!" I laugh in his ear, but I appreciate the embrace. "Amanda and the surgeon did it all."

"Your work starts now," he says in earnest. "You have a chance to do it better than I did."

What do I say? Social convention makes words like *You did just fine* or *You were a good father* spring into my mouth, hurtling over the truth in an effort to please and soothe, to remove the tension of reality.

Amanda rescues me. Or rather, Will does, by popping off, giving Amanda a chance to hold him up to Dad.

"Meet William," she says softly. Dad turns to her, arms outstretched, eyes on the baby.

"Wait," Pam and Amanda say in unison, then look at each other, surprised. "You need to wash your hands," Amanda adds to Dad, whose eyebrows go up.

But he goes to the guest bathroom off the foyer, water running shortly, Pam at his heels.

And when he returns, he holds up his palms and looks to Amanda for permission.

Her nod grants it.

Watching my father hold my son is a moment that will be etched in my memory until the day I die.

A day that will come one day.

A day when Will and Charlie will be there, I hope.

Amanda's eyes glisten as she watches Dad, who stares at Will, his throat jumping with a hard swallow. "He's beautiful," Dad says in a choked voice, closer to tears than I've ever seen him.

Oh, no. I can feel mine rising to the surface, too.

Long, fat tears roll openly down Pam's face as Amanda continues to nurse Charlie while she takes a bite of her gyro. Eyes averted, she's trying not to watch James. Maybe this is too much emotion for her.

Or maybe she's just that hungry.

"Welcome to our shared grandson, James," Pam says, her hand going to Dad's shoulder. "Can you imagine? We're connected now on a different level."

Extraordinary waves of feeling ripple across Dad's face, finally settling on something close to happiness as he replies, "I can't think of a better way to be connected to you, Pamela, than through these little boys. Our kids have done well, haven't they?"

She beams. "They have. I already have one more grandchild than I do children!"

Dad thinks for a second. "My kids have made it dead even. Three sons, three grandchildren."

"I'm sure Shannon and Declan are working on changing that ratio," she says softly.

Dad startles. "Really? Is there something I should know?"

Alarmed, Pam looks at Amanda, who shakes her head imperceptibly.

Recovering quickly, Pam simply says, "Oh, no. I just assume they want more." She rummages in the takeout bag and finds forks. "I brought plenty for everyone. Andrew? James? I'm sure you can find something you like."

For the next ten minutes, I stuff myself on spanakopita and kebab, Dad eating one handed as he watches Will with rapt attention. Other than Ellie, I've never seen a baby in my dad's arms.

And now he has my own child in his grasp.

Pride has a funny way of showing itself. Nothing I did was ever good enough for my father. Even being named CEO of Anterdec came with its own new set of expectations that I never quite meet.

But have a rousing night of unprotected sex, get my swimmers to produce two sons, and *bam*–instant approval.

A knock at the door makes us all turn. Dad's face lights up.

"Ah, yes! That must be Grace."

"Grace?" Amanda and I say her name in unison.

"She asked if she could come see the babies," Dad explains with uncharacteristic sheepishness. "I–I couldn't tell her no. She and her wife are leaving for a month-long cruise tomorrow. I should have told you."

Grace stepped in to fill the role of mother when our mom died. She's the closest person in my twins' life to a grandmother on the McCormick side. Until now, it hadn't occurred to me to ask her to be here.

I stand, cross the room, and let her hug me, her embrace big and warm.

"Little Andrew has two little babies now," she whispers in my ear. "Congratulations!" She smells of lavender, the same as always, and while I've grown taller and stronger over time, she's shrunk.

At seventy-one, not so surprising.

We walk into the living room, where Amanda's eating, her shirt and bra in place, and Dad and Pam each have a baby in their arms.

"One of you is going to have to surrender to me, because I need to huff a baby's head," Grace says pleasantly. "Oh. Right. Hi, Amanda. Now that you've had babies, you're just the backdrop, aren't you?"

"I practically blend into the couch," Amanda replies as Grace laughs and leans down for a hug. Poor Amanda makes a face as she tries to stretch. Well practiced in reading people, Grace pulls back fast.

"How was the surgery?"

"Fine."

"You had major abdominal surgery! Nothing about that is fine."

"They are." Amanda nods at our babies.

Grace softens. "Of course. But are *you* okay?"

"Time will tell." Her answers worry me. Dark circles under her eyes suddenly reveal themselves, and her mouth seems slack, turned down with exhaustion. I feel like an ass.

Today was too soon for people to come over.

Placing my hand on her shoulder, I lean down and whisper, "You want me to get rid of everyone? You look like you need some rest."

"I'm fine. Really. But if they're all here an hour from now, how about we reassess?"

I kiss her cheek, my protective streak intact. "An hour."

She nods, then looks longingly at the baklava. "Could you..?"

"Of course." I put two pieces on a plate and set it on her knees.

"Two pieces! I can't eat that much."

"You can," I answer simply.

Her gaze darts to my dad, as if she's worried about his opinion.

"Someone hand me a baby," Grace says, hovering next to Dad, who points to Pam.

The three of them laugh and figure it out, the handwashing ritual one that Grace performs without being asked. I suddenly feel young and old, all at once.

I'm the sandwich generation now. There's one above me, and Amanda and I created one below us.

My phone buzzes from across the room. I ignore it.

For the next five minutes, Pam and Grace and Dad roam between living room and kitchen, chatting and looking at the babies in better light, giving me the chance to eat and breathe. Amanda's eyes start to droop, and I prepare myself internally to send them all home soon.

Twenty seconds or so later, the front door code beeps.

"Who could that be?" Amanda asks.

Gerald walks in, stride steady, arms tight, face drawn in deep concern. Adrenaline shoots through me, spiking fast and hard, making me jump up and cross the room to him at the front door before I can think.

He's at my side, face impassive, which makes my gut clench. "We have an issue."

"A problem? Is Suzanne okay?"

"No, no. This isn't about Suzanne. It's about your family."

"My family?"

"I'm glad I'm on for Mort, because this is delicate."

"Get to the point. What's the problem?"

Something in his mask ripples. "More of an issue."

"Can it wait?"

He leans even closer and whispers, "A man claiming to be Amanda's father is at the gate."

"He *what*?"

"Right. Looks like a nicer version of the guy in Nashua. He's wearing a short-sleeved dress shirt and tie. Jeans. Hair's cut short. Not sure it's him, but probably is. Is it a problem? I'll get rid of him."

"No. Hold on. It's okay. That's Leo."

"Leo?" Dad's outraged voice comes at me from behind. Gerald and I turn. "Pamela's Leo? Her ex-husband?"

"Yes."

"What is *he* doing here? He's a felon! A murderer!"

Managing my father's emotional reaction on top of the surprise of Leo being here and the stress and joy of bringing the babies home is the last thing I need to deal with. Thankfully, Grace walks up and says to Dad, "James, can you help me with the baby?"

Dad can't resist his long-time executive assistant, and she knows it. Her gaze cuts to me as if to say, *I can hold him off for a moment.*

But not forever.

"I need to find Pam first," I murmur to Gerald, who nods and moves into the living room. I just hope Pam isn't holding one of the twins. This is going to be hard enough.

Peeling a grandson out of her arms would be an added gut punch.

"He has no right to be here, Andrew," Dad says to me, at my elbow again. Grace's cunning eyes take in the situation, sharpening at the word *he.*

"Who?" she asks Dad. Smart to defer to him.

"Pamela's ex. Amanda's father. A no-good deadbeat who killed a number of people in a drunk-driving accident years ago."

Grace's eyebrows shoot up. "He's here?"

"I thought he was in prison," Dad grouses, looking at me as if I've betrayed him by not keeping him apprised of Leo's whereabouts.

Just then, Pam appears, carrying Spritzy in a handbag, her face tight and closed off as if she's in pain. "What's going on?"

Dad opens his mouth, ready to blast her with his outrage, when Grace puts her hand on his elbow and he stops. He lets out all the air in his lungs, slowly, like a pinhole has formed.

"Leo's here," I say softly.

Pam flinches. "Here?" Her eyes blink rapidly. "Now?"

"Yes."

"Why?"

Until a few minutes ago, when Amanda had me hide Leo's gift, it hasn't occurred to me that Amanda might not have told Pam about our meeting with Leo. I hadn't assumed either way, but apparently, on some level, I had.

I had taken for granted that Pam knew.

And now I have to be the bearer of bad, bad news.

"He's out of prison," I begin.

"Obviously," Dad blusters.

"He served his time," I add tightly, ignoring him.

"James," Grace says softly. "Why don't we give them some privacy?"

"We need to give Pam and Amanda *protection*, not privacy!"

"Gerald's here and can do that. It's why Andrew has him on staff. You made a good choice in hiring him years ago," she says, massaging Dad's ego like a trainer for an Olympic athlete.

Pam's eyes flit to Dad, the bottom lids pulling up with an expression that says she doesn't appreciate his dominance, either.

"Let Leo in," she says firmly, until she looks at her daughter and hesitates. "If you want, Mandy."

"Mom, no. I don't want to upset you."

Pam squares her shoulders. "This isn't about me."

Dad can't help himself, interrupting. "It's most certainly not about that miscreant, Pamela! He has no right to–"

"*You* have no right to do this, James," Pam says to my dad, challenging him with a forcefulness Declan would admire deeply.

I know I sure as hell do.

"Excuse me? I'm trying to protect everyone from him."

"You're trying to assert your will over people who have wills of their own," she flatly declares. She looks at Amanda. "Do you want Leo here?"

Uncertainty fills Amanda's face, but she closes her eyes, looks down, and says, "We saw him a few weeks ago."

Time stops.

Just for a few seconds, but it's enough.

"You did." Pam says it flatly, sadly. Her reaction to stressful news is the same as Amanda's: A whoosh of air comes out of her. She's clearly struggling to control her reaction.

"I did."

"It's okay, Mandy. It's fine to see your father." Her Revere accent comes out, blooming under pressure; the end of the word father is cut off, the r consumed by the past.

"I know it is, Mom." Amanda looks up at Pam, eyes begging for forgiveness, understanding, empathy, compassion. "I had to. He reached out."

"He did?"

"Yes. Finally."

"FOR ANDREW'S MONEY!" Dad yells, as if we're all stupid and haven't pieced together some chain of facts he's pre-convinced himself is the truth.

"No," I say back loudly. "He hasn't asked for a penny."

"Not yet!"

"Not ever." Pam's mouth goes firm, set in a grim line. "Leo's not like that."

"How do you know, Pam?" Dad challenges.

"How did you know your late wife, James? I was with Leo for long enough to know the man. He may be a drunk, and a terrible father, and even an accidental killer, but he's not sniffing around our daughter so he can get money. He's here because he's trying."

"You don't have to see him, Mom. And we can send him away."

Gerald watches all of us with keen eyes, his quiet strength always a plus. Unlike in most situations, though, he speaks.

And speaks to Amanda.

"Amanda? It's your call. I can send him away. I can let him in."

She nods, then looks at Pam. "He brought a present for the boys."

"He did?" Her mouth softens. "What was it?"

"Red Sox hats and little onesies."

All of the blood in Pam's face drains out, her hand drifting to the back of a chair for support. "*Red Sox?*" she whispers faintly.

"I know, Mom. I know!" Amanda starts to cry. "He wants to try to make it right."

"He gave up that right long ago," Dad blusters.

"Did you?" I challenge him.

A deadly silence fills the air, my gut twisted in agony but my heart standing firm.

"Excuse me? What does this have to do with *me*?"

"Nothing, Dad. That's the point. Stay the hell out of it."

"Someone has to make sure they're protected from him."

"He made mistakes. He's trying to make amends."

"Some mistakes are too great to ever fix."

"Like when you blamed Declan for saving me instead of Mom?"

The front door code beeps at that exact moment, Terry's face popping in, Leo behind him.

"Hey, everyone! I came over to meet the babies and this is Leo. He says he's here to..."

No stranger to family tension, Terry's deep voice fades fast as his eyes ping from me to Dad, finally settling on Amanda with compassion. Quick to cross the room, he inserts himself physically between Dad and me, a wall between us and Amanda and Pam as well.

"What's going on?" Terry asks, voice calm yet firm.

"I was just explaining to Dad that people deserve second chances. Fathers, especially."

Terry's eyes narrow and he gives me a look that says, *Are you sure about that?*

"Leo?" Pam gasps, looking like a deer in headlights.

Leo's in the foyer, neck tipped up, eyes taking in the high ceiling, the double staircase, the whole nine yards. Because I grew up here, I don't think about how it looks to others.

But he lets out a long, slow whistle. "Heya, Pammy. Check out these digs."

My mother-in-law is one for polite laughs, so it's rare to hear her completely let loose, but now is one of those times. Raucous laughter, the nervous kind that bubbles out under tension, comes out of her like Silly String being sprayed by a four-year-old at the family dog.

"Leo," is all Pam can say in between giggles.

"Hey." Leo's gaze settles on Amanda. "Hi, Mandy. I hope you don't mind. You gave me your address and I know I shoulda texted or called but I was afraid you'd say no, and I didn't want to bug you. I didn't know if the babies had come yet, but I wanted to see you either way. A buddy lent me his car, but today was the only day I could use it and maybe it was wrong and man, I'm feeling like a jerk right now, so..." He takes a deep breath after all those words, unnerved by Amanda's silence.

All she can do is stare.

His eyes cast down, and his head dips into a submissive posture. Shoulders dropping, he turns back to the door. "I'll–I'll go now. I shouldn't've come."

"NO!" Amanda stands up, then bends over, clutching her pillow with one arm, Charlie with the other. In an instant, I'm next to her, the searing pain of this moment something I can practically taste.

"No," she says softly as I ease her down, taking Charlie out of her arms. "No, Dad. Please stay." Raised eyebrows and a sad smile are all she can manage as she looks at Pam.

Who nods.

Then walks out of the room toward the kitchen.

"Hello," poor Leo says to Dad. He shuffles closer to Amanda, his gaze on Will as he walks past.

Dad says nothing, eyes deadly.

Terry walks over to me and whispers, "Leo is *Leo* Leo? Amanda's dad?"

"Yes."

"Holy smokes."

"Uh huh."

"Want some whisky?"

I look at our father, who is watching us with the narrow-eyed expression of a man trying to figure out how to dominate. "Nope. Later. Need all my wits right now."

"How about I offer Dad a whisky?"

"Perfect."

Always able to work a room, Terry gives me an aggravated look that says he isn't a fan of Dad's, but he loves me enough as a brother to help out–but man, is this a pain.

All in one glance.

My quick nod says back, *I acknowledge your sacrifice, and thanks for saving me from doing it.*

Grace gives Terry a hug as he approaches Dad, who is suddenly focused on them and not on me. Leo, meanwhile, stands nervously next to Amanda. I'm on her other side, holding my son, who snurgles as he settles into the crook of my neck.

"You okay, Mandy? I can go."

"Stay," she says, looking up at the baby. "Stay and meet Charlie and Will."

"Those are the names you gave them?"

Her cheeks go pink as she nods.

"Fine names. Good, solid ones. No one ever picks on a Charlie or a Will." Tentative, Leo puts his hand on Amanda's shoulder. She gives him an apologetic smile.

"I'd stand up again, but that hurt."

"Hurt?" He pauses. "Oh. Right."

"I had a c-section. My incision is still really raw."

"Had to cut the babies out? That's tough."

"Want to meet him?" I ask as Leo looks at his watch.

"I—maybe I should go. My buddy really does need his car back soon."

"Not before holding your grandsons," I say firmly.

The juxtaposition of my own dad in the room with Amanda's dad, and the fury my father has for a guy he's never met, makes me realize their abandonment wasn't all that different. Dad parented from an extreme distance when it came to the emotional and day-to-day stuff, but up close when it came to high expectations and peak performance.

Which drove us away emotionally.

Leo tried, but like my father, he has limitations.

Don't we all?

What will mine be when it comes to being a good parent?

Handing Charlie off to Leo makes Amanda's eyes fill with tears, Leo's mouth quivering just as Charlie wiggles in his arms, the baby's head in the crook of his arm, Leo's shirt sleeve pulling up over his shoulder.

"Haven't held one of these since you," he says in a thick voice, talking to Amanda but not looking at her.

Just then, Pam comes back into the room, holding a sleeping Will. She comes to a dead halt as she spots Leo, as if she still can't believe he's here. Spritzy dances at her feet, doing the pee performance pet owners know all too well.

"I've got the dog," Gerald says, scooping him up and taking him unceremoniously out to the kitchen. A door slams and Pam opens her mouth.

Then shuts it, like closing a time capsule.

"Thank you, Pammy," Leo says, humble and hard-won, his arms dark with a tan, the shoulder cap white as a newborn's butt. The farmer's tan speaks to long, hard labor, and I wonder how much of that took place in prison.

"For what?" she asks, shoulders dropping with sadness.

"For raising a good girl. A good girl who is a mom now." He turns. "You done good, Mandy. You done real good, and I thank you for being kind to me."

Terry, Dad, and Grace are watching, all in a row, triplets holding highball glasses with amber liquid coping skills. Dad's mouth drops open as Terry gives a soft-hearted smile, and Grace tilts her head, taking it all in, her hand going to James's forearm.

Dad just clears his throat and kicks back another mouthful.

"Why wouldn't I be kind?" Amanda asks as Pam moves next to Leo, holding Will next to Charlie.

"Trade?" Pam asks before Leo can reply to Amanda.

"Sure. Whatever you want, Pammy. "

Amanda's crying openly on the sofa, watching her parents together like it's the greatest fireworks display ever, like she's watching a meteor, like a triple rainbow lights up her favorite water-fall. Luminous and ethereal, she's observing a wonder of the world, but a very flawed, human one.

Her parents trade babies and I hear a click.

It's Grace, an actual camera in her hand.

"Habit," she says as Dad rolls his eyes, but nostalgically. His hand goes to her shoulder in an affectionate gesture.

"You always took the photos and videos I wanted while I was at work," he whispers.

Terry and I catch the comment and Grace smiles at me, as if to say, *There's more to the story*.

I look at Leo and Pam, then Amanda.

There always is, I want to answer.

There always is.

EPILOGUE

T*en Weeks After the Birth*

"ARE YOU SURE?"

"Yes."

"The water doesn't have too many chemicals?"

"The doctor said it's fine."

"And you turned up the temperature?"

"It's ninety-three."

"Maybe that's too hot?'

"ANDREW!"

For a guy who is so commanding and sure in business, he's a softy and a worrywart with the babies.

I set Will down on the cushion of the chaise lounge, his body curled still, the startle reflex beginning to fade as he ages. They're ten weeks old now, and my C-section wound has healed enough that the doctors say I can swim.

So today, our boys swim for the first time in our indoor lap pool.

And *not* in front of their grandfather. This isn't the Olympic tryouts.

Andrew's in his suit, though he thinks it's silly, a formality we don't need in private. But I have a camera and for the sake of posterity, no one needs to see Dad or Grandpa in the buff.

One day, if all goes well, Andrew will be a grandpa, and I'll be a grandma. I think about this more and more as time passes.

As I get used to being Mom.

No one calls me that, yet, but the twins signal it in every way, from the latch that comes more naturally now as breastfeeding continues, to the quieting of cries when I pick them up at night. Two nannies and a night nurse means our life lives according to structure, schedules, and a sameness that is comforting, freeing me to heal.

Today is for us, though. The house is empty, the nannies off for the day, and my husband is fully present for this precious ritual.

A ritual bath of a different kind.

Charlie is in Andrew's hands, stripped of his diaper, each of us holding a naked baby.

One handed, Andrew descends the ladder with a wide-awake Charlie in his arms.

He halts.

"What if they poop in the water?" His consternation shows in the dropped brow, the frown hilarious.

"You're just realizing that's a possibility now?"

I get a flat look. "I had to be in the water with him to think about it." Charlie's legs are in, butt hanging off Andrew's forearm, eyes blinking rapidly.

"We climb out fast and let the filter do its job. But I don't think that'll happen."

Parenting two small babies means conversations like this, mostly revolving around poop. I thought Shannon was kidding when she said this.

Turns out my bestie was issuing a warning, not a joke.

Leaves in the trees over the enclosed glass solarium are a flaming mix of yellow, orange and red, a little green still dotting the lush branches. Fall in New England has a special kind of allure. Even if you've lived here your entire life, like I have, you see how special it is.

Crisp golds mingle with bright reds, the leaves falling and plastering themselves on the glass. It rained last night, leaving the air fresh, scented with dirt and woodsmoke, neighbors burning brush and wood stoves as the chill begins to hit.

We have Halloween costumes for the babies. They'll be pumpkins, of course.

Twin pumpkins.

A big smile crosses Charlie's face as Andrew goes in deeper, moving over a few feet from the ladder, holding on to the side with one hand, clutching Charlie in the other. The twins can't hold their heads up just yet, but they try, and Charlie pulls back off Andrew's shoulder for a few seconds as if looking up in wonder.

Then he settles in and kicks, just once.

"Yes!" Andrew says gently, grinning at me. "Good kick! We'll get infant swimming tutors here next month and start with you."

"Are you sure?" I ask, my heart exploding as I watch Andrew explore the water with Charlie, my hand on the ladder's railing, ready to join them. "I don't like the videos where they dip the babies all the way under."

"Some people start at birth," he reminds me. "From the amniotic fluid inside straight into the pool."

"Those were vaginal births," I remind him. "And those babies didn't have a mama who had surgery."

"Hey," he says tenderly. "No judgment. And no problem. We're not racing to turn them into Olympic contenders here."

"I know. And Mom agrees with infant swimming lessons, for safety reasons. It freaks her out that we have an indoor pool with little ones running around."

"Actuaries know all about the calculated risks." He doesn't say the word drowning, but I know what he means.

For the last ten weeks, since the birth, I've been a roller coaster of emotions as all the hormones needed to build the babies had to slowly leave my body so I could be just me again. My bones. My blood. My hormones.

My empty womb.

"We have locks and alarms. We're fine. But teaching them to swim is a joy. And I'll be here for every lesson."

"You said that, but – really? Can you be here?"

"Of course. Do you doubt me?"

"I – " A flash of the day Carol and Shannon were here runs through my mind. The day work took him away from me here in the pool.

"I mean it," he says firmly. "I'm changing my priorities."

"I know you are. I just worry you can't."

"Can't?"

"Sometimes what we want, even when we want it desperately, isn't possible if the structure of life fights us the whole way."

Andrew pulls Charlie off his shoulder, carefully putting the baby on his back in the water, Charlie's head in the crook of his elbow as he moves into the water deeper, tall enough to move easily through the water. There's a small lip on the edge, too, where I can stand if I'm unsure with Will.

"You're ready for this?"

"I think so."

"I'm here if you need me."

"You always are."

The first step down the ladder is slow, my body ultra-aware of all the ways I have to protect the baby. The second step puts my calf in the warm water, a light layer of steam beginning to form on the surface. Unaccustomed to this temperature, I let out a gasp of surprise, which makes Andrew laugh.

"It's so warm!"

Will squirms on my shoulder, my grip tightening.

"It is. And the view is fabulous," Andrew adds.

"If by view, you mean my ass, it's extra fabulous, given all the padding."

"The padding makes it fabulous, honey. What was already lovely is now extra lovely."

I suppress a sarcastic hah! He means it.

And knowing he means it makes me love him even more.

When my fabulous ass hits the water, I pause, the c-section scar a source of irritation. Two weeks after the birth, half the incision opened, unfurling like a broken zipper. Infection had set in and it drew out the healing process. Andrew insisted on waiting for the twins' first swim until I could be here, and as the water covers the scar, I feel nothing.

Whew.

Salt water and open wounds don't mix well, so the lack of feeling means the doctors are right.

I'm healed.

Will wiggles as his legs hit the water, and when I am in and holding on to the wide with my right arm, I turn him to face me, his smile like sunbeams. Andrew has Charlie on his back, still in the crook of his arm, and he's saying something to him in low, soothing tones.

For the next twenty minutes, we just float.

The twins love it, little coos and sighs their only language, smiles their currency we accept eagerly. Will and Charlie are identical twins, but we can tell them apart. Charlie's smile is crooked, the right side turning up a tinge more than the left.

Will sounds like a billy goat when he cries, and he's an innie. Charlie's an outie, though we're only discovering that recently, as the umbilical cord heals.

They are carbon copies of my husband, which makes him puff up to no end, though Mom swears they have my wide eyes.

Andrew and I trade off babies and he kisses my cheek, our eyes meeting, the gaze deeper and deeper as we just... float.

The water holds us.

And so does the silence.

"Do you hear that?" I whisper in Andrew's ear as he bends down to kiss Will's forehead.

"Hear what?"

"Nothing."

"Nothing?"

"No cell phones. No texts. No work crew or nanny or night nurse. No emergency meetings, no demands from your dad. Just us."

A funny look crosses his face, a mix of defensiveness, agreement, joy and sorrow.

And then he leans across me, kisses Will's shoulder, and looks at me again.

"If this is what nothing feels like, I want more *nothing*."

;)

THANK YOU so much for reading *Shopping for a CEO's Baby*. If you are suffering from "End of the Book Syndrome," you're in luck, because I have a BONUS EPILOGUE for you.

SECOND EPILOGUE

Mother's Day, the following year, Amanda's first

Andrew

"THIS ISN'T MORBID, RIGHT? WE'RE NOT BEING ghoulish," Shannon says as we haul two picnic baskets, two strollers, and three children down the long, winding asphalt path. Groups of people doing exactly what we're doing dot the walk, people in twos and fours, the occasional larger collection of people, like ours, circling their target.

"It is a little morbid. But it feels right. She should know her grandkids."

"She'll never know them. This is just as close as we can possibly get."

Declan passes us and says tightly, "We'll take what we can get."

"Look," I reply, knowing he hates every moment of this, "you don't have to be here. It was just an idea I had." Amanda and Shannon watch us carefully, wary eyes taking in the friction between me and my brother.

And then a bee buzzes by.

"Damn it!" I mutter, instinctively dodging it, looking out for Shannon, who has already noticed. This is why the twins are in carseats with bug nets over them, why Dec hates being outside with his daughter and wife who are vulnerable, too.

We don't know if the kids are deathly allergic like I am.

Like their grandmother was.

Like Declan's wife is.

It's the reason we're visiting our mother in a cemetery and not in person: a sting, a hyper-inflammatory response, and anaphylaxis, all caused by a piece of biological material the size of a lima bean.

Life is grotesquely unfair.

Death even more so.

My EpiPens rest inside the diaper bags, and we'll always carry three–yes, *three*–because the universe taught me a harsh lesson when I was sixteen:

Be prepared for every contingency. If you're not, the consequences are brutal.

Deadly.

No child of mine will go through what I experienced.

Not if I have a shred of control.

"There," Shannon says, earning a grimace from Declan as she points to Mom's grave.

We haven't been here since last Thanksgiving, and Mom's headstone is tipped slightly to one side. Amanda helps me right it, and she pulls up a weed that must have emerged since the groundskeepers were last here. She tickles Charlie with the long blade of grass and he giggles like mad, Will watching with a one-eyed squint that makes him look like Shannon's grumpy feline, Chuckles.

There's no joy in this trek, other than the fun of parenting babies and small children. Declan and I have taken a rare Sunday off to spend entirely with our wives and kids. Terry is with us, the affable, childless brother, who has morphed into the even more jovial uncle.

We three McCormick boys are here to visit Elena.

And for her to know her grandkids.

Kind of stupid, right? Don't blame me. Shannon started it when Ellie was born, and Amanda's easily influenced by her best friend. In a parallel world, I'm sure Amanda's living in a cult somewhere.

Or maybe I'm wrong.

Maybe she'd be leading it.

"Gamma!" Ellie chirps, the word dropping my stomach.

Grandma.

Mom never got to hear someone call her that.

"You look like you're on the verge of tears," Terry says to me, on my right, suddenly all emotion and nothing but low tones.

"I'm fine," I grunt.

"It's okay, you know. Dad's not here."

"What's that supposed to mean?"

"Exactly what I said. We don't have to pretend for him. You can feel what you need to feel."

"He's not a robot, Terry."

"No, but he's not exactly an empath, either."

"We're all somewhere in the middle."

"Dad's middle is *waaaaaay* on the other side of mine, Andrew."

Charlie grins up at us as if his Uncle Terry's words are the funniest thing he's ever heard. Now nine months old, he has a front tooth fighting to get out on the bottom, and dark green eyes like Declan's. A deep sadness pierces my heart as I let Terry's tone about our father ping around inside me, ricocheting off soft spots where it can do damage.

Will Charlie talk about me one day the way Terry talks about our dad? What about Will? Is there going to be a future in which my sons feel that I've pushed them away, but I'm so emotionally inaccessible I can't talk about it? That they can't talk to me? Will I draw boundaries around myself so strong I don't let love in?

Denial is powerful. Controlling the frame of reality is even more so. For so many years, I've been the closest to Dad of his three kids, and having my own children is changing that.

Alarmingly so.

We have choices in our relationships. I'll never make the same ones James McCormick did. *Does.* Amanda reminds me of that when the bleak worry hits hard. When I let it have enough oxygen to take a breath.

"Hey. Geez. I didn't mean to make you depressed," Terry says with a nudge. Concerned eyes meet mine. "But I won't sugarcoat the truth about Dad."

"You don't have to. It's just..." I look back at Charlie, his smile infectious. "We were like him." I point to my son. "And Dad..."

I don't have to finish my sentence.

"Dad isn't you," Terry says, arm going around my shoulders.

"And you're not him. We get to control our own lives, even if he thinks *he* should." Charlie grins up at Terry, who makes faces at the baby, which makes Charlie start to giggle.

"And besides, we're here to celebrate Mom."

"Can't talk about one without the other."

He ponders that for a moment, then concedes. "Fair enough." An insect buzzes near us, making me tense immediately, my eyes darting to Charlie.

We don't know. We still don't know.

Terry hasn't been outside with me, in the presence of a bug, in a long time. What surprises me the most in that moment is how alert he is, attuned to my concern. And then, to his own. Deep in the recesses of his mind, even though he wasn't there that fateful day when Mom died, he carries the circuitry. The wounded pain that forges a new loop, a reminder, an algorithm.

Grief does that.

So does love.

"Is there some plan?" he asks in a gruff voice that reminds me of our father.

"Plan?"

"A... ceremony, or some ritual or something, to honor Mom?"

"No," I say slowly, realizing we never thought about that. "We just came. We're just here."

Dec walks over, holding Ellie's hand. She looks up at Terry and says, "Uncatair!"

"That's so much better than Uncadoo."

"Is it?" Terry asks with a laugh as he swings her up onto his shoulders, Ellie's giggles flying on the wind.

"What's the plan?" Dec asks, echoing Terry, as Amanda and Shannon spread blankets on the grass near Mom's headstone, careful not to cover any places where coffins lie below.

"No plan. We're just here. Mom wouldn't need a plan, would she?"

"I don't know." Declan's face twists with confusion. "I don't know what she'd want. We never reached this point with her. I can tell you what Marie would want. You know what Pam would want. But Mom? We'll never know."

"What would Marie and Pam want?" Terry asks, hands on Ellie's ankles, looking so comfortable with a two-year-old on his shoulders that I wonder when–or if–he plans to settle down and have kids.

No way am I asking, though. Then I'd sound like Dad.

"Just... to be around everyone. To eat and talk. Play games. Watch the kids," Declan says slowly. "That's enough for them."

"The opposite of Dad," Terry bluntly states.

"Would it have been enough for Mom?" I ask.

"I think so," Dec and Terry say at the same time.

Ellie chooses that moment to pull Terry's beard, her little hands deep in the plushness of it. A few strands of gray make me calculate his age.

Thirty-seven.

He's on the downslope to forty.

Time really has passed.

"You three look like you're at a funeral," Shannon says brightly as she walks over to Declan and slides her arm around his waist. One corner of his mouth lifts, and gratitude for my sister-in-law floods me. She changed our entire family with one mystery shop.

And my wife rescued Declan from his own stupidity by making Terry, Dad, and me pose as employees at The Fort when Declan broke up with Shannon, all those years ago.

Good thing my brother doesn't make the same mistake twice.

Rescue can come in the most serendipitous of ways. Who knew Shannon's ninth cinnamon-raisin-horseradish bagel mystery shop, assigned to her by Amanda, would turn out to be the greatest day of my brother's life?

And the connection we all needed.

For the record, the guy who invented the cinnamon-raisin-horseradish bagel was fired two days after Shannon's final mystery shop. Bad taste combo.

"Thinking about Mom," Terry finally says to Shannon, who gives him a compassionate look.

"I wish I'd met her."

Ellie reaches from Terry's beard to her mom's head and gets a fistful of honey-colored hair. "Wan fly kite!"

Bzzzz

It's my phone.

They all groan.

"What?" I say, defensive. "I'm running a company."

"So am I," Shannon and Declan say together, making Terry laugh.

I look at my phone. It's Dad.

The babies will be perfect PR for the...

I stop reading the text.

I just *stop*.

"What's wrong?" Shannon asks, attuned to my emotions in a way that I just don't get.

"It's Dad."

Terry and Declan groan.

"What's he want?"

"To use the babies for PR."

From afar, Amanda shouts, "WE TOLD HIM NO!"

My meeting with Vince, the plans for the gyms, my conversations with Declan, all the emotions around Leo and Pam and Mom and Dad, and what Grace once said to me–*He's a limited man who thought he could show you love through achievement. It's the only love language he knows*–turn into a swirling dust storm of feeling in me, all of it spinning and spinning until I find myself in the eye.

The calm eye.

This is my one chance.

One.

And I take it.

Dad's text is there, so I press Audio. The phone rings.

"James McCormick," Dad answers.

"Dad? We need to talk."

"About what?"

The sun comes out from behind a white puff, like something in a children's board book, the sky gorgeous and bright. It's the kind of day where possibilities feel endless, worries are a mile away, and simple existence is enough.

Or, at least, we can delude ourselves into thinking that.

"About Anterdec."

"What about it?"

Dec looks up at me with a puzzled look as Terry crosses his arms over his chest, eyes narrowing, concern shifting to curiosity. Amanda senses the change in my brothers and, holding Charlie in a sling, reaches for Shannon's arm, bending over Will, who now has fistfuls of Shannon's hair in his happy grasp. Amanda whispers something, then they both look at me, too.

This is it.

Now or never.

Change comes gradually, then all at once.

Time feels compressed when my father has an expectation, but I let myself linger across the seconds, forcing him to wait. Project management software tells me I have 121 unfinished tasks, seven meetings tomorrow, and Gina's booked my travel for the next two years. All that I've achieved suddenly isn't a foundation supporting a growing tower of achievement.

It's a millstone crushing my heart.

"Andrew?" Dad barks into the phone. "Is something wrong? Are you hurt? Sick?" Genuine worry radiates from his voice, and that earnest emotion is what finally cracks me. It would be easy to stuff the words back down, especially in the face of Dad's humanity.

But it's because his caring is so rare that I must seize the moment and say what comes next.

"I'm fine, Dad. Better than ever."

"Oh. Good." Emotions tucked neatly back in the black box of his heart, he turns gruff. "Then what is it? It's about the public relations campaign with the twins, right? Great idea, if I do say so myself."

Amanda walks to me and my hand goes to her arm, gooseflesh greeting me as our eyes hold each other's gaze with an impenetrable lock. Her searching look makes me feel known.

"I bought a chain of gyms," I say, loud and confident, breaking my wife's gaze only to look at Mom's gravestone, to remember all the good. It would be so easy–it has been so easy, sadly–to think mostly about how she died.

But we came here to celebrate how she lived. And what she's missed.

The life that would have been, if circumstances were different.

Seventeen years ago, we didn't have a choice. Fate took our choice away.

But right now? Fate's not in charge.

"Gyms? Where does that fit into the Anterdec portfolio?" Dad asks, suddenly interested.

"It doesn't. I bought them myself, a year ago."

Keeping this secret has been hard, but worth it. I don't tell him Leo has a steady job working at one of the locations in Nashua, and how the gym in Dad's old neighborhood in South Boston is thriving.

I don't tell him because I can't.

Because if I did, I'd get, well, *this*.

"You *what*? Why would you do that?"

I say the most dangerous words in the world:

"Because I wanted to."

"What the hell are you going to do with a chain of gyms? You barely have time for your CEO job. I've been meaning to talk to you about some slippage I've noticed, especially since the twins were born, and –"

"That's just it, Dad," I say, interrupting, talking over him. He keeps speaking, as if bowling me over with louder words will make me back down. For twenty seconds, we both talk. The sounds mingle to form a kind of third language, one that holds a certain forlorn beauty.

The sound of people trying desperately to communicate but failing.

"*Dad!*" I finally say, the word long and real. "I bought the gyms to run them."

Amanda's hand flies to her throat, Charlie's little fingers already playing with her necklace. Eyes as big as hearts meet mine.

She knows.

She knows what I'm about to say.

"Run them? How can you do that?"

His question hanging in the air, I stare at my wife and realize she's crying, smiling and crying.

And then she nods.

Yes, Andrew. Yes.

I don't need her approval.

Yet it makes this so much easier.

"I can do that, Dad, because I quit."

"QUIT?" he thunders. "Quit *what?*"

Terry's mouth drops, then turns into a huge grin. Declan pinches the bridge of his nose and starts taking deep breaths, muttering something that sounds like *holy duck* over and over.

Ellie joins in.

And she doesn't say *duck*.

Amanda winds her spare arm around my waist, head tucked into my shoulder, nodding slowly against my ribcage as I say the words I need to say to rescue myself.

So I do.

"I'm resigning as CEO of Anterdec, Dad."

❧

Thank you so much for reading this bonus epilogue for *Shopping for a CEO's Baby*. Watch for the next book in the series by opening my future newsletters, or following me on:

Goodreads

Bookbub

TO GET A NOTICE WHENEVER I PUBLISH NEW BOOKS. There is definitely more coming in this world. <3

OTHER BOOKS BY JULIA KENT

Shopping for a Billionaire: The Collection (Parts 1-5 in one bundle, 500 pages!)

- Shopping for a Billionaire 1
- Shopping for a Billionaire 2
- Shopping for a Billionaire 3
- Shopping for a Billionaire 4
- Christmas Shopping for a Billionaire

Shopping for a Billionaire's Fiancée
Shopping for a CEO
Shopping for a Billionaire's Wife
Shopping for a CEO's Fiancée
Shopping for an Heir
Shopping for a Billionaire's Honeymoon
Shopping for a CEO's Wife
Shopping for a Billionaire's Baby
Shopping for a CEO's Honeymoon
Shopping for a Baby's First Christmas
Shopping for a CEO's Baby

Little Miss Perfect
   Fluffy
   Perky
   Feisty

Hasty

Her Billionaires
    It's Complicated
    Completely Complicated
    It's Always Complicated

Random Acts of Crazy
    Random Acts of Trust
    Random Acts of Fantasy
    Random Acts of Hope
    Randomly Acts of Yes
    Random Acts of Love
    Random Acts of LA
    Random Acts of Christmas
    Random Acts of Vegas
    Random Acts of New Year
    Random Acts of Baby

Maliciously Obedient
    Suspiciously Obedient
    Deliciously Obedient

Our Options Have Changed (with Elisa Reed)
    Thank You For Holding (with Elisa Reed)

ABOUT THE AUTHOR

New York Times and *USA Today* bestselling author Julia Kent writes romantic comedy with an edge. Since 2013, she has sold more than 2 million books, with 4 *New York Times* bestsellers and more than 19 appearances on the *USA Today* bestseller list. Her books have been translated into French and German, with more languages coming.

From billionaires to BBWs to new adult rock stars, Julia finds a sensual, goofy joy in every contemporary romance she writes. Unlike Shannon from Shopping for a Billionaire, she did not meet her husband after dropping her phone in a men's room toilet (and he isn't a billionaire).

She lives in New England with her husband and children in a household where everyone but Julia lacks the gene to change empty toilet paper rolls.

She loves to hear from her readers by email at jkentauthor@gmail.com, on Twitter @jkentauthor, on Facebook at https://www.facebook.com/jkentauthor . Visit her at http://jkentauthor.com

jkentauthor.com
julia@jkentauthor.com